BEWARE THE SMART KIDS

By Matthew J. Kushin

Praise for Beware the Smart Kids

In his remarkable debut novel, Matthew Kushin explores the delicate, sometimes painful journey to understanding, kindness, and that most precious of attributes, empathy. Saddled with self-doubt and a long simmering guilt, Kushin's main character steps outside himself to understand through another's eyes what it truly means to be isolated and reviled, yet remain true to who and what he might be. This is powerful writing, immensely engaging, and distinctive in both tone and theme. It merits a place on the bookshelf of any serious reader.

–Greg Fields, *Through the Waters and the Wild,* 2022 Winner, Independent Press Award for Literary Fiction

"With *Beware the Smart Kids*, Matthew seamlessly weaves philosophy, humor, and an honest look at teenage life in the twenty-first century. As the cast of characters search for meaning, purpose, and happiness, I couldn't help but see myself in each of them. The book uplifts the spirit, challenges the mind, and opens the heart towards a kinder universe. Plainly put, it will change the lives of those who read it."

–Derek Gallagher, high school psychology teacher

"It's hard to imagine how differently I could have seen life if I had read *Beware the Smart Kids* when I was seventeen. Once you enter the world of this coming-of-age story, you'll have a hard time coming back into your own without a positive perspective shift. A worthwhile read!"

–Shelby Daugherty, advocate for Appalachia

For my family

"I will not allow my life's light to be determined by the darkness around me." – Sojourner Truth

One

When I found out that he died, it wasn't like in the movies. I didn't fall out of my chair or start crying uncontrollably. No one whooshed over to wrap an arm around me and ask if I was okay.

I was sitting in a coffee shop working on my laptop when I got a text from Mrs. de León, my old high school teacher. Don Henley's "The Boys of Summer" started playing on the speakers overhead and all I could do was smile.

I'd forgotten that Mrs. de León had my number. It's weird how so much can happen in such a short amount of time after so much nothingness. It's weird how we fall out of touch.

Then, suddenly, a text comes in and we're zapped out of a coma. That's what happened to me, at least. He was dead and, *bzzz*, my past was alive again. It was as if Mrs. de León flicked a light switch in a dark room. And I found myself back in high school, reacquainted with tree branches dripping with color, the night sky cracking from the blast of a rifle, the body splashing into the river below, and my legs burning as I ran— back in that place where I saw for the first time what the universe could be.

———————————

We waited in the dark for the sound. It always

started as a soft groan in the distance. We had to stand real still to hear it plow through the cornfields and apple orchards to the north. As it crept closer, we could hear the bridge over the river begin to rattle. And we knew it was about time.

Branson and I stood at the ready. Anxious. Excited. Alive. Neil hid in the bushes, his binoculars locked on the bedroom window on the far side of the house.

Soon, the midnight train lumbered through Paxson. Its horn blared as the earth rumbled. Neil whispered over the walkie-talkie, "All quiet on the western front."

Think about how fast a bad grade ruins a good day. Branson and I put the party decorations up faster than that, finishing before the long train could roll away and leave behind a still town.

"Jester to Ghost Rider," Branson said over the radio. "Your mission is complete."

Neil's voice came back, "Roger that. Requesting a flyby."

"Positive, Ghost Rider. The pattern is empty."

Neil, his face in camo paint, shuffled out of the bushes. He ran in his hobbled way, jerkily across the lawn and into the cul-de-sac where Branson and I waited.

I whispered to Branson, "Where's the cake?"

"I put it by the mailbox."

It was Saturday night, the first weekend of June with summer break one week away. A few hours earlier, Branson, Neil and I were sitting outside Juanita's Taqueria on Main Street eating double-fried chimichangas. That's when Neil took a hot sauce bottle from Branson and said, "I got some Excedrin." Then he waved the bottle over his plate and used his finger to swirl the sauce into the cheese and guacamole. "If you want some, I mean. Helps with my hips and back."

I'd made it this far into the evening pretending the mountain range of purple welts on Branson's face didn't exist. Because that's what I did. Pretend that my friends were okay. Pretend that everything was okay. Pretend that the world wasn't teetering on a cliff's edge and that I wasn't sitting there watching it, too numb to feel anything.

Branson shook his head. "It ain't nothing."

I gave Branson that shoulder shake that says, 'I'm sorry. Chin up.'

Branson sawed his food with a plastic knife. "My mom's boyfriend-slash-dealer. I chased him off."

Neil shook the hot sauce bottle over his chimi. "Gone for good?"

"Made damn sure of it." Branson grabbed the hot sauce bottle back.

I dropped my fork. "Let's find where he lives and throw him an epic birthday party. Really bust his place up."

"Dude ain't from around here." Branson took a huge bite and chewed, glaring off behind us. Like a full minute passed. "Plus, If we found him, I swear I'd—I'd—" He swallowed. "Let's just have some fun, alright?"

"Don't look now, but here comes crazy Cammie Roland," Neil groaned between bites.

Cammie Roland was sweeping the sidewalk by the Lewis Real Estate Agency building two doors down from Juanita's Taqueria. She wore a fancy hat and was spinning and sliding as she swept, dancing with the broom as she belted the chorus to that old song that goes, "Oh, What a Night." The door opened and the owner, Mr. Lewis, emerged. Everything about him screamed, 'I got more money than the law allows.' My mom worshiped people like that. That's probably why she worked for the guy.

"Hello, Kardell. Oh, what a night, isn't it?" Cammie sang. And the way she said it, you could tell she really believed it. Mr. Lewis, who I had never seen smile or talk, did both. He agreed that it was beautiful out and he thanked Cammie for everything she did for the town. The sweeping. The trash collecting. How she got the fire department to string up lights every Christmas.

"Yo, we should celebrate her birthday," Branson smiled deviously.

I gave a fist bump across the table. "How have we not?"

Branson shrugged. But I knew he hated the Roland family. Cammie's son Ian shoved Branson into a locker in seventh grade where (Don't tell anyone I told you this) he cried for two hours before anyone found him and let him out.

"I concur. She's certifiable. It'll be a cinch," Neil said.

Mr. Lewis climbed into his Mercedes-Benz and Cammie waved as he drove off. Then, someone came around the corner. Someone I'd never seen before. He wore a beard and circular sunglasses that masked his face. From his hunched shoulders, a long black coat hung like a cape down to his shins. On his sockless feet, he wore the kind of strapped sandals that professors at the liberal arts college over in Wetton wear. His arms were held stiff by his sides. From his left fist, a dog leash ran out to a small white dog that dodged from object to object. The dog stopped to sniff a trash can in front of the Lewis Real Estate Agency building.

"Beautiful evening," Cammie said to the man. The man kind of smiled under his beard, or at least I think he did.

"Who the crap is that?" I mouthed.

Neil gaped.

"Death Row Barno," Branson said.

"Who? Why do they call him that?"

"My sister says he went crazy and killed a couple of students back when he was a teacher at Paxson High like 100 years ago," Neil said. "But some people say that he was broke so he robbed a bank, took everyone hostage under the age of 18, and snuffed them out one by one."

"That ain't what I heard," Branson said. "Word is, dude went bonkers and offed his whole family. Kids first."

Why had I not heard of Death Row Barno? Oh, right. My sister was never around to tell me that stuff and my parents never talked about anything except money and school.

Death Row Barno looked our way. *Could he hear us?* We stared down at our food. Then, his dog took interest in something behind him and he turned and followed the dog, disappearing into the darkness down the street.

"How is that nutbag out of prison?" I asked.

Neill wiped his mouth. "Prison overcrowding. Did you not pay attention in American Civ last year?" Then Branson said, "If there's someone who deserves a birthday party, it's that stain." And Neil and I agreed.

So that's how we got to standing in the cul-de-sac in front of Mr. Barno's house, about to light a 'birthday cake' on his driveway while the egg oozed down the siding of his house and the toilet paper dangled from tree limbs in the summer night breeze.

"Midnight Warlords forever," I said.

The guys echoed, "Midnight Warlords forever."

We put our fists together in a triple fist bump.

"Permission to fall back?" Neil asked.

Branson nodded. "Well done, soldier."

And I said, "See you at the rendezvous, Neil."

Neil saluted. Wincing, he trudged off down the street toward the high school. When he was out of sight, I plucked the paper bag with the dog poop inside out of the grass by the mailbox and placed it down on Barno's driveway. I asked Branson for the fuse and light and he handed me a birthday candle and lighter. I pushed the candle through the paper bag into the squishy center and lit the wick. I crouched behind the candle. With my phone held at driveway height, I snapped a photo—the 'birthday cake' in the foreground and some of the 'party decorations' in the background. Then, we ran to the high school, laughing the whole damn way.

If we were a song, it was "Teenagers" by My Chemical Romance.

We caught up with Neil on the away team bleachers at the football stadium. "Happy birthday to Death Row Barno," Neil smiled, rubbing his lower back.

"You alright?" I asked, pulling off my ski mask.

Neil nodded. "Roger dodger, you old codger."

Branson took off his Michael Meyers mask and gave Neil a 'what the hell are you talking about?' look.

Surfacing a vape, Neil replied, "Hey, when you're a 16-year-old in a 60-year-old's body and sports are out of the question, you get lost in a few books and movies." Neil passed Branson the vape. Branson took a pull and turned to me but I waved him off. "Might try out for varsity cross country next year," I said.

The boys laughed and Branson, smacking my arm, said, "This year, when you didn't make varsity, you swore you weren't going to try out again."

"Tore my hamstring a week before tryouts. Never got a fair shot."

"You've got so many excuses, No Land. Even you can't tell if what you're saying is fiction or reality."

I laughed—faked it—and stood up on the bleacher seat. "Look, our senior year is practically sitting in our laps. This has to be the best summer of our lives. If there's a party, we're actually going to show up to it. If there's someone we like, we're actually going to ask them out. Senior year is our year. No regrets. No excuses. Not even from me, got it?"

Branson said, "Your words to our ears" and Neil nodded while he hit the vape. So I put my fist out for a bump and said, "That's, what, the 12th birthday party we've thrown since last June?"

"Protecting the good people of Gotham." Neil saluted. "That's what this town needs, a Midnight Warlords flood light. Just like Batman."

"Customary photo?" I asked. Branson and I put our masks on. I got out my phone and we took a group selfie, thumbs popped, with the PHS lettering at the 50-yard line on the football field for a backdrop.

The next night I was lying in bed watching Lenny the True Love CEO on YouTube, trying to absorb the sage's wisdom. "Step one is to impress them," he was saying. A notification popped up on my phone: Battery

10%. I swiped it. "Show them your value," Lenny continued, "Show them the money."

A text from Branson: "Send photos [Pile of poo emoji][Birthday cake emoji][Clown emoji][Toilet paper emoji][Hatching egg emoji]." I swiped it away.

"You're fishing, brosef," Lenny espoused. "What do you have that they want? Put it on the line, cast it, and let your OAF"—pronounced like loaf without the L, the luminary of romance's acronym for Object of Affection Fantasy—"come to you."

I took out the red notebook I kept under my bed and thought, *What do I got that a girl like Gabi Meyers would want?* I scrutinized my room. Evidence of a palpable absence of social status hung above my desk—photos with Branson's arm slung over my shoulder at Dairy Queen in our scout uniforms, Neil and I showing off our builds at LEGO camp, the three of us smiling a bit too much at the Vietnam War memorial with Neil's grandpa.

An old kitchen chair with a bathroom towel draped over it was tucked halfway under the desk. Shelves were crammed with CDs, a Bluetooth speaker that couldn't play them, two once-prized Yu-Gi-Oh! cards in plastic stands, packs of Bubble Yum, a yellow LEGO Technic Jeep Wrangler, and cans of AXE Body Spray (Of all the things I'm not proud of).

A small TV and a Nintendo Wii were squished on the floor between a pile of clothes and the corner. The clothes pile resembled a bush and, to my mom's horror, it was taking root below the art: a Rage Against the Machine poster and a Che Guevara poster (For the look in his eyes, not the communism stuff).

There wasn't much to offer Gabi. Something told

me my OAF wasn't a Yu-Gi-Oh! girl. Then I saw the Jeep poster on the back of the door. I wrote, "Awesome car," in the notebook. Next to it, I wrote, "As soon as I get $5,000."

Another notification from Branson. "No Land! You get my text?"

"Seriously?" I groaned. This woke my cat Miles who stood, jumped out of bed, and knocked over the to-go cup I had left on the floor. I clicked the text, selected the camera icon, selected the photo I took at Barno's house and the group selfie photo at the football stadium from my camera roll, and hit send. I grabbed the towel off the chair, tossed it on the puddle of lemonade, gave it a few half-hearted dabs with my heel, plopped back in bed, and stared at the Jeep poster. I saw Gabi and me counting summer stars in my Jeep, top-down, seats rolled back, some beachy music low on the radio. The perfect night with my soulmate.

Eating together was a thing growing up in my house. We had these animated discussions about everything from who was going to win the pennant this year—my dad's favorite topic—to what we would do with our lottery winnings if we won the billion-dollar Mega Millions—my mom's favorite topic. The convos always started off simple before boiling into grand philosophical discussions. My sister, Sarah, was the best at them. She could have gone toe to toe with those European thinkers in the coffee houses back in the day because she read everything. Newspapers. Magazines.

Non-fiction books. Discussion forums from the far reaches of the Internet. And, she thought. I mean, she really thought about things like how the small was connected to the big.

But that all changed.

On the Monday of the last week of school, I ate cereal while Dad texted clients on his phone and Mom stared out past the succulents in the bay window, out toward the street where her eyes settled on some place in the past. I worked the puzzle on the Honey Smacks cereal box because my phone was charging at the kitchen counter. I was waiting for one of my parents to look in my direction, at least vaguely, so I could pick up my little blue pill, swallow it, and teeth smile. Always teeth smile.

My phone buzzed. Dad glanced up. He took off his reading glasses, stood, and, glaring out the window, groaned, "Ah, hell. Fitzpatrick was right." Death Row Barno was walking his little white dog down our street. Dad grunted, "They let that schmutz go free." Barno stopped while his dog sniffed our mailbox.

And I swear Death Row Barno stared directly at me through the window. I froze. *He knows*. Then, his dog pulled him off down the street.

"Who's that?" I asked. But my dad just said, "The fact that scum has got the gall to walk down the street makes me want to puke." So I peered at my mom but all she did was look away and offer her primary survival mechanism: a cold chill.

My phone rattled again. Then again. And again. I had so many notifications going off that my phone practically jittered off the counter. I jumped up to check it. Ten missed texts, one missed call from Neil, and two missed calls from Branson. Really? Branson would rather attend gym class in his underwear than face the awkwardness of talking on the phone.

The first text notification was from Branson: "You sent pics to study group."

I started to type "LMAO" when I realized, oh crap. No, no, no.

I swiped to the study group chat.

Omar (9:23 pm): [Photo of Señor Evans with marker stains on his butt as he writes on the dry erase board]

Cienna (9:24 pm): [Skull emoji]

Becky (9:25 pm): That's just cruel.

Yuvi (9:37 pm): 1 more week [Dice emoji]

Branson (9:42 pm): Last test brutal who help me cheat?

Omar (9:48 pm): Not going down for ur stupidity

Neil (9:49 pm): That

Yuvi (9:50 pm): Ur parents are from Mexico and ur failing Spanish?

Branson (9:51 pm): [Middle finger emoji] Grandparents from Mexico on one side of my family. That don't make me an expert

Becky (9:52 pm): I'm going to assume that you are joking and not turn you into Principal Anand.

Branson (9:53 pm): [Rat emoji]

Becky (9:53 pm): I know it's a surprise to you but some people have integrity and morals.

Branson (10:00 pm): Who got notes to study for test? Send pics

Branson (10:35 pm): No Land! You get my text?

Me (10:36 pm): [Nighttime photo of Barno's house with lit candle stuck in paper bag and tree with toilet paper draped over it] [Nighttime photo of camo-faced Neil, guy in Mike Meyers mask to his left, and guy in ski mask to his right, each giving the thumbs-up sign. Barely visible PHS lettering on the field behind them]

    Neil (6:24 am): Broken arrow
    Branson (6:26 am): Dude
    Branson (6:26 am): WTF
    Branson: (6:26 am): [Face screaming in fear emoji]
    Branson (6:26 am): Answer your phone
    Omar (6:27 am): For real its yall?
    Cienna (6:27 am): Dammmmn
    Yuvi (6:27 am): [Surprised emoji]
    Becky (6:28 am): OMG

Two

This was not good. Like the time I put my mom's Volvo in neutral, disengaged the parking brake, and sat quietly peering over the steering wheel as our car eased backward down the driveway and into the street to come to an abrupt halt astride the Fitzpatrick's azalea bushes.

I told my parents how I wanted to know how to drive like them. But since it was the second time that happened in a month, and the day after my dad found me pouring gasoline on a dandelion in our yard (An honest mistake, I assure you), they took me to a little office to do puzzles with a bald guy who asked gentle questions about school and home. A few months passed. One afternoon, my family sat in the man's office to hear his conclusion. He shared some terminology to describe me. Later, I asked my sister to help me understand and she got annoyed and said the man's fancy word just meant that I was "a handful."

In morning gym class, Branson heard from Yuvi that he had overheard Becky telling Jisoo on the bus that Becky was going to go straight to Principal Anand's office to show her the photos that I had accidentally sent to the Spanish II study group chat. So, we convened an emergency meeting of the Midnight Warlords in the bathroom by the cafeteria during lunch.

Neil turned on the faucets at the two sinks to muffle the conversation in case of eavesdroppers. "Deny everything," he instructed in a low voice. "Gramps says they usually can't prove anything, even when they say they can. We just need to keep our mouths shut. Anything they ask us, we say 'no comment' or 'I didn't see anything' or 'I don't remember'—stuff like that."

Neil's grandfather raised him. Gramps was a Marine in Vietnam. And after that, at least according to Neil, Gramps worked some secret job for the government. Although I'm pretty sure his grandfather was just a security guard at a museum in the city. Either way, the old guy knew a lot about military stuff, covert ops, interrogation, that kind of thing. He was also the closest thing we had to legal counsel.

We all agreed to a simple story: that's not us in the picture. We were not there. Nolan was just sharing photos he found online. And he doesn't want to get anyone in trouble, so he's not going to say where he found them. "They can't make you say where you found the photos," Neil advised, his hand on my shoulder like a mob lawyer. "That's like your constitutional right. Just act scared and say that you'll get beat up by the people who really are the Midnight Warlords if you rat on them. They can't make you say it if it'll get you beat up. That's like your constitutional right. Capiche?"

Nervous, I asked, "Don't we need an alibi?"

Neil said, "We were with Gramps at the movies."

Branson asked, "What if they call him?"

But Neil seemed unflappable. "Gramps lives by omertà, the code of silence. He is basically in the mafia, but for the government."

In fifth period, the word came down through the mysterious speaker box that hung on the wall above the door in each classroom—a relic from the Cold War or something—that I was to report to the principal's office after school. While everyone else rushed out the doors and poured into the sun-shining ecstasy of the last Monday of classes, I thrust against the stampede of students and toward the belly of the beast.

Now, when I get in trouble I tend to have to go to the bathroom a lot. So I stopped at the bathroom and tried to go. But I couldn't. This happens when I'm worried. I can't go to the bathroom when I'm worried. I have to go, and at the same time, I can't go. So I sat there on that cold toilet seat for a while warming it up. *Not this again*, I thought. Sitting in my toilet stall cocoon with teenage hieroglyphs—dicks and jokes like 'welcome to my humble commode'—carved onto the walls around me, I started wondering what would happen next. I knew that when I left this stall and went back into the world, I was no longer safe. I wondered, *how am I going to fight this?*

And I realized I was always getting into this situation. Trouble. Hiding. Fighting authority. I never had a plan. I never thought it through. I just kind of reacted. I guess I trusted my instincts. Or, maybe I just didn't want to face things so I never thought about them deeply enough to reflect on what I had done or plan for what I would do next.

I always just got up off the toilet before I really had time to think things through and went out to face things, because it's just easier that way. So that's what I did.

As I turned the corner into the locker-free hall of the administrative wing, I saw a figure on the far end of the long hallway moving in the other direction. The dim light of the hallway made it hard to see. But it felt like him. Death Row Barno. He was leaving, his back toward me, his trench coat swaying like the cloak of the devil.

I opened the door to the principal's office suite to see a frowning Mrs. Jackson, the administrative assistant. "Welcome, Mr. Sussman," she sighed. She told me to sit in one of the four empty chairs in the windowless waiting room. I sat in my default chair, the one in the middle of the room, and waited. I was trying to recite the story Neil, Branson and I had agreed on. And I was trying to think of anything other than that story. I counted the number of objects on Mrs. Jackson's desk—23, including a cool paperweight of the Eiffel Tower. I looked at the paintings on the wall. One was a field. One was flowers. One I couldn't tell what it was. I counted the height of the room by cinder blocks—13. I counted the width of each wall—the longer ones being 12 cinder blocks and the shorter walls being 10 cinder blocks. I pretended I didn't already know all of these facts about the waiting room.

The door to Principal Anand's office opened. Neil and Branson shuffled out in single file like ankle-chained convicts being escorted by guards, their shoulders sagging, vacuous looks on their faces. "The principal will see you now," Mrs. Jackson said, sounding less like an office assistant and more like a bailiff. I stood and headed toward my fate.

Branson mouthed, "Where were you?"

I mouthed back, "Bathroom."

He whispered in my ear as he passed by, "They got us by the balls." *Ouch*, I thought. Then I thought, *What horrible precedent inspired that saying, and wouldn't an arm or leg suffice?*

"Dead man walking," Neil announced dramatically

from behind me as I crossed the threshold into the principal's office.

Principal Anand motioned for me to shut the door. I did. I walked queasily toward the chair across from her desk because I had a sudden memory—real or imagined I wasn't sure—of our ball-crushing dictator stopping by shop class last year and conversing quite knowingly on the many uses of metal vices with Mr. Vanstrussen.

Principal Anand sat behind her mahogany desk, as always, and wore a business jacket with a flower lapel pin, as always. She must have had 50 different lapel pins. Today's pin was mauve. The suits were always beige or gray. She was the kind of person who wore a gold watch in the photo of her family at the beach. And when she looked at the framed beach photo sitting on her desk, I figured that she thought about how the salt water broke the watch.

"Nolan, your partners in crime have already confessed," she began. "I just want you to corroborate what they told me."

"No clue what you're talking about." *Stick to the story*.

"Nolan, is it fair to say we've gotten a chance to get to know one another fairly well during your tenure here at Paxson?"

"Fair indeed."

"You've certainly distinguished yourself among your peers." *Really, you're too kind*. Principal Anand folded her hands. "It seems that during your time here at Paxson, crossing lines has become a bit of your specialty. This time, you've crossed the fine line between souvenir and evidence when you shared those photos of you and your juvenile terrorist cell."

I wiped my sweaty palms on my shorts. "That wasn't me. That wasn't us."

"You see that scar on your knuckle there?" I looked down at the back of my hand. *Crap.* "You recall the thumb ring Branson wears? Or the military watch Neil wears? The same ones they wore when they came into my office this afternoon? The jig is up, Nolan."

"This is entrapment." It was a word I had heard Neil use before, a word I didn't know the meaning of.

Principal Anand's voice bumped up a level, "May I remind you that you have been suspended twice this school year, making that four times total during your time at Paxson High School. You have always had a need to draw attention to yourself, to stand out. Now you will. You will be the second student in the history of this school to succumb to the so-called 'Five and Goodbye Policy'—to be kicked out of school and miss your senior year with the people you grew up with."

"This is such bullshit," I blurted. *Time to fight.*

Principal Anand closed her eyes. When she opened them, her voice was soft and she said to me, "Nolan Sussman, I know you and your family have been through a lot. Pardon my intrusion, but are you happy?" She glanced at the beach photo on her desk when she asked this. Really, she did.

"I don't know. I guess. I mean, is anybody really happy?"

"Yes, Nolan. A lot of people."

"You're either born happy, or you're not, Principal Anand. That's just the way it is."

"I wholeheartedly disagree, Nolan." She wore a new watch now, an Apple watch. "Happiness can belong to anyone."

"If you say so." I slouched, legs spread wide.

"I care about your well-being, Nolan. I've been doing this a long time. When young people display the type of behavior that you've displayed, they need help. They're asking for help."

"Don't worry. I'm still seeing a therapist," I lied. Always lie about that stuff.

"Nolan, you're smart. You're not like your friends. You've got a 3.9 GPA. You've got A's in 4 Advanced Placement courses. Your SAT scores are excellent. You can get into a fantastic engineering program with your grades and your abilities. Why do you insist on sabotaging your life?"

"I don't want to be an engineer. Why doesn't anyone ever listen to me?" I felt like crying. I felt like getting up, grabbing that framed photo, and throwing it against the window, and the window breaking somehow and I could just jump through it unharmed and run, run, run away. Away from how adults have to squeeze you in. How they have to have a plan for everything. How everything has to fit neatly onto a label and into some adult's filing cabinet.

"Well, I've got good news for you," the principal said, "with your talent, you can do whatever you want for a career. What do you want to do, Nolan?"

I wanted to yell, "That doesn't help!" Telling me I can do anything is no different than telling me I can't do anything. I looked out the window toward the emptying parking lot, the last few clusters of students laughing and piling into cars. *That picture frame can't really break the glass, can it?*

"I don't know," I muttered. "I think I want to tell

stories. Like, I want to paint pictures in peoples' minds, but not with photos or graphics. I'm not sure, exactly."

"Okay, then do that. I'm sure you can be very successful. But you've got to stay out of trouble and not do stupid things like this."

I stomped my foot. "That's not me in the photo. Maybe it's them. But it's not me."

"Nolan, stop lying to yourself. You are your own worst enemy. If you don't realize that soon, I am afraid it will be too late."

"I swear that's not me in the photo. I didn't do anything."

Principal Anand pushed herself up out of her leather chair. "I am afraid you are going to have to complete your senior year at Middleview High," she said calmly and with what sounded like regret in her voice. "Because you were clearly using school grounds as part of your mischief, this is a school issue. Your fifth suspension means expulsion from Paxson. Your case will be sent to the School Board, who will vote on the expulsion next week. However, the vote is just a technicality. Despite your mistakes, I believe in you. I am going to do you a favor and request that the School Board seals your records, so you don't have to share why you are changing schools on your college applications. I hope you will not let your mistakes define your future."

———————————

My mom's palms pressed against her temples when I finally walked in the door. I didn't go straight home after school. Instead, I went for a run in my school

clothes. Then I sat alone in the football stadium bleachers and looked over the school campus. The old two-
story brick building. The fenced parking lot that used
to be tennis courts. The football field I always figured
my friends and I would sit on in fold-out chairs as we
waited for the valedictorian to finish their graduation
speech so we could throw our caps in the air. I sat there
with my digital recorder, a Zoom H1n portable microphone. I tried to capture the feeling of being alone at a
high school, the whispering breeze and the metallic
pings and plinks when I shifted on the bleachers, the
cars accelerating into the distance.

Mom sat at the kitchen table with a stack of papers
and her checkbook splayed out before her. "I thought
you had work this evening?" I asked.

She glared up at me. "You look slouchy. Your shirt
is too big. How have you not tripped? Those shoelaces
are a landmine. And do you bother to comb your hair?"

I placed my backpack down.

"What's wrong, Ma?"

"Don't you want to be presentable in life?" She
tapped her pen on the table with her left hand and
pushed her right thumb and forefinger against her forehead. "What are you going to do? What is your plan?"

The plan was no plan. But I couldn't say that, at least
not now.

"It wasn't me, Ma," I lied. "This kid at school is trying to frame me to get me kicked out."

"Who? Who would do that?"

I thought a moment. I hated lots of people. I just
wasn't sure who best to pin this on, at least in my
mom's eyes. "Dallas," I finally offered, referring to
Gabi Meyers' boyfriend Dallas Stone. He seemed just

as good a scapegoat as any. And since I always fantasized about getting rid of Dallas somehow so I could get Gabi, blaming him made the fantasy seem an inch more real.

"Why would he do that?"

"Because, I have enemies, Ma. People are jealous of me. That's just part of being popular." I did have enemies but the rest of it was a total lie. I didn't know the first thing about being popular. In truth, I had enemies for the same reasons everyone else does—because, as Sartre said, "Hell is other people." And high school is worse than hell.

"This is your fifth suspension. They're invoking the five-suspension rule."

"I know," I frowned.

"There's no bus to Middleview High from here. You can't afford to save up for that Jeep anymore. You'll have to get an old Saturn or something you can afford and drive yourself."

"I know, Ma."

"You had a chance to get a college scholarship. You got what it takes to go the distance, get your degree, and make good money. I want you to have more. But you're throwing our dreams down the tubes. Are you bent on destroying everything?"

"I don't know, Ma."

"That all you have to say for yourself?"

"The principal said they'll seal my records so no one knows I got expelled. I can still try for a scholarship."

"You don't need college," my dad said. He sauntered into the kitchen, the heels of his slippers dragging on the linoleum, from the dark cave of the TV room where he had been watching a documentary about geriatric rock stars riding motorcycles. "Look at me. I make a living, don't I?" He opened the fridge, grabbed a beer, and popped the can. "Here's what you do, you drop out before they can expel you. Beat them to the punch. Start working for me year-round. Put in a few years of grunt work, prove you can help me manage some projects, and soon you'll be earning good money."

"Terrance!" my mom bellowed, rubbing her temples, trying to buff something out of her head. "Really, you think being a high school dropout is setting our son up for success?" She turned toward me. "If you drop out, you'll end up living in a dumpster. Is that what you want, a dumpster?" If my mom wrote a book, it would be called *Everything That Can Go Wrong,* because, I swear, that's all she thinks about.

"Okay, okay," my dad said between slugs of beer. "What I'm trying to say here is, these teachers and principals get on a power trip and want to tell everyone how to live. That old Principal Anand treated me like I was dirt way back when. Just because I grew up on the low end of town. Believe me, she threatened to kick me out two or three times. She's all talk. And now feast your eyes." He belched involuntarily after he said this (Now you can say you've really met my dad). "A success. Own my own business. And she can't handle it. Here she is twenty-something years later still trying to get the best of me."

"What did I do to deserve this?" Mom asked the heavens.

It went on like this for a while. You know the drill. Mom goes crazy. Dad already is. My parents exhausted each other so fully that they apparently forgot to set a punishment for me, an oversight I thought it best not to point out. Finally, we ate dinner and I helped with the dishes.

I went upstairs and stopped outside the closed door—that torturous door I had to walk by to get to my room. I almost never looked at it. Instead, I would turn away, look at my phone, zero in on my door at the end of the hall, or close my eyes as I passed by. Yet, this time I stopped and stared at it. I saw the tape marks from old posters that used to hang on it and the scuffs from my childhood kicks against the bottom. I saw the dust on the handle.

I reached out and touched the handle with my pointer finger—the brass cold to the touch—and wiped a line in the dust. I heard my mom climbing the steps with what sounded like a laundry basket, so I scurried to my room.

Three

I got these ways of thinking I don't entirely understand. One of them goes like this: I'm more afraid of what *will* happen or what *did* happen than what *is* happening—what is *actually* happening right now.

That night, after I found out I was going to be expelled and taken away from everything I knew and my two best friends since elementary school, Branson and Neil—the kids who had seen me piss my pants after Hunter Gallo punched me in the gut in fourth grade and helped me cover it up so he and none of the other kids found out—I felt this numb way that I tend to feel when I am in it. I mean, really *in* it. Like a shitty moment where everything has gone wrong. And it's like this serene cloud that I'm floating on and all the crap is way far below me and I can't hear my parents screaming at each other, or the school administrators scolding me, or the burned-out teachers trying to give dated advice, or the assholes at school who always have everything going for them—the ones that call me Nolan Suspect and treat me like I'm a freak because they can look at me and see in my eyes that maybe I'm going to go crazy someday.

I was lying on my bed. But at the same time, I was on that cloud. *It's all ruined anyway, so what does it matter?* No school. No girlfriend. No Homecoming. No Jeep. No scholarships. No college. No future.

Unfortunately, that little high only lasts for a little while. And maybe that's why I do what I do. I get this buzz. This release. This touch of freedom. Complete freedom. When everything is ruined, nothing matters. You. Are. Free. And I don't care what anyone else says, but it is the only time I really feel safe. That I can sleep well.

Yeah. Maybe that's why.

If only it would last.

I awoke to daylight blasting through the edges of the blinds. I went downstairs for breakfast. My parents were gone. A note on the kitchen table read:

At work. Clean the house. Don't go anywhere. We'll talk tonight - Mom.

I texted Branson and Neil to share the news. They both got suspended, their second time each. Branson said his mom was, "too stoned to care." But he also said she threw a sleeve of Pringles and an open Go-Gurt at him. Neil's grandpa grounded him for a week. Gramps was disappointed with Neil, mostly for caving under the pressure of the school's interrogation. "Omertà," he reminded Neil. "Omertà."

So I cleaned for a while. I was taking a bathroom break when the house phone rang. As I came out of the bathroom, I heard the answering machine. Principal Anand's voice came on asking me to return to school for a meeting in her office at 2 pm. I picked up the phone and told her I would be there. She said, "Good. I look forward to it." And I said, "I'm glad one of us does," which was a stupid thing to say to a principal, but she wasn't my principal anymore.

Paxson is a town about as old as the United States with a main street of shops—including Juanita's Taqueria—that runs a few blocks from east to west. The town square sits in the center, an island around the

Paxson library. If you take Main Street in either direction, you are soon in farmland. If you follow Main Street to the edge of town going west, there's a small shopping center with a chain grocery store, a Dairy Queen, a cell phone store that used to be a Blockbuster, an okay pizza place, and an empty storefront that no business seems to want. Just off the other end of Main Street, is the Paxson Learning Complex, a patch of converted farmland where all the Paxson schools now stand.

Houses cluster to the north and south of Main Street. The nice houses—historic but renovated—are closest to the shops and the really nice houses—think McMansions—are up against the river on the north side of town. The south side of town has some nice houses, too, the closer you live to Main Street.

The Midnight Warlords lived on the southern side of town, with my house being the closest to Main Street. Neil lived a few blocks south. At the southern edge, just outside of town really, are two trailer parks and a paper mill. Branson lived out that way.

All of Paxson is maybe one and a half square miles. Since I liked to run, the good thing about Paxson was that I could run about anywhere I wanted to go. The bad thing about Paxson was that you could never run too far.

I texted my mom and dad to let them know Principal Anand wanted to see me, and that I was heading to school. My mom texted "What do you think she wants?" I replied, "No clue." And Dad replied, "Probably just wants to rub it in." And Mom replied, "Be sure to lock the house." So I did and I ran to the high school, passing the street where Death Row Barno lived, a small patch of woods separating the houses and the football stadium.

Catching my breath, I plopped into the chair across from Principal Anand who wore a gray suit and a yellow daffodil lapel pin. "There's been a development," she said. "I'm going to be truthful with you. I am more than reluctant about it. The man whose home you vandalized, Alexis Barno, called me this morning. He wants you to know that he forgives you."

"The murderer guy wants to forgive me?" I asked. "Okay. Whatever. Sounds good." The dictator developing the emotional capabilities of both being truthful and feeling reluctance coupled with a killer forgiving me felt a bit too Dr. Phil (Do all moms love Dr. Phil, or just mine?). I started to get up but the principal pointed to the chair. I eased down.

"Mr. Barno doesn't want to see you get kicked out of school. He is offering an olive branch."

"What's an olive tree got to do with it?" I deadpanned.

The principal sighed. "Let me offer a corollary. If this were a legal matter, it means he does not want to press charges. He says maybe it wasn't your fault that you vandalized his house. He says he believes someone put you kids up to this. He feels adamantly that you should not be kicked out of school."

"No shit?" I blurted.

"Nolan Sussman! Language!"

"Sorry," I said with a sort of surprised laugh. "Is this legit?"

"I haven't filed the paperwork with the School Board. So, yes, it's a possibility."

"So I'm free? I can come back to school next year?"

Her voice tightened. "There are conditions."

I started to speak, but she held up a finger. She picked up the phone and dialed the pad. She called my mom's office but my mom was unavailable, so she called my dad.

"Hello, Mr. Sussman. Yes. Yes, it's Principal Anand over at Paxson High. Yes. Sure. Of course. I do remember you. Sure. Uh-huh. A construction business? Well, good for you." The principal peeked at her watch, then out the window. "Yes, of course I mean it. Mr. Sussman, I have your son here with me. Do you mind if I put you on speaker?"

My dad's voice came out of the phone. "Hey, son, you there? What's going on?"

"Mr. Sussman," Principal Anand continued, "a community service opportunity has come up for Nolan. If he takes it, his suspension will be lifted, and his expulsion case dropped."

"Community service? Figures. I knew you were cooking up something over there at that school. Good grief. You hear that son? How you gonna save up for a car if you're cleaning water fountains and mopping floors at the school all summer?"

"Well," said the principal, "what's important—"

"Hold on a sec," Dad interrupted. I could hear his muffled voice in the background. Then, "Well, what does Nolan say?"

The principal faced me. "Nolan?" I didn't know what to say in front of my dad. Of course, I wanted to come back to Paxson and not go to Middleview. But dads say things that make it hard to know what to do. "He hasn't decided yet," the principal answered.

"Well, he's got to learn to make his own decisions. Isn't that what you're supposed to be teaching kids over at that school?"

"Yes, but there's something about this, uh, unique opportunity I'd like to speak with you about Mr.—"

"Look, I'm with a customer. Nolan knows the right choice. Give up his summer, give up his chance at a Jeep, and keep his butt in school and his mom happy. He'd be stupid not to take a get out of jail free card, right?"

After the call, Principal Anand took a few deep breaths, exhaling slowly. "Well, here's the deal. Mr. Barno needs help. He wants you to help him this summer with his home, which I understand, has been quite neglected during the time Mr. Barno was, well, away. I'm sure your parents know about Mr. Barno."

I nodded.

"Do you?"

"I heard about him."

She frowned and slid an envelope across the desk. "I talked with our legal counsel, twice. You must have someone above watching over you because, by some miracle, they've approved this. There are important forms you and your parents will need to sign— acknowledgments of risk and liability waivers. That is, if you want to move forward. Go home. Talk it over with your parents. They'll go over the paperwork with their lawyer."

My cheap parents having a lawyer? Yeah right. "Lawyer. Of course," I said.

"If they agree, and you agree, have them sign these forms and bring them back to me by Friday. Understood?"

I nodded, eyeing the envelope. Was this for real? A chance to have my life back? *Hell-freaking-yes. Sign me up.* Then I thought, *Nolan, are you crazy? What is Death Row Barno capable of?* He looked old and slow. But I had seen *The Silence of the Lambs* and I knew that old people aren't all homemade cookies and flabby hugs.

"For now, stay home this last week of school. If you go forward with the arrangement, then we'll call it, hmm, time off rather than a suspension." Principal Anand stood. "Frankly, every fiber in my being—" She paused and pressed her palms down her gray suit jacket. "This is your one shot."

———————————

"See that ghost walking by?" my dad asked. "When a man really screws up his life, that's what he looks like. Take a good long look, son."

Dad was talking about Death Row Barno, who was walking his fluffy white dog down our street. My dad and I stood in the driveway, me stretching before a run and my dad loading tools into his truck. So I looked at Mr. Barno because that's what my dad told me to do. I didn't know how I felt about Mr. Barno, except that I knew I felt some guilt and some fear—fear of Mr. Barno and fear that Mr. Barno might wave or nod at me and Dad would know that something was up. But he just walked by as if we weren't there.

My dad leaned toward me, "Know what I think about what you boys did to Barno?" I shook my head. "You did the right thing by putting that schmutz in his place. He knows he's not wanted in Paxson. No one else will say it to you, son, but this whole town's glad you did it."

I headed out on a run clutching my digital recorder. I ran south toward the paper mill and stopped by a playground. I leaned against the chain-link fence, turned on the recorder, and sat quietly trying to capture the pop of leather meeting leather as two brothers tossed a baseball.

I ran back toward Main Street and stretched in the square by the white library building. Two middle school kids held hands on a nearby bench. I tried to capture their sound—quiet stares, little giggles, the energy of nervous, sweaty palms touching. So much of the meaning is in the silence between the sounds.

I ran north toward the wider streets and bigger lawns and to a street sign that read 'Bridge ¼ mile.' I took a right, ran a ways, then made a slight right and crossed Main Street again. I ran toward Mr. Barno's house. When I got there, I panted in the street with my hands on my knees and studied his house at the end of the cul-de-sac. The night we threw Mr. Barno a 'birthday party,' it was too dark to see just how run down his house really was. I turned on the Zoom digital recorder and recorded myself laboring to catch my breath.

Gabi Meyers. The hottest girl at Paxson High School and maybe one of the most beautiful girls to ever step foot in our nothing little town—or anywhere I would ever go for that matter—stood in line ahead of me at

Juanita's Taqueria. Her highlighted hair fluttered in layers down past her shoulders where it draped over a short jean jacket that hung over a floral dress. The dress crested over her exquisite rear and fell carelessly off her smooth thighs. Everything about her seemed free and easy, put together and assured. She was perfect like that.

Branson, standing behind me, gave me a nudge forward and I bumped into Gabi. She turned around. "Oh, my bad," I fumbled. She gave that annoyed smile girls sometimes give and turned forward again. *Ouch.* I wanted so badly for her to think I was interesting.

Branson jabbed a finger into my kidney. I coughed and threw eyes at him. "Best summer of our lives," he mouthed. "Your words to our ears." I flipped him the finger behind my back.

"Hey Gabi," Branson said, "how's it going?"

She turned, gave a little wave. "Hey."

"You know Nolan, right?"

"Hiya Gabi," I said. *Hiya? What am I, a troll from Minneapolis?*

"Yeah, Trig with Mrs. Wilson, right?"

"Uh-huh."

"Cool. She's tough."

"Yeah, tough." *Come on Sussman, think. You're blowing it.* "So, do you have any special plans this summer?" *Special? What was that?* I sounded like a teenage Mr. Rogers.

"I dunno," she shrugged. "Probably just hang at the river."

"Yeah, me too." I mimicked her shrug. Not sure why. "I'll probably just hang at the river."

Gabi's eyes searched for something. "Alright."

"I'm getting a new car. Probably a Jeep."

"Mmhmm," Gabi smile-nodded.

"I'm saving up for it. Maybe I'll take you and your friends for a ride this summer?"

"Jeez, that's nice of you," Gabi glanced past me toward the door. "Maybe," she smiled with inviting symmetry, eyes alive. I smiled back. "So I'll see you at the river?"

Out of nowhere, Dallas Stone threw an arm over Gabi's shoulder. She accepted it like a favorite blanket, tucking into Dallas' side.

"Hey, look, it's president of the poop pals, captain of the crap club," Dallas smirked. His hazel eyes, Oxi-Clean white teeth, and million-dollar jawline were all characters in the act.

"It's Midnight Warlords," Branson announced, pulling up beside me and holding his rounded chin high. "Yo, I remember, we hit your place twice last summer. Word is, both times you spent the weekend power washing eggs off the side of your house."

"Fake news, Boogie Man," Dallas said to Branson.

Okay, quick aside. Nicknames are totally a thing here at Paxson schools. And they're not the kind you want. It's some masculine bullshit passed down to us from the 'Old Heads,' the generations of Paxson students that came before. A cultural inheritance that we were destined to pass on. You do something once and forever you've got this albatross. Branson was called Boogie Man because, well, in middle school he was constantly going nostril spelunking in class. I guess he didn't even realize he was doing it—just some bored habit. He would stick his discoveries under his desk to get rid of them. Some kid saw that behavior, pointed at it, named it, and that was that.

Dallas' nickname was Dallas. His real name was Domleck, which sucks. Since Dallas was the star of everything he did, some Old Head started calling him Dallas—you know, the football team with the star on their helmets—to make fun of him. In true Dallas form, he turned a weakness into a strength and took on the name with gusto. Someone should have nicknamed him 'Dumb Luck Domleck.'

Anyway, back to the story.

Hunter Gallo, aka The Shark, one of Dallas' lackeys and the clear favorite for the part as the punch-first-ask-questions-later villain in the next film in the *Creed* series, lumbered toward Branson. The Shark got his nickname because he had a shark tooth tattoo on his neck. I'm not kidding. The guy was in high school and he got a shark tooth tattooed. On his neck. How insane is that?

I was not ready to get punched in the gut again by this human stone face squisher thing from Mario Kart. I knew I probably wouldn't piss my pants the way I did in the fourth grade. Still (And, perhaps you can sympathize), I didn't care to risk having my reputation thwamped in front of the love of my life. Fortunately, Dallas called off The Shark.

Dallas stepped forward with Gabi in tow, a passenger in his muscular arm. "And I heard Nolan Suspect here is getting kicked out of school." Dallas shoved a finger in my face. "Way to blow up your future. I always knew you'd end up stuck in this town swinging a hammer for the rest of your life just like your old man."

My nickname, Nolan Suspect, was earned because I got in trouble so much that I became the prime suspect anytime something bad happened. I hated that.

"You guys are so inane. Lighting shit as your call sign gave away every house you've messed with. You were social rejects before, but now you cretins have made a lot of enemies." Dallas' eyes grew big. "And you've got no greater enemy than me." He flicked me on the forehead and I must have gone tomato-red-level embarrassed right there in front of Gabi. On the bright side, this was perhaps half a page below pissing my pants on the list of reputation-flattening experiences I might endure while in my OAF's direct line of sight.

Dallas shifted to Branson and gloved his face, giving it a taunting pat on the cheek. "And you. I can't wait to see which trailer park you'll be living in when I visit after college. Will it be the one you're living in now with your tweaker mom? Or, worse, the rank one by the paper mill?"

Branson shoved Dallas' hand away. "Boo-hoo-hoo Daddy, it's so hot out here. Do I really got to power wash the house?" Branson mocked, playing a baby rubbing its eyes.

"Order number 87," a voice called from behind the counter. The cashier held out a soda bottle. "Oh, that's me," Gabi said, sliding out from under Dallas' wing. Dallas disengaged, turning to follow his girl.

My heart was sprinting, my lips eraser dry. "It's Sussman," I fumed under my breath. "Nolan Sussman."

"Huh?" Branson asked.

"Let's just get our food and go."

Branson and I perched on the curb outside of Juanita's Taqueria and dug into our to-go bags like hungry strays. Branson, who was tall, looked funny sitting on the curb, his knees the knobbed upper edges of a pair of bony, brown isosceles triangles. "Freaking stains," Branson grunted, ripping the foil around his burrito. Some people are all knees and elbows and Branson appeared that way. Really, he was all balls and guts. Life had boiled down to that for my sidekick who once lived for splashing rocks in the river and bike races down the hill by the abandoned train station. And I wasn't sure if I should feel respect or sadness for Branson. So I felt nothing.

Neil hobbled toward us, a wooden crutch under his right shoulder. "What's the deal with the curb?"

"I thought you were grounded," I said.

"Gramps is away on a mission. I thought you were?"

"Not sure. Things are kind of in limbo. Guess I'll find out tonight."

Branson tilted his head, motioning toward Neil's crutch. "You alright?"

Neil nodded. "Yeah, my body's just bothering me something extra."

Branson squinted at me and wagged a nacho cheese covered finger. "Gabi Meyers is never going to date someone like us. Girls like that only go for alphas."

"She will," I said between bites. "Everyone now knows we're the phantom Midnight Warlords. That changes everything."

Neil peered into the restaurant through the window. "The only thing that does is put a bigger target on our backs. And B-Man's right, lionesses don't date hyenas."

"God, I hate Dallas," I said. Truthfully, part of me loved him. How could I not? I wanted to be him.

"Hey Nolan." Skyler Bell jogged up on the sidewalk wearing a Paxson High Cross Country T-shirt and running shorts. She checked her pulse and stretched. "Why y'all out here?"

I chewed while Branson played it casual. "Nice evening and all."

"Sweet," she said. "I'm gonna jump inside and grab something. Join you after." Skyler put her arm out in a hook. Neil grabbed it, and the two of them went inside.

"Yo. Why's she been hiding in them baggy overalls all these years?" Branson asked, his neck careened, his eyes on Skyler's backside. "Girl's looking fly in them gym shorts."

"Dude, come on." I hit Branson on the arm. "She's basically my sister. I mean, my mom's literally got photos of her and me in the bathtub together when we were like two."

"Glad you're not into her," he grinned, "'cause you two got way too much in common."

"No we don't. Just running," I said. "Hey, question. Did Principal Anand call you in on Tuesday?" Branson shook his head. "Do you know if she called Neil in?" Branson said he didn't think so and asked me what was up. "Nothing. You haven't heard anything more about Death Row Barno?" Branson spread his skinny arms out, "Just that he had a great birthday party." He laughed, rice and beans falling from his mouth.

I sat at my desk, my fingers tapping on the envelope Principal Anand had given me. That night, Mom pressed me about the community service situation. I assured her I was taking it. Dad reported to Mom that it involved cleaning alongside the custodians at the school. And that sounded sensible. Mom was relieved I was back in school and Dad seemed glad about Mom. They grounded me for the summer anyway. No hanging with Branson or Neil. I was to work with Dad all morning and he would drop me off at the school in the afternoon for my community service.

I opened the envelope to flip through the forms inside. I didn't want to read them. I just stared at the signature lines on each document. One for me, one for a parent. I signed mine in blue ink. Then I forged my dad's signature in black ink.

The next day, when my parents were at work, I dropped the envelopes off to frown-face Mrs. Jackson. It was the last day of our junior year and I didn't get to run out of the building with my friends. I didn't get to watch the seniors throw their papers everywhere while singing Alice Cooper's "School's Out," a Paxson tradition inspired by that movie about kids in the 1970s, *Dazed and Confused*. How much better it must have been back in the day when being young meant being free.

Four

What is it about the way my parents are that makes me lie to them? I chewed on this question, and some delicious Bubble Yum Watermelon, as I climbed out of my dad's truck on the afternoon of the first day of summer.

Is there a specific reason, or is it just because they are my parents and parents push their kids into corners the way generals push troops into battles? I quickly realized that comparison doesn't work because generals throw subordinates into danger knowingly and on purpose. Parents often have no clue.

Either way, I knew my parents absolutely couldn't know about Mr. Barno. They'd flip. All I had to do was make it through the summer pretending that I was doing community service hours at school on weekday afternoons and my life would go back to normal in the fall.

I just needed Dad to drop me off at the school before 2 pm. After he left, I would run to Barno's. When I was done, I would run back to school before 5 pm and wait for Dad in the parking lot. Mom would have nothing to worry about and Dad would have nothing to be, well, dad about.

"Thanks, Dad." I waved into the truck through the cab window.

"You betcha."

"Okay, heading into the school now," I smiled. "I'll see ya."

"Alrighty."

The engine idled. "So, uh, you heading back to the job site?"

"Yup." Dad's wrist rested on the steering wheel.

"Cool. Cool. Hey, sorry about this. I know you could use the extra hand."

"Nah, that's alright. I was young. Believe me, got into a few thorny situations. Just part of growing up, son."

"Yeah." I examined a fading line of paint on the parking lot asphalt. "You don't got to pick me up after if you don't want to. I can just run home. I mean, I do it all the time."

"Nah, a little 'mano a mano' time is in order. You'll be tired having worked with me all morning and then three hours here. What I wouldn't do now to be able to go back and get a few minutes riding with my old man in his truck." My dad could be completely aloof one day and then weirdly sentimental the next.

"Yeah, cool." I turned to leave.

"Hey, son." I stopped, turned back. "Just don't let 'em humiliate you. They do that with community service. Give you the worst jobs—scrubbing toilets, cleaning garbage juice out of dumpsters. You feel me?" That's another thing about my dad. Sometimes he was him, and other times he was trying to be some dad from like 20 years ago who was trying too hard to talk the way teenagers talked like 20 years ago.

"I feel you," I said. I always played along. It was one of our things. One of our few things.

As he drove off, C+C Music Factory blaring on the stereo, I walked toward the front doors of the school. Once he was out of sight, I started jogging to Mr.

Barno's house through the path in the woods by the football field that students sometimes used to smoke or cut class.

I hadn't decided yet if I was going to tell Neil and Branson about the Barno situation. On the one hand, I told them just about everything—except how I was basically getting a Master's degree in romance under the tutelage of Lenny the True Love CEO, nor how, when I got really upset, I found somewhere small and dark—a bathroom stall with the lights off or the interstice behind the stairs by the band hallway—and sobbed the weepy way that Sussmans cry. On the other hand, the Barno situation felt safer the fewer people knew about it.

When I came out of the woods, I was hiding under the droopy sun hat and sunglasses that I had stashed in my backpack. I got to Barno's house at the end of the cul-de-sac and stood in the driveway right by where I had lit the 'birthday cake' just over a week before.

Barno lived in a white one-story house with streaks of green and black gunk that grew in stripes along the vinyl siding. The house was shaped like an L, with the short part a garage. The garage door had a row of windows across it and they were all covered from the inside with newspaper. The driveway was a spider web of cracks with dandelion and hairy bittercress squeezing through. Bushes that were probably once manicured had gone Incredible Hulk and muscled their way over the half of the lawn closest to the house. They wrapped around the back, stopping at a privacy fence that ran to the forest behind the lot. The mulch beds were weeds, the bricks that lined them mostly buried. Fallen branches from nearby trees filled the yard. They reminded me of dead bodies in the way they made ghostly indents in the foot-high grass. Old leaves poured out of the gutters.

It was as if the thumb of a giant hand pushed the trees back and cleared maybe an acre of land and then the hand plopped the house down in the clearing amid a fortress of locust, cherry oak, and pawpaws. Nature seemed eager to take the land back.

What am I doing here? Maybe this was some kind of prison justice. Maybe Barno was luring me in to get his revenge. *Why do I suddenly feel like I can't breathe?* Maybe I should have told someone about the Barno situation so at least the police would have a suspect when I disappeared. Well, Principal Anand knew. So, yeah, at least my body would be found.

I imagined my parents sitting around the TV at home, cups of coffee clenched in their hands as they leaned forward, gaping at footage from a helicopter circling over Mr. Barno's house as people in blue coats dug a hole in a taped off section of the fenced yard. There would be another team of blue coats poking around a shed. There was always a shed in the backyard at these killers' houses.

It's going to be okay. He's old. He's a retired killer, not some mid-career striver.

I stumbled up a few steps onto a landing and stood before the front door, which hid under a pointy overhang. Webs with bug carcasses suspended in a miniature drama of frozen trapeze insects clung to every corner. The light in the doorbell was dead. The door was one of those kinds that had vertical windows on either side. They also were covered with newspapers from within. Blinds were drawn on the bigger windows to either side.

As I was about to test the doorbell, I heard something inside. It was faint, rhythmic. I pushed the doorbell. It chimed. A moment later the rhythmic sound stopped. Soon after that, the door opened a crack, and I heard the little dog scratching behind the door. A bearded face and sunglasses filled the crack. "It's you," Mr. Barno said.

"Appears so."

"Meet at the garage," he said.

"That one?"

He lifted the garage door by hand from the inside. It was a two-car garage. The left side was empty except for a faint stain on the ground. On the right side, I saw a green nineties-era Subaru Impreza wagon. The garage walls were lined with gardening tools, a ladder, an old push mower, and a workbench. Faded cardboard boxes—one for a crib, another for a playpen—were stacked in the corner. Everything looked and smelled abandoned.

Mr. Barno stood beside me in his black trench coat and sunglasses. Standing near him, I realized he was shorter than I had thought. Shorter than me. He looked…something. I wasn't quite sure. Not old necessarily, the way PopPop and Grammy Lulu had looked. No. He looked like the stuff in his garage: abandoned. And while his face was wrinkled around the eyes, the rest of it looked soft, almost rosy.

Now, I don't want you to mistakenly picture Santa Claus just because Barno had rosy cheeks and a beard. His nose was more pear than cherry, and he was thin, almost frail. But there was something in his face that did remind me of the elf in the red suit—a sort of lost boy look.

"Bees only get one stinger," he said. "No room for error." *Great*, I thought, *killer guy is into saying cryptic shit.* Then he told me about the work. Clearing debris from the yard. Cleaning out the gutters. Pulling weeds. Fixing a few loose shutters. Trimming bushes. Mulching. Edging and resealing the driveway. Regular mowing and string trimming.

He asked if I could do that kind of work and I told him how I did a lot of yard work at my house and how I worked construction with my dad. "I'm not big," I told him, "but I know how to work."

He smiled. "Then I shall leave you in charge of it," he said before telling me that when I was done I should just pull open the garage, put the mower and tools back, and leave. He said he would unlock the garage each afternoon before I arrived so I could open the garage, get the tools, and get to work. He pointed to two red plastic gas cans by the mower. "I assume you'll have to mow once a week. When they're empty, lay them on their sides. That way, I'll know to fill them."

I scratched my arm.

He said, "What's a bad day, anyway?"—more nutbag cryptic talk— and went inside.

I put on work gloves, grabbed the wheelbarrow, and started clearing branches from the yard. When my watch alarm chimed at 4:45 pm, I cleaned up quickly and ran back to the high school.

It took three days just to clear branches from the yard. On the fourth day, I put gas in the mower, cranked it a few times, and to my surprise, it started. The drudgery went on like this for a few weeks. I never saw Mr.

Barno. If I left a gas can on its side, it was upright and filled the next afternoon. The whole thing sucked.

I was lying in bed one Friday night in early July, staring at the Jeep poster on the back of my door and listening to the tinny speakers on my phone as Lenny the True Love CEO dropped pearls of OAF-luring wisdom. And the next thing I knew, I was thinking about my sister Sarah.

How it started was that I was daydreaming about my Jeep and how I would probably never afford it. So far that summer, I had saved $532. I needed over $4,400 more.

So that got me thinking about Mr. Barno's old Subaru in the garage and how all I would ever be able to afford was something lame like that. And that got me thinking about how Sarah used to drive an old red Subaru Justy. That got me thinking about how it seemed the Sussman fate was to drive crappy old Subarus.

And that got me thinking about how Sarah called Subarus 'twinkle cars' because their emblems had twinkling stars on them. And then I was thinking about how she named that crappy old car Rustin' Justin and how it didn't have a CD player so she had this tape with a wire on it that she plugged into a portable CD player and how she blasted all those great bands like The Get Up Kids. And how she drove me and Neil to LEGO camp and how we had an understanding not to tell our parents about the cuss words in the songs. And how she always smelled like something sweet, even when she smelled like cigarettes. And how she liked to mess up my hair and then squeeze me close to her.

I started to smile and I started to really miss her. And I started to think that she really loved that crappy old car. That got me thinking about love.

I felt alone and abandoned, and I wondered if people looked at me and thought I looked abandoned the way I thought Mr. Barno looked abandoned. Then I got mad. I got mad at my sister for not being here—not being here to give me advice on how girls think and what they want and how to get them to like me.

Want to know a secret? I've always just wanted people to like me. I've just never been good at figuring out how to do that. For Sarah, it was easy. People loved her. And she could have taught it to me. But she didn't. And she can't. She's gone.

I reached under my bed and grabbed a Converse All Star shoebox that had belonged to Sarah. I nabbed it from her room. Inside were two types of things.

1. Things I took: a few concert tickets from when she saw Something Corporate and Jimmy Eat World. One of the purple pens that she used to write songs. A shoelace from a pair of Doc Martens.

2. Things she gave me: a small stuffed tiger worn with love named Wolf. An old iPod wrapped in earphones. A piece of construction paper folded into a football triangle.

I didn't understand the football triangle. Had it belonged to her boyfriend who played on the Paxson High football team? I guessed she was trying to show me something I could do when I got older. "An outlet," she had said when she gave it to me. That was actually the last thing she gave me and the last thing she said to me. "An outlet."

I was interrupted by a YouTube ad for some body grooming device. Then, Lenny's soothing voice came back on. "Step two in my magic formula is to share your OAF's interests. When they look at you, they should see themselves. Got it, brosef? There are a few ways to do this. First tactic is, do the stuff your OAF does. If that OAF is into yoga, you get you some yoga pants, join the class, and start stretching those hammies." I grabbed my notebook and wrote this gem down. "Check the links in the description for 10% off purchases from sponsors mentioned in this video and remember, Lenny gets what he wants and so can you. As always, do right by Lenny and subscribe."

That night I had this recurring dream where I'm trying to communicate with someone but they don't understand me. Sometimes I'm talking gibberish. Sometimes I'm trying to write something down but the words in my head aren't the words that come out on the paper. I told my old counselor about the dreams, but she wasn't the kind of shrink that was into dreams. She was the kind that was into medication. Which is fine and all. I think the blue pills do help. But it'd be nice to have someone to talk to about dreams.

On weekends, I was allowed to go for runs, get a few hours away from the house, that kind of thing. "Just no Neil and Branson," Mom said.

I kind of followed the rules. I texted the guys late at night and deleted the conversations before bed, just in case my parents checked my texts. Mostly we texted memes, bitched about whatever, and made promises of how fun senior year would be. Sometimes they texted me photos they snuck of kids having fun around town or down at the river just to torture me. There was even a picture that Branson snuck of Gabi and Becky sunbathing on a rock in the river, which I felt a bit slimy about. Branson got fired from two summer jobs—one at the grocery store and one at the pizza place.

Neil went out of town for a few weeks with his grandpa, supposedly because Gramps had a mission somewhere in South America. When we asked him to text us photos of his trip, he said he couldn't "put Gramps' life at risk like that."

Branson claimed he'd made out with Cienna twice at parties when she wasn't even that drunk. When pressed whether anyone actually witnessed this, he said it was a passionate affair that Cienna wanted to keep on the down low. Two days later he texted, "We broke up. It was mutual, bro."

One day, I just couldn't take it anymore. I took the path beside the boat launch, where you needed to use a stick to push the undergrowth away so the grasses and sedges didn't deposit ticks on you, to where the roofless shell of a decomposing stone building jutted out amid the trees at the edge of the riverbank.

This shallow spot in the river, Paxson Ford, is where troops crossed during the Civil War. These days, it was a secluded swimming hole. At a little cove of sand and shell, some fabled Old Heads had hung a rope swing from a tree that dangled over the river, installed a few old beach chairs around a fire pit, and somehow built a small wooden pier atop stacked rocks. If you were in high school, you could come and sit in the shallow water or wade out into the river to sunbathe on the large gray rocks scattered about. Middle schoolers got chased off. And only select people got invited to The Jungle, the legendary parties that happened here on summer weekend nights.

I lay out on a rock in the river hoping to see Gabi. No luck. After an hour or so, I climbed down from the rock and waded to shore. I perched on a beach chair, got out my Zoom recorder, and captured the sounds—the bugs, the breeze, the river. I sat quietly, listening.

"Yo. He lives," called a voice. I turned to see a smiling Branson with a towel over his shoulders wearing a pair of gym shorts and Adidas flip-flops. His hair was braided and dyed red.

"Holy shit man," I jumped up and gave him a hug. "Looking good."

"Thanks," he bowed to show off his hair. "You still on house arrest?"

I cursed an affirmation and he said, "I pity you, dude. Missing the best summer ever. I've made out with two total babes. Get this, Neil and I might crash a party at The Jungle next week."

"Worst summer ever," I muttered.

"Dude, I've been telling you. Screw your parents. Just live while you can."

"I know. Just can't risk it." I bit my lip so hard I was surprised it didn't bleed. "Can't blow my shot at coming back to school in August."

"Your loss." He pulled the ends of the towel up and down on either side of his torso. "Looking for your girl, Gabi?"

I swatted at a bug. "Was hoping to run into her down here."

"Lots of people been going to the waterpark in Hendersonville. Maybe she's there. Oh, saw her last week at Main Street Custard with Dallas. Those love birds were leaning over the table at each other and all that."

I gazed out over the river. "I'm not worried about Dallas." This was true because the luminary himself, Lenny the True Love CEO, was lighting my path now.

"Dude, you should be. Dallas is her perfect match. They're both going to be on the yearbook committee and in student government senior year. I overheard them plotting it. Plus, they both play lacrosse. As for you, No Land, you're a scrub with no car. No sports. No student clubs. No status. Just like me and Neil. Man, we're Midnight Warlords. We're outsiders."

"That all changes this year," I said, eyes locked on the glistening water. "I'm going to ask Gabi to Homecoming."

"You for real? Only way that changes is if you get rich. That's my plan. Make my millions and get up out of this town. Then I'll finally be happy, man. Finally."

Did those kids just flip me off? I was jogging down Mr. Barno's street one afternoon, my hat drooping low over my face. Two kids went by on their bicycles and out of the dark corner of my vision, I swear I saw them both flip their knuckles up off their steering wheels.

At Mr. Barno's, I had cleaned the gutters, trimmed the bushes back to Dr. Bruce Banner levels, pulled the weeds, excavated some semblance of the mulch beds and the bricks around them, and re-mulched and re-lined the beds with the bricks. I had also edged, filled the cracks, and resealed the driveway, which took for-ever.

I figured the work was about done. But I arrived that afternoon to find a note asking me to power wash the walkway and clean the siding. By the workbench, there was a bucket, a few gallons of some kind of cleaner, a pair of rubber gloves, and a pressure washer nozzle for the hose. So I started on that.

As I was leaving that evening, a few adults stood in the driveway of one of the homes on the street. When I jogged past them, they got quiet. One of them, a woman in capri pants holding a binder, turned and inspected me.

The next day, I was up on the ladder cleaning the siding when I saw the binder woman standing in an-other driveway talking to the homeowners. I started to really have to pee. I tried to hold it in as best I could, but as someone who had regrettably peed his pants at the unfortunate age of nine, I knew holding it was a los-ing battle. I got down off the ladder and knocked on Mr. Barno's door. No answer. I knocked again. Waited. Finally, I ran around the corner and rushed to the woods behind the house.

After going, I was walking along the privacy fence back to the house when I heard something on the other side. *Maybe he's digging a hole, the hole he plans to bury me in*, I thought. So, of course, I needed to see the hole and any accompanying shed. I tiptoed to the fence and pulled myself up quite stealthily the way I figured Gramps does, or at least the way he does in Neil's head.

Mr. Barno was on his knees in fresh red mulch at the base of a red oak. He reached his left hand out and grabbed hold of the air in front of him. With his right hand, he picked up a pair of pruning shears from beside a watering can and cut the air a few inches off the ground directly below his left hand. He turned and motioned like he was putting something into a vase, but his hands were empty. Completely empty.

Five

One night, I went for a run up to Main Street. I peered in the window of Main Street Custard, but I didn't see Gabi. I walked by Juanita's, but I didn't see her there either. I did see Skyler Bell who told me she liked my running shoes.

"Oh, thanks. Hey, have you seen Gabi?" She hadn't. "How about Dallas?" Hadn't seen Dallas, either. "Okay. Thanks. Well, catch you later."

"Hey, Nolan."

"Yeah?"

"Haven't seen you around much."

"Yeah. Been busy."

"Will I see you at school?"

"Yeah, sure." I turned to leave. Then I had an idea. "Hey, Skyler. Didn't your older brother play lacrosse in high school?"

"Um, yes," she said, dragging her s. "He was the goalie the year they won regionals."

"Cool," I nodded. "Hey, you think he could show me how to play?"

"He's away at college. He taught me how. I could, maybe, show you what he taught me?"

"Yeah, why not?"

"Sweet." Skyler smiled. "When?"

"My schedule is kind of crazy. Why don't you give me your number and I'll text you?"

"Would you like something to drink?" Mr. Barno's voice came out of nowhere. I shivered involuntarily (I guess I'm more like my mom than I want to admit). I was in the garage getting more house washing cleaner on a Friday in mid-August. "Didn't mean to startle you."

I placed the cleaning solution on the workbench and turned toward Mr. Barno. He stood smiling on the step from the garage into the house, the door open behind him. "No worries. You didn't," I said. *Seriously, could you be creepier?*

"You needn't relieve yourself in the woods. The house is old, but it's got indoor plumbing," he smiled.

"Oh I didn't want to bother—"

"No bother," he interrupted. "You work hard. Just as you said you would. I appreciate all you've done for me. Come on in, I've got some lemonade. It's just the stuff from the packet. But I add extra sugar." His smile morphed from impersonal to a friendly grin.

Alright, Nolan, this is how the ending begins, I thought. Next stop, you'll be wrapped in duct tape and trash bags in a hole in this nutbag's backyard. But even though I thought that, I decided to go inside anyway. I'm not sure why. I guess it was his grin. It felt, I don't know, genuine.

As I was about to step up the stairs and into the house, Mr. Barno said, "No smartphones." I squinted at him. *I'm pretty sure I saw a horror movie that started like this.* "Life is not somewhere else," he said. "Life is right here in front of you." I put my phone on top of a cardboard box by the door and went inside.

His little white dog, Dodger, greeted me with a wag. "He's a rescue. We've only been together a few months."

I squatted to pet Dodger. "Really? You two seem like pals."

Mr. Barno smiled. "I'm happy to have him and he's happy to have me. It's that simple."

I followed Mr. Barno and Dodger through the laundry room and into the kitchen. The kitchen was small and dated, and the countertops were cluttered with dishes, pots, pans, food boxes, and mail. There must have been seventy books stashed in corners, along walls, under countertop ledges in dozens of piles stacked five, ten, fifteen books high.

But it was, like, magical. Sunlight poured in through skylights.

Art hung everywhere. It was mostly paintings of flowers—purple and yellow flowers. The whole house was this way. Flowerless vases with marbles or little rocks at the bottom filled with water occupied any available space on every flat surface—the round kitchen table, the coffee table, the windowsills.

Plants, actual ones with actual green leaves, were scattered around—vine ones here, big elephant ears there.

Everything felt alive yet frozen in time. The tan leather couch that lined the wall in the TV room. The old thick kind of TV with the curved screen. An off-white computer monitor, also the old thick kind, on a desk beside a tower computer that had a telephone line running out of it and into the wall.

The back wall of the house, where the kitchen bled into the TV room, was floor-to-ceiling windows with a sliding glass door in the middle. By the door, I saw a bag of organic fertilizer and the watering pot and sheers I had seen Mr. Barno with in his backyard some days before.

And the music. All kinds I had never heard before. Pianos. Violins. Horns. Acoustic guitars. Wind instruments I didn't recognize. Sometimes the sounds of birds or waves were mixed in. It had a soothing wisdom to it, a knowing I can't describe.

"So next week is your last week, isn't it?" Mr. Barno took off his trench coat. Underneath, he wore stone-washed jeans, a purple and yellow T-shirt, and he had a few bracelets wrapped around his wrists. He took off his sunglasses. His eyes were soft, almost kind.

I scratched at the back of my neck.

"Think you can help me get this place in shape before you head back to school?"

"I can try."

Mr. Barno chuckled. "Are you excited to be heading back to school? Your senior year starts the week after next." He walked to the fridge.

"This wasn't exactly the summer I had in mind."

"I imagine it wasn't," Mr. Barno chuckled again, opening the fridge and taking out a pitcher of lemonade. "I'll never forget the summer before my senior year. Don Henley's *The End of the Innocence* had just come out and I blasted it on my Sony Walkman. I must have played that tape until it wore out. I saw a girl that summer at the pool and I just knew."

His grin grew. "When senior year started she was seated right next to me on the first day of classes. Every other girl's name was something average. Jane or Mary. But not this girl. The teacher said her name during roll call as if she was reading Shakespeare. Celeste. I repeated that name in my head over and over. Celeste. Celeste. That was the year that everything changed." He poured two glasses of lemonade, picked one up, and left the other on the counter.

"Jeez, you really know how to cheer a guy up," I deadpanned.

Mr. Barno pointed to the glass on the counter. "Maybe this is the year everything changes for you."

I picked it up. "Maybe."

"Here's the thing. You never know what little moment, like hearing someone's name for the first time, will send ripples into the future that will affect the rest of your life." *Like the first time I heard your name and now I'm here about to be ax murdered?* "Anyway, the world is so different now. They put a lot of pressure on you young people. Pressure to get it all figured out. They don't let you discover anything anymore. Careers, not jobs. Plans, not life." He sipped his lemonade and let out a satisfied 'ah.' "That stuff weighs on your mind?"

"I guess," I said, looking around the room for an ax tucked in the corner. "Senior year will be all about figuring out my career. They've got a whole day at the high school—Fridays—where seniors work on that. It's called Gold Day."

"The world is so different now," Mr. Barno shook his head. "So where are you on that journey?"

"I just know I want to be important," I shrugged, "like an influencer."

"A what?"

"An influencer. It's a person on social media who influences people to go places, or try things, or buy things. They live these amazing lives and have tons of followers."

"If you want to be important, all you have to do is be kind to other people and mean it."

I snorted a doubtful laugh, though he had said it sincerely—not in the cheesy or forced way that teachers say that kind of thing. I guess I just felt uncomfortable. Mr. Barno put his lemonade down and walked into the family room. I stood there awkwardly a moment before following him.

"Who's that?" I pointed to a photo of a young woman holding a cat, her mouth open so wide in a smile that her eyes were practically closed. She clutched a cat by her cheek. And you could feel she treasured that cat. She had a joyful beauty that held my gaze. I had never seen someone, in person or in a picture, look so happy in my life.

"That? That's Celeste." Mr. Barno picked up the photo and I could see that her joyful beauty held him too. "She would have turned fifty-two this year."

He put the photo down. "You've lost someone, as well, haven't you Nolan?"...

I was lying in bed one night when my door opened and Sarah slid quietly in. She put her finger to her mouth and kneeled beside me. "There's something better out there for me," she whispered. She had this look on her face. A look I didn't understand. She placed Wolf, her small stuffed tiger, and an iPod with earphones wrapped around it on the bed. I touched Wolf. "To remember me by," she whispered.

She kissed me on the forehead and stood. "Oh,

yeah." She pulled a folded paper football from her pocket and placed it beside Wolf and the iPod. "An outlet," she said. She squatted, pulled me close to her, and held me awhile in the quiet of my room. I didn't know what to say so I just smelled her.

She smelled sweet, as always. After a while, she stood, wiped her nose with the back of her hand, brushed her hair from her face, turned, and slipped out of my room…

I scratched my back neck. "How did you know that?"

"Your loss is written all over you, Nolan. I can see it in everything you do."

"You miss her still?"

"Boy, do I miss her," Mr. Barno said. "But that's alright because I talk to her all of the time."

"How did you get over losing your wife?"

"What do you mean?"

"Well, you seem so happy." It was true. One of those things you don't realize until you say it. Then once you say it, you still don't understand why you think it. Maybe it's not something you can think. Maybe it's something you can only feel.

"I am happy."

"How can you be happy?"

"Loss is part of life. In fact, I seem to have lost my lemonade."

"On the kitchen counter," I pointed.

Mr. Barno chuckled. "Sorry about that." He walked over and took a sip of lemonade. "One day, we lose our lemonade. Another day, we lose someone we love. Finally, we come to the day where we lose our mind." Mr. Barno laughed harder. "How can I not be happy?

This is my life. It's the only life I get." He glanced around. "I have lost a lot but I still have a lot. I've got a place to rest. I can still cook and enjoy food. I can still hear music. Oh, and books. I have books! The sun is shining. There are birds in my yard. I have flowers." He motioned toward the empty vases on the coffee table. "I'm not alone. I've got you here to help me. That makes me happy."

I laughed awkwardly. "Me? So what? I'm the kid who pranked your house. Why would you want me around?"

"Because you're worth having around. You may not see that in yourself. But I do." My face got red. "So how about you?" Mr. Barno asked. "Are you happy, Nolan?"

"I don't—" I paused. Thought. Happiness wasn't something I thought much about. It seemed so… so off-topic, so lacking emphasis in day-to-day life. "I don't think so." I pushed my lips to the left and sucked my right cheek in. "No. The truth is, I'm not happy." My shoulders sagged. "Man, this sucks."

"What sucks?"

"Realizing that I'm not happy."

"Balderdash," Mr. Barno smiled. "It's great."

"It's great?"

"Correct. It's great."

"What's so great about that?"

"It means you can finally do something about it."

I snorted. "What's there to do? Like most things in my life, it's out of my control. My parents annoy the crap out of me, but I got no choice about that. And thanks to you, I haven't chilled with my friends all summer. Oh, and this totally perfect girl I like? She's in love with this popular kid named Dallas."

"It's that bad, huh?"

"Yeah, and, I'm supposed to be getting ready for college. But I don't even know if I want to go to college. If I don't go to college my dad will be happy, but my mom will be devastated. And if I do go to college, my dad will be judgmental and my mom will be happy. And she will be pressuring me the whole damn time. She wants me to get a business degree so I can make lots of money. And what I want to do doesn't matter."

"Of course it matters."

"Not to my parents. Not to the school."

"Well, humor me. What do you want to do?"

"I don't know, exactly. I want to help people see the world in a different way than they already do."

Mr. Barno smiled. "That sounds exciting. Is that why you carry that device with you everywhere?"

"The digital recorder? Yeah, I guess."

Mr. Barno crossed his arms. "Do you think that if you can find out what you want to do, then you will live," he made air quotes, "happily ever after?"

"Yeah, I think so."

"You're wrong."

I stepped back. "How do you know that? You don't know anything about me."

"Happiness is what I know. You, my friend, are not happy and it breaks my heart."

I turned away and sucked hard on my cheek.

"I taught a class called 'Well-being and a Meaning-ful Life' at the high school before, um," Mr. Barno paused, "well, before I took a hiatus for a while. I can tell you that finding your calling will bring you joy and fulfillment. I'm sure you will be great at it. But it won't bring you the kind of lasting happiness you think it will."

For feeling reasons, not thinking reasons, I knew that what Mr. Barno said was true. "Well, then what will make me happy?"

Just then, the alarm on my watch began to chime.

"Looks like that's a conversation for another day," Mr. Barno said.

"But—"

"I'll see you next week, Nolan."

Six

I blew past the 'Bridge ¼ mile' sign. I was running so fast that if my life was a Saturday morning cartoon, the draft from me gazelling past the sign would have blown it down. But, alas, my life was very much not a cartoon.

I left Mr. Barno's house at 4:47 pm and knew I only had a few minutes to get to the high school before my dad. But my mind was racing and when that happens the only nondestructive thing I know to do is to run with it.

So I didn't run to the high school. Instead, I came up over the hill, past the imitation European bed and breakfast that overlooked the river, and there it was. The bridge. Well, there were two bridges actually. But I'm talking about the car bridge, not the train bridge. The train bridge was a few hundred yards downriver. So there it was. The car bridge.

On our side of the river, across the road from the bed and breakfast, is a small parking lot with one of those signs historic towns like Paxson put up to mark historic stuff. People stop to read the sign and walk the sidewalk on the car bridge. Sometimes, especially in autumn, they sit on the bench that overlooks the river. I sat on the bench, took out my Zoom recorder, pressed record, and waited.

Waited for Sarah.

I sat for a long time. Nothing. Just cars on the car bridge and, eventually, a freight train on the train bridge, the blare of its horn echoing off the cliffs below.

As the train rumbled south into the distance, I heard someone approaching and peeped back the way I had come. She wore a jacket and held a duffle bag slung over her shoulder. She walked past me sitting on the bench—didn't even look my way. When she got to the bridge she stopped a moment, eyed her watch, then kind of glanced around as if taking a picture in her mind. She seemed to spot something on the other side of the bridge and started to jog with this heavy bag swaying over her shoulder along the pedestrian walkway on the bridge. I knew where to look next. I swung around and set my sights on the top of the hill by the bed and breakfast.

Maybe a minute passed. A shoeless boy came running over in his pajamas. Tears streamed down his face, blowing in streaks back across his cheeks. He ran so fast. If only he could run faster. He stopped at the bridge, clutching the railing. Panting. His eyes locked on the far side of the bridge.

Across the river, I saw her sling her bag into the trunk of a blue car. The boy righted himself and screamed for his sister, "Sarah! Sarah come back!" She shut the trunk, opened the passenger door, and disappeared into the car.

If only I could run faster.

I stood and wiped the tears from my cheeks.

The truth is that when someone leaves home, home leaves the people left behind.

When I finally calmed down, it was 5:31 pm. *Crap. My dad.* I needed to get home stat. Every extra minute late was a nail in my coffin. *Has Dad knocked on the high school door and if so, was anyone there to answer?* If there was someone there, it would be a custodian and my web of lies would be ripped to shreds once they told my dad, "I think you're mistaken, buddy. There is no student on summer community service."

In my experience, dads do not like to be mistaken or called buddy.

I was too exhausted to run home fast. I needed a ride. But who could drive me? Neil didn't have a driver's license. I wasn't sure if that was by choice. And Branson's mom would never let him borrow her busted old Dodge Caravan. *Who else both has a car and doesn't deplore me?* I scrolled frantically through my contacts. *This is normal, right, to have almost no friends in high school you can count on?* Dwayne Albertson from LEGO camp. *Yes! Wait, crap. He moved two years ago.* I stopped at the kids in my Spanish II study group. Okay. *Most of them don't have cars and the few who do, Becky and Cienna, wouldn't pick me up.* I scrolled back up. *But the ones who don't have cars would definitely pick me up if they had cars, right?* Skyler Bell. *Yes, Skyler would give me a ride. See, I have friends.*

I texted her and she said she was on her way. Minutes later, she swooped into the parking lot, swung the car around like a stunt driver so the rear was facing me, halted with a screech, poked her head out the window, and called to me, "Heck in the what is going on?"

"Rock in the road. Didn't see it," I called back. "Nice driving. Holy crap!" I limped to the car. I was faking it and I felt like a total piece, especially knowing that Neil's limp was real and if he knew I was faking immobility he would hurt betrayal-level deep. But the excuse I texted Skyler was that I rolled my ankle running, and maybe it was sprained.

Skyler drove a yellow hatchback Volkswagen Rabbit, which was aptly named given the speed at which she drove. It had a bumper sticker that read, "Honk if you have a small brain," with a drawing of a goose.

I hopped in. Her maroon boot slammed the accelerator and we were arcing onto the road before I could grab my seat belt. Branson was right, Skyler had nice legs. And the way her hair blew all over her face as she drove made her look different than before. Cute. I could see why he liked her.

A song blared. A guy with this beautifully creaky voice sang about filling out forms to get into heaven and all the people you meet waiting in line to meet God.

"Who is this?" I asked as the evening air whipped around us.

Skyler stopped singing long enough to say, "Paul Simon. Paul and I are exclusive." We listened to another song. This Paul Simon guy was really talented. As we pulled into my driveway, Skyler added, "Musically, I mean. Like, I'm not like dating anyone or anything."

Inside my house, the questions came fast and hard. "Why weren't you at the school? Where were you? What were you doing?" I wanted to answer that I was at the bridge thinking about Sarah. Missing her. Hoping to see her on the far side of the bridge, walking toward me, her bag over her shoulder. But Sarah was an unspoken word in our house. And the bridge was a place I no longer went to, a place I vowed not to be found at by my parents again. I loved my parents. They annoyed me, yes, and they didn't understand anything. But they were mine and I loved them and I wanted so bad for them to believe that everything was finally okay with me.

Mom buffed her temples. "You were with Branson or Neil, weren't you?"

It was easier to argue than to tell the truth. Easier to fight with them than to say I'm sorry and I love you. Easier for them to be disappointed with me than to worry about me. So I lied and said, "I wasn't. I wasn't anywhere. Um. I was waiting for Dad, and, like, I saw Skyler. Yeah, and she was upset because her boyfriend broke up with her or something. I asked her for a ride home. But then she, like, started crying so I told her to pull over and she just unloaded on me."

"Then why didn't you text me and save me the trip?" Dad asked, leaning against the fridge. He sounded hurt. "I waited awhile. Almost got out the truck to look for you." I pictured him in the parking lot bobbing his head to House of Pain's "Jump Around," a deflated tinge in his voice as he rapped the part of the song about coming to "getcha" because I wasn't there to be got.

"I forgot, jeez. She was all bawling her eyes out." This seemed as good a time as any for an exit, so I thundered upstairs. At the top of the stairs, I shook with this feeling of being adrift and tried to anchor myself by focusing on Sarah's bedroom door. And the next thing I knew I was sliding down the hallway wall sobbing, "Sarah come back."

On the last weekday of summer, I snuck to Mr. Barno's house after my dad made me promise to either:

A. be at the high school at 5 pm, or

B. text him if I was getting a ride from someone else, no matter what.

When I got to Mr. Barno's, I veered around the side of the house to the spot where I had seen Mr. Barno cut invisible flowers at the base of a tree in his yard. I jumped up a few times to see the yard again, just to make sure I saw what I thought I saw. And yes, there were no flowers at the base of the tree. I did see smooth stones around the edge of the red mulch that encircled the tree. Some of the stones appeared painted.

I reached my recorder over the fence and pressed record.

After, when I was inside the house, Mr. Barno asked me to go to the hardware store. He handed me a shopping list—pressure-treated lumber of different sizes, pressure-treated boards, deck screws, bags of concrete mix, et cetera. "The house is in good shape outside and in," Mr. Barno said as he poured lemonade for two. "Thank you for your help this week. Are you up for this errand? It's getting harder for me to go out now. You'd need to take the car. You can drive, yes?"

I put an open palm out. "Indeed I can" (Okay, so, I didn't exactly have my driver's license. I had a permit and had never driven alone before).

"Freaking awesome," I said to myself when I turned the key and, somehow, the engine started on the first try. I blasted the fans to freshen the air and poked around a bit. The car smelled. Not in a bad way—just in a stale air kind of way. A few cassette tapes lay under a glaze of dust in the center console. A few more tapes were crammed into a shelf by the radio. A graveyard of brittle cigarette butts lay twisted like mealworms in the ashtray.

Inside the glovebox was a car registration form for Celeste Barno from the year 199-. The ink was so faded I couldn't read the last number. Maybe a three. Maybe an eight. I also found a folded pink sheet of carbon paper. I opened it, saw it was a police citation, and, flush with guilt, shoved it into the glovebox.

I blindly grabbed a tape and put it into the player. "Smooth Operator" by Sade began to play and I gave myself the old wink and gun in the rearview mirror and pulled out of the garage.

As I was strolling through the hardware store parking lot, my dad came out of the double doors pushing a cart full of chair rail and paint. I practically dove behind an SUV. He went by, his phone tucked in his ear. I scurried inside, got everything on the list, and carefully drove back to Mr. Barno's house.

Mr. Barno was sitting on the couch reading a book when I came inside. "Where were you? I was looking for you." He sounded like he was accusing me of something, but I wasn't sure what.

I held up a bag of screws. "At the hardware store."

"Right," he sighed. "The hardware store."

"I got everything on the list. Just got to get it out of the trunk. Where do you want it?"

He placed his book down. "Through the gate in the fence and into the backyard. I'll meet you there."

"Cool."

"Thank you, Nolan," he said as I put the last of the lumber on the pile. "That's all for your last day. You've been a big help this summer. Truly."

"But we're not done."

"There's more?"

I dusted off my hands. "I want you to teach me about happiness."

He folded his arms. "You do?"

"Yes. Can't you teach me?"

"Don't teach anymore," he shifted. "That was a long time ago."

"I don't care that you aren't a teacher at the school. I care because you're happy. And, well, I want to be happy, too. I asked you what will make me happy and you said we'd talk about it later."

"No," he said, tucking his hands behind his biceps so that his fingers were under his armpits. "Don't teach anymore."

"Please. I want to be happy like you."

"The answer is no. I'm sorry. It's just not a good idea."

"Why'd you convince Principal Anand to give me one more chance, then? Why did you save me if I don't get to be happy? What's the point then if there's just going to be—"

He cut me off, "Another miserable kid in this town?"

"Yes," I gasped. "Yes."

"Because I needed help." He turned away. "Had nothing to do with you."

I reached out and grabbed his shoulder. "That's a lie and you know it." My eyes began to well. *Why is he acting this way?* "We both need help. We both need each other."

"Our work here is done."

"Don't do this. Don't give up on me."

He stopped. "Do you see those flowers there?" He pointed to the base of the oak tree. I shook my head.

My hand fell to my side. "But you want to?" he asked, his near eyebrow raised.

I didn't know what he meant. "Yeah," I said, "sure." Then I added, "I can see all the other ones," motioning to the rainbow of flowers in the beds all around us inside the fenced yard.

Mr. Barno eased onto a metal bench. "You said you work construction with your dad, isn't that right?" I nodded, rubbing snot with my knuckle. "You're a good builder, aren't you?" I nodded again.

Mr. Barno waved for me to sit. "Suppose you could help me build it?" I sat next to him facing the lumber. "And in exchange, I will help you."

"Cool," I said. "Okay. I mean, yes. Yes, I can do that. Just tell me what to build. After school. I'll find a way to come then. Don't worry about that."

Mr. Barno put his veiny hand on my knee. "The most important question you must answer is: 'is the universe kind?'"

"Is the universe kind?"

"Yes, I'm paraphrasing a quote from Albert Einstein. He used the word friendly. Einstein said that the important question each of us must answer is whether the world is friendly or not. But I prefer the word kind."

I sat beside Mr. Barno and thought about this question. Or, at least I tried the best way I could to understand what he was asking me. I wasn't sure about the universe, but I knew that high school wasn't kind. If it was, there wouldn't be people like Dallas Stone and that creature, The Shark, prowling the halls. And high school was my universe, really. So no, the universe wasn't kind. But I didn't tell Mr. Barno my answer because when I opened my mouth to speak he closed his eyes, drew his tongue up and down his mustache, and said, "Be with the question."

I tried to 'be with the question' for a while that afternoon on my run to meet my dad, during dinner as we ate in silence and the TV news droned on, and as I lay in my bed staring at the contents of my room. Is the universe *kind*? Is the *universe* kind? *Is* the universe kind? But, soon I found my way to my phone, or my phone found its way to me. Not sure which.

I hopped on Gabi's Instagram feed and scrolled through her pics. The most recent one, from yesterday morning, was of her and her brother at the beach. Probably Ocean City. No, there was a picture of her at sunset wearing a loose-fitting Paxson Lacrosse T-shirt—a tanned shoulder revealed—and jean shorts on the boardwalk from the day before. Definitely Rehoboth Beach.

I scrolled. More beach photos. Seems like she spent most of the summer there. No pictures with Dallas though, so that was good. Further down I found pictures of her, Becky and Jisoo holding their lacrosse sticks up at a summer lacrosse league game. Then, her and Dallas at the river. *Dang she looks good in that red bathing suit. And Dallas, that show off with his abs flexed. They're flexed right? That's not his resting ab-state, is it?* I pulled up my shirt to compare Dallas' toned landscape to my barren, clammy wasteland of a chest and stomach. If I was the lead singer of a cover band, it would have to be called: Imagine Muscles.

Next photo: a photo of her, Dallas, The Shark, and Jisoo around a bonfire at a party at The Jungle. Then, a selfie of her and Dallas in a booth at Main Street Custard, smiles to the ears. Then there was a video. I clicked play.

Gabi was in her bedroom, a very pink and organized bedroom with lots of pillows and plush animals, and she was sitting at a desk looking over her laptop into the camera. "Hey lovies, just working on my app to 'Cuse. Gonna get this done tonight, click submit, and send my dreams out into the world. Hope they turn orange! Love you all. Stay tuned!" She kind of shrieked with excitement and just as the video cut off she glanced off camera and smiled. *Was she smiling at someone?*

I sighed, slid off my bed to the floor, and lay there feeling like wet socks. *Is the universe kind? Clearly not when it comes to love.*

Strangely, studying is the thing I've always been good at. Maybe because the goals are clear, the rules are clear, and the results of your efforts are clear. Doesn't matter what's going on around me. Doesn't matter how I feel inside. The material in the textbook, on the board, in my notes is unaffected. Emotionless. Empirical. Reliable. When everything is in chaos, a math formula doesn't judge. When you're in trouble, an historical figure doesn't chide you.

I may not be good at a lot. Other kids might beat me in just about everything—sports, clubs, money, cars, abs, popularity, self-control, million-dollar jawlines, general levels of sanity—but I whoop them when it comes to school. That's how I compete.

I grabbed a pen and logged into class for tonight's lecture with Lenny the True Love CEO. "Remember, Step two in my magic formula is to share their interests." *Ah, yes I remember. Teach on sage.* "The second way to do that is by conveying that your wants are their wants. Listen to the music they like and show them that you like it. See the kind of clothes they like to wear and wear clothes that match their style."

I paused and studied my notes. *What kind of music does Gabi like?* I tapped to her Instagram feed. There was this one old video I'd seen where she and Jisoo were lip-syncing to Justin Timberlake.

Okay, I knew I couldn't pretend to like that.

I started re-watching my esteemed professor's lecture. "See the kind of clothes they like to wear, and wear clothes that match their style. For example, I'm wearing this slick hoodie from USC that my people at College Threddz n' Stylez hooked up. Now, everybody knows I went to UCLA. Go Bruins! But, my girl Tanya goes to school at USC. You get me? Write that down."

That's it! Thank you, oh wise one.

"Check the links in the description for 10% off purchases from sponsors mentioned in this video and remember, Lenny gets what he wants and so can you." I paused the video and finger-hopped down to the link to College Threddz n' Stylez.

"Welcome to The Jungle," Branson said. He said it in a cool way, not in the 1980s leather pants kind of way my dad says it when he sings that Guns N' Roses song.

Branson and Neil met me at the entry path to Paxson Ford. A bonfire raged and people drank to Eric Kemp plucking his guitar while girls belted out "Margaritaville" lyrics. Others encircled a keg of beer. *How'd they get a keg down here?* A few folks sat huddled on the dock, passing something back and forth. Nearby, a guy splashed a few girls in the shallow water. *The Shark?* In deeper waters, swimmers with underwater flashlights were spotlighting the river bottom. Here and there were the faint sounds of couples copping feels in the dark.

An hour earlier, I was asleep in bed when the vibration of my phone woke me.

Branson (10:33 pm): Come down to jungle. Dank party. Everyone here. [Palm tree emoji][Fire emoji]

Me (10:33 pm): You serious? The jungle? No way parents let me.

Branson (10:33 pm): Yes. Wait till they asleep. Sneak out. [Smiling face with halo emoji]

Me: (10:34 pm): Not trying to get busted. [Knife emoji][Face with crossed-out eyes emoji]

Branson (10:34 pm): Gabi here.

Me (10:55 pm): Sounds like parents in bed.

Branson (10:57 pm): YOLO. I know is dated but true. Your chance with Gabi tonight.

Me (10:58 pm): Waiting 10 to make sure asleep. Then on my way.

"Sure it's cool we're here?" I asked, spotting Dallas sitting beside Gabi at the bonfire.

"Yeah. Last night of summer. No one cares. Everyone's hammered." Branson gave me a fist bump. A "whhhhoaa" sparked over the noise followed by a splash. Then laughter. Someone snatched the rope swing as it whooshed by the ledge.

"To Camp Warlords," Neil waved. His usually clammy, pale skin was summer gold. "You first," he said to Branson. Branson swayed as he walked and Neil leaned heavily on his crutch while he followed as the clumsy robot. We went down a short path to an opening where a log sat at the edge of the party.

Branson reached behind the log and revealed a bottle, "Beer?" I shook my head. Branson grinned, "More for me."

I peered over the log and saw five beers left in a case of twelve. "Thought we made a drinking pact. Two beers max."

Branson shrugged, twisted the bottle cap, chucked it over his shoulder, and took a sip. His face contorted but he seemed to try to hide it. He shifted his grin toward Neil, "Need one?"

Neil lowered himself shakily and slipped and fell on his rear. Branson and I grabbed Neil's shoulders and helped him onto the log, Branson and Neil laughing the whole time. We sat a bit as they drank and talked about things that I missed out on. I gazed through the trees toward the bonfire, but I couldn't see Gabi.

I turned to see Neil rolling a THC vape pen between his fingers. He took a pull and said in what I think was an impersonation of a book character, "The herb lifteth me up and settith me down gently," before giggling.

I didn't want to be a party pooper, but I rarely drank and had only ever tried cannabis exclusively with Neil. I kind of liked the way it made music better and video-games cooler. But I couldn't think straight, let alone talk, when high. Plus, it sometimes made me really paranoid. And I was planning to talk to Gabi. So when Neil offered, I shook my head. Neil took a hit and said, "I don't do it just for the goofballs, you know. It helps my pain." I knew. He wasn't old enough to get a medical marijuana card, but if he had been, he would've qualified.

"I'm pulling rank. Give me beer." I looked up. The Shark loomed over us.

Branson stood, swayed. "Hell nah, man. Get your own." He chugged the bottle in his hand.

The Shark's muscles tensed. "Keg's kicked. Give me a beer."

Neil grabbed his crutch and pulled himself up. "Here, take mine." The Shark swiped the beer, turned, and left. I helped Neil down to the log. He asked me if I was still grounded. I said that once school started on Monday, I was free.

"Status update on the Jeep?" he asked.

"About $2,000 short."

A woozy Branson stood. "Sssenior year starts next year. I mean, week. Thisss is our year. Next week," he laughed. "Jjjust like you said man, jjjust like you said. Gotta. Gotta make it the most fun we've ever hhad. Nolan's back man. He's back. Time for the Midnight Warlords to re-u-nite."

"I'm not about to get in trouble again," I said, trying to get Branson to not talk so loud and sit down.

"No worries, my mannn. The pppranking stuff is

done. Finito.”

"More beer. Now.” The Shark had returned.

"Get fffffucked. I'm not gggiving you my beer,” Branson slurred.

The Shark spoke in a low, sharp tone. "Boogie Man, I'm trying to fucking enjoy the last night of summer with that fine-looking lady down there.” He grabbed Branson by the shoulder and swung him so they both were facing the silhouette of a female standing at the water's edge. "So give me a fucking beer or I'll turn you into Boogie Boy right here in front of everyone.”

Out of the corner of my eye, I saw Neil reach slyly behind the log.

"Branson, just give him a beer,” I said.

Branson shooed me with a swat of the arm. "Ifff he wants my beer, hhhe can go get it.” He chucked his bottle against a tree. It smashed. A malty firework.

I jumped to my feet. Neil pushed himself up slowly, holding something behind him. "Come on Shark, drop it,” Neil said.

"Get bent, pip-squeak.” The Shark grabbed Neil, picking him up. Neil's crutch fell and something fell, too. A rock. The Shark marched down the path toward the river, Neil thrown over his shoulder. Neil screamed. "My back, my back!”

Branson yelled for The Shark to put Neil down. I stood, frozen, staring. Branson gaped at me, "Come on!”

"I can't. I can't get in trouble.”

"Are you kidding mmme right now? Hhhe's one of your bbbest friends.”

"I'm sorry.”

"Did you forget second gggrade? He was the ooonly

kid who was nnnice to you. Even I was a ppprick to you bbback then."

I reached down, picked up the rock and we ran toward the river. The Shark stood on the dock holding Neil under his arm like a designer dog. The music died. The swimmers' lights spotlighted the dock. Silence fell over The Jungle. Everyone waited and watched. Branson and I halted at the edge of the dock.

"This disrespectful cripple is going for a swim," The Shark howled.

Tyler Pratt-Baldwin stood from his perch on the dock and soothingly said, "Hunter. Hunter, my man, relax. Be chill."

"Piss off," The Shark barked.

Tyler, with the tact of a hostage negotiator, said, "Dude, it's Neils on Wheels. He's harmless, man."

The Shark laughed, "Neils on Wheels. Best nickname ever." He gave Neil a noogie. Seriously. A sixth-grade fucking noogie. Neil fish-squirmed.

Tyler chuckled along, telling The Shark that someone brought weed and that a few people were smoking it in the dilapidated building. "Last joint man. I just had a hit a minute ago. It's fire. Let's get some before it runs out."

"They got beer, too?"

"Pretty sure," Tyler smiled.

The Shark dropped Neil on the dock and jogged toward the old building. Neil crashed onto his side. "I'm right behind you," Tyler called to The Shark who was already out of sight. When we got to Neil, he was clutching his ribs.

"Neil, Neil, you alive?"

Neil opened his eyes. "The Shark lifteth me up and

settith me down gently." And he laughed hysterically.

Tyler kneeled down and helped pull Neil up. "You steady?" Tyler asked, his arm around Neil's back.

"Thank you," Neil smiled.

I ran back to Camp Warlords, scooped up Neil's crutch, and ran back to the dock while Branson puked off the dock's edge into the dark below. Tyler and I helped Neil onto his crutch. "You guys alright?" Tyler asked me and I replied, "I think so. Hey, Tyler, thanks, man. Really." Tyler stood there with this half-wasted smile on his face. Everyone stared at us, but he didn't seem to notice or mind. I added, "We owe you one."

He shook his head and pushed his multi-color dyed hair back over his scalp. "No you don't." Then he reached out and messed up Neil's hair the way an older brother does. "I see you," he winked. "The Midnight Warlords." And with that, he turned and sauntered away.

Eric Kemp came in right on cue with an acoustic version of the Beastie Boys' "Fight for Your Right." And the party started back up.

Neil, with the crutch under one arm and his other arm draped around my back, murmured, "That's Tyler P.B. Tyler Peanut Butter. He talked to me. Oh, man. Oh, wow. He's so freaking cute." Then he smiled. And for the first time in forever, I couldn't find an ounce of pain on his face.

I tried to get Neil to leave but he said he'd wait at Camp Warlords for Branson to sober up. I didn't say bye to Branson. Honestly, I was pissed at him. My sister had this line in one of her songs. I don't remember how she phrased it, but the point was: the things about the people we love that make us stronger also make us weaker. When she sang it I asked her, "Then who'd want to be in love?" And she told me I was too young to understand.

So, yeah, the drinking. I liked it back when we were just starting. Sophomore year, everything changed. Branson would drink and act real stupid. He'd throw things. And finally, he'd puke and sober up and have this kind of amnesia about what he'd done. One night after sobering up, he said to me, "I've got that Hurtado family thread in me. Don't let me pull it." He held it together after that. Two beers max. But here he was senior year, yanking on that thread.

Secondly, I was pissed about Neil. Not at him. At me. The Paxson nickname Neils on Wheels started because Neil showed up to eighth grade in a wheelchair. Things were getting worse. His one leg was swollen red at the ankle and knee. He never said why. I just knew he went to a special doctor a lot and it was hard for him to walk.

One day I called him Neils on Wheels because... I don't know. It was just easier than asking questions. It was supposed to be an inside joke. Like, the way guys prod each other out of love. Unfortunately, other people found out about it. Neil became Neils on Wheels. He said he got so sick of people calling him that. I guess he figured he'd just use a crutch. But the crutch caused him terrible back pain. It was a lose-lose. I haven't seen him in a wheelchair in public since. And that's on me.

As I walked down the dark path away from the party, my phone's flashlight guiding the way, I came across two people on the path in front of me. A guy and a girl all over each other in this drunken embrace, the girl's leg wrapped around the guy and the guy's hand up the girl's shirt. I squeezed by. They were so into each other that they didn't notice me. But I noticed them. It was Dallas and Gabi.

At the boat launch, I sat and listened to the water lap against the concrete. I swear, sometimes I could have disappeared into the silence between sounds—the purgatory after the river licks the shore before it slips away, the anticipation of something better, the wisp of air between the pounding of a runner's feet, the pause before the next breath. The time it takes a voice to travel from one side of the river to the other. I wished I had my recorder. I took out my phone with the intention of using the record app.

My fingers found their way to my text thread with Skyler. I typed: "Hey it's Nolan." It was almost midnight. I hovered over the send button. Then, I forced my thumb onto the button—like there was this fight between my mind and myself and somehow I won. I put the phone down and just as I wrapped my hands around my knees, my phone vibrated.

Skyler (11:57 pm): [Smiling face with smiling eyes emoji] I know.

So we texted a bit:

Me (11:57 pm): Oh right
Me (11:58 pm): You awake?
Skyler (11:58 pm): Yes, silly.
Me: (11:58 pm): Oops. Duh. My bad
Skyler (11:59 pm): [Smiling face with smiling eyes emoji] It's no problem.
Me: (12:00 am): So about lacrosse. When can you

teach me?

    Skyler (12:00 am): How about next Saturday?

    Me (12:00 am): Cool. Noon at town square?

    Skyler (12:00 am): [Smiling face with smiling eyes emoji] Okay. I'll bring you a stick.

    Me (12:01): Right. Good idea

    Skyler (12:01 am): [Zzz emoji] Goodnight Nolan.

    Me (12:01 am): Night

Seven

I remember Sarah getting ready for her first day of senior year in high school while I lay wrapped in a blanket on the floor in the hallway outside her bedroom. I was nine. High school started earlier than elementary school and so it became our thing. We didn't talk. But I was there with her as she leaned over the dresser toward the mirror to put on a little makeup or perfect her hair. If it was a good day, she sang the songs she wrote. If it was a bad day, she sang other peoples' songs.

On the first day of school my senior year, I ran down the stairs. I made it. Back to Paxson High. My parents never found out about old Mr. Barno. Summer was a waste. But it was behind me. Things could go back to normal now.

"You look nice," Mom said. "Finally. Who's the girl?"

I put my arms out so Mom could see my new orange Syracuse Lacrosse T-shirt. "Thanks, Ma. No girl."

"I get it. Too cool to tell your mom. Thinking about college at Syracuse, then?"

"Maybe."

She scrunched her nose the way she used to. "Hey, I need you to promise me something. No trouble this year."

"Okay, okay. No trouble."

"I'm serious. I need you to promise."

"Okay. Sure. I promise."

Mom hugged me and I kissed her on the cheek. I could smell the tears starting, "I just can't have you getting kicked out of school. If something were to happen, well, your dad and I, well, right now we can't afford to pay for private school."

I eased back. "We're broke?"

"No. It's nothing to worry about, hun. The housing market has cooled off a bit. That's all. And Mr. Lewis seems a little concerned."

"Why does this always happen to us?"

Mom wiped her eyes. "Hey, don't say that. We've got a lot going for us."

"I worked all summer. I'm still $2,000 short of what I need to buy a Jeep."

"I know you want that car, hun."

I grabbed a Pop-Tart and tossed it in the toaster. "I gotta have it. Everyone else is getting a car but me. It's not fair."

"Don't give up, hun. Just a few more months of working with your dad."

I gulped some OJ. "Hope so. Just tired of waiting."

She patted me on the shoulder and gave me a squeeze. "I know. Speaking of waiting, that bus isn't going to wait for you. You better go."

I wrapped the hot Pop-Tart in a napkin. "Okay, Ma. Love you."

"Love you."

I ran out the door, glanced back at the house, and took a mental photo while Mom stood in the doorway waving.

The social hierarchy at Paxson High School was intertwined with the building's architecture. They say power always consolidates and that was true at The

Sect, or main intersection, where the most popular kids had lockers closest to where the two major hallways crossed.

That's where you could find the football team, lacrosse team, yearbook committee, SGA, et cetera. It was our Beverly Hills and residents included Dallas and his entourage and Gabi and her clique, the Honey Bun Girls—no clue where that name came from. Popularity worked outwardly in concentric circles. Rings of status. Less popular sports, band and theater kids, the moonshiners who constantly skipped school to hunt and fish, goths and kids who dressed like anime characters.

The Midnight Warlords inhabited a desolate outpost by the cafeteria known as The Desert. There we huddled amid the burnouts, the clueless, the egalitarians, and the unaffiliated.

Heading through The Sect on my way to my last class of the day, I finally saw Gabi in the crowded hallway at her locker. I turned toward her and waved so she could see my orange T-shirt. She smiled and opened her locker. I smiled back. *Lead me to the Promised Land, Lenny!*

The last class on Mondays was Government & Military with Mr. Green. The rumor was that Mr. Green fought in Iraq and Afghanistan, was a little hard of hearing because of an IED explosion, and, in his finer moments, forgot this was a high school and not a boot camp.

I came into the classroom, slung my bag down on an empty seat to hold it for Neil, and overheard Yuvi saying to Omar, "So get this. My mom's going all Captain Mom and trying to help a couple of those Justice

League parents to get this petition going to force that serial killer guy to move."

Omar asked, "Can they do that?"

Yuvi said, "Don't know. She says his house is too close to the school and it makes the parents uneasy. I guess there's some law about criminals or something and a mile radius around the school."

Omar said, "Well, shoot man, I can't say I've ever agreed with anything your mom has done." Yuvi and Omar guffawed. "But I wish them luck. That guy deserves to hang. He's a lunatic."

I leaned in. "Who you talking about?"

Omar said, "Death Row Barno."

And I said, "How do you know? You ever talked to the guy?"

They both leaned back and kind of glimpsed at each other, their faces big. Then Yuvi said, "Looks like Nolan's wearing some guilt about hitting Death Row Barno's house."

I said, "Shut-" A bugle interrupted me. Mr. Green stood erect at the front of the class facing the flag that hung by the door. He was playing "Reveille," which I had heard he does at the start of each class.

After the blare, Mr. Green put the bugle in his drawer and pointed to the chalkboard where a quote read: "War presents itself as necessary for self-protection, when in fact it is necessary for self-identification." *– Finite and Infinite Games: A Vision of Life as Play and Possibility* by James P. Carse.

Neil was late, which was typical. It took him a while to get from class to class. When he came in, he was wearing his *Top Gun* T-shirt under a military surplus store bomber jacket (August heat be damned), which was also typical (Neil perennially claimed that his first day of class outfit was necessary to 'set the tone' for the school year).

After class, Neil, Branson and I met at our lockers where I told them my dad was picking me up so I could get to work.

Branson cracked his knuckles. "I thought you only work Friday afternoons and weekends with your dad during school?"

I told him I was trying to save up money to buy that Jeep, so I was working Monday afternoons too. When they were gone, I jogged to Mr. Barno's house.

Mr. Barno opened the front door and I announced, "I'm here for my first happiness lesson. It's 3:05. I told my parents I was training on Monday afternoons to get ready for cross country tryouts. I have to be back at the high school before 5 pm so my dad thinks I was practicing. I've got just under 2 hours once a week to learn about happiness. Will that be enough time?"

"Well, let's get to work," was all he said. So we worked in the backyard for a while. Mr. Barno had drawn schematics and the first step was to dig a few holes around the tree outside of where the stones were.

After an hour, I wiped the sweat from my forehead. "When are we going to have the happiness lessons?"

Mr. Barno handed me a glass of lemonade. "Doesn't work that way."

"Can we start with love? I want to get Gabi Meyers to fall in love with me."

"Why?"

I leaned on the shovel. "Because, when I get Gabi, I'll be happy."

"I'm afraid we can't start there."

I shifted my weight. "Why?"

"Loving someone comes much later."

"Why?"

"Well, if you want someone to love you, you first must love yourself."

I swayed the shaft of the shovel side to side. "Seriously?"

He drew his tongue up and down his mustache. "We must start at the beginning." He reached out and I handed him the empty glass. "I didn't say this would be easy, Nolan. If you want to find true happiness, you have to face some truths. They may be hard truths. But if you work through them, then happiness you will find."

I let go of the shovel and it fell. "You don't know me. You don't understand me. Why are you acting like the shrinks my parents try to chase me down with like I'm a wild animal? It's not fair. You all just make assumptions about me."

"You're right. I don't understand you. And you don't either. Here," Mr. Barno put a hand on my elbow and led me toward the tree, asking me to avoid stepping on the flowers that weren't there. "Stop," Mr. Barno squeezed my elbow. "You're crushing them." I apologized. "Sit down against the tree, just be careful of the flowers," Mr. Barno instructed.

I sat and squeezed my legs tight. The air smelled of something familiar. The soap in Mr. Barno's bathroom? Jasmine? He sat with his back against the tree next to me, put his hand on the back of my neck, and said, "Close your eyes. Just breathe."

I sat there a bit and tried to breathe. I tried to breathe in the way I thought he wanted me to.

"Stop," he said. I opened my eyes. "Be. Be with it."
I closed my eyes and started over.
Something happened.

Soon, I was sitting in a chair that lined the hallway of the police station. I don't mean in my head, like a memory. I was really sitting in the chair. My dad surged out of a room crying.
"Dad," I called.
He marched past me down the hallway and outside through a door.
"Did they find her?" I asked when I finally caught up to him in the parking lot.
He shook his head, turned away from me, and said, "If she crossed the bridge then she's out of state. They said that makes it harder."
"Where'd she go?"
He didn't speak for a while. Then he spat and said, "We don't know."
I kicked at a pebble. "When will she come back?"
He spat again.
"It's not fair," I said.
He grabbed a wad of his shirt off his chest. "Stop. Stop. Stop. Stop. Be a man."
"But I miss her," I cried.
He swiveled around and crouched down, the skin on his face tense, his lips sharp as a blade. Tears in his eyes. He grabbed me on either arm. "Then why did you act that way? Why couldn't you just be, shit, more like your sister? God, Nolan. It's like you're waging total war and nothing can survive on the edges."
I lost control, went limp, and sobbed hard. I re-mained on my feet only because he held me there. It

took a while but as I calmed down, his grasp loosened. I snorted and rubbed my knuckle under my nose, my vision blurry from crying.

"I'm sorry," he said finally. "I shouldn't have. I just wish. Maybe. If everything hadn't. It's hard being a parent. Maybe your mom and I would've noticed something. We could have been there for her. Anyway, it's not your fault. It's. Well. When you've got two kids, well, you've got two kids."

I said, "I love you, Dad. I. I'm sorry." I knew to say sorry, even when I didn't understand why. I guess everyone is that way. My dad let go of me, righted himself, turned, and walked to his truck. He opened the passenger door and stood there looking at me. I ran over and climbed in.

Back under Mr. Barno's tree, I opened my eyes. The last trickle of a river of tears oozed down my face. "What kind of tree is this?"

"Nolan, our first lesson about happiness is actually about fear. If you want to understand someone, really listen when they talk about their fears. Everyone has at least one great fear that motivates the choices they make."

I wiped my cheeks, sucked back phlegm, and waited until I thought I was steady. But my teeth chattered when I asked, "How do I know what they fear?"

"Listen closely to what they talk about most. Their fear is hidden behind the thing they care about most. A police officer will talk about keeping the community safe. He's telling you that his biggest fear is crime. You could say his life is focused on the fear of crime happening to the community. But that's missing the personal aspect of fear. Fear is about what will happen to us. The police officer's big fear is that he or his family will be the victim of crime. His biggest regret would be that he didn't do enough to stop that from happening. On the other hand, a basketball player will talk about everything she is doing to win. She's getting in shape, she's practicing her jump shot, she's watching videos of great players. She's telling you that her greatest fear is losing, both on the court and in life. Her biggest regret would be if she didn't work hard enough and ended up being a loser, however she defines that."

I took a fistful of my T-shirt. *Stop. Stop chattering. Be a man.* "Okay, you want me to listen to people and learn their fears?"

He slipped his hand out from behind my neck. "Mostly I want you to listen to yourself and find your fears."

"I'm not afraid of anything."

"Correction, Nolan. You're afraid of everything. But what do you fear the most? What is it?"

"This is a load of crap." I stood.

"Your choice." Mr. Barno wiped his hands together. "Your life. Your happiness. I'm just the teacher. But I'm not taking attendance. This isn't high school."

"Alright." I slid back down. "Okay. Well. Um. I guess I'm afraid of getting in trouble. Like, I hate getting yelled at or being told I'm stupid or that I can't do anything right."

"That's funny, isn't it? You seem to be good at getting in trouble."

I snorted. "Yeah, I guess so."

"Why are you afraid of getting in trouble?"

"I dunno. I guess I don't want to disappoint people. Maybe I don't want them mad at me."

"That's interesting. Why's that?"

"I guess I don't like being labeled bad."

"What happens to you when you get in trouble and are labeled bad?"

"I get really pissed off."

"You want to protect yourself and fight back? Or, maybe you strike out and hurt someone else before they can hurt you?"

I folded my hands in my lap. "Yeah. Guess I do that."

"Why do you think you do that?"

"Well, I guess I feel that people don't like me. They don't want me. They don't—"

Mr. Barno interrupted. "They don't love you?"

I closed my eyes and nodded the tiniest nod. Mr. Barno pushed himself up slowly. He leaned against the tree and his voice sounded worn. "It sounds as though you have a big choice to make. Live by fear or live by happiness." I opened my eyes and saw he was clutching the tree, sort of anchoring himself to it. "That's all for today, Nolan."

"But—"

"That's all for today," Mr. Barno repeated. He walked unsteadily away from the tree and into the house.

Eight

Okay. I'm not crazy. Alright, who am I kidding? But I'm not that kind of crazy. I'm not the 'seeing and hearing things that aren't there' kind of crazy. I'm more your 'whoa, that guy just did that, is he crazy?' kind of crazy. Or, if you want to get clinical about it the way my old counselors did, I'm sure there's some word they got in that big gray dictionary book, or whatever it is, that shrinks use to put a label on you—like the terminology the bald guy told my parents when I was 6 years old. My kind of crazy has resulted in me being called lots of things. Some are: too sensitive, too much, marches to his own beat, in need of a good kick in the rear, and on the fast track to nowhere.

Good things have been said about my kind of crazy, too. For example, Mrs. McBryde from fifth grade called me an exceptionally bright kid who just needed to be challenged academically (Okay, I'm kind of bragging there but Mrs. McBryde was an amazing teacher. Wherever you are, thank you Mrs. McBryde. And sorry about the fish tank).

Point is, not one person ever told me that I *experienced* things that weren't there or that I *momentarily time traveled*. No one ever said that I was loopy, or whatever.

I didn't know what to think about what happened under that tree at Mr. Barno's. I didn't tell anyone about it because maybe they would start calling me loopy.

And I'm not that kind of crazy. I'm not like old Cammie Roland.

But life's weird. Something that seems so crazy (Sorry I'm using that word a lot. I just don't know what else to call it) can happen and it's all you can think about for the rest of the day. Then, you go back to school and see new teachers, and try to pretend that when you tripped on your way up the stairs in front of everyone it wasn't a big deal, and also that it really wasn't a big deal when you saw some junior driving a new Jeep.

The next day: Pop-Tarts, school, cafeteria pizza, Gabi' smile, music, parents. Rinse and repeat. And you kind of lose sight of that crazy thing. Like, maybe it didn't happen. Maybe you imagined it. Maybe that's just an ordinary tree in Mr. Barno's backyard.

Right.

Anyway, Fridays were Gold Day—the day we had to figure out what we wanted to do with the rest of our lives. In the afternoons, I had two classes back-to-back: Senior Seminar I - College Prep, and Senior Seminar II - Senior Project.

Senior Seminar I was a boring class everyone took and the only class that Neil, Branson, and I all had together. It helped you learn about college—like, how to pick a college, how to pick a major, that kind of thing. The highlight was a field trip to Wetton, a small college a half hour away. Whoopee.

Senior Seminar II was a class for 'high achievers.' Kids who didn't get put into it—like Neil and Branson—took a different class which was basically just extra time to do homework. Lucky bastards.

Or, maybe not.

I felt pride about being the 'high achiever.' I felt ashamed, too. Neil was brilliant. But when you look incapable of some things, I guess people treat you like you're incapable of everything. And Branson, well, maybe he had a lot on his mind because he never seemed to focus.

"This class is the culmination of your education," Mrs. de León said on the first day of Senior Seminar II. The way she stood made you know she had expectations. Plus, she just looked smart—she wore librarian glasses, lots of bright jewelry on her olive neck and wrists, a long skirt, and her hair was up in that always perfectly messy way. "It'll be part senior project, part college prep."

I raised my hand. "Um, I thought the college prep class was our college prep?"

Mrs. de León was the senior guidance counselor and taught two classes, both on Fridays: this class and Introduction to Journalism. Word came down from the Old Heads that Mrs. de León had been famous once, but it was never quite clear what for or why she'd be here if she was.

"Yes and no. Think of Senior Seminar I as an exploration of college. Senior Seminar II is where I help you get into a great school. I'll teach you to select a school worthy of your talents, write an eye-catching college essay, find scholarships that match your abilities, and help you fill out financial aid if needed. This class is a formula for college acceptance success. Your senior projects will demonstrate your talents."

The good thing about the class was that Gabi Meyers was in it (Skyler Bell was, too). At the end of class, Mrs. de León asked everyone to turn in our senior year plan for applying to colleges. As I walked by her desk, Mrs. de León asked for my plan. I held my empty hands up.

She glanced over her glasses at me. "I've reviewed your academic performance. Your best bet is to apply for data science or engineering. You're a sure bet for any state school, although you can be choosy and get into several highly ranked programs nationwide." She pointed at me. "However, you've got to put in the work. Only you can."

"Yeah. I know everyone wants me to make Paxson proud and all. Well, maybe not my dad."

"What does your dad want?" She sounded as if she actually cared.

"Um, he doesn't really believe in college. Says it costs too much. He won't let me take out loans. Says not to mortgage my future. If I go, I got to take out loans without him knowing. Maybe you can, like, help me fill out the forms or something?"

Mrs. de León folded her hands. "I hate to tell you, Nolan, but you need your parents' detailed financial information to apply for college loans."

"Oh." I tried to smile. Maybe knowing there was no college in my future made things easier. Surprisingly, I felt disappointed. *I guess I want to go to college? Or do I just not like losing choices?*

"Scholarships exist for a reason, Nolan. Any money set aside?"

"A few thousand bucks. For a Jeep."

"Cars are depreciating investments. Despite your father's, um, outlook, an investment in education returns appreciably."

"But everyone—"

"You'll need a scholarship that covers the full tuition. I know just the one. It's called Building Our State's Future. Five students are selected statewide each year. You have a great shot at it. It lets you go to any state school with a full ride to study engineering. The catch? You'll be working for the state for three years after graduating."

She pulled a folder from a tray on her desk, flipped through it, and selected a sheet of paper. She placed the paper on top of the folder and held it out. "The folder contains all the scholarships I've compiled for every degree. This paper has the details about the scholarship I'm talking about and a list of possible degrees within engineering."

I took the stack and read: building construction, chemical engineer, civil engineer, electrical engineer. I glimpsed at her, "You think this is for me?"

"This is your chance, Nolan. You can succeed at this. All you have to do is fill out some personal information, send in your transcripts and your SAT scores, and write an essay about why you want to study engineering. I'll cut you a deal. I'll get the transcripts and your test scores together, and you write the essay. We'll do the forms together. The deadline is in two weeks. Start now, for work conquers all things."

I held the lacrosse stick. *This can't be too hard, right?* Skyler had shown me how to hold it, how to throw with it, and how to do something with it called cradling, which didn't seem to have any purpose.

Skyler backed up. "Ready?"

I held up the stick the way she showed me. She eased her stick back and snapped it forward. The ball took to the air. I held the stick in front of me to catch it. I missed. The ball smacked me on the forehead.

"Oh my gosh. I'm so sorry." She ran over kind of giggling but sort of looking sympathetic. I couldn't help but laugh. It was too embarrassing not to. "You'll get it," she said as she scooped up the ball. "The first time with my brother was a dis-aster."

"Why don't you play on the team? You're pretty good and all."

"Just isn't my vibe." Between sentences, she pulled her lips in as if she was thinking really hard even when she was talking casually. And I don't mean this in a bad way, but she never seemed to be thinking too hard. What I mean is that everything seemed easy. Like she just knew. She thought fast. She made decisions fast, just like how she drove fast. And she seemed at peace with everything being fast. All that change. All that motion. Everything going by.

I tried to hand the stick to her but she pushed it back playfully. "No quitting." So we tried again and the second time the ball hit the side of the stick and fell to the ground. We tried again and again. Soon I was able to catch the ball. Well, sometimes.

She pulled her lips in and asked me, "Why don't you play sports?"

I motioned at my body, "Not really quarterback material." She chuckled in a way that made her chipmunk dimples show. We talked about how I liked to run and I told her about my hamstring last season before tryouts and she put her hand on my forearm and said she hoped

I would go out for cross country this year. I told her I might, and when I said it, I really hoped I would too. But the truth was that I had no time to train for tryouts anymore.

"So, Mrs. de León is pretty intense," she said, walking to grab her water bottle by a bench.

"You're telling me. Where'd you say you want to go to college in your college plan?"

Her voice perked. "Good question. My goal is to get a degree in Culinary Arts Management at the City College of San Francisco. My dream is to manage a sustainable restaurant, and maybe own my own one day. It might just start out as a coffee shop and bakery. But I'd grow it into a full restaurant."

"Whoa," I said.

"What?"

"Just jealous. Got no clue what I'm gonna do."

She started walking in no particular direction and I followed her. "Life's about figuring out the price of your dreams and paying it. My dad says it's that simple. What's with the recording thing? I've seen you doing that. Is that what you want to do?"

"Just a hobby. Originally, I got it because Branson said he wanted to DJ. I wanted to help him. I was trying to learn about audio stuff. I figured I'd get some, like, atmospheric recordings he could use. But, typical Branson. He never did anything to become a DJ. Then he said the plan was to be a rapper. He never actually tried to rap. In his mind, he's going to be rich and famous. I hope he is someday. He just doesn't seem to be trying, though."

"Maybe he's just doing some mental accounting." She stopped. "Like you."

I stopped, too. "What do you mean?"

She sat in the grass. "Figure out the price of your dreams and pay it. Seems you haven't figured out the price or you're not willing to pay it."

"Correction. I haven't figured out the dream."

She pointed to the grass next to her. I sat. "Dad has another saying for that. It's something like, 'shift the opportunity, not the restriction.' Like, the restriction that your mind is projecting on the situation."

"I like that," I smiled. And I meant it.

"You're just recording stuff for no reason?"

"Let me ask you this. Do you listen to the freight train when it passes through town?"

"Sure."

"Me too. I always listen. Most people don't. They just want the train to go by so they can cross the tracks. They treat that stuff like it's the space between the important moments in life. They're wrong. The ordinary is never ordinary if you're paying attention. I record what most people ignore to try to understand what life is really about." I gazed into her eyes—tried to at least. "Speaking of dads, mine taught me the whole 'the ordinary is never ordinary' thing. Mine taught me that ignoring the wrong moments is the worst mistake you can make."

She brushed aside a lock of sun-bleached hair. She had the kind of eyes where you can't quite tell what color they are and you wonder if maybe they change from the light or from some other reason that only females understand. "Gosh, Nolan. That was deep."

I didn't know what to say because all I was saying was the truth. So we sat quietly side by side and that was enough. Then she asked, "Can I listen?"

"Let me find you something good."

"You've got your recorder with you?"

"No. But I download my favorite recordings to my phone." I flipped through my phone and found the sound I had recorded after I finished texting Skyler the night of The Jungle party. It was the sound of that night—the good and the bad—as the river lapped against the concrete at the boat launch.

When it finished playing, she said, "I like how your world sounds."

I just stared at her with this dumb smile on my face. I wasn't looking at anything in particular about her, just all of her. And the thought came out of nowhere but here it was: *if I could record Skyler—her energy, her being—, what would that sound like?*

Then I saw Branson walking down Main Street. I hopped up. "Hey, I'll be right back." I ran over to him.

He peered over me. "That Skyler? Tell her I said what's up."

"Sure man. She's teaching me lacrosse."

Branson patted my shoulder. "I see where this is go-ing. But I'm telling you man, Gabi and Dallas are tight."

I thought about what Skyler had said about figuring out the price and paying it. "Homecoming isn't until October. I've got time."

"Meeting of the Midnight Warlords next Friday. Our old spot. See you there?"

I sucked on my cheek. "No man, count me out."

Branson cracked his knuckles. "Come on, dude. What're you afraid of?"

"Nothing," I said. "Not one dang thing."

"That's my guy," Branson smirked. "I'll see you

there then, cool?" Branson put a fist out.

I eyed it for a moment. Then, I bumped it and pushed air out through my nose. "Yeah. Sure. I'll see you there." He walked off down the street. I turned to head back to the grass but Skyler was gone.

———————

Mr. Barno stood outside of the stones that encircled the red oak tree in his backyard. His eyes closed, the bugs of late August whirling around his head. I swatted gnats from my face as I stood nearby, the pile of lumber at my ankles. He was perfectly still, gnats or not. Finally, he said, "Tell us, tree. What work will we do today?"

I hadn't seen his schematics yet. All I had seen on the previous Monday when we started the project was the backs of a few sheets of creased drafting paper which he had removed from a pocket, unfolded, and consulted. He did the same thing today when I arrived. He looked at the schematics, looked at the tree, smiled to himself, folded the schematics, and put them back in his pocket. Then, like I said, he stood by the tree with his eyes closed and, I guess, sort of felt the mood of the air or something.

The week before I had dug two holes on the far side of the tree and one on the near side. It seemed the next logical step was to dig the final hole. *What's the holdup?* Maybe 5 minutes passed before Mr. Barno walked to a spot in the yard and said, "We will dig here."

"Not going to be symmetrical if we dig there," I

said, pointing to the other holes. I walked over to a spot about five feet from him and said, "We should dig here so everything is squared."

Mr. Barno stared at where I stood. He stared at the base of the tree. "You are sure?"

"Yes," I said. He said okay and walked toward the lumber. I grabbed the shovel and started digging while he measured and marked posts. "What's the lesson today?" I asked, tossing dirt.

Without looking up, he said, "I told you last time that the happiness lessons don't work that way."

I stopped. "What do you mean?"

He marked a post with a pencil and said, "I teach only what emerges from the student. I will not give you a syllabus and we will not go in any order. However, when I have taught a happiness lesson, I will make it clear and I will review it with you. We will let the lessons flow naturally from the project."

"The tree project?"

"Yes, the tree project. The life project. It's all the same. The lessons will present themselves if you allow them to."

I got maybe ten inches down when my shovel struck something hard. A rock. No surprise there. I'd dealt with several at the other holes. I started working my way around the rock. But it was wide and I couldn't find an edge to get leverage under. After several minutes, I was sweating really bad.

I got some lemonade and got back to work. Still, I couldn't find my way around that rock. The hole was growing wider and wider but not deeper. Finally, I reached the rock's edge. Then I hit something else. A tree root. Thick. The shovel left a green fleshy gash in the root.

I went back the other way. Soon, I made it to the edge of the rock on the other side and started digging down. When the hole was dug, I glanced around and realized how badly I had torn up Mr. Barno's yard. I tucked my chin and wiped my face on my T-shirt. "Sorry about your yard. I'll fill it in and put some seed down. It'll grow back."

Mr. Barno sat on the metal bench just kind of looking past me. I let go of the handle and the shovel dropped to my side. "What?" I asked. He sat quietly. I turned to follow his eyes and I noticed the other three holes. "Crap, this hole isn't symmetrical with the others," I said. Then, it hit me. I had dug a hole right where he had told me to dig in the first place.

I feel bad admitting this, but I got mad and grunted, "How'd you know? Why didn't you correct me?" It was hot. Humid. Buggy. Sweat in my eyes. Shirt drenched. I had been digging, then resting, then digging for what must've been an hour.

He stood. "While we have the shared goal of completing this project, we have different agendas. My agenda is to complete this project in a way that spreads harmony."

"Yeah, me too."

"Your actions say otherwise. We are working, but we are not in unison."

"What're you talking about? I'm trying to help you, aren't I?"

"Think, what is your agenda, Nolan?"

My eyes stung from sweat and I wiped them on my shirt but it was drenched so I wiped them on my sleeve. "To get this freaking tree project done. Isn't that your agenda, too?"

"Yes, it is. Then, again, it isn't just to get it done. It is to get the project done harmoniously with you and with the tree. The way you engage with this project, with me, and with the tree says to me that you want to be right more than you want to be free."

"Free? What're you talking about? I just want to help you so you help me. Isn't that harmony?"

Mr. Barno walked over to the exposed tree root and put his hand over his mouth. "Why did you hurt the tree?"

"It was an accident. Come on. I mean, I'm digging. How was I supposed to know the root was there?"

He kneeled down and touched the gash in the root. "This isn't harmony."

"Okay, so how do I do what you want me to do?"

He searched my face. "Wrong question. It's not about what I want."

I flapped my arms against my thighs. He ran his tongue up and down his mustache and, for some reason, seeing him do that made me realize I was being a jerk to this person that I needed and that needed me. "I'm sorry. Tell me what you mean about doing this project with harmony. How can I do that?"

"I can't tell you how you should do it. I will tell you how I do it. I do it by listening, by compromising, and by finding a way of doing things that make the best of my abilities and minimize my weaknesses. I do this while considering your strengths and weaknesses and your needs. I do the same with the tree."

"I don't get it."

"Kneel down beside me," he said. So I did. "Here, put your hand on the root, close your eyes, and listen."

I put my hand on the root in the dirt, just over the gash where his hand had been. Mr. Barno gave me an assuring nod. I sensed that he wanted me to close my eyes. I closed them. Okay. So keep in mind that I'm not the loopy kind of crazy. But I felt a shrieking sound. I didn't hear it. I felt it. You understand? The shrieking sound traveled from the tree root into the nerves of my hand and rushed over me the way an electric shock does. I yanked my hand back and opened my eyes. "What was that?"

Mr. Barno put his finger to his ear. I closed my eyes and listened. I was afraid of the shock and the sound but Mr. Barno's hand took mine and held it to the tree root and I felt the shrieking sound again. "The tree is afraid we'll damage it," I said, opening my eyes.

Mr. Barno nodded. "In whatever you do, ask yourself how you can do it in a way that brings about harmony." He whispered those words to me as if the tree were a baby he had just coaxed to sleep. Of course, that's not why he whispered. He whispered because now we shared a secret.

Nine

I sat in the back of the Senior Project II classroom waiting for Mrs. de León to start class on the second Friday of the school year. I always sat in the back of my classes. I didn't like people sitting behind me. Call it the panoramic view of life. I was interested in people, but I wasn't necessarily interested in knowing them.

Yes, I also wanted to have friends and be popular, and go to parties, and make out with Gabi Meyers who was sitting at the front of the class with a Syracuse T-shirt on, her legs crossed and her hair way up so the nape of her neck was showing—a neck I wanted to kiss someday.

But every time I tried to let people into my life, I somehow ended up pushing them away. Like my sister Sarah. Or, I ended up discovering that they were terrible people. Like her boyfriend Rafe. That's the hard part about having a panoramic view.

I suppose that's why I just stayed interested in the hypothetical of other people. The reality part was just too messy.

I didn't want to screw it up with Gabi. Didn't want her to shun me. And she was definitely not a terrible person. Because she was Gabi Meyers. She was perfect. The problem was, if things didn't happen with her soon, what hope was there for Homecoming?

Maybe Mr. Barno is right. Maybe I am afraid of everything.

I got up and moved to the front of the class. The one

good thing about this class was that, as talented as he supposedly was, Dallas Stone was not in it. I sat next to Gabi and smiled at her. *A life of fear or a life of happiness, right?*

She was looking at her phone. Then, she looked at me.

"Syracuse," I said.

"Huh?"

"Syracuse."

"Yeah," she smiled.

"Yeah," I said.

Then a pause sort of settled over us and I didn't know what to say. *Don't let this moment go, you idiot. Think. What Would Lenny Do?*

"Syracuse," I said again.

"Yeah. Syracuse." Her eyes poked around the room.

"So are you applying there? I mean, to Syracuse."

She started tapping her pink pencil on the desk. "Uh-huh. Sent my app in early decision."

"Oh, yeah. Me, too. Early decision."

She smiled. "Cool."

"Yeah, engineering." I nodded a bit too much.

"Right on. Rad. Engineering. That's the big bucks."

"Dollar, dollar bills, y'all." I said it in the loud way my dad says it when he listens to Wu-Tang. It was an impulse. A Dad and me thing. An embarrassing, you just ruined your chances with Gabi Meyers, thing. *Well, that's that. I'm never getting a chance to procreate.*

She put her hand over her mouth. I couldn't tell if she was saying 'oh my God' to herself or what. It took every bit of strength not to punch myself in the face right there.

When she moved her hand, she was smiling. Even

stranger than that, she kept talking to me. "I'm thinking of public relations or marketing. I applied early decision for marketing because my mom went to school there and I can totally get in. Truthfully, though, I think I want to study public relations. I hear it's not hard to switch your major once you get in."

Public relations. How beautiful. I had no idea what it was. Though I could tell it was a great thing to be studying.

Okay, be cool. Don't be eager. Just sound casually interested. "Yeah. Public relationships, I mean, relations. It's, like, super important. Yeah. I'm big on relationships." *What the crap was that? Big on relationships?*

She squeezed her eyebrows down and something happened. She laughed. A little bit. But it was a laugh—a laugh that went pop as if she had tried to hold it in but couldn't. Then she said it. "You're kind of funny."

"I am," I said impulsively. She laughed at that, too. Just then, Mrs. de León started class. *Hey, that wasn't bad*, I thought. *You came across as confident and Lenny the True Love CEO is always preaching confidence.*

That day, Mrs. de León assigned our senior project. I remember she said it was due in May and it would bring together everything we had learned during our time at Paxson. She kept saying, "Senior project is your capstone achievement." I didn't pay attention to the details. How could I? I had just engaged in one of the pinnacle minutes of the last four years of my life. Gabi Meyers and I talked. I initiated. And she laughed at something I said and called me funny, or at least, kind of funny. This was my capstone achievement.

When I sort of came to, Mrs. de León was wrapping up class and saying, "What you choose to do your senior project on is up to you."

After class, I couldn't wait to give the guys the play-by-play of my romantic exchange with Gabi. But Mrs. de León had me stay after class. She wanted to know where my Building Our State's Future scholarship essay was. "Nolan Sussman, the deadline to apply is one week."

I told her the truth. "I just don't know what to write. I can't get into it."

Mrs. de León took off her glasses, glared at me dead in the eyes, and said, "Start now, for work conquers all things."

Afterward, I scurried toward the stairs. And that's when I saw it. It hung on the bulletin board between the elevator and the stairs: a pink flier with big black letters that read, "Save the Youth of Paxson." Underneath, in a smaller font, it read, "Wednesday, September 13th at 4 pm in the Paxson Library Auditorium. We're Protect Paxson, a group of concerned parents and students. Help us lobby our local government to force the relocation of Alexis Barno, a convicted killer who served 25 years in prison."

Branson and Neil were sitting in the away team football bleachers when I arrived, napkins and wrappers littered everywhere from the football game earlier that Friday night.

Neil was leaning over Branson's phone as the two of them inspected something.

I plopped down next to Branson who tilted his phone so I could see a picture of a black box with a matrix of gray buttons and a row of knobs. He grinned, "Dank drum machine, ain't it? I'm getting a laptop, too, to plug it into. Soon I'll be dropping my own beats and in the music business for real." I could smell the beer on his breath.

"Can't wait to hear your songs, B-Man," Neil said.

Branson ruffled Neil's hair. "I got you, my man, so long as you join my entourage."

"So what's up?" I asked, giving Neil and Branson fist bumps.

"The drum machine and the laptop," Branson said.

"Dude, I snuck out to look at a photo you could've texted me, seriously?"

"Nah, man. Not the picture. The how. I need you shysters to help me find a way to buy them. I need like $1,800."

"I got an idea. Get a job and don't get fired." I was serious but also teasing.

Neil did his best Arnold Schwarzenegger impression, "Do it! Do it now!"

Branson cackled, "Impossible!"

We sat there. The blaring horn of the midnight freight train lingered as a sonic fog over town. After a while, I stood. "I got nothing. This has truly been a worthwhile use of my waning teen years, but I'm turning in. Branson, good luck. I'll learn some audio editing and we can figure this music stuff out together. Cool?"

Branson rubbed his neck. "What if I get a gaming laptop instead? I hear them videogame streamers make bank."

I turned to leave.

"Hey, No Land," Branson grabbed my arm. "You're asking Gabi to Homecoming, right?

"Absolutely."

"Now's your chance, man. I saw Dallas talking to Natalia Valentine after school the other day. The way they were standing, something's going on between them."

I punched at the air the way boxers do and threw my arms up in victory.

"Since you're not planning on asking Skyler. Well. Shoot. Ever since I saw her in those running shorts, girl's been running through my mind."

I must have seemed surprised because he made a puzzled face at me and said, "Friends before femmes, right?"

I gazed out onto the football field. "Hey, can I ask you guys something?"

They were quiet.

"What're you afraid of?"

"Nothing," Branson wadded up some trash. "Don't ask stupid questions." He chucked it.

"Come on," I urged, sitting. "I'll go first. I've been thinking maybe I'm afraid I'll never really be loved. Like unconditionally, the way it is in the movies and on social media."

"Thanks for sharing that." Neil reached his arm behind Branson and patted me on the back. "I'll go. It's knowing I'll never fit in because of who I am. I just want to find my place. Maybe that's what college is."

"You fit in with us," I said, reaching over and patting his shoulder.

Branson elbowed Neil playfully. "For sure. Midnight Warlords forever."

We all smiled but didn't make eye contact. If we hadn't been teenage guys, then maybe I could have told them how much they meant to me.

"Alright. I'll go. I'm scared of being a nobody. Of having nothing." Branson smeared a wrapper into the bleachers with his heel. "What if I ain't ever rich?"

"Don't say that," I said.

Branson hung his head and muttered, "If I don't change my situation, this is it. Stuck in this miserable town with this miserable life. Sometimes, I get so down that this is my life that I just. I can't take it. I just want to run away. I swear I'll—" He stopped. "Dang, Nolan, I didn't mean that."

"It's okay," I said.

"I just want to matter." Branson sat quietly, his chin in his palms. "I'm done sitting around. I'm going and getting my happy ever after. Look, I got an idea. I was hoping one of you fools would have a better one. But here's the plan." He rubbed his hands together. "So Mr. Lewis, right? He's stashing cash in a box in his garage."

"How the hell do you know that?" I asked.

"Last summer, when Neil was out of town and you were grounded, I was out of beer one night. I went garage hopping, you know, looking for open garages with fridges in them. I always go to the rich neighborhoods for that shit. Well, it's real late. I'm walking down the street in the dark past the Lewis house. And I see his garage is open and there's a light on. But I can't see because of the trees. I sneak into his yard and hide in the trees and I can see him standing by a shelf. Dude's putting something in there and—"

Neil said what I was thinking. "That could've been anything."

"Let me finish. He goes inside the house through a door in the garage and I sneak into the garage to check the fridge. No beer. I spot an open bottle of liquor on a workbench. But it's right by the door and I can hear him inside. So I'm leaving. I'm sneaking around the side between the Mercedes and the wall where the shelf is. I look inside, flip open the top of the box, and there's a load of cash. I'm talking stacks of $100 bills. Just then, the door opens and Lewis steps into the garage. I duck. He pours a drink and walks down the middle of the garage. Doesn't see me. Okay? Dude sits in a lawn chair in his driveway staring at the stars and crap. I crouch in the garage until my legs are numb. Finally, he's snoring and I make my break for it." Branson laughed. "Get this, I'm running across the lawn, but my legs are asleep. I fall. Dude wakes up. Starts yelling, 'Who's there?' He's all cursing some lady named Wanda. I jump up, jelly legs and all, and get the hell out of there."

"Why would a rich guy be stowing cash in his garage?" I asked.

"Who knows, maybe—"

Neil interrupted, "I know why. He's going through a messy divorce. It was on the front page of Gramps' newspaper. Bet old Lewis is hiding money so his wife doesn't get it."

Branson cracked his knuckles. "Doesn't matter why. We're taking it."

This was a horrible idea. And an exciting one. I hated Mr. Lewis. Maybe because he owned most of the buildings, most of the land, and half the homes in

Paxson, including ours. Maybe because my mom worshiped him even though he worked her to the bone. And definitely because the Midnight Warlords had always been too scared to prank his house.

Neil asked Branson, "How much loot's in that box?"

"A three-way split? Probably ten thousand dollars for each of us. No doubt."

Neil pretended to hold a walkie-talkie. "Requesting mission Lewis Stakeout."

I wanted to see Mr. Lewis passed out in a lawn chair with his garage open. I guess I wanted to know that a bulletproof guy like him was vulnerable. So I pulled out an imaginary walkie-talkie and replied, "Permission granted."

The hair on my arms stood as if my arms were covered by a thousand tiny pencils. I knew that what Branson was suggesting was not a couple of kids doing pranks for kicks. Stealing money was real crime. And real crime can land you in prison.

Ten

Pink Save the Youth of Paxson fliers. Tucked into the flag of the mailboxes on Mr. Barno's street. Every house. Including his. That's what I saw when I ran to Mr. Barno's house on Labor Day (My parents had work. Dad was driving real far to source wood flooring for a client. Since I get carsick on long drives, I got out of it).

I spent the day pouring the gravel and concrete footers for the posts in the holes around the tree. It took forever because Barno was acting strange. He appeared pale, depleted. He didn't talk.

Not at all.

As frail as he was, he was usually tenacious. Always moving. Always doing.

But not today.

Today, he would go inside for a while. Then he would come back out and give me this surprised look as if I wasn't supposed to be there. I started to get paranoid that maybe he was going to call the cops on me. I'm not sure why. But I know that look when I get it.

Afterward, I sat on the bench to rest. Mr. Barno usually had a pitcher of lemonade that we sipped on as we worked.

Not today.

I said, "Man, it's humid," while he sat in the grass behind the bench looking at the flowers. Real flowers—ones I could see. "Jeez I'm thirsty," I said over my shoulder.

No response.

When I feel uncomfortable, sometimes I just start talking.

"I screwed up," I said, more to the tree than to him. "Got time to fix it. But I won't. Got this teacher. She's great and all. But she wants me to apply for this engineering scholarship—got until Friday to write this essay. And I can't. I just can't. I know it's the right thing to do, the good thing. I should get this scholarship, go study engineering, and do the right thing, the good thing. Be the good guy everyone thinks is buried somewhere inside of me. If that's true, why do I keep doing bad things? Why can't I do good things? I swear I deserve whatever bad comes to me for all my screwups."

"Only in our culture could a person focus on the bad. What about all the ways in which you try? All the people you help just by being in their lives? The impact you've had? Have you made someone smile? Have you helped someone? Yes, of course you have. What about all your progress despite the hooks in you? Gradual is good. Most miracles go overlooked."

I peered over my shoulder at him, his back still to me.

"I had a teacher friend who wanted to see the northern lights. Talked about it incessantly. Never had the money to head north to see them," he continued, speaking to the plants. "When I brought my chess set to his house, we always played. One day, he gets a telescope. Says he wants to see a shooting star. Stops playing chess. I go over. He's staring through that telescope. Stops talking when I'm there. Never lets me look in the telescope. Well, one night there is supposed to be a meteor shower. He invites me over. His face is stuck to that telescope. Watching. Waiting. We're sitting on his back deck, which looks out over this field. He's looking, he's looking. Waiting for those meteors. Then, I hear something. I look out and there is this bear twenty feet away. Sniffing around. Then I see something small and I realize it's a bear cub. Then I see another one. These two cubs play with each other. Tumble around. They bite at the mom's fur, trying to get her to play. At first, she doesn't want to. But the cubs persist. I witness an amazing moment these bears have together, playing. Then, they leave. That was a special night."

"What did your friend think about the bears?"

"I don't know."

"He didn't say?"

"Never saw them. He was glued to that damn telescope."

"You weren't like, 'holy crap, check out these bears!'?"

Mr. Barno turned toward me. "I did exactly that. I whispered it. Didn't want to startle the bears. Either he couldn't hear me, or he was so focused on what he was doing that he wasn't listening."

"That meteor shower must've been amazing."

Mr. Barno stood and walked toward the bench. "Sadly, no. Some clouds roll in. Boy is he mad. He stands there cursing at the clouds. At the clouds. How silly is that? Then, when he has given the clouds a mouthful, he starts yelling at himself that he should've known to drive a few hours to where there was no cloud cover."

"So you're saying the meteors were bad? He should've been looking at the bears?"

Mr. Barno sat down beside me. "No. Let go of good and bad. How do things being bad help you?"

"Like, in my own life?"

He nodded.

"Guess it helps me know where I stand, how I stack up. And it helps me know where other people stand—if they're on my side or not."

"Give me an example."

"Well, like, if I'm doing a good job. Like I said earlier, I'm screwing up because I'm not completing the scholarship application. I don't want to be an engineer. But, I need money to pay for college. The right thing would be to do the scholarship application and not be so selfish and boneheaded."

"And where would that get you?"

"Well, I know I'd hate it."

"Then, why are you so hard on yourself?"

"I just hate letting my mom down."

"What do you think your mom really wants for you?"

"To make lots of money."

"Maybe. She probably sincerely believes money will make you happy. She may be wrong. But, she sincerely believes it."

"She's wrong."

"What she really wants is for you to have a happy, satisfying life. She doesn't want you to suffer in the ways she has. All parents want that—to mitigate their child's suffering. They just don't always know the best way to do that and they're usually blind to that fact.

Your mother's heart is in the right place. You have to learn to help guide her."

"Never thought of it that way."

"Let's return to things you've said both today and before. You frequently talk badly about yourself. Today, you've called yourself a bonehead, said you screwed up, and implied that you're doing the wrong thing by not applying for the scholarship. Another day, you said other people see you as bad. I'm starting to think that you see yourself as bad."

"Not true." I picked at a callus on my hand. "I'm—" Maybe he was right. *How often have I called myself a bonehead, or worse? How often have others labeled me as bad? Do I believe what others say about me?* "Maybe I deserve for bad things to happen to me."

"Balderdash. Stop cursing at the clouds." He pointed upward. "They're just clouds. Forget good. Forget bad. Look at the situation just as it is."

I started to well up. I swallowed hard to hold it in. *Stop. Be a man.* "You don't get it. My sister ran away when I was little. No one's seen her since."

Mr. Barno put a hand on my knee. "I heard about that. I'm so sorry."

"What you didn't hear is that it was my fault." I turned away and blotted tears with my sleeve. "Jeez, man. I was getting in trouble. My parents were spending so much time on me. I didn't get it then. But I understand it now. And I think—well—she just fell through the cracks. Lots of yelling and fighting between my parents, and me, you know. And. And, my sister was going through her own stuff. I knew. My parents didn't. No one was there for her. Understand? She left. With her boyfriend, Rafe, this amazing guitarist everyone worshipped. She wanted to be the lead singer of a band. I don't know if she ever got to."

"Angry at yourself?"

I stared at Mr. Barno's hand.

"Blame yourself?"

"Mmhmm."

"Punish yourself?"

"I guess. I deserve it."

"Balderdash. You deserve compassion."

"Compassion? What for?"

"We're all suffering. I don't believe your sister left because of you. But you do. You suffer a lot. If a baby drops her bottle and cries, do you blame the baby? Does that stop her crying? What if you yell at the baby? Ignore the baby? It's the baby's fault, right? Those things won't help. That's why a mom picks her baby up and tries to ameliorate her suffering. A baby needs someone to be there for her more when she is crying than when she is smiling. The same is true for non-babies. When we're in pain, we need more compassion, not less."

"Trust me, my sister left because of me."

"Okay. Your pain is coming from self-judgment. I accept that. You've decided to punish the baby inside. Does it feel good?"

"No. It feels like I've got a hurricane inside of me and I'm standing in a house that's about to blow over, and I'm screaming my head off, but the wind won't stop."

"Ah, you paint a vivid picture. I know that feeling. I signed up for a picture-perfect life, and it didn't work out. I've lost someone I love. You've lost someone you love. I feel great compassion for you. And I feel great compassion for myself. We are suffering."

"I don't want a pity party."

He let go of my hand and showed me his wrinkled, empty palms. "I don't pity you. I feel compassion for you. It's different. I've made some terrible choices in my life. Spent twenty-five years in prison. My punishment didn't end when I got out. I'll suffer for the rest of my life. Should I pile on and exacerbate my suffering? I did that for the first ten years of my sentence. It didn't bring my wife back. It didn't change my circumstances. Make sense?"

I nodded.

"I don't want pity either," Mr. Barno continued. "But I'd take compassion, if someone offered it—if they accepted me, including my mistakes. We're flawed, but not unworthy of love. Let's choose to accept that."

I reached out and took his soft hands in mine. "I know you're not the monster people say you are. You're a good person, and I'm sorry about your wife."

"Thank you, Nolan. I appreciate your compassion," he smiled. "How you feel inside dictates much of your happiness. Pay attention to how you perceive yourself and what words you use when having a conversation in your head. Be a little kinder to yourself."

"Thanks. I'll try. I promise."

"So far we've covered two lessons. You know what they are?"

I let go of his hands. "I forgot. Wait, could I borrow a pen and paper? I should write this down."

"Perhaps inside the house, in a drawer. Hurry," Mr. Barno said with a smile, "Or I might forget."

"What about my recorder? Can I just use that?"

"That's easy."

I ran into the garage where Mr. Barno made me keep my stuff. I grabbed my recorder and ran back. I pressed record. "Go ahead."

"Lesson One is to choose happiness over fear. Lesson number two contains several steps. They are necessary to arrive at the end goal on your journey to happiness. Lesson Two begins with letting go of notions of good and bad. Accept things as they are. Make space for everyone and every moment. This includes yourself—that's vital. When you're open to the world just as it is, you'll arrive at the goal of Lesson Two: compassion. What's compassion? It's realizing that everyone—ourselves included—is hurting. Because all people have pain, all people deserve kindness and support."

I sat, trying to absorb what Mr. Barno was teaching me. He sat there with me. Still. Silent.

"What do you want to know? I see a question on your face."

I told him how I'd heard rumors about him and how people said he was a rapist, a murderer, a serial killer. That he had killed young people, young people like me.

"I am whatever others see me as. That's up to them. I know that I was convicted of vehicular manslaughter—for acting negligently with a vehicle resulting from alcohol intoxication. That's a fact. I don't hide from it."

I couldn't look at him when I asked, "What happened?"

"Please turn off the recorder now." He stood. "Let me show you something." Sometimes when he walked, Mr. Barno tucked his left arm straight down behind him. Then he reached his right hand back and clutched his left elbow. He walked this way to the tree. I followed and stepped instinctively over the flowers that weren't there, just like Mr. Barno did. We sat and leaned against the tree. He put his hand on the back of my neck and I breathed the way he had shown me.

Soon, I was there. In the backseat of some nineties-era convertible. A Chevy, based on the steering wheel logo. Mr. Barno was driving and Celeste was in the passenger seat, the top down on a summer night.

He smiled at his wife. He was much younger, with side-parted brown hair and no beard. But his eyes were the same, youthful and kind. "Are we going to tell everyone at the party tonight?"

Celeste lit up the night sky with her beauty and her big smile. Just seeing that smile made me smile. She was just like the picture. She put her hand on his in the center console and peered out into the darkness.

We slowed to a stop at a four-way stop sign.

"I'm not sure," she said.

"I think we should."

Her eyes were red now and a tear hung off her cheek. She lit a cigarette.

"Honey, please."

She mashed it out in the ashtray.

We started forward. A car slipped through the four-way stop to our right. It T-boned an oncoming car.

"Oh my!" Celeste yelped.

Mr. Barno pulled into the median. As soon as he did, the lights and siren of a police car awoke. "We should stay a minute. Might need to give an eye-witness report," Mr. Barno said, getting out of the car.

Celeste handed Barno gum. "Don't let them smell your breath."

"Only had two," he said, taking the gum. "I love you." He walked toward the accident.

I stayed in the car with Celeste. We watched as the officer gave the driver who failed to stop, a college-looking female, a sobriety test. The officer handcuffed her and put her in the back of the police car. An ambulance arrived. The other driver, an elderly man with a cut on his head, clutched his chest. The medics helped him into the ambulance. Mr. Barno came back to the car. "That's ironic."

"What?"

"Officer Danenza was on his way to set up a sobriety checkpoint on Route 40."

We drove out of Paxson as Main Street turned into Route 40. The convertible sped up. The lights receded and darkness abounded on either side. The sky, open and endless, flowed through us.

We turned down a country road and whipped around the bends and hills. We must have been late to wherever we were going because Barno parked in the grass at this old farmhouse in the country and he and Celeste ran across a big yard and into the house.

I guess they didn't know I was in the backseat because they didn't invite me in. I sat crammed in for a long time. I'd never been on this country road. Never been to this house.

I could see all these people through the window.

Later, Celeste pressed through a screen door and down a few steps into the grass. She sat on a swing and sipped at a bottle. She smoked a cigarette and gazed at the stars. Mr. Barno came out calling his wife's name. He ruffled toward her.

She stood. They got rigid and sharp in their movements, pointing this way and that. Celeste ran shoeless toward the car, toward me. Mr. Barno chased her, a bottle swinging in his hand. He caught up to her just in front of the car.

I could hear him now saying, "I want to tell everyone. Tonight."

Celeste shook her head woozily. "No, it's Quin's night. Let's not bring our news into this."

Mr. Barno said, "You shouldn't be drinking that."

Celeste stiffened, "Don't tell me what to do."

"Honey, I love you. We should be celebrating, not fighting."

"How?" She lit a cigarette. "I'm in mourning."

"I know. I loved Portia, too."

"She wasn't your mom."

"I'm sorry."

"Stop."

"I'm just—"

"Give me the keys."

"Why?"

She reached into his pants pocket and took them. He didn't stop her.

"I love you. But I need to be alone right now. Please, let me go be alone. Stay. Quin's your best friend. He needs you here. He doesn't need me. It's fine. I'll be fine."

She got into the car and started it.

Mr. Barno jumped in. "Honey," he pulled the parking brake up. "You can't drive like this."

"Then you drive. I can't be here. I want to go home."

"I can't. I drank too much. Can we wait an hour? I'll sober up."

Celeste pounded on his chest and he wrapped his arms around her. She started to sob, kind of like how my family sobs in that weepy way.

"When will we share the news?" he asked.

She wiped her face, leaned back, and searched his eyes. "When we're both ready, sweetheart. Just not now."

"Okay," he said. "Okay. You are my heart. You know that, right?"

"You're mine. Either you drive or I drive. But I'm going home now."

He sighed. "No more drinking. No more cigarettes. You have to stop. For our family."

I don't want to see this.
"I don't want to see this!" I yelled.
"I don't want to see it!"
Get me out.
I want out.
Out.
"Out!"
"I WANT OUT!"

Mr. Barno pulled his hand from my neck. I felt the tree against my back.

"I don't want to see this. I don't want to know."

"It's okay," he said soothingly. "I don't hide from it. I don't want you to either. We have to know our fears. We have to talk about our fears. These are my fears and my regrets. I've already lived them. I accept them. Can you? Can you accept me?"

I closed my eyes. Breathed. It took a while, but it worked.

Mr. Barno was lying in the grass, twisted and bleeding. Covered in shards. Behind him, the convertible hugged a tree as though the lights on either end were arms wrapped around the trunk. It looked so peaceful, though the light fell jaggedly onto the grass. The dewy grass. The long, dewy grass where Celeste lay.

The tree, a massive red oak—easily 100 years old—stood at the brink of a bend in the country road. I saw the lights on in a house on a hill. Soon, the siren of an ambulance screamed quietly in the distance below an open sky. It reminded me of the way, if you really listened, you could hear the freight train far off before you ever saw it or heard its horn.

The peace shattered when the ambulance came over the hill. A medic tumbled out and sprinted to Mr. Barno. He pounded on Barno's chest and did CPR. Amid the commotion, I lost sight of Celeste. Two medics huddled in the shadows beyond the reach of the headlights. A police car arrived. Next, a fire truck.

Then I saw something.

A police officer's jacket draped over a mound in the crooked light where Celeste had been.

Mr. Barno shot up, coughing.

"Sir, sir, are you alright?"

"Celeste, Celeste!"

"Sir, calm down."

"Where's Celeste?"

A police officer, the same guy from earlier that night, squatted beside Mr. Barno.

Mr. Barno didn't talk for a while. He just sat there, his body drooping. The police officer asked Mr. Barno if he knew what happened and Mr. Barno said, "No. Uh. I was driving. Taking a turn. And. Uh. I guess. I guess too fast. The tree. That damn tree came out of nowhere."

Back in Mr. Barno's backyard, before I opened my eyes, I saw two blurry faces. Teenage boys.

When I ran home that day, I ripped the pink flier from Mr. Barno's mailbox, and from every mailbox I passed.

Eleven

When I let someone down, they give me that look.

Mrs. de León gave me that look after class on Friday, the deadline for the scholarship. I didn't write the essay.

Her version of the look had a lot wrapped up in it. Confusion. Disappointment. Surprise.

And I was pretty proud of myself because when I saw that look I thought about what Mr. Barno had said—the look was neither good nor bad.

It was a look.

I watched it on her face, on her whole body, when I told her that I didn't want to be an engineer. Just to make sure she knew, to preempt any idea my mom might someday plant in Mrs. de León's mind, I told Mrs. de León that I didn't want to be a businessperson either.

And you know what else that look got me in its 'wasness'? Moved out of Emerging Business Leaders United and into Introduction to Journalism for my Friday morning Gold Period One, the period where we had to take a class paired with a professional club.

See, I asked Mrs. de León what she wanted to do when she was my age. And she said she wanted to be on the radio. I asked her if she ever was. And she said yes, she started as an intern for some local radio station, built up her portfolio, and landed a job in Chicago. She started a podcast—way before they were a thing—doing everything herself, including the audio production.

And guess what? She fell in love with audio production. Well, I told her about how I liked to record stuff and how I wanted to help Branson someday with his music, and I said I just had to know what audio production was. She told me. I must have seemed pretty interested because that's when she told me that every Friday the kids in the journalism class help the school news club by pre-recording all the morning announcements for the following week.

"Can you really get my class changed?"

"I'm your guidance counselor," she winked. "I can do anything."

She opened a notebook and asked me for my cell phone number. I told her that I'd never given a teacher my cell phone number before. She said that since she was the news editor, she needed to be able to contact student journalists at any time. Like the real world.

Just like that, I left class knowing that next Friday I would be taking Introduction to Journalism for Gold Period One with Mrs. de León.

You know what else? I left class feeling pretty good for once.

Afterward, I saw Skyler in the hallway in her trademark look: overalls. She was holding her phone on a stack of books and seemed to be texting with someone.

Sometimes, Skyler wore overalls with paint stains on them, but not today. And to be honest, she was cute in those overalls. The way she was when she drove me home that day from the bridge. The way she was when she taught me lacrosse. It felt weird. To think that about Skyler, I mean.

I liked how she painted diamonds on the bottoms of

her shoes and how, when the paint wore off, she re-painted them.

I liked the way her arms were smooth and the way her T-shirt made this little upside-down V at her shoulders. You don't hear a lot about arms when it comes to looks. But I'm an arms guy if that's a thing.

I liked her nose ring and her long hair, too. I liked her smile. Her dimples. The little scar she had just above her left eyebrow that I knew was from when she fell off a trampoline at her fifth birthday party.

How her eyes defied color.

That made sense for Skyler—eyes that defied color.

"Hey Sky, where'd you go the other day?"

She turned away and kept texting.

"What gives?"

She turned back. "The other day?" She shrugged. "You seemed out of the moment."

"Um, yeah. No. That was just Branson."

"What'd he want?"

"Nothing."

"Nothing? Alright, whatever."

"Hey, you alright? You seem kind of. Kind of something." Girls never made any sense.

"Yeah. Of course."

We stood there. Teenage statues. I had the feeling that if Skyler had been sitting, she'd have been sitting on her hands.

"Alright. Cool. Hey, what's that Paul Simon album we listened to in your car?"

"Paul and I are exclusive. And when I'm exclusive with someone, I'm exclusive with someone."

"You know I could look it up, right?"

"I still won't cheat. Love is love."

"Alright. Okay. I admire that."

"You doing the whole Homecoming thing?"

"I might. You?"

"Thinking about it. If the right guy asks me."

"I think Paul Simon's a bit old for you." She didn't laugh. *Bad joke?* "Anyway, I blew my chance at college."

"Why?"

"Missed a scholarship deadline. My only shot."

"Well, I have to go. Still have a dream to chase. And if you'd believe in yourself the way others do. Well." She sighed and gave me a little wave before leaving.

I called after her, "Cook for me sometime? I want to experience your dream."

Skyler turned to face me, her books clutched to her chest. "Yeah, okay. Except I don't cook." She shook her head and walked away.

Mr. Lewis lived by the river. We tubed down the river every summer—every summer except last summer. You couldn't see the house from the river. But you could see the property.

There was a little island in the river where kids stopped to fish and teenagers stopped to drink. A stream, maybe 20 feet across and a foot deep, ran between the island and the mainland. The water felt colder there.

A wood stairway with railings zigzagged down the cliffs from up on the Lewis property. A wimpish waterfall drooled off the cliffs and into the stream, then the water flowed down the stream to where the island ended and the stream joined the river.

Up there on that cliff, above the stream, the gray house hid. Concealed among the trees. Looming.

I had never seen the property from the street. Not until tonight.

The driveway was lined with these low-lying lights like the place was a freaking airport. And Neil, Branson, and I—dressed in black, our faces in camo—squatted in the trees by an iron gate.

I sucked on my cheek. "You didn't mention any gate or wall."

"Don't freak out. We just jump over it." I could smell something on Branson's breath. Alcohol. But not beer.

"And Neil?"

Neil gave me the stink eye. "I can do it. Don't you start treating me any different."

"Alright. Alright. This is dumb."

Branson put his hands together for Neil to stand on. "No Land, you want that Jeep or what?"

We helped Neil over the high stone wall that ran along the front of the Lewis property.

Neil tumbled over with a crash.

Branson leapt up. He clung to the wall's saddle, peddled his feet against the stone, and rolled over the top.

That might've looked easy, but Branson was tall. I backed up, took a few steps, and threw myself at the wall. No dice. I tried again. This time I got a hold of the saddle. I scratched my feet frantically against the wall and somehow managed to pull myself up.

On the other side, I felt the sting of a few nicks on my palms. "What now?"

"Just got to creep up a bit and we'll get a clear shot of the garage."

We wormed behind Branson through the trees, careful to stay in the woods and off the winding driveway. "Hold up here," Branson whispered. We could see the garage. It was open, the lights on.

Music played from inside the garage. A woman sang and it felt as if she knew pain that nothing could touch. I was glad I wasn't that woman. As sad as I had ever been, she was sadder.

I scratched my neck. "What now?"

"Like I said, hold up." Branson shushed. "Jeez, No Land. You a Midnight Warlord? Or, you someone else now?"

Neil took three pairs of binoculars from his bag and handed them out. The three of us lay on our stomachs propped up at the elbows. I scanned the house and property through the binoculars. It was boxy—a bunch of perpendicular cubes with tall windows. On the outside, all of the walkways were curvy and edged with low lights and exotic plants.

We must have waited silently for half an hour.

I thought about what the hell I was doing here. *What's wrong with me? I should be home in bed, not on the edge of blowing up my life.* Then I watched my friends. I knew high school wasn't forever. Fun was a passing phase. *In 20 years, will I be doing anything remotely this exciting? Probably not, unless wearing khakis and fake laughing with co-workers is considered exciting in middle age. Probably in 20 years, high schoolers will be dressing like I do now and calling it vintage. God, then I'll really need a shrink.*

Then I thought, *Man, I know Mr. Barno wouldn't*

like me thinking this, but I'm a freaking idiot.

Branson whispered, "Ask her?"

"What?" I whispered back.

"Gabi. Homecoming."

"Oh, yeah. Soon."

"A girl like that, you need a big plan. I'll probably take Skyler to a nice dinner and ask her there."

Neil pulled his binoculars from his face. "A nice dinner? Been on any dates yet?"

Branson replied, "A couple. Not sure if they are dates or whatever. But we've been hanging out."

Neil whispered, "Kissed her yet?"

"Nah, not yet. But I bet she's a good kisser."

I started to get real annoyed. I'd never kissed anyone romantically.

I know, pathetic.

I didn't know if Branson had ever made out with someone. He claimed he had—both Cienna and some unnamed 'total babe'—, but that didn't mean anything. I knew Neil had made out with a college guy once.

Am I seriously going to be the last person ever to make out with someone?

Or, what if that's not what I'm annoyed about? No. *But, what if?* No. *I like Gabi Meyers.* Yeah, but. *Shit. What if I like Skyler Bell?*

Neil put the binoculars against his face. "My life would be complete if Tyler kissed me on the dance floor. Too bad Tyler Peanut Butter is way out of my league. And besides, I'm, I'm not going."

"You crazy?" Branson whispered. "If we're going, you're going."

"You don't get it. It's bad to be the sad queer kid at the dance."

"Forget bad," I whispered. "Be you. Have fun."

Neil sighed. "That easy?"

The door inside the garage opened. We watched intently as Mr. Lewis stepped down into the garage. He held an envelope. He placed it on a workbench and lazily poured a drink of booze. He sloshed it back, pounded his chest, and poured another.

Then he grabbed the envelope and scuffled around his big Mercedes-Benz to a shelf along the wall.

I zeroed in on the envelope in his hand. Twice he took cash from the envelope and shoved it into a cardboard box. He pushed the box back, put a towel on top of it, and set some spray bottles and a bucket in front of it. Then he slogged along the wall and fell into a chair on his driveway.

Later, outside of the gate, Branson put his hand on our shoulders and pulled us into a huddle. "Y'all in?"

Neil popped a thumbs up.

I said, "Not sure. There's something shady about Mr. Lewis."

"No Land, this is your chance to get that Jeep while you're still in high school. Your take is like 10 grand. Screw that guy. He owns everything, even the trailer parks. Remember the Robinsons? Used to live next to me. When they couldn't make rent, dude kicked them out. Just like that. Middle of winter. Once threatened to kick us out, too. This is a victimless crime. We're like freaking Robin Hood and that greedy dude is, like, you know, the bad guy from that story."

Neil said, "The Sheriff of Nottingham."

Branson threw Neil a fist bump. "That's my man."

I stood there scratching my arm while remembering something Mr. Barno said to me the first day he invited me in: "You never know what little moment will send ripples into the future that will affect the rest of your life."

I told Branson, "Let me think about it."

I went home, lay in bed, and stared at my Jeep poster.

I thought about ripples. And I thought about my future.

Twelve

You can only read the back of a cereal box so many times before the nutritional information gets interesting.

Come on parental figures, look my way so I can take my pill and teeth smile.

Dad texted clients.

Mom stared out the bay window.

Finally, Mom looked at me. *Look alive!* I grabbed the pill, flung it in my mouth, gulped OJ, and teeth smiled.

She faced me, but her eyes seemed somewhere else. "I just need you to do good in school this term and get into college."

"I know, Ma."

"I have some news."

"I know, Ma. We're out of Pop-Tarts," I motioned toward the cereal bowl. "I'll live."

"No, hun. Important news. Mr. Lewis is. Um. Not well. He's dealing with a lot. And see. We had a meeting on Friday and he informed us that he's. Basically, he's just not able to focus on the business right now."

I dropped my spoon. "He fired you?"

"No. Firing happens when you get in trouble. I'm not in trouble. I'm just sort of on leave from work."

Dad didn't look up. He must've already known.

"For how long?"

"Indefinitely."

"Jeez."

I wanted to hate Mr. Lewis, but I don't know, I felt bad for him. He was suffering and no one deserves that. His suffering caused Mom's suffering—caused my family's suffering. Then I felt like shit. Two nights before I was hiding in his trees, targeting him.

I did what I always did when I wanted to make things better: improved upon reality (Or as cynics like to call it, I lied). "Hey, great news. Mrs. de León told me I've got a good chance at getting into engineering school and making real money. I'm applying for this scholarship that pays for all of my tuition. Can you believe that?"

Mom straightened up. "That's great, hun."

"I love you, Ma. It'll be okay. I can work extra with Dad and use the money to help out with bills. I've got a little saved up, too."

"That's for your Jeep."

"It's just a car."

Mom stood, water in her eyes. She sniffled and murmured, "Thank you." Then she pulled a smile together and left the kitchen.

Dad glanced up at me. It was weird. He looked different. Less like a stone, more like a person. "That was nice of you." He put his glasses on the table and set his phone down.

"You going to start eating leftovers again for breakfast?"

When I was a kid and my dad's business was struggling, all we ever ate were leftovers. My dad was even eating meatloaf leftovers once for breakfast from a half-empty baking dish—a meatloaf I had no recollection of my mom ever baking to begin with nor us ever having had for dinner.

Meatloaf is like that. Strange things happen when it's around.

Dad said he didn't think so. "I ain't dead yet. Long as I'm living, I'll work to provide for this family."

"Who said you were dying?"

"I ain't. I didn't."

"You're okay, right?"

"Yeah, son. Just an expression."

I thought about Mr. Barno and harmony. I was making harmony in my home. It felt nice.

Thinking about Mr. Barno got me thinking about how he said he met his wife, Celeste, back when he was in high school.

"You like Don Henley's music?"

"Love the Eagles. You know that."

"No, I mean, his solo stuff."

"The only solo one I know is 'The Boys of Summer.' Love that song."

"Really? You never play it."

"Sometimes dads need a song that's just theirs."

"Why that song?"

"Well, that song's about a guy who longs for this girl that all these other guys like. And he's determined to stick around after the other guys run off."

"And?"

"I was that for your mom."

How come I knew about how Mr. Barno fell in love, but not my parents?

"How so?"

He picked up the cereal box and slowly rolled up the bag inside before putting the box down. "I decided I'd always be there for your mom, even after she got pregnant with your sister. We were teenagers. I started construction full time with PopPop. Your mom tried college. But once Sarah was born..." Dad scooted his chair back, leaned forward, and put his hands on the table. "Love takes sacrifices."

My dad never talked about this stuff. I rushed to the next question. "How'd you know you loved Mom?"

He eased back. "Actually, I didn't know at first. We were friends and we dated a little. Then, she was dating this guy named Craig." He eyed the light fixture above the table. "Ya know. See son. Some guys. It's hard to explain. Some guys don't take responsibility. Some guys are boys of summer, like Craig, you understand?"

Not really. "Yeah. Yeah, Dad. Of course."

"Eventually, your mom and I realized we loved one another. And when you love someone, you take care of them. Like I said, sacrifices." He stood and ran his hand through my hair. The last time he had done that I was probably 8 years old. "Good talk, son."

The quote on the chalkboard when I sat down in Government & Military class that Monday afternoon was: "The two most powerful warriors are patience and time." – Leo Tolstoy.

It was September 11th—the fourth week of the school year—and Mr. Green stood a little taller, wore a little American flag lapel pin on his polo shirt, and donned military socks (I know because he also wore no shoes that day. Not sure why). When he played "Reveille," he held a few of the notes sort of mournfully. During lecture, he made several vague references to the 'enemy within.' I wrote that down and circled it. No clue what it meant.

This was Neil's favorite class. He leaned so far forward in his chair that his chin was practically out past the front of his desk. I think Neil saw Mr. Green and pictured a young Gramps.

Mr. Green. An American hero. A guy who loved his country so much that it haunted him.

Maybe that's what love is: this thing that haunts us.

I wrote that thought down in the margins.

Then, for some inexplicable reason, it occurred to me that Mr. Green was probably the only teacher in America who still used a chalkboard.

Toward the end of class, Mr. Green delivered announcements. Most teachers did them at the start of class. Not Mr. Green. Mr. Green did things "non-linearly" (His words) to "prepare us for the chaos and uncertainty" (His words) of "the battlefield of life" (You guessed it).

If it was a special announcement, Mr. Green would erase the quote of the day and put up a special announcement quote. He did that this time. The quote was: "Know thyself, know thy enemy. A thousand battles, a thousand victories." – Sun Tzu.

"Voting for Homecoming court commences now." Mr. Green nodded at Becky who stood and dutifully distributed notecards.

He continued, "My fellow Americans, and Raúl our welcomed guest who represents our allies abroad in good faith, you are to cast your votes at your seventh period class. For the unthinking among you, that would be this class. Enter who you are voting for on the lines on your voting card and place your card in the box.

This'll be a fair and secure election, I assure you." He picked up a box with a slit on top of it and shook it. "Remember your solemn oath. And write clearly. You may nominate up to ten people. Homecoming court will comprise of the eight students who receive the most votes. Eight dedicated souls who will represent this institution admirably. And, yes, you may nominate yourself. An unwillingness to vote for yourself portends a failure of self-confidence." He tapped his wooden lecture pointer against the quote on the chalkboard. "Votes will be tallied Friday. Homecoming court will be announced next Monday. Godspeed."

Neil turned and passed me a voting card. I stared at it for a while.

Then I wrote down three names: Gabi Meyers, Neil Filipowicz, and Tyler Pratt-Baldwin.

I left the rest blank, got up, and cast my votes.

An envelope rested in the shade on the welcome mat by Mr. Barno's front door. It was folded and wrinkled like someone had tried unsuccessfully to jam it between the door and the seal.

I picked it up. The words, "Important: Last Warning," were printed at an angle in red. The return address was the Paxson Community Bank. The addressee, Mr. Alexis P. Barno.

I tucked it in my back pocket, put my phone and recorder under a bush, and went inside. Things were that way now with Mr. Barno. He expected me to just walk in without knocking. "Hey Mr. B. It's me," I called.

Mr. Barno read on the couch while Dodger sprang off it and rushed me, tail wagging. Barno stared kind of blankly like it took him a moment to recognize me. When he did, he smiled.

I said, "Big day today. We're installing the posts, right?"

"Posts?"

"For the project."

"Why are you here? It's Saturday."

"Mr. Barno, It's Monday. I came from school."

"Oh."

I told him about my mom and how she was on 'indefinite leave' from work and how I did what he taught me: I brought more harmony into my home when my mom was sad about her job. I told him how I volunteered to work with my dad after school every day of the week except Mondays to help make extra money. "I told Mom I was going to get that big scholarship that pays for all of college, the engineering one. It all went nicely. I mean, it was the most peaceful conversation I've had with my parents in a long time."

"That's great, Nolan. I'm happy for you."

I smiled big—big as my mouth would go. It felt good to feel good.

"Remind me about the scholarship."

"The one with the essay I was telling you about I didn't want to write."

"Of course. When's it due?"

"It was due last Friday. But. Yeah. Um. I ended up not applying for the scholarship. I just kind of told Mom that so she'd stop worrying so much. You know, harmony. Not hurting Mom, right?"

Mr. Barno cocked his head. "Harmony isn't about

lying."

"But it was, like, a white lie. Something you say to help."

"Balderdash. Dishonesty is a cut that doesn't start bleeding right away. What happens next?" Mr. Barno sounded stern, a tone I had never heard from him before.

"I guess I figure I'll tell Mom I didn't get the scholarship. She'll be disappointed and all. But." I thought a bit. "Yeah, I guess she'll be pretty devastated. Sorry. I'm kind of crazy to get my mom's hopes up over a lie."

"No labels. No good, no bad, no sane, no crazy. You're not crazy."

"That's a relief because I don't want to end up loopy like Cammie Roland."

Mr. Barno tossed his book on the coffee table. "Cammie's not crazy. She was a student of mine."

I felt bad for making his voice sound the way it did. "She was?"

"Yes, and one of the last Smart Kids."

"Smart Kids?"

He crossed his arms. "Nothing."

"Come on, what?"

"An unofficial after-school club of sorts back when I taught at Paxson."

"What was it about?"

His voice softened a tad. His face did too. "Eh. It's the kids that stick out in my mind."

"At least tell me why it was called that."

He scratched his head. "Let's see. Before prison of course, I ran into some students at the pizza place and they asked me to sit and chat. Somebody made a joke about me sitting with the smart kids. They liked that, being called the smart kids. Eventually, it grew into a regular thing."

"Cool. I'd have joined the Smart Kids if I was your student back then."

"You're the last Smart Kid." The way he said it, I couldn't tell if he was glad about that or not.

I grinned anyway. *The last Smart Kid.* "And Cammie's not crazy?"

He tucked his hands under his armpits. "In this town, there are myths about success that adults get wrapped up in. Cammie chose to stay and help improve Paxson. People look down on her for not meeting expectations—their expectations. Of all people, I figured you could understand that."

Man, that shot through me. I tried to change the subject. "Hey, I got some fortunate news. The girl I like, I think her boyfriend is cheating on her."

Mr. Barno closed his eyes and put his hands over his face. He said through his palms, "How is that fortunate?"

"If they break up, I got a shot at her."

"Will profiting off of misery bring greater happiness to you?"

"I mean, if it gets me a chance to be with her. Then, yeah, there are winners and losers in life. It's my turn to win. My turn to be happy."

He pulled his hands away from his face and glared at me. "Is that harmony?"

I made some 'I feel dumb' grunt.

"Remind me, what lesson are we on?"

"We've done two so far. Lesson One was happiness not fear. Lesson Two was compassion not judgment."

Dodger jumped back on the couch and rested his

head on Mr. Barno's thigh. "Okay, time for Lesson Three."

"Hold on, I'll grab my recorder." I ran to the front door and hurried back. I pressed record and gave Barno a nod.

"What?" he asked.

"Ready for Lesson Three."

"Oh. Eh. You'll have to remind me."

What is this, a test to see if I'm paying attention? "We talked about Cammie Roland not being crazy. Then I was talking about this girl Gabi who I like and how her boyfriend is a possible cheat."

"Right. Have we explored the importance of harmony yet?"

This confused me. We were talking about harmony minutes before. And we talked about it the other day. "Yeah, the tree root thing."

"The what?"

I pointed out the sliding glass door to the patch of dirt that I had yet to cover with seed. "You know, the gash I put in the tree root."

Mr. Barno squished his eyebrows together. "But it's not solidified as a lesson yet?"

"No."

"Then Lesson Three is to move toward harmony with others and with yourself. We think people must. Um. They should." He grew quiet and petted Dodger. "Where was I?"

"Uh. About thinking people should something or other."

"Eh. Right. Here's one. Did you know more people are lonelier today than ever before? Humans yearn for deep connection. Why, then, can't we accept anyone that doesn't fit our expectations, that isn't precisely how we think they should be?

"You mean, like how people treat Cammie Roland?"

"Yes, her. But not just her. If we don't meet our own expectations, why is it that so many of us can't accept ourselves?"

"I don't know."

He stood and moved to the kitchen. "What is one of the greatest contributors to happiness?"

I 'hmmd' a bit, following him to the kitchen. "Success, like a great job. Money. Nice car. Cool stuff. Being attractive so people want you. Maybe fame—"

Mr. Barno interrupted. "It's relationships. Having strong relationships is one of the best predictors of happiness. Spending time with people face-to-face, the way we are doing now."

"I call B.S."

"No B.S."

"Friends? Family? Sounds too simple of an answer."

He got a pitcher of lemonade from the fridge. "We're losing our human connections. We're spending more time alone and when we do interact with others, it's through a screen."

"But, like, people make me nervous," I said. "What if they don't like me? Or judge me?"

"I understand. We place no trust in one another. We only trust our way of seeing the world. We lash out and cut others down. We've suffocated our ability to communicate. In a world like this, it's no wonder other people make you anxious."

I reached for the glass of lemonade he held in an outstretched hand. "Okay, so I'm confused about the

Gabi's boyfriend maybe cheating on her thing. You just said that relationships make us happy."

"Is this young lady going to be happy if her boyfriend is cheating on her? If her boyfriend was happy, would he be cheating on her?"

"No. But. Well, I can't do anything about that. What does it matter if I benefit from it?"

He poured himself lemonade. "It won't bring you happiness to cheer for the unhappiness of others. How could destructive thinking bring greater joy in the long run? Don't create walls between people. There are too many as it is. If you put your energy toward wanting others to be well, you'll feel a greater connection to them."

"But I want Gabi. Why should I care about her boyfriend Dallas?"

"Do you want Gabi to be happy or do you just want her for yourself?"

"I want her to be happy."

"Doesn't sound like it. Sounds like you want her to meet your expectations—be the girlfriend you want, help make you feel good about yourself, help make you feel less alone."

"This is hard," I groaned. "I don't like it. So what if I want something? You're the one who said things are neither good nor bad. So I can want whatever I want."

"When did I say that?"

"Lesson Two. You said no good, no bad."

"Oh. Right, that's true. You *can* want whatever you want. Doesn't mean it'll make you happy. Doesn't mean it'll bring happiness to others. Lesson Two was about not judging situations and being more accepting of them, right?"

"Uh-huh."

"That's not an excuse to do whatever you want, consequences be damned."

"This is dumb. I don't get any of it. I thought you wanted me to get the girl and be happy."

"I would never say anything about wanting you to get a girl. That's your rigid expectation." He shook his head. "People who run against the wind do a lot of huffing and puffing, don't they?"

I moaned. My eyes drifted off to a mound of dishes. I slid to the sink and started washing them.

"What if this girl. Eh?"

"Gabi."

"What if Gabi doesn't like you?"

I thought about Skyler. Thought about how she was made of Paul Simon, of art that stained her overalls, of dreams in which she owns a restaurant. Thought about the smile on her narrow face and how her teeth were rounded a tiny bit. Thought about the last time I saw her when she was standing in the crowded hallway clutching her books to her chest—free but holding onto something. *Holy shit, I like Skyler Bell.* "Well, there's this other girl, Skyler. But my friend Branson is obsessed with her."

"You must let others choose who they love. If one of these young women loves you, that's their choice. Clearly, someone is going to have their heart broken. Not everyone can be happy in every situation. You can't force someone to love you. You can love someone for who they are. That's it."

"This is heavy stuff. Can you, like, break it down for me?"

"Eh. I'll try. Let's see. Move with things, not against

them. That's harmony. If you find yourself being certain or rigid, take a step back. It's not possible to have all your expectations met. Be flexible. That's harmony. Build things up, don't tear them down. That's harmony. Make sure others' needs are met. That's harmony."

"Okay, so how do I do this harmony thing?"

"There are lots of ways, but patience and love—with yourself and others—are two of the best ways I know."

"Sorry. I'm trying."

"No sorry. Gradual is good. Most miracles go overlooked. I've said that before?"

I nodded. "Patience and love. Thanks for being patient with me. Sorry I annoyed you." I stopped the recorder.

He stepped toward me and put a hand on my shoulder. Then he gave me a hug. I had forgotten hugs existed. "You didn't annoy me. Look, it is time I tell you something. Something difficult." He buried his upper lip and gazed at the project in the backyard through the window. "My moods these last few weeks, please know they have nothing to do with you. They're a symptom."

"A symptom?"

Mr. Barno closed his eyes and touched his palms together. His belly expanded and contracted. "My mind—my memory, my thinking—is slipping away. Many moments are clear as water, others murky like lemonade. Still other moments are opaque like Pepsi. I get by with lemonade. Pepsi, not so much. I'm getting less water, more lemonade and Pepsi."

"Oh." I studied the haze in my glass of lemonade. "One day we lose our lemonade. Another day we lose our mind. You said that to me once, right?"

He squeezed his eyes closed and breathed slowly. "That day is sooner than later."

I surfaced the envelope from my pocket. "This have anything to do with it?"

He unsealed his eyes. His body slumped. "Some things are worth forgetting."

I handed him the envelope. "What's going on?"

"Let's get to work and we'll talk. There's much to do and not much time."

We went into the backyard and worked on putting the posts up. While we worked, Mr. Barno told me his predicament. When he went to prison, he put his sister in charge of using his savings to pay the mortgage on the house. This was his and Celeste's home, and he was determined to return to it someday. When that money ran out, he had his sister tap into his retirement account. His sister passed away two years ago and there was no one to help pay the mortgage. "I try to keep up with the late payments and interest, but—this may be hard for you to understand—I forget. Money is drying up. I tried to find a job, but no one in this town will hire me. Thought about working in another town, but I'm not allowed to drive."

"What's in the envelope?"

He pointed to where the envelope sat on the metal bench. I walked over, picked it up, ripped the edge, and slid the letter out. I didn't understand all of it, but basically, the letter said that Mr. Barno had two months to pay the rest of the loan in full or the bank would foreclose on him. He owed $22,876.42.

I plonked onto the metal bench and surveyed the backyard. *He's going to lose everything? He can't. He just can't.* "Jeez, I wish I knew how to help," I said in this really pitiful, forlorn voice. I felt like grabbing the shovel, digging a hole, and crawling into it.

Mr. Barno held his arms out the way people at sports games do when they're making letters. His letter was a T, palms up, and I pictured some actor in a musical about to break into song. Behind him, the tree and the posts we had just installed were his set. "You have. Celeste. You. This project. These are my wellsprings of joy. And true joy stays with us forever."

Thirteen

Tuesday night. I couldn't sleep. My brain was a videogame platform character in a side-scroll game. My brain was Mario. My thoughts jumped, ducked, and dodged obstacle after obstacle. But the platform wasn't Nintendo Wii. The platform was life.

I was stuck in World 17 Year Old.

Too many obstacles.

Next obstacle: the mysteries of love.

I grabbed my phone and downed some Lenny the True Love CEO YouTube videos. He had a series called 'Lenny's Love Ratings,' where he discussed the virtues and flaws of various celebrities—social media influencers, movie stars, musicians—and what each celebrity would be like to date. He had, like, a scientific, proprietary formula he used to do his ratings. And I was hoping that I could figure out what that formula was if I watched enough videos. I figured I could use the formula to decide between Gabi and Skyler. Tragically, after watching the series for over an hour, I conceded at 1:07 am Wednesday morning that not even the good professor's wisdom could help me make sense of the Gabi and Skyler predicament.

Another obstacle approached: Mr. Barno's situation.

I had about $11,500 saved from almost three years of working with my dad. I was approaching my $13,000 Used Jeep Fund target. But if I used the money on Mr. Barno instead, and if I did the Lewis job, and if my take in that was $10,000, then I'd have $21,500. That was about $1,500 short of what Barno needed. Maybe the bank would be okay with that for now and Barno could pay the rest of the money in a month or two.

Maybe I can do it.

Maybe I can help Mr. Barno.

Then, an obstacle popped out of the ground: Mom no longer working.

Maybe I'd need my savings to help my parents get by, instead.

Another obstacle came bounding toward me: the Save the Youth of Paxson people.

This misguided mob was holding a meeting Wednesday afternoon at the Paxson Library to try to force Mr. Barno out of his house. If they succeeded, paying off the bank loan wouldn't do any good.

Can't miss that meeting. Got to gather intel. I had to give my dad an excuse so I could get out of work.

Fake an injury? Say there's a big test? Yes, that's it. There's a big test Thursday in AP English and I need to study with some kids after school. I'll tell Mom it's important for my college app and tell Dad there's going to be a girl I like there. That'll satisfy them both, right?

Then I realized, crap. Another obstacle swooped down from the sky. At some point, my parents were going to ask me when cross country tryouts began. And I didn't even know when they were. Or maybe my parents forgot about why I wasn't working on Mondays. With me working all the other days now, maybe it would slip through the way lots of things did with them.

Then again, lots of things didn't slip through with them. *Crap*.

Too many obstacles.

At 2:19 am, I couldn't take it anymore. I snuck out of the house in my PJs and wandered around in the chilly air. Then, my legs decided to run. I ran through empty Main Street. Ran through the vacant parking lot at the high school. Ran to Mr. Barno's house.

I stood on a log, reached over Mr. Barno's privacy fence, and teased the gate latch open with a stick. Inside the backyard, I tiptoed to the oak tree.

I almost stepped on Mr. Barno.

I nearly screamed.

He was curled into a sleeping bag beside the smooth stones that surrounded the tree the way I used to sleep by a campfire back when I was a scout.

I slid around him and over the invisible flowers. I crouched against the tree trunk and was about to close my eyes when he lifted his head. "Who are you here to talk to?"

"Nobody," I frowned, sorry for waking him. "Just didn't know where else to go."

His eyes smiled, "I talk to Celeste every night."

That about made me cry.

"There's a little magic, a light that guides each of us." He rested his head and, before drifting back to sleep, he assured me, "You are not alone."

I wanted to shake him, wake him up, and ask him what he meant. But, I don't know, he seemed so happy sleeping there.

I closed my eyes and breathed the way he had shown me. And it happened. I did the momentary time travel thing. The loopy thing.

I was standing wide-legged on the hood of a blue sports car, clutching a baseball bat way up over my head.

I smashed it down on the hood. Then I smashed it again. Again.

I vaulted off onto the high school parking lot asphalt. I swung at the lights. Smash. Buckshot of plastic shards blasted against my chest and arms.

I cocked back for another swing. The bat wouldn't move.

I spun to see the blur of a fist.

The asphalt rammed against my head.

I opened my eyes. Everything was shattered. Blue. Orange. Plastic.

Blinked.

A few high school students congealed into mini sky-scrapers off across the parking lot.

I rolled my head back and peered over my shoulder. My sister's boyfriend, Rafe, stood over me, the bat swaying by his side. He looked evil the way Branson's mom looked sometimes when she was on the verge. He kicked me on the ass and legs. Over and over.

I screeched and writhed.

He raised the bat menacingly.

Closed my eyes.

Sarah shrieked, "The hell is wrong with you?"

Tell him, Sarah. Stop him, I thought.

I cracked an eye open. Saw Sarah standing by Rafe's side, her arms clasped around his waist. "Nolan, what the fuck! The hell is wrong with you?" She glared down at me.

I tried to talk. Tried to tell her I saw what happened. Saw Rafe punch her hard last night in the driveway when I was counting the stars through my bedroom window. Saw her fall. Saw him spit on her. Call her some word. Storm off.

Saw her get up. Whimper. Run after him.

Saw him shake her.

Saw them kiss.

I tried to talk. But my mouth was empty.

Didn't matter. Sarah and Rafe were gone.

I lay beside Rafe's blue Mitsubishi Eclipse.

Shattered.

I tried to find the students across the parking lot. Had they seen?

No. Gone.

I shoved my hand into my mouth. Bit until my fingers bled.

Wept.

How do you tell an adult that you saw your sister get knocked to the ground by Rafe, the musical genius that everyone worships? How do you tell your parents?

How, when everyone else turns away?

How do you ask your sister why she kissed a guy who hit her? How do you ask her what the space between those moments was like for her, the space between being hit by Rafe and kissing him?

You don't. Not when you're 9 years old.

You clench your teeth. Learn to bite hard.

I was back. Sweaty. Shivering. Mr. Barno slept peacefully by the tree.

That was the thing. Mr. Barno had peace. I didn't.

I didn't have anything.

Mr. Barno had Celeste.
I didn't have anyone.
That wasn't true.
I had the lessons. I had Mr. Barno.
I had hope.
I got up, floundered to the fence gate, and, gasping for air, ran home. As I ran, I thought about what Mr. Barno had said in Lesson Two. It wasn't good or bad what I had done to Rafe's car. Done to Sarah. Done to my family.
It was love. Love for Sarah.
The sky was purple, the sun just around the corner.

Fourteen

"A war of attrition." That's what Mr. Green called the Pacific Theatre of World War II. "We were getting whooped. Shellacked. There's no denying that. I love this country. You do, too. But, my fellow Americans—and Raúl—here's the harsh truth. In the early going, we were no match for the island nation of Japan. Fear not. Soon, our industrial might was firing on all cylinders and we stuck it to 'em and stuck it to 'em good. The lesson? Don't awaken a sleeping giant, especially one with superior resources." He paused to gulp water. Little sweat pimples dotted his forehead. This guy really loved to teach. You had to admire that. "We have 14 minutes and 27 seconds left of class. Your task? Engage the textbook in the productive reading protocol."

The unit was about government, warfare and industry. The textbook said that in 1941 alone, the United States launched more vessels than Japan did during the entirety of World War II. It said that the Battle of Midway was the turning point and that after that time, the U.S. built almost three times as many aircraft carriers as Japan.

I tried to 'engage in productive reading,' but I was bobblehead tired with concrete-heavy eyelids. Mr. Green didn't notice. His attention was on the still trees outside the window. He always faded off after assigning us to read quietly. His thousand-yard stare, I guess. Behind him on the chalkboard, the quote of the day read: "We are not retreating. We are advancing in another direction." – Douglas MacArthur.

I had told my parents that I had an AP English test to study for so I couldn't work with Dad that afternoon. Guess what? They didn't even blink. So after school, I went and sat at a lunch table under a tree and attempted homework. I could've hung out with Branson and Neil, but I just didn't feel like it. I didn't even go to the lockers to catch up after school.

I woke up, face matted to my notebook, a puddle of drool on the pages. Checked my watch. It was 4:30 pm. *Shit! The Save the Youth of Paxson meeting!*

I shoveled my stuff into my backpack and ran downtown.

Throughout its history, the Paxson Library building was a butcher shop, an old schoolhouse, and a jail cell. By the entrance, one of those historic signs sprinkled around town boasted that 'a public whipping post and a pigpen were once situated on the external western wall of the building.'

In the library, a heap of people spilled out of the auditorium—a classroom-sized room with chairs where they projected *The Wizard of Oz* on a screen once in a while—and into a narrow aisle of books. I squeezed into a spot on the floor near the rear of the mob. A child. On the floor.

Inside the auditorium, a woman boomed, "We must protect our youth from that man. Many of you lived here in the 1990s when, due to his immoral actions, we lost several cherished members of this community. Preventable deaths. Senseless deaths. I present Exhibit A. This is a copy of the October 7 19—"

A voice cut in, "Hold it higher up!"

"Thank you, Avani. For those who can't see in the back, I'm holding the *Paxson Chronicle*. The headline reads, 'Paxson High teacher convicted in fatal car crash sentenced to 25 years.' The article states that Alexis Barno's blood alcohol level was twice the legal limit. Let me repeat that, twice the legal limit. Three people died because of his drinking that night. Three people that will never have a chance to breathe the air that scum freely breathes, or to walk the streets that he walks among us, in our town. Our town. Not his. Ours. Beautiful souls are no longer with us because of this impetuous, selfish, moral-less man. This is just one instance in which—"

The woman's voice faded into the background as I clung to the words: 'three people died.' *Three people?* I only saw Celeste Barno's body at the accident. *Who did I miss?*

Next thing I knew, a man's voice was saying, "As your mayor of 20 years, I look out and see many neighbors, many friends. Now, I understand this is upsetting for members of our community. I empathize. My son Tyler goes to school alongside many of your children. That said, I have held discussions with local and state officials, including the Attorney General of our great state. There exists no statute that prevents Alexis Barno from living near a public school. Such laws are confined to sex offenders and Mr. Barno is not a convicted sex offender."

"He's worse!" a male voice bellowed.

The mayor made a sound like he was gargling rocks. "Excuse me, Patrick. I have the floor. As I was saying, Alexis Barno was convicted for aggravated vehicular manslaughter while under the influence. Yes, he knew that road well, knew it was dangerously winding. He clearly disregarded that, driving aggressively and well above the speed limit. Nonetheless, as a jury of his peers determined in a court of law, while Alexis showed a reckless disregard for human life, the deaths were involuntary. He's served his sentence, paid his debt to society. You may dislike this fact, but no one can stop him from living where he lives."

The crowd jeered and booed the way crowds did in the old movies Gramps sometimes had on when we hung out at Neil's house.

The woman who spoke earlier called out, "Mr. Barno is a murderer. He killed my brother and he did it with malice."

"Mrs. Meyers, please. May I caution you that some may find your words slanderous? You are well aware that your brother's death was an accident."

"Am I? Am I really, Michael? How can you stand idly by? You, sir, have lost the faith of this community. So help me God, this will be your last term in office."

More jeering. The crowd simmered as the mayor marched out of the auditorium. A few minutes later, clusters of parents and teenagers filed out, exchanging sharp words and explosive gestures.

My parents shot out, passing me. Didn't see me sitting on the floor. *Close call!* Someone was blabbering at them. Dad gesticulated. Mom buffed her temples.

I went up and down the aisles, pretending to look for books while waiting to ensure my parents were gone. From the other side of the Mysteries & Thrillers aisle, I heard the voice of the woman who said Barno killed three people. I squinted through a crack between the books. A heavyset woman in a pantsuit embraced a woman of stubborn elegance in a dress, shawl and heels.

It was Yuvi's mom, Avani, in the pantsuit. And I realized that the lady who was talking earlier in the auditorium was Gabi's mom, Penelope Meyers.

"Penelope," Yuvi's mom consoled, "don't trouble your soul, my dear. Fate has intervened."

Gabi's mom dabbed tears with a tissue.

Yuvi's mom continued, "You mustn't tell anyone, alright? This is my career we're talking about."

"Oh, get on with it, Avani."

"The bank. It's foreclosing. Mr. Richardson had me mail Barno his final notice. Hang in there, my dear. A few months and that awful man will be on the street. And, please, please, this is our secret."

I never did this kind of thing—never skipped school or snuck away for lunch. But this was crisis-level shit.

Apparently, a lot of high schools let students leave for lunch. Paxson High was not one of them. Leaving Paxson without permission could get you suspended. Yuvi and Omar had pulled it off unscathed three times. At least, that's what they claimed.

The way to do it, they said, was to hide in the bathroom on the way to the cafeteria.

"When the hall's empty, run like hell out the double doors by the gym. Hide behind the metal storage container where they keep the football helmets and stuff. Be patient. Narcs will be doing their rounds (We had two narcs that drove around campus in an old minivan.

Their job was basically to catch teenagers being teenagers and penalize them for it). Once the narc-mobile turns the corner, make a break across No Man's Land (About 50 yards of asphalt parking lot) to the wooded path," Yuvi counseled. The path was the same one I used to get to Mr. Barno's house.

Omar added, "The morning of the day you're planning to skip, park the getaway car on the street that serial killer guy lives on. Then you're free to drive wherever for lunch."

They both recommended Dairy Queen. Of course, I didn't tell them I was going to Mr. Barno's house—didn't tell them that I wasn't fiending for a DQ Blizzard.

I made it undetected to the storage locker outside the gym doors. I knew Principal Anand's office window faced No Man's Land. I was betting everything on her not being there or not looking out the window. Expulsion. Finishing my senior year at Middleview High. Or, becoming a dropout and living in a dumpster, just like Mom had warned. Those were the risks.

Now, I'm not from an overly religious family (The one teaching my parents seemed keen on relaying to Sarah and me, drawn from my mom's Catholicism and my dad's Judaism, was that guilt should be ever-present in our lives). Yet, I once saw a guy in a football game my dad was watching double tap his chest and point to the sky after scoring a touchdown. So I did that.

Then I ran.

Ran through No Man's Land like my butt was on fire.

I made it to the trees and dove headfirst onto the path. In a battle, when you make it through No Man's

Land, you know you've survived (According to the movies I've seen at Neil's house). I had no clue if I had survived—if the principal or the narcs saw me. I would find that out when I returned to school. That is, if I made it through No Man's Land on my return trip.

At Mr. Barno's house, I put my phone under a bush and knocked on the door before letting myself in. It hadn't registered before, but the mess in his house, the mess we had cleaned over the summer, was starting to grow back.

I found Mr. Barno in the backyard working on the tree project without me. "You're late."

"It's Thursday."

"Lift this," he said. I stepped up a ladder and helped him hoist a cross beam up. He stepped up on another ladder and I placed my side on the top of my ladder. I hopped down, ran over, and held his end while he hammered.

I called over the noise, "There's a group trying to force you out of your house. Seems like much of the town supports them. There was a meeting yesterday. And the popular girl I'm into, Gabi, I think her mom's one of the people in charge of the group."

He stopped swinging the hammer but kept his eye on the board. "Is the last name Meyers?"

"Yeah. Penelope Myers. You know her?"

He started hammering again.

"You knew about this?"

He put the hammer down and inspected me. "Mrs. Meyers does not have harmony. She has fear. To her, I am bad and she is doing good."

"And?"

"And I understand her suffering. I know its source. I cannot blame her. Fear can disrupt the harmony in a community, can't it?"

"If the community knew you, they'd know you're a good guy."

"The sun's out. You're here. The birds sing. My mind is mostly water with a drop of lemonade today. That's good enough for me. I don't worry about others' thoughts."

"Aren't you mad?"

"What good is mad?"

"But if they take your home, they take everything—your place to be with Celeste, the tree project."

He picked the hammer up.

"How can you act like this?"

"Live by fear or live by happiness."

"Then why bother? Why am I holding up this stupid beam?"

"Move forward. Always. We control what we can. That is all."

"You're just trying to be tough, like my dad. But you're not. And, well, I'm no longer sure he is either."

"I am being realistic. Have you heard of impact bias?"

"No."

"Look it up sometime. In essence, we humans overestimate the impact things will have on us. We think negative events will leave us buried under devastating emotions forever. The same with positive events. We think that if our dreams come true then we will be forever elated. Yet, most things don't impact us as much as we think they will. We're more resilient than we give ourselves credit for."

"Well, if I was you and I lost my house and my connection to my wife, I'd be pretty devastated."

"I will mourn. For a little while. But it won't destroy my life. I'll move on. One tree cut down is not the death of the forest. I can plant more trees. You can too. If things don't work out with something you put your heart and soul into, you can go on."

I stamped my foot.

He descended the ladder. I followed him over to the other side of the cross beam and I held it up while he hammered it to a post.

"Who else was killed in the car accident?"

"Hand me a nail."

I did. "Who else? I heard three people died, not just Celeste."

Mr. Barno stood on the ladder and as he hammered, he said between swings, "Two boys… Summer before their… first day of high school... Camping in a tree fort… in the oak tree…. Built it themselves… One boy was climbing… up the ladder when… we crashed into… the tree… crushed him… Other boy… in the tree fort… Knocked out… fell… Broke his neck… Died in the hospital."

I closed my eyes and massaged my memory of the car crash while Mr. Barno hammered away. I conjured the image of Mr. Barno and an EMT pounding on his chest. Celeste, lifeless under a police officer's jacket. And two medics huddled in the dark. They must have been attending to the boy who fell out of the tree. In the distance, there were headlights wrapped on either side of the old oak's trunk. The other boy must have been pinned between the car and the tree on the far side. I was glad I never saw him.

Suddenly I remembered. After the crash, before I opened my eyes back in Mr. Barno's backyard, I had seen something, hadn't I? Two blurry faces. Teenage boys.

It all made sense. That's how Mr. Barno killed Gabi's mom's brother. He was one of the boys. That's why she wants to kick Barno out of town. *She wants revenge*, I thought. *She doesn't fear Mr. Barno. She hates him.*

I told Mr. Barno I had to get back to school before lunch break was over. I left and ran down the street. As I turned onto the path through the woods, I saw Mr. Lewis' big Mercedes-Benz sloping onto Mr. Barno's street. I ducked into the trees and watched as Mr. Lewis passed by. He parked in the cul-de-sac and got out. He walked up to the driveway, took his sunglasses off, and propped them atop his fedora. He glanced around a bit. At the garage. The siding. The landscaping.

I made it back through No Man's Land and ducked into the bathroom to wait for the lunch period to end. When it did, I slithered into the crowd, just another kid on his way to class from the cafeteria.

My class after lunch was Spanish III with Señor Zunk, or 'Funky Zunky' as he was known on account of his unidentifiable musk. Some claimed to experience an aroma of expired cat food and cafeteria Hi-C in Zunk's presence, while others cited a potpourri of stale vending machine Cheetos and lightly urinated on hamster cage shavings. In either case, Zunk was tolerable, so long as you sat in the back of the class. Which I, of course, did.

I spent the first half of the period watching the classroom door and expecting the narcs, or the dictator herself, Principal Anand, to bust in and drag me away kicking and screaming. Banished to the School Board's version of a gulag: Middleview High.

When that didn't happen, my mind drifted to Mr. Lewis. *What was he doing at Mr. Barno's?* I thought and thought. *Oh, that's it. Sly old bastard.* He was scoping out the condition of the house. A Real Estate guy like that? He must know people at the bank—possibly Yuvi's mom, Avani—who tipped him off to the fact that Barno's house was on the verge of foreclosure. Mr. Lewis must be planning to swoop in, buy Barno's house cheap, and make a bunch of money renting it.

Fifteen

My first day of Introduction to Journalism with Mrs. de León took place on the Friday morning of the fourth week of school. I was behind my classmates, but she helped me settle in.

Mrs. de León ran the class real serious, the way I guess a newsroom is run. The cool thing was that she let our interests and talents guide things. For example, if a student was interested in being on-air talent, they got to do that. If a student wanted to be an editor, they got to help edit the script.

It was a small class. Only nine of us.

Tyler Pratt-Baldwin and a girl who had just moved from Pittsburgh but was uber popular already, Linda Woo, were the on-air talent.

Since I wanted to learn about audio production, I got to help Vavara Pushkin, the student in charge of all the audio recording, editing, and mixing. Mrs. de León said, "Watch Vavara and learn from a master." Vavara was responsible for recording the show. And I was to help her do sound checks, work with the levels of the talents' voices, that kind of stuff. After recording the show, the 'fillers'—ums, uhs—and popping sounds needed to be edited out, the intro and outro music needed to be added, and background music needed to be laid under the voices. I was to help her with that, too.

Varvara's parents were Russian. She was the kind of person whose neck had muscles. I pictured her flattening my face with one hand while tossing back vodka with the other. Everyone called her Rocket Red (Though her hair wasn't red. I heard it was actually a reference to some obscure comic character).

I said hi to her.

She gave me a slight nod.

"So, you can show me the ropes?"

Another slight nod.

I got a sense that everyone looked at Vavara and saw marching troops in fur caps. And nukes. Lots of nukes. I guess I saw those things, too.

Other people in the class included:

• Becky Stone – Girl that ratted me out to Principal Anand. Probable future state prosecutor. Also, Dallas' twin sister. She lived with their dad whereas Dallas lived with their mom

• 'President' Jamal Young – President of the SGA, chess prodigy, and guy who already had his own charity helping estranged housecats. His social media posts comprised an irresistible alloy of his vaunted smile, stylish clothes, and retro dance moves alongside suspiciously fluffy cats. Last I checked, he had over 400,000 followers

• 'Lucky' Jack Ono – Star baseball pitcher who once got hit in the balls by a line drive and was called Lucky because his jewels didn't explode

• Randall McCullough – A moonshiner. That's all I know

• Hunter 'The Shark' Gallo – A sharkish humanoid you've already met

I watched Varvara work silently on the computer at the editing station while I took lots of notes. When Mrs.

de León circled over to us, I impulsively told her about an idea sprouting in my mind about my senior project.

"I want to do a podcast about life in Paxson. I'll, like, interview teachers and students. I'm thinking I can do 5 episodes, each one exploring a different aspect of life in Paxson today. At the school. Maybe in the town even. I sort of want to tell the story of this place in a way that people can understand and relate to, no matter who they are, old or young. What do you think?"

"It's a start. A bit broad. But a start." Mrs. de León rubbed her palms together, her loose jewelry tumbling on her wrists. "Write me up a page about the idea for class this afternoon. I'll let you run with it, see where it goes."

"Shit's getting festive." That's how Branson described the Homecoming decorations going up in the hallways at school (Homecoming was still a few weeks away, but here in Paxson we milked the excitement for all it was worth). Our mascot was the Saxon. We were the Paxson Saxons (How lazy is that?). The decorations included banners with poorly painted warrior guys in horned helmets doing the Captain Morgan stance over bears with X's over their eyes. Other banners contained phrases like "Bury the Bears."

Neil, Branson and I huddled at our locker out in The Desert.

"Alright. Thought about it. I'm in for," I looked around to ensure no one was eavesdropping, "the thing. The thing we talked about the other night. By the river."

Neil shook a fist. "Operation Nottingham is on," he whispered.

Branson offered me a fist bump. "No Land is a Midnight Warlord after all."

We were talking low but I kept feeling like we were too loud. "Here's the deal. No dookie celebrations. We leave our smartphones at home. Midnight Warlords take this job to the grave. You stains get caught, you keep your mouths shut this time. Got it?"

Branson grabbed my shoulders and shook. "Finally getting that Jeep."

I shushed him. "Who knows."

Branson cracked his knuckles. "Yo, relax. There's no way we get caught for this."

"Oh, and we bring a step stool next time for the wall. My dad's got one I'll borrow."

We parted ways and headed to our classes.

After first period, I cut through The Sect on my way to AP Physics. I saw Gabi camped at her locker—the door open, her face practically inside it.

I waved. But, nothing.

Following AP Physics, I was on my way to the cafeteria when I heard a very Tarzan-esque howl. Three football players stampeded past me from the rear. Behind one, a lassoed stuffed bull swished across the hallway floor (I guess it was the mascot for the team our school was slated to play that week). The teammates clustered together, bouncing on their toes. Then they smacked hands with someone coming toward me and sped off around a corner.

That someone was Dallas Stone. He sauntered past me, his arm adorning Natalia Valentine. She wore her green and gold cheerleader outfit over her curvy body.

Dallas had a football jersey on with sleeves rolled up. *His muscles deserve their own Instagram account*, I thought (Turns out that actually already existed. As I later found out, a sophomore named Evie Katz started it as a private account for Dallas' fangirls).

Hands shook my shoulders. "You hear?"

I swung around to a high-five from Branson. *What the?* We were fist bump people. Not high fivers.

"Dallas asked Natalia to Homecoming. She said yes. He broke up with Gabi. Your dreams are coming true, man. The door's open. Jump through it and ask Gabi to the Homecoming dance."

I couldn't believe it. I walked to class in a sort of daze, Branson beside me chattering on about Homecoming this and Homecoming that.

After lunch, I was supposed to go to the weight room for my exercise class. Weights weren't really my thing, but I wished they were. So when I was given a choice to fill a free elective, I picked Intro to Weight Training. That's where I was in life: needing an introduction to weight training. What girl would be impressed by that?

Anyway, what I ended up doing after parting with Branson, was marching through The Sect to Gabi's locker. Branson had psyched me up, what with his high five and all.

She stood there, her face shoved in the locker like before. "Hey, Gabi. You okay?" I tried to say it in this soft tone so as not to startle her.

She didn't reply.

"Gabi. You alright?"

She slammed the locker closed. "What?" Then she saw it was me. The muscles in her face loosened. "Oh, hey. Syracuse guy, right?"

"Name's Nolan."

She swooshed hair out of her face. "I know that. It was a reference to our convo a while ago."

Two amazing things here:

1. She remembered talking to me

2. We had a reference. She referenced us.

"So you okay, Syracuse girl?"

She smiled. "You're the only one who has asked me that. None of those Honey Bun Bitches have bothered."

"Noticed you seemed kind of off somewhere this morning. Then I saw Dallas."

"No loyalty, that one." She put her hands on her hips. "Natalia got selected for Homecoming. So did Dallas. Guess who didn't?"

"Me?"

She sniffle-chuckled and punched me playfully on the arm. "You neither, huh?"

"So close."

"They're going together. That's his big dream. Be crowned Homecoming royalty and dance in front of everyone. You know he lobbied against changing the titles from king and queen to royalty last year?" She made a mock Dallas voice, "Homecoming tradition." It was a pretty good impression. "Wants it to be him and whatever girl he's with."

"Who all got nominated?"

"Dallas and Natalia, of course. Dallas' twin sister Becky, Tyler Pratt-Baldwin, Jamal Young, Reese Hightower, and this new girl who puts out, Linda Something-or-other."

"Yikes. Possible incest."

Gabi chortled. "God, I hope. I will seriously die happy if he does win and he ends up having to dance with his sister."

Then, the unthinkable happened. She gave me a friend hug—the kind where girls put their cheek on yours and wrap their arms up under your arms like vanilla-scented uppercuts. "Thanks, Nolan."

After the hug, I winked at her. It just happened the way old people fart out of nowhere sometimes. *A wink. How weird is that?*

"Not going with anyone to Homecoming?" she said.

"Nah. You?"

"No."

"Well, if you need a date."

Gabi snorted a little. She rubbed her eyes. "You're sweet."

"So, that's a yes?"

"Well, are you a good kisser?" She winked at me. I mean it, really, she did.

"Ye— yeah." *Is she flirting?*

"Cause I only go to Homecoming with guys who kiss like movie stars."

She is flirting with me.

"I think. Um, yeah I could definitely accommodate that."

"Tell you what, I'll think about Homecoming," she smiled. "Got to run to debate, then yearbook. Check ya later, Syracuse guy."

She did that little wave hot girls do. She spun, her hair twirling, and glided down the hall. Her backpack bounced above her perfect rear.

I watched her—watched her walk away. Gabi Meyers. *The* Gabi Meyers. I felt like she had a string she was pulling behind her, the way that football player had dragged that stuffed bull. And Gabi's string was around me. I wanted to follow her. Wanted to talk to her more. Wanted to know what she had to say. What she liked. What she thought. What her favorite food was. What kind of music she liked. What her kisses were like. What she slept in. Wanted to know how Dallas could be so stupid.

I thought all that in the 10 seconds or so it took Gabi to disappear into the crowd. When I turned around, I spotted Skyler parked halfway up the stairway to the Social Studies Wing. She was looking my way, her books clamped to her chest. I smiled. Waved. She scurried up the stairs.

I don't remember my Introduction to Weight Training class that day. I assume it happened. I assume I was there. After, I went to seventh period—my last class of the day, Mr. Green's Government & Military class. When I entered, Mr. Green stood at his tidy desk. This was how he greeted students before each class, with one arm tucked behind his back.

We made eye contact, something I've never been good at. His big gray eyes penetrated through me and I sensed that he must have killed a lot of people. With eyes like that, you kill people. That's what they're for.

Or, maybe it was that after you've killed a lot of people, you develop eyes like that. Maybe Mr. Green had regular eyes once. Soft eyes. Kind eyes. Kind eyes like Mr. Barno. Maybe Mr. Green used to be someone else. Maybe he was just a kid named Dennis once. A kid who kissed someone under the high school bleachers and said, 'I love you.' A kid who'd had his heart broken by that same someone and cried more than his dad allowed him to. A kid who loved his parents before he ever loved his country. A kid who never imagined being a killer. A kid who imagined war was a videogame or a movie, the way Neil did. A kid who became Mr. Green.

And then I had this thought that didn't make a ton of sense but at the same time, it kind of did. Like a momentary epiphany—the kind you have just before you wake up and that you forget about the second you see your bedroom ceiling.

The thought was: *A tragedy of life is that most of us end up like Mr. Green.*

I took my seat in the back of the class and eyed the chalkboard. The quote of the day read: "You may not be interested in war, but war is interested in you." – Leon Trotsky.

Mr. Green played "Reveille." "Alright, get out your notebooks and prepare thy soul for more chaos, more uncertainty. What do you see here? A quote. A famous one ascribed to Trotsky. Yet, that odious Marxist may have never uttered it. In fact, novelist Fannie Hurst may have spoken a slightly different configuration of these words. Now, as students of conflict, you must come to grips with the immutable fact that the facts themselves are in question. The record of who did what to whom under what circumstances is perhaps less a matter of certainty than a matter of conjecture, the product of the competing interests of fallible humans. If we cannot agree as to whether a person said something, what can we agree upon? Who does the truth belong to? The victor? The counter-revolutionary? Soon, we will engage in the debate protocol. So take vigorous notes. Later today, class will be divided into teams and a battle of qualifications will ensue in class on Wednesday."

Sixteen

"I did it. I asked Gabi to Homecoming."

"Congratulations."

"Thanks!"

"How do you feel?"

"Nervous. She hasn't told me her answer yet."

"All good things in time."

"It's going to be amazing. She's got to say yes. Real soon I'll buy this Jeep I want. I got enough for a used Jeep now, but I'm saving up to get one with big tires and a lift. What if I get it in time to take Gabi to Homecoming? Then, Dallas and his minions and everyone else will know that I've arrived—that Nolan Sussman isn't 'Nolan Suspect' anymore. Yeah, I can get my Jeep in time. And they'll know when they see that Jeep and see I've got Gabi on my arm."

"Sounds as though you've got it all planned out."

"Yes. I'm so freaking happy."

"Which one, eh, is she?"

"Gabi? She's the one whose boyfriend might be cheating on her."

"Have you heard the saying, 'All is fair in love and war'?"

"No."

"Good. Forget I ever told it to you."

"What was your favorite thing about Celeste?"

"My favorite thing about Celeste was Celeste."

"So what's the happiness lesson today?"

"No lesson today."

"I'm doing it. I'm getting this whole happiness thing."

"I see that. Grab that board, will you? Let's get to work."

———————

Skyler Bell was sitting at a desk in the Introduction to Journalism class when I walked in Friday morning. "Hey Sky, didn't know you were in this class."

"Didn't know you were."

"Started last Friday."

"Doctors appointment that day."

I took the desk beside her. "Cool, cool."

She sat there spinning a pencil, her body bent toward the window.

"Still not telling me that Paul Simon album, huh?"

She reached into her button-covered backpack for her notebook. "That album was too recent, anyway. You got to start with his earlier stuff."

"Alright."

She leaned toward me. "'Still Crazy After All These Years' and 'The Obvious Child.' Those are two songs for you."

What is she trying to say? I played it off. "Oh cool."

She shifted away, crossing her legs. "Branson asked me."

"Asked you what?"

"To Homecoming."

I sunk an inch.

"Took me to that French restaurant, the bistro, last night."

"Oh. On a Thursday night?"

"Yeah."

"That is romantic."

"Yeah. It was really sweet." She straightened herself up and brushed her hands through her long hair. "So I guess I'll see you and, um, at Homecoming."

I plunked my chin into my hands. "What?" *She said yes to Branson?* "Yeah. Oh, right. Yeah. Absolutely."

"Quiet. Quiet. Gather around." Mrs. de León made an upward gesture with both arms. We all stood and approached her desk. "As chief editor, I'm going to assign each of you a story. We're adding a new segment to the weekly news. One day a week we will have original journalism conducted by you, our intrepid journalists."

Several students clapped. One cheered. These kids were all in.

"This list of topics I'm passing around contains important issues facing the Paxson student body. Beside each story is a due date. I've ordered them such that what I believe will be the most challenging stories are due later in the term. This will make things fair. Starting the week after next, we'll have our first story due. It'll be a preview of Homecoming and our football team's big game against the Cherryville Bears."

Lucky, who stood next to me, passed me the sheet. I scanned it.

Homecoming. Band funding. A new end-of-school day traffic pattern under consideration following a minor accident during the after-school rush between a school bus and a student driver. An infestation of mice in the cafeteria. That kind of thing.

The final story, due the last week of school before winter break, was about Protect the Youth of Paxson.

"Becky, you're on the accident story. I want quotes, on record, from the student and the bus driver. Got it?"

"On it."

"Jamal, I want you on band funding. You're a numbers guy and I need someone who can dig into the budget and hold the administration accountable."

Jamal smiled his best smile. "Can I do the mice in the cafeteria story? I think I know a fan-flipping-tastic solution."

"Yeah, alright."

"I got you, Mrs. L."

"Hunter, you're on the Save the Youth of Paxson group. They're making a lot of noise about a former Paxson teacher, Alexis Barno, in their effort to force him to move at least a mile away from the school. But no one's heard Mr. Barno's side of the story. I need someone who can get that interview with Mr. Barno. Think you can handle it?"

"Excuse me, Mrs. de León." I raised my hand. "Can I cover that story?"

"You're new. Hunter has been in this class since the start of the year. It's his story."

"Please. I think I can get that story."

"It's going to be a tough one to get."

"I can do it."

Mrs. de León took her glasses off and chewed one of the temples. "Alright, alright. Nolan, you're on Barno. Hunter, you're on band funding."

"You won't regret this," I said to Mrs. de León.

"You will," Hunter—The Shark—grumbled at me.

Mrs. de León assigned the rest of the stories before moving on to the weekly discussion prompt, which was a warm-up to get our "juices flowing" as she liked to say. "If you could interview one living person, who would it be?"

We went around the circle, starting with Jamal who said he'd interview Warren Buffett because he was such a great businessman. It went like that. Oprah. The president. The Kardashians.

When it was my turn I said, "My sister, Sarah, because—"

There was a knock on the classroom door. "Hold that thought a moment." Mrs. de León stood and slid to the door. She told us she would be right back. The door closed behind her.

"Teacher said the person's got to be alive," The Shark barked at me.

I yelled, "Don't you ever—"

The Shark hurled desks out of the way. He barreled toward me like one of those massive Decepticons, tossing cars and people aside in the *Transformers* movie.

No exit. Hemmed in between the desks and the circle of people. I braced my feet and tried to grow back that inch I had lost earlier during my conversation with Skyler.

The Shark. Nose into an arrow. Jaw tight. Razor teeth. Eyes bulging. Ears red. Neck all sharkishly thick.

Towering over me. His chest inches from my face.

"Say something else." He did that rage whisper thing. "Say something else and the story I'll be writing is your obituary."

The crowd seeped away through the rows of desks.

That's when I saw it clearly. "That's not a shark tooth tattoo on your neck. It's a birthmark." It was. It was a birthmark.

I pointed at the birthmark. Turned to my classmates. Saw Skyler. Her hand in front of her mouth.
Then.
Black.
Red.
Rattling.
I staggered.
Head hot.
Throbbing.
Stumbled into a desk.
Dazed.
Grunted. No air in my lungs.
Caught myself.
Steadied my arms.
Pivoted toward the shark.
Hands up. Ready for the next blow.
That hurt.
I glanced down. I didn't pee my pants this time. May wonders never cease?
Didn't hurt that bad.
Tyler rushed between us. "Back off, Shark!"
Didn't kill me.
The punch didn't kill me.
No peed pants. No knockout blow.
Still on my feet.
The Shark shoved Tyler, who tripped over a chair and spiraled to the floor.
"Go buff one, you confused freak."
I hurled my pencil at The Shark. "Lay off him."

His big shark head and black eyes swiveled and locked onto me. "Make me."

"Not scared of you," I trembled. "What are you so afraid of that makes you go around being such an ass to everyone? You're such a miserable excuse for a person."

The Shark flexed. Fists in wads. Arms the size of monster trucks. Mouth open, ready to chomp.

A body lurched into view. A fist took flight, striking The Shark below the eye. A thwack pinged off the walls. The Shark's face puttied. His eyes rolled like slot machines. He crumbled, his knees and arms falling Jenga pieces.

Vavara Pushkin.

She turned. Strolled back to the editing station. Sat. "Vavara do not permit any battlings."

I wobbled over and tumbled down next to her. "Thank you."

She held up the audio editing headphones in her fist. "We are one people."

"I thought you didn't speak English."

"Nothing, not even Vavara, is what seems."

Just then, Mrs. de León appeared in the room. Seeing the mess and The Shark climbing up a chair, trying to get to his feet, Mrs. de León revved into interrogation mode.

Vavara erected herself and declared, "I did the punch out on the shark boy. He made lookie-lookie at me and called me a little bit of words I do not like."

Mrs. de León escorted The Shark and Vavara to the administrative wing where punishments would be doled out. I don't know why The Shark didn't drag Tyler and me into it. Maybe he lived by omertà, just like Gramps.

Tyler came and leaned over the editing station. "What you working on? Can I listen?"

"Haven't really done anything yet. But I'm hoping, eventually, to make a new intro for the morning show."

"Vavara's going to get suspended after that. Now's your chance to take over."

"Don't want to take anything. The spot's hers. Just want to help."

"That's cool of you." He pushed purple nail-polished fingers through his hair. "Thanks for standing up for me back there."

I scanned the room for Skyler. And through the haze in my punch-drunk head, I had this horrible thought as I searched for her: *I don't even know what to look for.*

Seventeen

My sister's favorite band was The Get Up Kids. Her favorite album by them was titled *Something to Write Home About*.

Man, that pissed me off. *You love an album so much and you can't even do what it suggests, write home?*

Did she not have something to write home about? Where was she? What was doing? What was she doing yesterday? Right now?

I thought about this at night more than I should. I'd drift, unmoored in bed when I really needed her—needed someone to talk to. And I'd wonder why she never wrote. Not once.

I was sprawled in bed on Friday night thinking about what The Shark had said. Sarah was dead.

No.

Maybe.

But no.

Could she be? Is that why she never wrote?

It couldn't be. She was definitely alive.

Then, I started to wonder if that's what Lenny the True Love CEO was, a surrogate for sibling advice. I thought all this while his videos played, my eyes transfixed on the light from my smartphone. Lenny was saying, "You got 'em to this stage. Your OAF is on the hook. You're reeling that fish in. Step three is going to go against your instincts. It's not easy. This is pro-level advice. Time for a huevos check. Ready? I believe in you. Step three is to ignore your OAF. That's right. Ignore your OAF. Play hard to get. Scarcity creates demand. That's economics, brosef. Nobody wants something they can have any time, like pickles on a McDonald's burger. You're no slimy pickle. You're filet mignon."

Ignore them? But I don't even have my OAF yet, I thought.

I put my phone down, reached under my bed, and excavated the Converse All Star shoebox. I opened it and stirred its contents around. I dug the paper triangle football out of the box. I swung it in my hand, pretending to throw it against the ceiling.

Suddenly, I did. I got mad and flung it against the ceiling and it fell on my chest. I picked it up and chucked it at the fan light. It fell on my arm. Then I flicked it with my finger and it spun off into the dark.

I didn't want to be mad. Didn't want to be mad at my sister.

What good was this anger? Where was it getting me?

She was gone. Gone. Gone, gone. That kind of gone. What good was mad? It just was.

I wanted to love. Wanted to love my sister. Wanted to love people. My parents. Love life. Love the mornings. Love Mr. Green. Love Mrs. de León. Love my future, whatever it was going to be.

I did love. I realized that. I loved Mr. Barno.

I wanted to be able to love other stuff, too. I wanted to love myself.

I got up to look for the paper football, using my phone as a flashlight. But I couldn't find it.

My phone vibrated.

Unknown (11:06 pm): [Orange emoji]

I responded:

Me (11:06 pm): ? Who this

I put the phone down.
Vibration.

Unknown (11:07 pm): Guess

I replied:

Me (11:07 pm): Dunno someone who likes OJ a lot just like me

The reply came fast:

Unknown (11:07 pm): Noo [Crying laughing emoji] syracuse oranges for syracuse gguy
Me (11:07 pm): Gabi?
Gabi (11:07 pm): Smartt this one
Gabi (11:07 pm): Thats ssyracuse girl 2 u
Gabi (11:07 pm): [Winking face with tongue emoji]

Holy shit. How'd she get my number?
I started to type that question but stopped myself.
This is good. Don't question it. Just keep going.

Me (11:08 pm): [Smiley face emoji]
Gabi (11:08 pm): Why arrent youu at Tylers jam?

Um, cause I wasn't invited. No. Don't say that.

Me (11:08 pm): [Skull and crossbones emoji]
Gabi (11:08 pm): Me 2. [Crying laughing emoji] Drank 2 much jjungle juice
Me (11:08 pm): 4 beers for me
Gabi (11:08 pm): Tthats all?
Me (11:08 pm): couple vodka sodas. Lost count
Gabi (11:08 pm): Kewl
Gabi (11:08 pm): I leftt anyway. Was SO lamee
Gabi (11:08 pm): Fact or fiction
Me (11:08 pm): What is?
Gabi (11:08 pm): No goof. Thats thhe game. Pick 1
Me (11:08 pm): Fact I guess
Gabi (11:08 pm): No. U tell me sumthin I guess which it is
Me (11:08 pm): [Thinking face emoji]
Me (11:09 pm): I didn't really apply to Syracuse early decision
Gabi (11:09 pm): Easy. Fiction
Me (11:09 pm): [Thumbs-up emoji]
Gabi (11:09 pm): My turn
Gabi (11:09 pm): My mom such a bitch
Me (11:09 pm): Fact?
Gabi (11:09 pm): Shee tries to control my entire liffe
Gabi (11:09 pm): She hhas to control EEVERYTHIN
Gabi (11:10 pm): My stepdad
Me (11:10 pm): What?
Gabi (11:10 pm): Nuthin
Gabi (11:10 pm): Syracuse gonna rule!! [Cocktail glass emoji][Party popper emoji]
Me (11:10 pm): [Clinking beer mugs emoji]

Gabi (11:10 pm): U go

Me (11:10 pm): Hmm

Me (11:10 pm): My moms been sad for so long I think thats just who she is now

Gabi (11:10 pm): O. Im sorry.

Gabi (11:11 pm): Wait. Fact right?

Me (11:11 pm): Yep

 Gabi (11:11 pm): Ill go

Gabi (11:11 pm): Dallas cheated on mee

Me (11:11 pm): Hopefully fiction

Gabi (11:11 pm): FACT

Me (11:11 pm): [Enraged face emoji]

Me (11:11 pm): Im sorry

Gabi (11:11 pm): Boys ssuck

Me (11:11 pm): So Ive heard

Gabi (11:12 pm): LOL

Gabi (11:12 pm): My turn again

Me (11:12 pm): K

Gabi (11:12 pm): Dallass Stone sux at life

Me (11:12 pm): Fact [Pile of poo emoji]

Gabi (11:12 pm): [Clapping hands emoji]

Gabi (11:12 pm): shhh

Me (11:13 pm): What

 Gabi (11:13 pm): I like talkin 2 u

Me (11:13 pm): Same

 Gabi (11:14 pm): Think I might ralph

Me (11:14 pm): Want me to hold your hair

Gabi (11:19 pm): [Candy emoji]

Gabi (11:19 pm): Nighty nite Nolann

Me (11:19 pm): You mean Syracuse guy

Me (11:22 pm): Night Syracuse girl

I hovered over my phone hoping for another text. When it didn't come, I climbed into bed.

Later, my phone vibrated.

Gabi (11:53 pm): U gonna aask me again or what
Me (11:53 pm): Huh
Gabi (11:53 pm): Homeecoming

Is this for real?

Me (11:53 pm): Serious. This is Gabi Meyers right?
Gabi (11:53 pm): No. Its Gabi fromm Sesame Street. LOL
Gabi (11:53 pm): Course it is goof
Me (11:53 pm): Prove it
Gabi (11:54 pm): [Photo of Gabi, blurry eyed, smeared makeup, sitting beside a bed in her bedroom wearing a Syracuse Orangemen lacrosse T-shirt]

Okay. Okay. This is it. The fates have smiled upon me. Don't know why, but I've pleased the Homecoming gods!

Gabi (11:55 pm): Welll
Me (11:55 pm): Yes
Me (11:55 pm): I was just planning to do it up big you know
Gabi (11:55 pm): Sweeet but am over that bunk. U cann ask me like this
Me (11:55 pm): Will you go with me to homecoming?
Gabi (11:56 pm): Ssuree

Eighteen

Mr. Barno's house seemed to be shrinking on the inside, victim to the sprawl of dishes in the kitchen, the stacks of books in the corners, mounds of trash on the counters, and a bag of spilled dog food in the family room. The water in the vases had a film. I figured the invisible flowers were wilted. But Mr. Barno didn't want to waste time cleaning up inside.

The tree project. That's what mattered.

Mr. Barno took a few minutes to feel out the project and look over his schematics. I gave him his time and space. Meanwhile, I set up the Zoom recorder nearby. After Mrs. de León assigned me to get the interview with Barno, I made what my dad likes to call 'an executive decision' to record all my interactions with Mr. Barno. Barno didn't know I was doing it but I had two good reasons:

1. When any spontaneous happiness lessons came up, I didn't want to have to interrupt Mr. Barno so I could start recording. I didn't want to further derail his deteriorating concentration and memory.

2. In case anything relevant came up that would help me with my Save the Youth of Paxson story assignment. I guess it was a little sneaky, but I knew Barno probably wouldn't remember I was recording anyway.

We got to work installing boards perpendicular to the crossbeams. "Huge news." I stood at the base of the ladder and passed boards up to Mr. Barno. "That girl,

Gabi, she said yes. We're going to Homecoming together."

"Congratulations. Who's that again?"

"This girl I like."

"What do you like about her?"

"She's really, really pretty. Popular. Smart. Head of the debate team, yearbook editor, student government vice president, and the captain of varsity lacrosse. What's not to like? She's perfect and her ex-boyfriend is too dumb to see that. Basically, she's everything I'm not."

"What are you not?"

"Well, I'm not—"

"Don't want to hear it. Want you to think about it."

Mr. Barno and I worked quietly for a while setting the boards down.

I climbed down to get the hammer and a box of deck nails. "I mean, I can show you her social media, if you don't mind me bringing my phone in. She looks perfect. There are photos up there with her ex-boyfriend. And they just—they look perfect, and I want to look that way with her."

Mr. Barno stood above on the platform. "'Comparison is the death of joy.' Not my words. But. Eh. Can't remember who said them."

I searched for the hammer and box of nails.

"When's the last time your parents got a new car?"

I shrugged. "My mom. Couple of years ago, I guess."

"Why?"

"No clue."

"Something wrong with the old one?"

"Not that I know of," I said.

"Did anyone else on your street get a new car?"

"Uh. I think so. Yeah. Across the street. Mrs. Fitzpatrick got a Mazda SUV."

"Before or after your mom?"

I thought a moment. "Uh, I think before. I remember my mom was obsessed with that Mazda."

"You know that if your neighbor gets a new car, it increases the chance that you'll buy one?"

"So my mom got a new car because the neighbor did?"

He called down, "Appears so."

"That makes no sense."

"Live your life, not a copy of someone else's."

"Yeah, but this isn't a car," I said. "Gabi's out of my league." I paused. "And, well, I'm competing with her expectations from dating popular guys. So, I kind of have to copy the popular thing or else."

"If I paid you $15 an hour, would you enjoy that?"

I laughed. "You're not paying me at all. That'd be awesome."

"Sounds as though you'd be pretty happy. But, what if you found out one of your friends made $20 an hour."

This one was easy. "I'd want you to pay me $20 an hour."

"Why?"

"I guess I'd feel less valuable than my friend."

"But maybe your friend is doing really hard work or work that requires years of schooling that you chose not to do. Additionally, with your $15 you can still buy the same stuff you could before you knew he made $20."

"Wouldn't matter," I called up the ladder.

"Why not? You were happy making $15 before."

I smirked. "Not anymore."

"All of these cases have one thing in common. You're making the mistake of relying on points of reference, ones that are irrelevant but salient—"

"What do you mean salient?"

"I mean something you can easily recall or access such as seeing a nice car in the driveway across the street."

"Alright."

"You're using these salient points of reference that have nothing to do with who you are to decide about your own life. Just because someone lives across the street from you and gets a new car, doesn't mean you should go buy one. Finding out someone makes more money than you doesn't devalue the money you're making. Just because a guy who gets girls acts a certain way, doesn't mean you should. We soak in our environment as points of reference even if the comparison isn't similar or fair." Mr. Barno reached down and I handed him the box of nails. "Just be you."

"I can't. I got no sports, no clubs, no car, no status. I'm No Land. That's what one of my best friends calls me. Literally, a guy who has nothing. Got no track record of getting girls. And girls need to see that. They're into guys who've had other girlfriends because it means the guy must be, I don't know, desirable or something. I mean, seriously, I pissed my pants in elementary school, and I've been a reject ever since. All I'm known for, all I've ever been known for, is screwing up and getting yelled at. They say girls like 'bad boys,' but that's total bull. They like James Dean looking guys. Not actual guys who get in real trouble."

"I pissed my pants the other week. So what?"

I laughed. He did too.

"I'm not joking, though we've got to learn to laugh at ourselves," Mr. Barno said. "What're the consequences of being so hard on yourself?"

I stared up toward Barno but the sun was in my eyes. "The consequences? It pushes me to be better."

"And the insults you're hurling at yourself, they're helping your happiness?"

"Oh yeah, Lesson Two, right? Acceptance leads to compassion."

"You said this young lady, eh, Hallie, is perfect."

"Gabi."

"Let go of perfect. It's not possible for someone to be perfect but it's possible to love someone while knowing they're not perfect. It's not possible to be perfect ourselves but it's possible to love ourselves while knowing we're not perfect."

"No. This girl is literally perfect."

"Why do you use social media?"

"It's the lifeblood of my generation. It's how we discover. How we communicate."

"Never used it. Never will."

"Well, you're old." I still couldn't see him up there because of the sun. And I didn't want to climb up yet. I just felt I needed to be down here. "Sorry. I didn't mean that."

"That's not untrue." He sighed and grew quiet. "Wish I could remember facts the way I once did. But." He sighed more deeply. "Well, there's research. People who study happiness. They say we make many incorrect judgments when it comes to other peoples' happiness. I can't remember the details. But. Eh. Give me a minute." Mr. Barno sat down. I stood there and inspected the branches by my head. "Oh. Hey, Nolan."

"You alright?" I called.

"We were talking, weren't we?"

"Um. Other peoples' happiness. We make bad judgments about it."

"Right. Yes. Have I told you that people aren't as happy as we think they are? That we tend to think they don't get as unhappy as they really do?"

"No."

"Everyone experiences the ups and downs of life. Even this young woman you like. Eh. You say she had a boyfriend or am I imagining that?"

"I did. Said they were in lots of perfect photos together on her Instagram before they broke up."

"Sounds as if they had serious relationship issues. That sound happy?"

"Well. I mean, when they were happy, they were really happy."

"People on the Internet aren't as happy as they look. That can't be news to you, Nolan. Just think. I bet you've got some exciting or happy photos on social media, but are you always happy? Are you always doing exciting stuff?"

"No."

"Can you go inside and get some paper and a pen? I think it'll help me organize my thoughts."

After I got the paper, I climbed up and we got to work hammering the boards. Occasionally, Mr. Barno would stop and write something down.

When we finished securing the boards, Mr. Barno said, "Next, we build the railings. What lesson number are we on?"

"Um, four," I said.

"Regale me. We must rely on your memory, now." We climbed down the ladder.

"Lesson One was happiness not fear. Lesson Two was compassion not judgment. Lesson Three, I'd call it harmony not rigidity."

"On to Lesson Four."

"Okay."

"Let's talk about perfection. I'm going to pretend to be you." Mr. Barno read from his paper. "There are a lot of qualities about, eh—"

"Gabi."

He continued, "—that I find attractive. She's beautiful. Smart. Hard working. I admire that. Lots of people like her, which tells me she likely has some great qualities. She's got a lot going for her."

"That's basically what I said, it just sounds like an old person's saying it."

"No," Mr. Barno said. "I complimented her but I didn't say she was perfect. I left space for her imperfections. That's realistic."

"Okay. Fair."

"Now, you try doing it, but talk about yourself. Mention some strengths and some of your qualities or areas you want to improve upon."

"I am, um, good at school. I can run pretty far without getting tired. I'm taking a new class at school where I'm learning about audio recording and editing. That shows that I'm into learning new skills. I got some good friends, even though, well, you know, we've been together a long time. So that shows loyalty. Obviously, I want to get better at dating girls. Finding love. I'm working on that. Let's see. What else? I guess I've always being kind of emotional and just sort of impulsive. Yeah. And I could get better at that. I mean, I am getting better, but I got room to grow. I'm trying to improve my relationship with my parents. I'm trying to do this happiness stuff and, honestly, I'm noticing it's starting to work."

"Very good. You have good qualities and areas for improvement. So does the young woman you are into. That's realistic."

"I see what you mean."

"I know identical twins, one's named Perfection and the other's named Misery," Mr. Barno said.

"This reminds me of the acceptance not judging thing we talked about in Lesson Two. Like, accepting responsibility for my decision not to do the scholarship and owning up to telling my parents."

"Scholarship?"

"Long story."

"Something you told me about before?"

I patted his back.

"It's alright. It's where I am."

I tried to smile. Only half of it showed up. "What I'm getting at is, if I look at it another way, you're kind of saying I'd be happier if I lowered my expectations, correct?"

"Balderdash. Expectations and goals are essential. However, there are at least two problems that can occur. One is having unreasonable or rigid expectations."

"Yeah, we talked about that in Lesson Three," I said.

"It's strange. I remember people from long ago and things that happened long ago really well. Stuff I've learned is there, broadly at least, if I dig. But things from a week ago, yesterday, an hour ago, well, that's hit or miss."

"Our brains are so weird," I grinned.

"Thank you." It wasn't just his words. Barno's kind eyes said thanks, too. I wasn't sure what for. "Can I tell you a story?"

I nodded.

"Had a student long ago who everyone—his parents included—expected to be someone. But being that someone made him miserable. Sadly, there was no room for him to be anything but exceptional. Great wasn't an option. It caused a lot of anguish. A problem, then, is how we respond when expectations are not met. Many things aren't life and death, yet we act as if they are. It's a formula for misery."

"Kind of like figuring out exactly what I want to do?"

"Figuring things out doesn't guarantee happiness. Not figuring things out doesn't guarantee unhappiness. It'll never be the case that your happiness will depend on something turning out one way or another. But thinking that's how happiness works is a great cause of unhappiness."

"It's possible to be happy no matter which path I choose?"

"Yes. It's an inconvenience, not a catastrophe."

"What is?"

"Most every problem. There's no such thing as perfect. Your life will never be perfect. No one's life will ever be perfect."

"Feels like you're telling me Santa Claus isn't real. That all this I've been taught about striving for a perfect life is a lie."

"If all you ever do is expect things to be perfect, you're setting yourself for a great deal of disappointment. Make room for imperfection, and love life and other people not despite the imperfections, but because of them. This house is wonderful, it's not perfect. My life is wonderful, and it's far from perfect. This town is wonderful, but—"

"Definitely not perfect," I laughed.

Mr. Barno chuckled. "You got it. Yet I am grateful for all of these things. If you remember one thing from our time together, it is this: be grateful. Find as many ways as you can to be grateful. I know two other identical twins whom I much prefer. Their names are Gratitude and Wonderful." He put his hands on my shoulders and searched my eyes when he said all of that. And I guess because I had said the thing about Santa Claus a minute before, I remembered about how, when I first met Mr. Barno, he reminded me of Santa. Maybe it was because he and Santa were that rare kind of boy who grew up but never lost touch with his heart. "Celeste—the love of my life—was an amazing, wonderful person. Not a perfect one. She made mistakes, had flaws, and struggled at times, like all people. I loved her because of it. Did everything I could to love her no matter the cost. I don't regret one minute of that."

Nineteen

On Wednesday night I sat at my laptop and scoped out the Lewis property on Google Earth. I zoomed in and out, trying to get a better lay of the land—trying to figure out a few escape routes if things turned sour. You know, just in case.

Since the property was in the woods, most of what I could see was a green canopy and a shadowy outline of the house and garage.

I moused around and found a long and narrow clearing. A red shed and a square gazebo—or at least two objects sharing their resemblance—stood at one end of the clearing.

On the other end, I spotted some grainy blue and white objects with a half-moon mound behind them. I spun Google Earth around every which way. But I couldn't figure out what that part of the property was.

I thought about what I did know. I had seen the house from the spot by the driveway where Neil, Branson, and I hid the other week. And I had seen a little bit of the property from the river on our tubing trips.

Then I remembered a clacking noise, a chain of explosions that rippled across the river and echoed off the distant mountains a few summers ago when we were tubing. I remembered because Neil started acting all *Full Metal Jacket* or something, diving off his tube into the river, and pretending to shoot back at the shoreline. That happened near Mr. Lewis' house, right? I couldn't remember for sure. Maybe it was further down the river. In the outskirts of Paxson, a lot of people shot…

Did Mr. Lewis go back there and shoot guns?

No way. My imagination is just—just hunting for things to worry about. Just coming up with excuses to back out.

It's okay to be nervous about Operation Notting-ham, I told myself. *It's risky but something you got to do to save Mr. Barno.*

I shut my laptop and got up. Needed a distraction. I shuffled over to the old TV and Nintendo Wii. I grabbed a controller and was gearing up for some Mario Kart when I saw the paper football Sarah had given me splayed open on top of the Nintendo Wii—the football I had flicked the other night and couldn't find. The tape had torn from the football's corner where it had once sealed a tab into a pocket. I picked the paper football up and saw in tiny print 'DONT HATE ME.' It was my sister's handwriting.

It's a secret message!

'Don't hate me.' *What does that mean? Why? What'd you do, Sarah?*

I rolled back onto the carpet and observed myself in the TV's reflection. It's a shame we can see what we look like sometimes—all that confusion.

Wait, is this a reference to…?

I soared across the room. Crashed onto the bed. Snatched the old iPod from the Converse shoebox under my bed. Flicked it on. Popped the earphones in. Spun to the Get Up Kids. Found the song "Don't Hate Me." It was from their first big album, *Four Minute Mile*.

The singing started before the instruments, "Forgive me…" The song had a raw, frantic, kind of fizzy sound to it. The singer asks the listener for understanding for running off and finding something the singer needs to find. And he tells the listener it is okay because he promises one day to return.

It is a reference to the song.

As I listened, I unfolded the paper football. Inside, written in tiny print, was a note. A note from Sarah.

Holy Noley,

First off, Oh Noley, don't hate me. Im not running away. I'm running toward. Running toward the life I never knew I had.

I need to discover who I am. Who I really am. I'm leaving to go find my dad. My real dad, Craig.

Our dad isn't my real dad. I saw my birth certificate when Mom took me to get my license. What a screwed up way to find out. How could they lie to me for so long?

Didn't let Mom know how she broke my heart.

It took a year of feeling like an imposter. A walking lie!! But I got the courage to look my real dad up online. I found his address. I'm gonna surprise him.

How are ya, kid?

How's school?

Got a girlfriend yet? I don't know when ur gonna discover this letter so not sure what to ask. Hope it's not too soon so I got time to get far away.

I bet the girls are gonna luv U. U got a gr8 smile & the bluest eyes & deep down I know ur sweet.

I realize now that U saw that night. I know U luv me & thats why U did what U did to Rs car. I'm so freakin' sorry.

R is ok. Not so bad. I wanted to leave without him & he lost it. Doesn't make it ok.

Got a knife with me. Took it from the garage. If R tries anything again, I'll dice him up crazy emo girl style. LOL. U can see it on the TV news & ull know Im ok.

After, R & I are gonna head out on tour on the road. R says he knows a drummer & guitarist that are both increds in New Jersey. Gonna go there first & practice a few months. Imagine that I'll be playin' with artists from where Saves the Day & The Early November are from. When ur older, U can come to one of our shows.

Write me at Craigs address below. I doubt 9-year-olds have email addresses. If u do, I dunno it. LOL. When ur older, write & tell me an email address & I'll write U emails cuz I don't want Mom & Terrance to find letters in the mail. Don't want to see them ever again. Don't want them to find me. I won't write U for that reason. So U gotta write me & tell me an email address, ok bud? Promise!

Don't tell Mom & Terrance. They don't know how phucked up this is. He's not my dad. U understand right?

I think teenagers, we are shards—dangerously sharp bits and pieces of the broken parts of our childhood. Know what? That's ok because we are beautiful the way crows are beautiful.

I've got to go forward because that's all there is to do. We all fit in somewhere.

Keep going forward, Nole. Promise U will or I'll come back & kick ur ass!

Sorry for everything. Forgive me?

Guess this is goodbye for now.

I'm ur half-sister, but I'll always be ur full brother. Ur not alone. I'm always with U Noleyboo. I know U hate that name but I luv it.

Luv,

Sarah

Craig Diffendaffer – What a dumb last name. Sussman is way better. At least U got that. Maybe I'll keep Sussman too. Sarah Diffendaffer. LOL.

3125 Trough Rd.

Mecklenburg, WV

P.S. Leavin you my iPod with all my music. There's even a few songs I recorded. Demos. They're not that great. But will be someday. Music is everything and everything is music, right?

I must have read the letter ten times. One hundred times. I don't know. I just read it over and over. Read it out loud under the light of my cell phone. Read it to my cat, Miles.

Lots of thoughts—lots of scattered thoughts slammed inside my skull.

The first one was, *Holy shit. My dad, Terrance Sussman, is not Sarah's dad? And who the hell is Craig?*

Why didn't my parents tell me about Craig? Why didn't they tell Sarah?

I careened in the direction of anger before I stopped myself. What good was anger?

Sarah was gone.

She was gone because of anger. Because of pain.

Maybe Mom and Dad had a reason. I mean, they were parents and parents historically didn't have any good reasons for the stuff they did. But who knows? Maybe they did. Maybe this was the one time in the history of the world that two adults who joined in marriage had a good reason for a decision they made.

It was possible.

Unlikely.

But possible.

And maybe I could give them the benefit of the doubt. Maybe I could choose happiness, not fear. Compassion, not judgment. Harmony, not rigidity. Gratitude, not perfection.

Then I thought, *An outlet. That's what Sarah meant when she said 'an outlet' to me the night she left.* I could write to her. That was my outlet. I could write to her and tell her about my life. And she would write back.

But that was? That was eight years ago. *When Sarah was 17. I'm 17 now.* What chance did I have that this Craig guy still lived there? Even if he did, what chance did I have that he still knew how to contact Sarah if she went to New Jersey and then, who knows where? Would Craig even help me?

Why didn't Sarah just leave me an email address to reach her by? What was that about?

And then. And then I realized something that changed everything: *Sarah wasn't running away from me. Sarah leaving wasn't my fault. She wasn't running from us. She was searching for Sarah.*

Sarah was a crow. Crows are beautiful. *Maybe I'm a crow, too.*

Twenty

I took Gabi on a date on Saturday evening. I didn't know where to take her, so we went to Main Street Custard. But that's not the point. The point is, I asked her over text message, and she said yes. So, at a little after 8 pm, we met at the booth by the window and while we sat there, I realized I didn't really know what to talk about.

The good thing was, she seemed to know what to talk about. I mean, she talked almost the whole time. Occasionally she asked me a question and I answered it. At first, my answers were long, but they got shorter as the date went on.

Her hair was up in a way that showed her neck. Small earrings clung to her ears and her nails and makeup were done in a way I had seen her do in her photos online. She wore a tight black shirt with a silver necklace and a black and white checkered skirt, even though it was late September. She could have been a model, really.

I thought I might wake up and realize I was dreaming, but that didn't happen. I actually was on a date with her in the booth in the bay window that looked out on everyone walking down Main Street.

Gabi held up her phone. "I'm going to send you a link to that shirt. It'll look great on you."

"Okay." I was wearing a shirt, tie, and jeans because I didn't know what else to wear on a date. Though I was starting to think the answer was not a shirt, tie, and jeans.

"You've totally got the bones. And I love your shoes. Converse. Retro style."

"Thanks. My sister introduced—"

"I think you just get those black jeans and the shirt." She tilted her head, eyeing my hair. "I'm thinking chop a little off. Maybe something spikey, kind of punk. That's on brand for you. Don't know. Let me sleep on that."

I patted my scalp. "So, uh, what's your favorite band?"

"Oh. Um. Yeah, whatever's hot. Long as it's got a good beat and you can dance to it, ya know?"

I licked my spoon. I swirled around the chocolate puddle coalescing in the bowl. "Cool. Grew up on pop punk and emo. Little bit of ska. Always just stuck to that music."

"Yeah. Great." She was leaning forward, which I thought was a good sign. Her arms were crossed and when she talked her high ponytail occasionally brushed her shoulders like those big spaghetti brushes in a carwash. I know that's not a very flattering description. But that's what I thought of (At least I didn't say that to her). "Homecoming. Here's the plan. We meet at Jamal's for pictures. I'll text you the time. For the corsage, my dress is an ocean blue. Arm band or wrist corsage works perfectly. Jamal's dad is covering the limo, so no worries there. It'll be me and you, Reese and Jamal, Cienna and Maxine."

I ate a spoonful of melted ice cream.

"As ya know, there's a big jam afterward at Dallas' house. A football team thing. So, I'm not sure we'll go.

Jamal said he might throw something, though. Anyway, we'll see. Can ya get some alcohol?"

"Definitely," I said, unsure of how to pull that off. Maybe Branson could help me. I wanted to ask Gabi if Branson and Skyler could be part of our Homecoming group. But, if Jamal's dad had already ordered the limo and it had limited space, well, then.

"Perfect. Homecoming is my favorite. Totally love it. It's going to be wild. Schnapps is best if you can get that. But, Jägermeister is fun, too."

"Yeah, schnapps and Jäger. Love it," I said. "Probably can get both." *No I can't.* "Definitely." *Why'd I say that?*

She reached her hand across the table and touched my forearm. "You're the best, Nole."

"So you're liking, uh. You're liking that cookies and cream, huh?"

"Yeah, yeah, absolutes." She leaned back. "Hey, thanks for getting this."

"Is that, like, your favorite?" She hadn't eaten more than a spoonful.

"Sure. Kinda. I like, um, Rocky Road, too. How about you?"

"Definitely mint chocolate chip. So, you said your mom was, um?"

"A total bitch? Yup. And I don't even want to get into my stepdad."

"Okay. Cool. I'm sorry."

"Not your fault."

"Lacrosse. Love it. Only reason I don't play is, you know, it's like, I hurt my hamstring in cross country, and it just keeps getting injured. So."

She pushed her eyebrows up. "When do you think we'll hear from Syracuse, early November?"

I swallowed hard. "Definitely early November." I scraped at the bottom of the bowl. The puddle was so small that even tilting the bowl didn't give me enough drops to gather onto the spoon.

Gabi picked up her phone and started scrolling through it. "No way, have you seen Reevo Bella Martineeni's latest post? Ya know Reevo, right?"

I rolled the spoon in my hand. "Definitely."

"How is that bitch so perfect? If only—" She did a deep sigh that was coated in despair.

"Love Reevo." I picked up my phone and scrolled around, too.

Maybe twenty minutes passed.

"Gotta run," Gabi said. She stood, slid into the booth beside me, and held her phone up for a selfie with me. She kissed me on the cheek—or held her lips against my cheek—while she snapped a photo. "Thanks, Nole. You're the best." And with that, she slipped out of the booth and was gone.

I kept my eye on Gabi's Instagram profile the whole walk home. Nothing.

Later that night, I was lying in bed staring at the Jeep poster on the back of the bedroom door when I got a text from Gabi.

Gabi (11:03 pm): Thx forr 2night
Me (11:03 pm): [Smiley face emoji]
Gabi (11:03 pm): Do uu think Iam pretty?
Me (11:03 pm): Of course
Me (11:03 pm): You are beautiful

Gabi (11:03 pm): Ur sweet ssyrace guy [Kissing face with smiling eyes emoji]

Gabi (11:04 pm): Factor Fictton

Gabi (11:04 pm): My tuurn

Me (11:04 pm): [Smiley face emoji]

Gabi (11:04 pm): Whatt can Ido 2 be mor like themm?

Me (11:04 pm): Like who

Gabi (11:06 pm): Ur turn

Me (11:06 pm): K

I needed something good to tell Gabi to get her interested in me. I mean, beyond the Syracuse lie dance thing I was doing.

Everything I had said on the date bored her to the edge of death. There was no juice, no chemistry. Rocky Road and Mint Chocolate Chip. Schnapps and Jägermeister. That was it.

Me (11:07 pm): Promise you won't tell anyone

Gabi (11:07 pm): this isgood

Me (11:07 pm): Promise!!

Gabi (11:07 pm): [Thumbs-up emoji] Absoluttes

Me (11:07 pm): Ive been helping Barno since summer

Me (11:08 pm): The guy your mom hates

Me (11:10 pm): You there

Gabi (11:11 pm): I now hwho he iss

Gabi (11:11 pm): Nurdeded moms brothrr

I didn't know how to respond. I typed a few different things. What I finally sent was:

Me (11:13 pm): Really sorry about your moms brother. It was an accident. I hope your moms okay

While I waited for a reply, I tried to picture Gabi. How much had she drunk since our date? Where? With? Maybe she didn't want to know it was an accident. I wished I never had sent anything about Mr. Barno, about me working with him. Finally, I sent:

Me (11:16 pm): Don't tell anyone about me and Barno

Several long minutes later:

Gabi (11:21 pm): Iwont
Gabi (11:21 pm): nite

I checked Gabi's Instagram profile the second I woke up. She had posted the picture of her kissing me on the cheek at Main Street Custard 10 hours previously, which, by my math, was about midnight last night. It had 156 likes and lots of comments with surprised emojis and encouragement like "get back out there girl" and "get some you sexy bitch." I didn't understand why female friends called each other bitch. I guess it was kind of like the Neils on Wheels nickname.

You know that feeling when your throat is really tight, like someone sprayed a bunch of spray paint or something in your face, and your stomach is where your lungs go, and your lungs are nowhere? And it's like your feet are concrete but your knees are jelly and your hands get cold and your head gets hot? That's how I felt when I got onto Mr. Barno's street, faced his house, and saw a crowd of people buzzing around in the cul-de-sac.

They had signs in their hands that I couldn't read because I was behind them, and the signs faced Mr. Barno's house. And they were shaking the signs, thrusting them up and down, and waving their fists. They were talking, lots of them. It reminded me of a crowd of students in the auditorium before assembly.

I didn't know what to do. I hid on the path in the woods and listened. Finally, I decided to just make my own path in the direction of Mr. Barno's house through the woods. I went over, under, and around all kinds of branches and thickets. Got pretty scratched up. And, eventually, I got behind the privacy fence in Mr. Barno's backyard and hurled myself over it.

I found Mr. Barno sitting in the grass in his backyard smiling at the tree project. We had finished the platform, which stood on the posts we had installed onto the concrete footings. The platform—which was about 10 feet off the ground—encircled the tree, leaving a gap between the platform and the branches of about a foot all the way around. We had also finished half of the railing around the platform. I didn't know what would come after we finished the railing. Maybe we'd be done.

I waved. Mr. Barno gazed at me. He had that kind of suspicious look on his face—confused, alone.

"It's me, Nolan."

He didn't move. Didn't say anything.

I sat down next to him and just stared at the project for a long time. The cacophony in the cul-de-sac drummed on. After a while, a woman's voice overtook the crowd through a megaphone. "We are Save the Youth of Paxson. We know you can hear us, Alexis. My name's Penelope Meyers. I know you know the name Meyers because you killed my older brother, Joshua, during his senior year of high school. He was going to be a great quarterback and do wonderful things playing in college, maybe even the pros. He was some-one who was going to make this community proud. And you took that—took that from all of us, from my parents, from me. Listen to me, you coward, hiding in your home. Come out and face me."

The mob urged Mr. Barno to come out to the cul-de-sac. But he didn't move, not a blade of grass shifted beneath him. Gabi's mom, Mrs. Meyers, came back over the megaphone, "I have one last thing to say to you. I will not rest until you are gone, gone from this neighborhood, gone from this town. You understand? I will not rest." The crowd howled taunts at the house.

Mr. Barno said to me, "When'd you get here?"

"Just now," I lied (I know, I know).

"My time here with Dodger is short."

"What's going on with the bank?"

"The bank?"

"The foreclosure thing."

"Oh. Not to worry. I've got some money. Will that be enough?"

I asked Mr. Barno to show me, and he told me to go inside. On the kitchen counter was a stack of opened mail. I dug through it and finally found the envelope from his retirement plan. The document inside said he had $4,285.21 in the account. I went back outside and told him that he didn't have enough to pay off the bank.

"I don't think we should work on the tree project today," I said.

Mr. Barno agreed. "Tell me about your life."

"Remember that girl I told you about, Gabi?"

"I'm sorry, Nolan. I don't. Are you dating now? How's it going?"

"No need to say sorry," I said. "The dating is alright, I guess."

"Not enjoying it?"

"I am. I'm just, I'm kind of over that initial rush. Like, we went on a date and—I don't know—it wasn't how I thought it would be. She kept talking about boring things, like the yearbook and debate club. Then, for some reason, she talked about how I dress and stuff."

"And?"

"I tried to ask her about music and stuff she's into—tried to show interest in her interests by bringing up lacrosse. I don't know, she's gorgeous, smart, and popular. But, I guess when I do better next time, then, you know, she'll really like me."

"When, when, when, when, when. That's your go-to word. When I get a girlfriend. When I figure out what I want to do. When I do this. When I get that. Stop with when. Young people wish their lives away—rushing past right now and into some distant, imagined future."

"Well, that future is happiness and I'm wondering when I'll finally arrive at it. I keep trying, and trying, and I make a little progress, and I think I'm almost there, and then something happens like that bad date with Gabi and I plummet back down."

"Be realistic, Nolan. The happiest people in the world are not that way every day of their lives."

"You don't got to try to make me feel better."

"I have a memory of you looking at the photo of Celeste holding a cat. Is that memory real?"

"Very real."

"That's a photo, Nolan. Celeste wasn't happy all the time."

I realized he was right. I remembered his wife in the Chevy convertible that summer night and she seemed distraught. "What was going on with Celeste?"

"Her mother died suddenly. A stroke. Celeste became inconsolable. Weeks turned into months. She started drinking and smoking. Even when… It was sad. I tried to get her to stop. But grief…" Mr. Barno stroked his beard slowly and tears made wet stripes down his sagging face. "Happy moments are important. But chasing happiness won't work."

"Why won't it work? This is maddening."

"Because of this thing called hedonic adaptation. Look it up sometime. Basically, when good things happen, we get a happiness boost, but it only lasts a little while. When you get a good grade, you feel as though you're on top of the world, don't you?"

"Of course."

"But you come back down, right?"

"Yeah, there's always another test to study for."

"Same thing when you're sad. It lasts a little while then you're back to your baseline, your typical level of happiness. You can have high swings—let's say you win the lottery—and low swings—let's say you had gotten kicked out of Paxson High School last summer.

But they're always just swings. Pleasure. Pain. Back to your baseline."

A light rain began. It gently dampened my head and shoulders.

"Instead, seek a fulfilling life. Eudaimonic happiness—a deep sense of happiness that comes from a meaningful life filled with love, friendship, the smell of this rain, peace, joy, harmony, trust in our fellow humans, time spent with loved ones, the pleasure available to all of us in trees, dogs, the stars. The happiness that comes from making a meaningful contribution to the world."

"This sounds impossible," I moaned through the drizzle.

"It's hard. Not impossible. Changing your circumstances isn't the solution. The changes must be in how you relate to your circumstances."

He stopped and we sat there getting wet for a while. "I don't remember the percentages. Been a long time. But researchers have found that only a little bit of our happiness comes from our circumstances. And let's say half of happiness comes from our genes. The rest of your happiness is up to you."

I pulled my sweatshirt up over my head, tightened the strings, and tried to be with what Barno said—with the sky and the smell of early October rain and the sensation of the drops all over me. Soon, I noticed that the chanting and banging of the crowd out front was gone. The mob had left. In its place, I heard a continuous symphony—as if every hair on my body was listening and there were no spaces between the sounds of the raindrops on the house, on the ground, on the tree, on us. And I felt so grateful just to be able to hear the world like this—to be fully a part of it for the first time.

After a while of sitting there in the rain with my eyes closed beside Mr. Barno, he whispered, "Happiness."

Twenty One

I met Neil and Branson out at our lockers in The Desert.

"What's the plan for Homecoming?" Neil asked.

"You're coming?" I grabbed Neil and hugged him. His crutch fell away, and I had to pick it up afterward and hand it to him.

"Yeah, yeah, I'm going stag."

"Cool. Can either of you score me some schnapps or Jägermeister for Homecoming?"

Both said they would try, but neither had a solid hookup.

"How's that journalism class with Tyler Peanut Butter?" Neil asked me. I wasn't sure why people called Tyler that, other than P.B. were the initials of his hyphenated last name. Maybe because everyone—except The Shark—liked Tyler the way everyone likes peanut butter.

"Class is awesome. And, honestly, Tyler's a lot cooler than I thought."

"When we meeting up?" Branson asked.

"About that," I said. "Do you guys mind, if um, well. Gabi wants to go with Reese and them all. And, the thing is, Jamal's dad's paying for a limo. But it only fits, like, so many people, you know? So. Yeah, I got to do pictures with Gabi at Jamal's house. Can I just, maybe, meet you guys at the dance?"

Branson stared at me all crooked. "For real? You barely hang out with us anymore and now this?"

Neil held a hand up in front of Branson. "It's cool. We get it. This is your big thing now. Gabi. Your dream. We're happy for you."

Branson peered over me. "Hey Sky-sky," he called. He galloped over to Skyler and gave her a hug right there in the middle of the hallway. And a kiss on the cheek, too. "Day-um, looking fine." She smiled in her skirt and hugged him back and they sort of swayed there like I bet French people do under the stars by that river in Paris when they're in love. But, since this was high school in Paxson, apparently people embrace-swayed by the lockers under distinctly un-romantic fluorescent lights when they were in love.

My heart pounded so hard I could hear it in my ears. *Are they actually in love—real love the way people in Paris are in love?*

Branson kissed Skyler on the cheek again, told her goodbye, and strutted off down the hall.

I wanted Skyler Bell more than I ever had before.

She wasn't a friend I had a crush on. She was what was missing.

I said "later" to Neil and caught up with Skyler. "Hey, what's up, Sky?"

"Hey."

"You and Branson, huh?"

"Yeparoo. You and Gabi, huh?"

We walked a bit, her a half step ahead.

"I'm thinking about renting a tux for Homecoming. Or should I just wear the suit my mom bought me last year for my cousin's bar mitzvah?"

Skyler stopped. "People don't wear tuxes to Homecoming."

"Yeah, but I really want to impress."

She started walking.

"Hey, where you going?"

"Class."

"What're you wearing to Homecoming?"

She stopped, glanced back. "A dress, Nolan."

"Overalls made into a dress? That'd be cute."

She walked off. "Why are you making fun of me?"

I caught up to her. "No. No. I'm sorry. I. Ugh!"

As she walked, she said, "And the fighting in class last week? I thought you were someone else." She regarded my new black jeans and shirt, her taste buds seeming to register somewhere between surprise and dissatisfaction.

"I wasn't fighting." I stopped. "I am. I am someone else."

She kept going.

"What about you? Skirts?"

No reaction.

I formed a megaphone around my mouth with my hands. "What gives? Why won't you talk to me?"

She turned, faced me. "Me? Why won't I talk to you? Ever since you got popular, you have completely ignored me. It's like I never existed."

Popular? "That's not true."

As she walked away, she stuck her elbow out. Then, a hand popped up—as if pointing at the fluorescent lights—and waved curtly as if not to say, 'see you later,' but to say something that words can't.

———————

I watched the driveway from my bedroom window that night. Rain again, the window pocked and blurry. I had the iPod earphones in. I couldn't get myself to listen to Sarah's demo songs—didn't think I could handle hearing her voice. Instead, I listened to all the saddest songs I could find. "Konstantine" by Something Corporate. "Your Own Disaster" by Taking Back Sunday. "Transatlanticism" by Death Cab for Cutie. "Cautioners" and "Claire" and, of course, "For Me This is Heaven" by Jimmy Eat World. "This Song Brought to You by a Falling Bomb" by Thursday.

I started thinking about how, from this window, I saw Sarah all crumbled on our driveway. The worst part was how Rafe spit on her after knocking her to the asphalt. I wanted to hate Rafe so much, but I couldn't. I tried to clench my fists—tried to get my face all hot with rage. But there was no rage left in me.

Then I thought about love and how my sister sang that lyric she wrote—that sad and beautiful lyric that expressed how the part of the people that we love that makes us stronger is also the part that makes us weaker.

I had this ah-ha moment, this thought that she was singing about Rafe. But then I had this tragic feeling that maybe she was singing about her and me.

"The Last Song I Will Ever Want to Sing" by Moneen came on. And I started to sob. I fell to the ground into the fetal position. Weeping. Trembling. I crawled to my bed, dragged a blanket off it, and hid beneath the blanket on the carpet. Crumbled, like my sister.

In the middle of the night, I snuck into Sarah's bedroom—the first time I had been in there since I broke in the night she left and took the shoelace, pen, and concert tickets. I ran my hand silently across her music keyboard.

I brought my red notebook to school the next day and tried to write a letter to Gabi during classes. It seemed we could only really communicate well late at night through text messages. I just wasn't good at talking to girls. I figured I'd write the letter and then I'd text it to her tonight in pieces. But I didn't know what to say. I wasn't profound with words the way my sister Sarah was.

I wanted to tell Gabi that I was drawn to her—that I wanted her, and I didn't know why. I wanted to tell Gabi that I didn't want to want her anymore. But I couldn't stop myself.

So I tried to write a letter to Skyler, instead, and tell her I wanted to confess my love to her. Wanted to go to Homecoming with her. Wanted to dance cheek-to-cheek with her. Smell her. Hold her hand. Kiss her. Lay in a field with my head on her chest, her arm wrapped over me. Wanted to talk about Paul Simon and her dreams of school in California. And my dreams, the ones I had at night where no one could understand me. And our dreams.

But I didn't write anything in that red notebook all day. I was buried under this thought that Gabi didn't love me because I didn't do cool things and Skyler didn't love me because I didn't have beautiful things to say.

That night I decided to text Gabi and just act like everything was normal:

Me (9:55 pm): [meme of Michael Scott from *The Office* dancing]

Me (9:55 pm): LOL just practicing my dance moves for homecoming

Me (10:03 pm): Whatcha up to

Gabi (10:07 pm): Grr. Big fight with parents

Me (10:07 pm): Im sorry

Gabi (10:10 pm): Im sorry to do this to you [Loudly crying face emoji]

Me (10:10 pm): ?

Gabi (10:12 pm): Ur the best Nolan but Im sorry I can't go with you to homecoming anymore

Oh.

Gabi (10:13 pm): Ur really sweet. It's not you. [Heart emoji][Heart emoji]

Me (10:14 pm): Its ok

Me (10:14 pm): I understand

I didn't, but.

Gabi (10:14 pm): Me and Dallas may be getting back together

Why?

Me (10:14 pm): No worries

Now what do I do? I felt the way I did when Mrs. de León told me I couldn't apply to college without my parents' financial information—kind of free and kind of gutted. Like something was taken from me before I got to really have it. Gabi was no longer mine if she ever was. Skyler never would be.

Me (10:15 pm): Im happy for you
Me (10:15 pm) See you at the dance
Gabi (10:16 pm): And school
Gabi (10:18 pm): We're still friends?
Me (10:19 pm): Definitely
Gabi (10:19 pm): [Smiling face with smiling eyes emoji]

I put the iPod on. Music played. I didn't listen to any of it. It just sort of hovered around me. Then I got up and carefully peeled the Jeep poster from my bedroom door. There was no anger in me to rip it off the wall. It was this weirdly tranquil feeling.

I think I was asleep. I know I was in my bed. My phone vibrated.

Gabi (11:17 pm): Can I ask u somethin?
Me (11:17 pm): Of course
Gabi (11:18 pm): U ever feel hopeless?

Hopeless? Gabi?

Me (11:18 pm): Yea. Used to feel that way all the time
Gabi (11:19 pm): Me too and I still do
Me (11:19 pm): How can I help [Crying face emoji]
Gabi (11:21 pm): Its only in my head right?
Me (11:21 pm): Those feelings are common. Youre not alone. It's gonna be okay.
Gabi (11:23 pm): Doesnt feel that way
Me (11:23 pm): I know
Me (11:23 pm): Do you want to talk

Gabi (11:25 pm): Absolutes. Ur sweet
Gabi (11:26 pm): Meet at the bench in Overlook Park
Me (11:26 pm): When?
Gabi (11:26 pm): Now

I got to Overlook Park as fast as I could. It was on the cliffs above the river near the train bridge. There was a great view of the trains when they crossed the bridge that I used to love to come and enjoy when I was a kid. I'd climb on the rocks and count the boxcars.

I sat down next to Gabi. She didn't say anything. She just put her head in my lap and sobbed. It was cold and all I had on was a sweatshirt. Her hands were tucked into the sleeves of her jacket, her head wrapped in a white knit cap. I could hear the midnight train rumbling up north through the orchards and fields. Not long after that, it crossed the bridge under a full moon, and I felt Paxson's familiar quaking. That night I really listened to the train's horn.

Gabi strained, "Everyone feels a thousand miles away."

"I'm not."

She took my hand and squeezed it. "Does anyone see me? I'm so tired of looking this way. Feeling so, I don't know, alone."

"I'm not sure what you see in the mirror, but I can tell you that every guy at school must see what you don't. You're beautiful."

Gabi wept. This night was the opposite of those dreams I had where everything I said was gibberish. I was awake and what I said made perfect sense, but she wasn't listening.

She sniffled, "That's just crap guys say before they touch you." She wept hard for a while then sighed, "Oblivion." She sat up and she put her hand on my cheek and started to kiss me on the mouth. It tasted of everything I dreamed it would.

It's just that I couldn't kiss a broken girl who just wanted someone to kiss her. I wasn't that kind of guy. I pulled my face away and said, "There are other kinds of guys, too."

I held Gabi's head to my chest and rocked her back and forth—not in a romantic way like how Branson had swayed with Skyler, but in a way I hoped could make Gabi feel less broken.

I never knew that someone as widely desired as Gabi Meyers could feel so alone. Mr. Barno was right, we're all suffering, even the most beautiful people in the world. Loneliness was something we all shared. The sad thing was, realizing that wasn't at all comforting.

Twenty Two

After Senior Seminar II, Mrs. de León wanted to know how things were going with the Mr. Barno story I had begged her to assign me. I told her I was working on it, and I promised to get the interview she wanted.

"Can I ask you something?"

"Sure, Nolan."

"If you had this awesome career, why'd you move to Paxson?"

"Paxson is a lovely place. And I came back to make it even lovelier."

"Came back?"

"I grew up here, Nolan. Went to high school in this very same building."

"You did?"

"Yes, of course."

"If I leave, I'm never coming back."

"Don't be so sure."

"Can I ask you something else?"

"You may."

"Did you know Mr. Barno?"

"Yes," she said. "He taught me. I knew him well. There was a gang of us that got together to eat pizza and talk about life with him. I learned more in those evenings than I have learned anywhere else—college, on the job. That man saved my life. He helped me see meaning, purpose. It's my responsibility to pay that forward."

Whoa, Mrs. de León was a Smart Kid. "I bet he was a good teacher."

"He was a great teacher with a kind heart. He cared, maybe too much. But he was beloved by the students and admired by the staff. Many thought he would be principal someday."

"I know about the car accident and all. What I don't get is, how can someone so loved become so hated?"

"You're the journalist. That's for you to find out."

————————

Two weeks to Homecoming.

It didn't matter.

Everything kind of looked different after the Gabi thing. I was going alone. Or maybe I wouldn't go.

Maybe I'd just sit in my room and doomscroll everyone's posts from the football game and the dance. Or maybe I'd put on the iPod and dance on my bed with Miles to the *Nothing Gold Can Stay* version of "Hit or Miss" by New Found Glory.

Beneath a dome of gray, Mr. Barno and I spent Monday afternoon working on finishing the railing on the tree project. Mr. Barno seemed lost inside himself. His eyes were glazed donuts, his face hollow, his beard frayed like a bird's nest that a WWE wrestling match had taken place in. He worked methodically, anyway. I guess it gave him something to do.

Finally, I asked him, "What's going on with the house?"

"What do you mean?"

"The bank."

"What bank?"

"The letter demanding money."

"Oh, I must've thrown that away." He walked over to the base of the tree, leaned down, and sniffed the air. "I can't believe they've survived this late into the season. I better cut them and bring them inside."

I wanted to tell him that there weren't any flowers there. Wanted to say, 'Get your head out of the clouds. The bank stuff is what's real. Serious. Definitive.' Instead, I told him that I was no longer going with Gabi to Homecoming and that she said she might be getting back together with Dallas.

He waved me over. "Sorry to hear that. How do you feel about it?"

I could smell Mr. Barno and he stunk. I mean, really funky. I didn't say anything because, how do you tell someone they need a shower? "I feel okay about her and me not going together. It's weird, if you had told me that Gabi Meyers would dump me before we were ever really dating, I'd have guessed I'd be devastated. But I'm not."

"How you feel isn't weird."

"It's not?"

He reached for my hand. I helped him up. "I want to start teaching you about cultivating a happy life before I lose everything. I've been meaning to do that. I believe that if we did some special lessons, the way I did long ago with an after-school group of students I mentored, it could really help you."

I explored him standing there the way you might explore a picture of a beautiful person. Maybe because Mr. Barno was a beautiful person. A different kind of beautiful. The most beautiful kind of person you could know. He had his heart. And I wanted to believe there were many other people that are beautiful like that.

"I want to start now. We don't have much time." He cupped his shivering hands in front of his face and blew on them as if blowing magic dust. "What you're talking about is hedonic forecasting, or when we make predictions about future emotional states. There's this thing called hedonic adaptation, where we tend to go back to our general level of happiness quickly after experiences that make us feel up—like someone saying yes to Homecoming—or down—like someone saying no to Homecoming."

I thought about interrupting him. That would be awkward. I knew it was the disease and not him that had forgotten that we were already doing happiness lessons and that we had already talked about hedonic adaptation.

He continued, "With hedonic forecasting, we are predicting how emotionally intense some future event will be. In your case, you forecasted that being dumped would be devastating. But you're recovering. The reason for that is immune neglect. We fail to realize how good our coping skills are at helping us overcome the bad stuff. If you can remember these concepts, then you can do two things that I suggest. First, choose to live with less fear and worry because the feared pain is often greater than the actual pain. Most people don't do that. They multiply their suffering by manufacturing pain in their minds in anticipation of bad things. They get buried under this manufactured suffering, under fears and worries of things that may never happen. What I'm trying to say is, we live as though things will be worse than they often end up being. But you can't go back in time and say, 'Oh that bad thing I was so worried about didn't happen. Let me undo that unnecessary worry and sorrow.' That anguish has taken its toll on you already. Second, be comforted knowing that in our darkest times we have the capacity to cope and persevere. We are adaptable. We seek the silver lining."

"Like how you once told me that most things are an inconvenience, not a catastrophe?"

"I said that? I'm smarter than I look." His mouth smiled, but his lost eyes didn't join in.

Hedonic adaptation. Hedonic forecasting. Immune neglect. They all made sense conceptually. But, well, some people—like my mom, Gabi, and Gabi's mom— seemed so sad in real life.

"Do you think Gabi's mom will ever forgive you for killing her brother in that car accident? Is her psychological immune system just not working?"

"Killing her brother in the car accident? That's not what happened."

What? He didn't die in the car accident?

"Don't take my word for it. These concepts that I am teaching you aren't mine. They've been studied by smart people at places such as Harvard. Let's see, what other lessons can I teach you? We've got to cram what normally takes months to teach."

"Mr. Barno." I gulped. "I don't know how to say this. We've been doing happiness lessons for a while now."

It was as if someone dropped a violin mid-stroke. "We have?"

"Let me show you." I went and stopped my recorder from recording and then I played back for him all four lessons we had previously recorded.

Mr. Barno started to talk. His knees jiggled and he collapsed. In a moment I was beside him in the grass, my arms wrapped around his frail shoulders. And I know it's selfish, but I just held him there and thought over and over, *It's too soon.*

———————

On Wednesday night I was studying for an AP Calculus test. I was on my laptop with Mr. Barno's words yanking the steering wheel of my attention away from the practice problem set on my desk. These words: "Killing her brother in the car accident? That's not what happened."

I Googled 'Joshua Meyers' and discovered that a zillion people had that name. I tried 'Joshua Meyers Paxson' and found one relevant entry: a link to an old *Paxson Chronicle* article about the Paxson High School back-to-back state football championship team. I guess in the 1990s, not everything that happened ended up online the way it does now. I clicked the link to the chronicle's website—the Internet version of a 6-year-old's family portrait—but it brought me to a 404 page.

Just then, I got a text from Gabi.

Gabi (8:23 pm): Sorry about the other nite. Wish u hadnt seen that

Me (8:23 pm): It's okay

Gabi (8:23 pm): [Person facepalming emoji] Sorry I kissed u

That was a first.

Me (8:23 pm): It's okay. Really

Gabi (8:23 pm): Thx for being my secret best friend [Detective emoji]

Me (8:23): Any time

Gabi (8:23 pm): Hehe

Gabi (8:23 pm): Really tho. Ur sweet [Heart emoji]

Gabi (8:24 pm): I mean as a friend

Me (8:24 pm): I know. Im cool with being friends

Gabi (8:24 pm): Rad because u really are cool. Ur kind and u listen

Gabi (8:24 pm): U made me feel safe. Is that weird?

Me (8:24 pm): Thats what friends do [Smiley face emoji]

Gabi (8:25 pm): Im just kinda [Face with head-bandage emoji] right now

Me (8:25 pm): I understand

Gabi (8:25 pm): Thats the thing about u. U understand

Gabi (8:26 pm): U know every other guy would have taken advantage of me that nite and u didnt

I started to type: 'No they wouldnt have.' But I stopped. Because, really, I didn't know that. I just knew what I would do—who I was. And I hoped there were other guys like me too, for Gabi's sake, and for Skyler's sake, and for Sarah's sake, and for everyone's sake.

Instead, I sent her what I knew for sure:

Me (8:27 pm): Im here if you ever need a friend

Gabi (8:27 pm): You = [Smiling face with halo emoji]

Gabi (8:27 pm): Big news. Dallas and I are a no go for homecoming

Me (8:27 pm): Im sorry

Gabi (8:27 pm): Im not

Gabi (8:28 pm): So what do you say [Woman dancing emoji]??

Me (8:28 pm): ?

Gabi (8:28 pm): Will you be my date to homecoming?

Gabi (8:28 pm): Just friends

Gabi (8:28 pm): PLEAASSEEE

Me (8:29 pm): Can I wear a [Person in tuxedo emoji]?

Gabi (8:29 pm): A tux? Sure! Hehe

Me (8:29 pm): Yes. If I can wear a tux and we go as just friends

Gabi (8:29 pm): Absolutes [OK hand emoji]

Me (8:29 pm): [Man dancing emoji]

Gabi (8:29 pm): Hey can I apologize about 1 more thing

Me (8:30 pm): No [Smiley face emoji]

Gabi (8:30 pm): Grr

Gabi (8:30 pm): Well then can I get a redo?

Me (8:30 pm): [Back arrow emoji] approved

Gabi (8:30 pm): LOL. I want to buy u ice cream and hear about the music u like.

Gabi (8:30 pm): Can we do that instead of going to Jamals for pictures? Im over that scene

Me (8:30 pm): Absafuckinlutely

Twenty Three

Gabi and I started playing a new game over text messages. Fact or Fiction was out.

The new game didn't have rules. It didn't have a name either. The way it worked was that we just shared about ourselves. We played before breakfast, between classes, and all afternoon long up until bed every day. She liked it because, as she told me over text, I was someone who looked beneath the surface. I wasn't sure what that meant, but since it had the [Detective emoji], [Smiling cat with heart-eyes emoji], and [globe emoji] alongside it, I figured it wasn't a bad thing.

I had never texted so much in my life. I didn't mind. I guess texting is just the honest way to communicate.

Gabi wasn't Gabi. I mean, she was. But she wasn't. It was confusing. Not in a bad way. It was like there was the Gabi you saw and the Gabi you didn't.

Some things about Gabi:

She hates ketchup and mustard unless they are on a hotdog. But it must have relish on it too. Otherwise, she won't eat the hotdog. She only eats corn if it's on the cob. She never wears lipstick or lip gloss because she doesn't like the sensation of them on her lips. No one ever notices (I sure didn't). Her favorite food is peaches, but she doesn't like to eat them in front of others—too messy. Her favorite drink is black cherry soda.

She tends to run hot. She wears light jackets, never heavy coats. She broke her wrist during summer lacrosse two years ago. She got a spider bite on that same wrist the night before. An omen?

Her favorite song isn't one that just has a good beat like she had said when we were on our botched date. Her favorite song of all time is the Eva Cassidy version of "Fields of Gold." It always makes her cry in a good way. She misses her Nana.

She doesn't like Mexican food, but she used to hang out at Juanita's Taqueria because the other popular kids liked it. She drank the black cherry soda whenever she went.

She used to do a lot of things she didn't like. I didn't ask what. But she used to try to find something good in those things she didn't like, like black cherry soda. One day, she just stopped trying to find something good in the bad. And things just got worse. She didn't say what.

Maybe 200 feet back through the woods, my dad's step ladder was tucked behind a bush near the gate to the Lewis property. I had lifted it all stealth-like from our garage on my way to meet Branson and Neil.

It was a little after 10:30 pm on a crisp Friday, one of those autumn nights when you first notice the air is thinner, less welcoming than it was a few days before. Something had left Paxson for the year—some comfort found in the warmth of the nights, the crickets, and the frogs that called you to them. And you knew that something would not return until next May. For now, our part of the country would slowly darken, and people would recede indoors to hide from the world.

We had climbed over the high stone wall and wormed on hands and knees through the trees to the same spot we used the last time to spy on Mr. Lewis' garage. Branson's plan was for Neil to stay hidden at the lookout spot and scan the house with his binoculars for signs of Mr. Lewis. Neil had one of Gramps' bird callers. If we were in danger and needed to abort, Neil was supposed to use it to send us a signal. It was a crow call, this little tube thing you blew in to attract crows so you could shoot them.

As for Branson and me, we were to creep to our attack position—a landscaped area with a big rock and bushes maybe 20 feet from the garage. On our way to the attack position, I would throw rags over the low lights that lined the driveway to make it harder for Mr. Lewis to see us during our escape if things turned south.

My job in Operation Nottingham was to be the 'rabbit.' What that means, for the uninitiated, is that I was the guy who made noise and ran like hell if necessary to draw attention away from the person taking the biggest risk, which was Branson. In other words, it was a failsafe thing where I was a diversion so Branson could get away if Mr. Lewis came out into the garage while Branson was in there. When I drew Mr. Lewis' attention and he came running after me, Branson could sneak out of the garage.

Because I was the fastest and I was already going to be twenty-odd feet away from the garage stationed at our attack position while Branson would be in the garage grabbing the money and shoving it into his backpack, I figured rabbit was the safer of the two jobs.

And anyway, I had done the rabbit thing before and it had never been needed.

In the event of retreat, the fallback position was in the trees about a quarter mile up the road where the road bent. In that scenario, the last person over the wall had to grab my dad's step ladder and run with it. I was adamant about that. No evidence left behind.

I was really hoping the last person wouldn't be Neil.

"I'm so amped," Branson whispered as we lay under the cover of the lookout spot scanning the Lewis house. "Just like the old days, back when we were all, like, the boys of summer and shit. Remember that summer before sophomore year? Best of our lives. Everything was possible back then." He had that damp look on his face and I didn't need to smell his breath to know he'd been drinking.

"The boys of summer in their ruin?" Neil's eyes were in his binoculars. "That sounds ominous. Don't be ominous before something like this."

I gathered the rags from my backpack. "That's not how the song goes."

Neil whispered, "It's a poem by Dylan Thomas."

And I was like, "No, it's a Don Henley song."

Neil put the binoculars down, reached into his backpack, and took out his smartphone.

I glared at him. "Dude, no phones."

He tapped away on it. "My bad."

"Jesus, man. That was the rule. This whole thing, I swear—"

"Said I'm sorry. Jeez."

"Lose the phone. We got to run it back to the fallback position. We'll grab it on the way out."

Neil wore this kind of scared look that I had never seen before. I don't know, his eyes seemed real big, his nose all flared. I was used to seeing the high cheeks and wrinkled nose of pain on Neil's face. Used to his wide-open mouth when laughing. Used to his perked eyebrows when excited. Used to the way his jaw clenched when he tried to hide pain. But scared was a new look. "I'm slow, if something happens."

"Who you going to text? We don't got our phones."

Branson pushed my arm, "Chill bro. It's all good. Mine's in my bag."

Amateurs, I thought. *Branson I get. But Neil? He's a professional.* I picked up Neil's binoculars and scanned the house. The garage was open. A chair was in the driveway. But Mr. Lewis wasn't around. I saw something small and white in the corner above the garage. *Was that here before?*

"Found it. 'I See the Boys of Summer' by Dylan Thomas." I rested the binoculars and Neil read the poem quietly. Now, I don't like poetry. I can't make any sense of it. But when he read this part, I thought I might implode: "These boys of light are curdlers in their folly, Sour the boiling honey."

I lay there in the dark and gazed at Neil and Branson. And I just thought about that poem and how I had soured so many things.

Branson whispered, "Alright, let's do this."

I stood up.

"Stay low."

"I'm leaving."

Branson reached for me as I retreated into the trees. "Dude, what the fuck?"

This is not harmony. This is not compassion. This is fear. This is fear. This is not what Mr. Barno would want.

I threaded through the branches. Branson grabbed me from behind.

I sprung back. "This is not harmony."

"What?"

"Nothing. I can't do this."

"You're no Midnight Warlord. Never were."

I yanked my arm away.

"You're out. No cut. No Jeep money."

"I don't want it."

"Don't come begging."

"I won't."

"More for me and Neil, you pussy."

I walked away. As I walked through the trees, I saw a fox in the bars of moonlight that striped the forest floor. We observed each other from a distance as I passed by—two intruders hoping the other could keep a secret. When I got to the wall, I decided I was taking my dad's step ladder. Screw Branson and Neil. I wasn't going down for them.

I got over the wall and was folding up the ladder when I realized what I had seen above the garage door.

A security camera.

I rushed back over the wall and through the trees. Neil was at the lookout spot, his camouflaged face squished against the binoculars. I tugged his arm. "Where's Branson?" Neil pointed. Branson was half-way to the attack position, yanking out the low lights.

I sprinted to him. "Security camera." I jabbed my arm toward the top of the garage. I yell-whispered, "He'll catch us."

Branson stood there.

"If we get kicked out of school and lose control of our lives, I don't want that kind of prison."

He rushed me. Shoved me. I tumbled backward.

Flung his backpack. Leapt on top of me.

We rolled on the driveway grunting and shoving hands and elbows, grappling like wrestlers. Choking. Breaking free. More grunting. He bit me through his ski mask. I bit back through mine.

Suddenly, Neil was on the ground yanking us apart.

And somewhere in that, Neil caught an elbow on the jaw. He cursed in anguish and, on hands and knees, careened toward the lookout spot where he vanished into the shadows.

I lay there coiled on the ground sucking wind.

Branson was hunched, his back to the moon, knees on the ground, face buried in his arms. Convulsing—a throbbing wound.

And I felt it in my lungs. Something was definitely gone from the air. And I wasn't sure now if it would come back next May, or ever again. I pulled myself up and as I trudged away, I declared, "It's over."

Twenty Four

Gabi Meyers and I threw the double doors open to the high school gymnasium and paraded into the Homecoming dance. I had on a tuxedo with a very Scottish-looking plaid cummerbund—the only tuxedo I could get on such short notice. Gabi wore sparkly jewelry and a blue dress cut above the knees. We had earphones in—me with my iPod and her with her smartphone—and had synched up our music to play "All My Best Friends are Metalheads" by Less Than Jake as our entrance song.

I don't know what song everyone else was dancing to—what song was playing on the sound system. Gabi and I just cruised onto the dance floor and danced to our own playlist.

I didn't know if I would ever really be cool or accepted or whatever you're supposed to want to be in high school. But in those moments dancing with her I was so much more than those wants.

It was our dance. Our moves. Our tempo. Our rhythm.

We had something in the air and in the music between us—some kind of something much different than what I had once thought I wanted from her. It was woven with the knowledge that the other person was cracked in a lot of places—like my sister Sarah's crows—, and with a comfort that lets you know the other person will be there for you because you had so many cracks that an extra pair of hands was needed to hold you together. And that was more than enough. So much more than enough.

I wasn't a Midnight Warlord and Gabi wasn't a Honey Bun Girl. We were people who still had our hearts.

Gabi took my hands, and we swung side to side for a few songs. Then, we bounced up and down when the songs led us to. We danced to "Hit or Miss" and "Ballad for the Lost Romantics" by New Found Glory, "Ocean Avenue" by Yellowcard, and "Here it Goes" and "Sweetness" by Jimmy Eat World.

Hot. Sweating. My hair all messed up. Her hair flat and wet from perspiration. And she couldn't have been more beautiful to any other guy in the world than she was to me during those songs that we danced together at Homecoming my senior year. Because I saw her. And I saw that she could be herself with me and that I could be myself with her. And I didn't need her any other way.

And when she smiled at me as she danced, I saw in her eyes that she saw the same things I did.

She sang as we danced like she knew the words. Maybe she did. Maybe every Smart Kid knew those songs. That's what she was, a Smart Kid—kids who had pain and were learning to dance with it, who wanted to live with an open heart, who wanted a world where more people were that brave.

Later, the winners of the Homecoming court were presented. The winners were initially announced at halftime of the football game when Gabi and I were at Main Street Custard eating mint chocolate chip and peach ice cream and talking about music and how I didn't really apply to Syracuse and how Gabi didn't actually want to go there—that's what some of the arguing at home was about. She wanted to go to a liberal arts college. And I told her about my sister. And she told me about her stepdad. And about Dallas. And she showed me the bruises and the invisible scars. And I helped her look up a counselor and urged her to talk to the police.

A voice came over the sound system announcing the entrance of the two winners of Homecoming royalty. The voice was Mr. Green's and he spoke with his drill sergeant enthusiasm. "Welcome, my fellow Americans and distinguished guests. I proudly present to you your Paxson High School Homecoming royalty." He picked up his horn and did a rendition of the sax riff from "Baker Street," proving to us students that "Reveille" wasn't the only song he knew. "Tyler Pratt-Baldwin and Becky Stone."

Colored lights flashed onto the far doors. They opened and two silhouettes emerged through fog beneath an archway of green and yellow balloons. Tyler wore a golden shawl over a black gown. And Becky wore a strapless green dress. And the two of them strutted hand-in-hand onto the dance floor. We all stood in a semi-circle around the dance floor and cheered—I was a part of that semi-circle, part of Paxson, not off in the back with a panoramic view.

A slow song started. Tyler raced to the DJ table and whispered something to the DJ. The song "The Fox" by Ylvis kicked on and everyone from the Homecoming court rushed onto the dance floor and they did some kind of flash mob dance. Everyone except Dallas and Natalia.

Natalia brushed past me and Gabi. Dallas rushed after her. By the bleachers, Natalia rammed her finger at Dallas' nose. "We were supposed to win."

Dallas barked, "Chill the hell out."

But she didn't. "This was supposed to be my night. Me queen, you king. Our picture-perfect Instagram moment. I thought you were a winner, Dallas Stone. But the only Stone that's a winner is your sister, you loser."

Dallas seized her wrist. "You didn't win either."

Natalia shook him off. "Oh shut up! That's because your heart wasn't in it." She stripped her corsage from her wrist, slung it to the ground, and smeared it with her heel. He grabbed his hair and when he saw Gabi and me watching, he kicked the bleachers and stomped toward the exit. Natalia picked the corsage up and heaved it at him. "Because you still love her," she screeched, jabbing a finger in Gabi's direction. Natalia stalked after Dallas and the two vanished through exit and outside into the darkness.

Gabi and I cackled like nine-year-old kids blitzed on soda and candy. "I don't get why anyone would want to be popular. I'm so done with it."

"What do you mean?" I asked.

"The popular kids are all so miserable."

We trickled through the crowd to the refreshments. I stared at Skyler and Branson swaying to a slow song out on the dance floor. I wanted Skyler. I'd fallen in love with her from the sidelines.

I felt Gabi beside me, felt this person who was safe—who was out of everyone's league because, as Mr. Barno had taught me, you must learn to love yourself before you can love someone else. And Gabi still had that road before her.

But with Skyler, it felt dangerous—dangerous to love her. I knew what Mr. Barno had gone through and lost for love: everything.

What was there to do? Branson and Skyler. Dancing close. Gazing into each other.

I spotted Neil on the far side of the refreshments table talking eagerly with Mr. Green. I could tell that Neil was a little drunk because he was barely using his crutch. Mr. Green didn't seem to notice.

I handed Gabi my iPod. "Wait here, okay?" I ran over to Tyler who was waving his hands like a conductor over Jamal and Reese as they danced cheek-to-cheek.

"Hey Tyler."

"Oh, hey." Tyler hugged me and swayed with tipsy glee.

The Shark drifted past, pulled by his date. He gave us the sharkish look. But The Shark's date forced him to the dance floor where she buried his face in her, shall we say, copious bosom.

I told Tyler, "I'm not doing the Midnight Warlord thing anymore. But I made one exception with it being Homecoming and all. Can I suggest you leave Dallas' party before 11 pm? The cops may be tipped off about it then. Oh, and I'd avoid being near The Shark's truck when he leaves tonight as I got a feeling he'll be raging pretty hard."

Tyler howled.

"You see that fine looking gentleman over there?" I pointed to Neil. "It would mean the world to him if you asked him to dance."

"That cutie? How's a boy like him here alone?" Tyler slinked toward Neil. They returned, Neil with this soft smile beneath his glasses.

Under the lights, Tyler held his other hand up. Neil took it. And the two glided over the dance floor to "Get Lucky" by Daft Punk. I went back to Gabi and got some refreshments.

"You like her, don't you?"

"What?"

"Skyler. You've been watching her ever since we stopped dancing."

"Uh."

"I don't mind, Nolan. We're friends. We don't own each other's night."

I scratched my arm. "I think. Maybe."

"You think or you know?"

"I know."

"Isn't that your best friend that she was dancing with?"

"Yeah, Branson."

"You all not talking?"

"Some stuff happened."

"Need an ear?"

"Thanks, but I'm alright."

She took my hand in hers. "You should talk to Branson."

"No clue where he is."

On the dance floor, Skyler and Neil were talking over Tyler's shoulder while Neil and Tyler slowly danced to a song I didn't know. Neil pointed toward the male locker room. Skyler planted her hands on her hips.

"I think I know where Branson is."

Gabi pushed me. "Go."

I found Branson in the stalls in the back of the locker room, his arms hooked around a toilet bowl, his chin on the seat. A gray suit jacket was wadded on the tile behind him.

"You alright?"

He peered through the storm in his eyes at me. "What'dya want?"

"Just to say what's up."

"What's up," he moaned.

The place reeked of cleaner, urine cakes, and fresh vomit. "Nothing really. Came with Gabi. Thought I might find you—"

"Big fucking Nolan. Cool guy now. Nolan Coolpants. Mr. No Loyalty Coolpants."

I squatted. "Look, I'm sorry about Operation Nottingham. It's not right. Mr. Lewis is in pain. And it wasn't worth it, anyway."

He rested his chin and closed his eyes. "What about my pain? You got no clue what my life's like."

"I know I don't. I just wish it wasn't like this." I paused. "You know where Skyler is?"

"She's so pretty." He swirled his neck and retched. "And now I've ruined her Homecoming."

"Hey man, as a friend, I think you're pulling too hard on that Hurtado family thread."

He dragged his sleeve across his mouth. "Forgot that No Land's got a problem with drinking now. Cool guy's too good for everything." Licked his lips.

"No, I got a problem with your relationship with it."

He held an arm out behind him and presented me with the finger. Puke came in chunks. And I didn't want to leave him there, but when I got up and got a wad of toilet paper from the stall next door and came back, he wouldn't take it from me. So I left. Left my friend there suffering and that nearly drove me to tears.

Back in the gym, I swiveled, trying to spot Skyler. No luck. Then Gabi pointed me toward the exit.

The Shark, both his flat top and his suit wet and limp, splashed into the gym through the exit doors. "Listen up dick bags! Who's the dead man who let the air out of my truck tires?" The music pulsed on. No one turned their heads toward him or broke their rhythm.

I sidestepped Hunter (The Shark no more), thrust through the door, and bumped into Skyler just outside the exit where she huddled under an overhang. She palmed her eyes, her bare back to me, the red straps of her dress scrunched between her folded shoulders. "I just want Branson. He's okay, right?"

We were boxed in, walls of torrential rain on three sides, cold splashes misting my tuxedo pants. "Not sure. He's pretty wasted."

"Why?"

I shrugged but realized she didn't see.

"Can you help him?"

"I don't think that's wanted."

She turned. Her colorless eyes spotlighted me. "By him or you?"

I must've been pretty sweaty.

She stroked her corsage.

I tucked a finger under her chin the way I figured a French guy would. "I'm worried about you."

"Don't go there." She tilted away.

"Why?"

She dipped into the waterfall, breaking the wall. In an instant, she was a red blur. I lunged after her, my hair and clothes quickly drenched. "Wait!" I grabbed her glossy arm. "Why can't I go there?"

She froze in the parking lot, tucking her arms in tight which squeezed my grip loose. "I was certain we were finally… that we were meant to be. Tried to send you every possible signal. Waited and waited. But the moment passed. I'm with Branson now. I love him."

I searched her face through the downpour. The lifeless smell of wet asphalt and the whoosh of water flushing underfoot engulfed us. When I finally spoke, I mustered, "But I didn't… I ignored those moments. I didn't know... Just like my dad. And. And he was right. Ignoring the wrong moments. Worst mistake you can make."

"I'm sorry. I tried." She spoke with finality.

"But I love you now. Why can't we try now?"

"Don't say that." She mopped a lock of wet hair from her face. "We just missed each other. That's all."

The wind shifted. The rain eased. "That's all?"

I wanted to grab her on the shoulders, pull her close, and kiss her. Kiss her into wanting me, into loving me. But her narrowed shoulders and downcast chin said she wasn't mine to kiss. And I wasn't the kind of guy who forced a kiss on a girl who didn't want it. I knew now that there was too much of that going on.

Instead, I crossed my arms as the frigid rain nails were hammered down on me. "I love you and I don't know how not to."

Her face hardened. "You can't just love someone when you decide it's time. It doesn't work that way. You've got to love them when they need it, in the way they need it. Love isn't on your schedule, Nolan. It's something you grow and cultivate, not something you just declare."

The smeared makeup on Skyler's face. The rain glazed on her cheeks. They weren't mine to kiss.

And it wasn't my place to try to steal her from Branson. I started to say that I also wanted to be there for Branson. But…

A fist crashed into my cheek before I could open my mouth.

Suddenly, I was sprawled in a pool in the parking lot, my shoulder twisted, my knee burning. I lifted my head. Water poured down my back. I caught a bleary sliver of Skyler rustling toward the gym door in her heels, one arm over her head and the other tucked into the loop of the arm of a tall, gray suit. Branson.

I rolled onto my back and cradled my shoulder. The rain pelted my face. Then something else hit me. I was horizontal in about the same spot in the high school parking lot as I was when Rafe had knocked me down years before. This time I didn't want to know if anyone saw. I closed my eyes and cried—not the weepy, hiding kind of tears, but the loud, convulsing kind.

When Gabi found me sometime later, my right cheek hot and my rental tux sodden, she helped me to my feet. Her eyes said she saw my bruises—and not just the one on my cheek. She handed me my iPod and asked me if there was a song I wanted to dance to. "No," I quivered in the pair of puddles that were now my dress shoes, "I'm all out of songs."

Gabi fished her phone from her purse and plugged one earbud into her ear and one into mine. "My first boyfriend used to play this over the phone late at night to me in eighth grade. Sweet kid—like a middle school version of you." "Time After Time" by Cyndi Lauper played. Gabi pillowed her head on my soggy shoulder, and we bobbed gently in the storm, the parking lot lights casting down on us, a glittering constellation of raindrops encircling our shivering bodies. And I felt both closer to and further from love than I had at any point in my 17 years.

Twenty Five

Rejection. The gloomy lake that reflects all your cracks and holes. And your upside-down-ness in the glass of the water's surface lets you see how you must look to everyone else—this insurmountably flawed and unlovable freak.

When I realized Gabi and I wasn't going to happen, it was okay because Skyler. Skyler was smart and cute and quirky and funny and artsy. She was the hidden gem the guys in the movies discovered. It made perfect sense, discovering I loved Skyler. And now this?

I tried to understand. I knew that Lesson Four taught me that I should forget perfect. Did that also include things that made perfect sense?

Will anyone ever love me?

I tried using what Mr. Barno said in what amounted to Lesson Five. *I've got a psychological immune system that will help me recover from this. I will go on. I'm strong. I will be laughing and obsessed with some other girl in a matter of, what, weeks, months... years? When? What if this is the one time that my psychological immune system fails the way Penelope Meyers' system failed after her brother died?*

Skyler loved Branson.

Branson and I were no longer best friends, my jaw ached sufficiently to know that.

Some things we don't recover from, right? How did Barno move forward after the accident?

I felt sniffly—still shivered from the frigid rain the night before. I wished I could have dodged those raindrops. *Really? Trying to dodge raindrops*, I thought. *That's like cursing at the clouds.*

I thought of the woman who sang that sad song I'd heard in Mr. Lewis' garage. In a small way, I wanted to sing like her—wanted to bellow my pain to my sleepy-eyed parents sipping their coffee at the breakfast table.

"We need to talk," Dad said abruptly.

Mom added, "Your dad and I didn't want to, well, we wanted you to enjoy your Homecoming."

"The Frosted S'mores Pop-Tarts are an awesome surprise. Appreciate you, Ma." Mom had gotten the s'mores flavor as a special post-Homecoming treat. "I'm just not hungry right now."

Mom cupped her mouth and whispered to Dad. "Is he hungover, Terry?"

"Ma, you know I can hear you, right? And no, I didn't drink" (If you're keeping score, I didn't lie this time. Gabi and I failed to get our hands on any booze).

Dad reached across the table for the Pop-Tarts. "Hook a brother up."

Mom shot Dad the stink eye.

"Alright," Dad sighed. "The mom of the girl you went to Homecoming with, Mrs. Meyers, called your mother the other day."

Mom squared up on me, "Did you get handsy with her? Is that what the bruise on your cheek is about?"

"No. No, I didn't 'get handsy,' ma. Can't I just be friends with a popular, smart, gorgeous girl who's to-tally a lot of fun to hang out with and who is also secretly a really cool dork?"

"Then explain this." Mom pointed at my face. "Because if you got handsy and she didn't want you to, I'll clock you myself."

"Branson did it," I moaned, elbows on the table. "He sucker punched me. That ignoramus thought I was trying to steal his girlfriend. But I wasn't."

"Oh hun, Branson, your BFF?" Mom rocked forward and back.

Dad took a healthy bite from his Pop-Tart. "Sounds like his girl wants you."

"Incorrect, actually." I reached across the table and grabbed the other Pop-Tart. "I'm not good with the ladies."

Dad extended a hand for a high five. "Sounds like you are to me. Making suckers jealous. And stretching up to the pros and scoring a big-time Homecoming date. Atta boy. A chip off the old block. Didn't know you—"

"Anywho," Mom whistled.

"My hand's getting cold here," Dad groaned. I accepted his high-five half-heartedly.

Mom tapped the table and repeated, "Anywho."

"Alright, Nancy. Alright. Anyway, Mrs. Meyers told your mom that you've been hanging out with that schmutz Mr. Barno and helping him with yard work or something."

Mom squeezed my arm. "I told her that's not possible. That you work with your dad and you're training to try out for sport after school."

Sport? I thought. *Jeez Mom.*

Mom pulled her hand away. "But she insisted."

Dad tossed his glasses on the table. "We want to know why she would say a harsh rumor like that. That could really hurt this family."

"What your dad's trying to say is, there is a lot of negative sentiment about Mr. Barno and we don't want people falsely thinking you're associated with him. It's a small town. Word gets around."

"You guys want Mr. Barno gone the way Mrs. Meyers does?"

Dad folded his arms. "Mr. Barno is, look, he's a bad man. Back when your mother and I went to Paxson High, bad things happened—bad things that affected many of us who now got kids at that school."

"I know about the car accident," I said. "But it was just an accident. A mistake. What about that whole learning to forgive thing you're always preaching, Ma?"

Dad washed Pop-Tart down with a gulp of coffee. "Not just the car accident. That came a few months after something else that Mr. Barno did."

"Did the other thing have something to do with Mrs. Meyers' brother Joshua?"

Mom nodded.

"What was it?"

Mom cradled her coffee mug. Dad attacked the last bites of his Pop-Tart. Finally, Mom wiped her eyes and said, "Joshua was a classmate of ours. Everyone loved him. Played football with your dad."

Dad chewed. "Best damn quarterback this town's ever produced."

I dropped my Pop-Tart onto the plate. "Barno served 25 years in prison. Why can't people just leave him alone?"

Dad grabbed the bottom of his chair and hopped back a few times, turning to face the refrigerator. He spoke as if lecturing to the appliance and not to me. "Mr. Barno got the maximum prison sentence possible for the car accident. That was this community's way of punishing him for both the accident and for the other thing he did to our friend, Joshua. You see, son, there wasn't enough evidence to charge that scum for—"

Mom wept. "For killing Joshua."

Dad, still addressing the fridge, added, "In this community, we look out for one another. That's how justice is served."

Mr. Barno would never intentionally hurt anyone, right? Why would Mr. Barno kill a Paxson student, anyway? And what was Barno's connection to Joshua?

"Whatever you think Barno did, it's not true." I waved my Pop-Tart, but no one was looking at me. "I've been helping him. And he's been helping me. Maybe he made mistakes a long time ago. But he's a good person."

Dad surged to his feet. "What do you mean helping him?"

"Um. For like." I couldn't look at my dad. "My teacher. She assigned me this journalism story. I have to. Um. I got to interview Mr. Barno for a class story. Mrs. de León. It's just an assignment."

"How is that helping him?"

"Um. Right. I just mean. Like, when I've gone there and interviewed him, I'll, like, help take out the trash or something. You know, just to, like, build interviewer rapport and stuff."

"Oh." Dad's voice softened.

Mom added. "If it's just for class."

"When you're done with the assignment, you're not to see that man anymore. Got it?"

"Yeah. Yes. Got it."

Dad turned to Mom. "Call Penelope and explain it's an assignment. He's not doing it by choice."

Mom gave Dad a tight nod.

Man, that Pop-Tart got cold. I couldn't finish the rest. We all just sat there. Lumps of flesh. Then, Mom piped up, "Oh, I forgot. Good news. I'm starting back up with Mr. Lewis on Monday."

I turned and fixated on the fridge. "Who's Craig?"

I heard Mom off to the side say, "Craig?"

I kept staring at the fridge. "Sarah's dad, Craig. Who was he?"

Dad sunk into his chair. "Why are… who told you about Craig being Sarah's dad?"

"Rumors," I lied. "At school. It's a small town, you know. Word gets around."

My parents explained that Craig was a guy my mom dated in high school. Craig got her pregnant and Craig got scared. And he said the baby wasn't his. And then I remembered what my dad said to me when I asked him about Don Henley's music: "Some guys don't take responsibility. Some guys are boys of summer, like Craig, you understand?" And I understood my dad this time.

Before that day my parents had only ever been parents to me. Whatever had come before them becoming parents had just been, I don't know, this black hole. This nothingness. One day they were parents. That's how their lives started. With Sarah. That's what I thought at least. But I had that all wrong.

I told Mom and Dad about Rafe and how he hit Sarah and spat on her and how that's why I smashed his car up. And I told them how I saw Sarah run away with Rafe that night at the car bridge.

Dad stared at the fridge a lot that morning. "Why didn't you tell us?"

I told Dad, "I don't know."

And Mom cried and cried. "Is that why you always went there, to the bridge?"

I told Mom, "Yes," and cried too.

"Oh hun, it breaks my heart to know you went through that alone."

I didn't tell my parents about the letter from Sarah or why she ran away. I kept my promise to her. I don't know why. I guess that's what being a brother is. I knew my lies and omissions about Mr. Barno and Sarah that morning went against everything I'd learned in the happiness lessons. I wasn't perfect. I was a work in progress. And I just felt like some stories weren't mine to tell.

Later that day, I texted Gabi to ask her why she ratted me out to her mom.

Gabi (12:35 pm): Panopticon mom checks my phone. Must have seen ur text to me about it. Sorry I usually purge my texts every couple days but forgot [Person facepalming emoji]

Me (12:35 pm): She saw your texts that you were drunk then

Gabi (12:35 pm): Crap. Yup.

Gabi (12:36 pm): This should be fun

Me (12:36 pm): Change your phone password dork

Gabi (12:36 pm): Grr. Not allowed to. Big Brother will take my phone away.

Gabi (12:36 pm): Why u helping that creepy killer dude anyway?

Gabi (12:36 pm): [Knife emoji][Ogre emoji]

Me (12:37 pm): It's the other way around. Hes helping me

Gabi (12:37 pm): ??

Me (12:37 pm): Wish I knew how to explain it to you. But hes not a bad guy I swear

Gabi (12:37 pm): Not sure I believe that

Me (12:37 pm): I know [Sad face emoji]

Gabi (12:37 pm): Be careful [Heart emoji]

Gabi texted throughout the day to see how I was handling the Skyler rejection. And I told her and she listened, or read, or whatever you call it.

That night I deleted my Instagram account and un-installed the app from my phone. I didn't want to see pictures of Skyler. I found myself moping around and staring at her profile, over and over, and it just hurt too much.

Also, I didn't want to see Gabi's profile because I knew the girl in those photos wasn't the real Gabi. The real Gabi was my friend and you had to look past what she wanted you to see, or what you wanted to see—I'm not sure which—to see her.

Oh, and I unsubscribed from Lenny the True Love CEO, too.

Before bed, Gabi texted me:

Gabi (10:25 pm): New game

Gabi (10:25 pm): When one person shares something bad the other replies telling them something good in their life to be thankful for.

Me (10:25 pm): Whats it called

Gabi (10:25 pm): Come on try it

Me (10:26 pm): K

Me (10:26 pm): Whats it called

Gabi (10:26 pm): I dunno. Does everything need to have a name?

Me (10:26 pm): Yes

Gabi (10:26 pm): [Smiling face with smiling eyes emoji]

Gabi (10:27 pm): Ok. It's called boomerang. Something bad goes out. Something good returns.

Me (10:27 pm): Acceptable

Gabi (10:27 pm): LOL. Cheer up buttercup.

Gabi (10:27 pm): So ur having the shit day. The game starts with you.

Me (10:27 pm): K. This may not make any sense

Gabi (10:27 pm): Try me

Me (10:29 pm): I feel like this dream I used to always have. Im stuck on this hill in this field. Im on one side of a giant piece of glass and everyone else is on the other side and I can look through the glass down to where all the people are. But they can't hear me or see me

Gabi (10:30 pm): [Boomerang emoji] coming back at ya

Gabi (10:30 pm): I hear u. I see u. U have ur family and u have me. And Im pretty freakin cool if u ask me. [Nail polish emoji] So dont sleep on that.

Me (10:31 pm): I like this game.

Twenty Six

The red sign menacing Mr. Barno's front yard was for the Lewis Real Estate Agency. Underneath the big sign that included a photo of Mr. Lewis in his trademark fedora, was a small, second sign that hung by two chains. It read 'Listing Coming Soon.'

I asked Mr. Barno about it while we worked on the finishing touches of the tree project. He reeked of body odor again and I tried not to get too close. "Time for me to move on," he said blankly. "It'll be good for the community."

I had been helping Mr. Barno with his mail and trying to stay on top of the bank situation. The last letter from the bank said that, unless they received full payment, they would start the foreclosure of the home on November 1—in a few days. Barno would have six weeks after that to get out or the police would show up and escort him out. Six weeks, which they said was very generous. That's what they were, they said, a 'community bank' that was 'very generous.' I guess sly old Mr. Lewis got a deal with the bank so his real estate agency could sell the house.

Mr. Barno handed me a hammer and told me to put the last nail in the tree project. It secured a post attached to a railing. The post held up a string of outdoor lights that we had woven through the tree branches above the platform.

He rested against the railing and looked out over the yard. "Celeste loved lights." He pointed below us. "Before the tree was here, we. Hmm. Something was here. Eh. And lights. I remember lights hanging all over the yard."

"I thought the tree had always been here."

Mr. Barno shook his head. "No. Not while she was alive."

"Congrats," I raised my glass of lemonade. We had done it. We had built a wonderful tree fort around the oak tree.

Mr. Barno raised his lemonade and we toasted. "Thank you, Nolan, sincerely. This exists because of you." His hand massaged the grain of a railing board. "Now that we've built it, I can be here with my wife. Not just talk to her. But be with her. Here. Together. I can see her smile. Hold her. Smell her. Even if it is only a few times before I must go, it'll have been worth it."

"I'll leave you to be with her." I slid into the hole in the floor where the down ladder was.

"Stay." He sat down on the platform and patted the boards beside him. "Sit with me." So I did. He gave a child's smile. There was that Santa Claus angle again. "Nolan, I want to introduce you to Celeste."

I followed his lead, closing my eyes and breathing the way he'd taught me. And together we did the loopy thing. But this time, well, I'm not sure if it was momentary time traveling or what. Because when we opened our eyes, we hadn't gone anywhere. We remained in the tree fort in Mr. and Mrs. Barno's backyard.

When she saw Alexis, Celeste beamed her big, open smile. Those gorgeous teeth. Cheeks high. Eyes pinched into crescents. She wore an oversized plaid shirt—probably one of his—and a pair of old jeans. She looked as though she had been gardening, her jeans patched with brown, hands powdered in dirt.

Celeste fell into his arms, locking her hands around him. They clung to each other the way you would if you were freezing in a storm and the only warmth was the body of the person who loved you—as though the thing keeping them alive was that embrace. Alexis tucked a hand into Celeste's hair and cradled her head delicately against his chest. She squeezed and her hands indented into his sturdy back.

They were ageless. Strong. Together.

I shut my eyes, embarrassed to be intruding on their reunion, and that's when I noticed the sound. A gentle hum, the way Grammy LuLu would hum to me when I couldn't sleep. I strained after the barely audible sound. I hadn't caught when it started. Its presence made its prior absence known. Some people are always with a tune, I guess. The music just follows them. Celeste had that.

"I want to introduce you to someone." I heard Mr. Barno say. I opened my eyes. Celeste's outstretched hand pointed at me. I got to my feet.

Eagerly, she shook my hand and squished her eyes into crescents. "Heard a lot about you."

"Hi. Hey." I cleared my throat. "Really? It's, uh. It's wonderful to meet you, Mrs. Barno."

She bounced and gave me this big hug. "Thank you."

"I didn't do anything."

Celeste grasped my elbows and, man, did she have a tight grip. "You're exactly how I pictured you."

I tried to pull away because, you know, I was hugging someone who was, well… dead. Dead, dead. But she didn't let me. She hugged me, tighter this time. "You've been looking after my rascal and, oh, from the bottom of my heart, thank you, thank you. I can't do it all by myself, you know. He's a child, really."

"Sweetheart," Mr. Barno said, "careful not to crush the air right out of him."

"Oh hush, Lex," she teased.

I smiled, trying to stifle any tears. "Your husband saved me."

"No." Celeste danced over to Alexis and kissed his cheek. "No, you saved him."

"Barno!" A voice somewhere far away called. It called repeatedly, "Barno! Barno where the hell are you?"

Celeste took Alexis' hands and rubbed them. "I have to go."

He kissed her on the forehead, sniffed her hair, and without saying a word, turned and climbed down through the hole in the floor. I leaned over and watched him descend the ladder. At the base of the tree, I saw them. Flowers. Purple and yellow. Each flower was made of layer upon layer of pedals that fanned out in concentric circles.

I turned back to wave goodbye to Celeste, but she was gone.

I scrambled to the railing. And from up there I could see my parents' heads just over the privacy fence. I ducked.

"Open up, Barno."

I heard the fence gate open.

Mr. Barno's voice: "Can I help you?"

My dad's voice: "We're Nolan's parents."

Mr. Barno: "Welcome. How are you?"

Dad: "Listen up, pal. We don't want you corrupting our son."

Mr. Barno: "Corrupting?"

Mom: "We've lost one child already. We simply cannot afford to lose another."

Dad: "You don't even remember us, do you?"

Mr. Barno: "I'm sorry. Eh. It's not—"

Mom: "Stay away from Nolan. You hear me? If he comes by here for that interview, tell him you changed your mind. You can't do it."

Mr. Barno: "Oh yes, Terry, right? And Nancy? I remember you both from—"

Mom: "Enough with the niceties. He's my son. He's got a future. College. A career. A family. You're not going to ruin his future the way you did—"

Dad: "That's right, pal."

Mr. Barno: "Mr. and Mrs. Sussman, please. I hate to be the one to tell you this, but it's not your life. It's Nolan's. It's not your problem to worry about, it's his opportunity to grow. Why don't you try putting a little more faith in Nolan and a little more faith in yourselves and see what happens for your son?"

I heard the gate shut. Then, banging and my dad yelling, "Don't you shut that! Don't you dare shut that!"

I squinted between some boards and saw Mr. Barno hunched in the yard. I lay on my back and tried to press myself into the boards, hoping my parents wouldn't see me, and gazed up through the branches.

I heard a car racing in the distance. Closer. Closer.

I sat up. Opened my eyes—didn't realize they had been closed. Peered over the edge. It was dark, starry, the moon pinned to the edge of the sky. A flash of light whirled around a corner and in an instant, I saw her. Celeste. Knuckling the wheel of the Chevy convertible. Alexis in the passenger seat, his hands braced on the dashboard—their eyes wide in terror, bodies leaning against the momentum of the skidding car, as if their counterweight could keep the car on the road.

The Chevy screeched onto the grass. Toward the tree. The tree I was in. Up in a fort, clutching the railing, bracing—just as Celeste and Alexis were—for the lights and steel barreling below me. Then a scream. "God, no!"

A thunderous crash. The tree quaked. I was thrown onto my back. Stiff. Unable to breathe. As I lay paralyzed looking out into the night sky, I thought I saw purple and yellow flower pedals puff up into the air just beyond the edge of the tree fort, then flutter down.

Finally, I could breathe. Could move. I clawed my way to the far edge of the fort to see what I knew I would, Mr. Barno and Celeste scattered in the grass. *I've got to help them*, I thought. I dragged myself to the hole in the fort where the down ladder was. But when I poked my head through, I wasn't there anymore—wasn't at the accident. It wasn't night. I was looking down into Mr. Barno's backyard. It was light out. Mr. Barno was stretched out in the grass, holding his chest, wheezing, "Call an ambulance."

The gate swung open. My dad slid down beside Mr. Barno. I dropped through the ladder hole to the ground. Dad saw me, and before he could get mad, he melted into a look of relief. He tossed me the keys, "Start the car."

At the hospital, I plunked into a chair beside my parents and waited and waited. I texted Gabi to distract myself and told her what happened. She said she was coming to the hospital. I didn't know what to say other than to ask her if her mom would be mad. She just replied that she was on her way.

Finally, a short nurse in scrubs and a blue cap with yellow smileys on it approached us. "I'm Savannah. You're the family?"

My dad started to say no, but I blurted, "Yes."

"Alexis had another heart attack. The good news is that he survived it. Look, his cognition will presumably further deteriorate. The dementia is, look, well when the brain doesn't get enough oxygen… As you know, dementia is progressive. This event will probably accelerate that. Frankly, we're not sure how much more his heart can take."

"Oh," I gulped.

"He told us that you've been helping look after him. Is it, Nathan?"

"Nolan. Yeah, yes. I have."

"Has he seemed unusually confused? Hallucinations. Imagining things. Anything of that nature?"

I scratched my neck. "No, no, not that I can think of. When can we see him?"

"Now's fine. Ready to come back?"

Dad held Mom's hand on his lap and they both nodded, Mom motioning me to follow the nurse. Just then, Gabi scuttled through the automatic doors. She raced over and threw her arms around me. Over her shoulder,

I saw my mom give me two thumbs up while my dad did this erratic shoulder dance.

Mr. Barno shared a room with two other people. The nurse pulled back a wraparound curtain. Inside, a breathing mask palmed Barno's face and there were tubes and beeps and clanks and big machines and bags hanging on rolling coat hangers. It took me a while to get myself to look at him. Gabi and I squeezed into two chairs right by his bedside. I took his hand, careful not to touch the tape and the tube sticking out of it.

He seemed to try to smile, his voice muffled by the mask. "Who is this good soul to your left?"

"My friend Gabi."

Gabi leaned toward the bed. "Nice to meet you, Mr. Barno."

We sat beneath the beeps and clanks and just watched each other. And in between the noises of the machines, I listened for the sound of Celeste—that low, gentle hum. But I couldn't hear it. I wasn't sure if it was because it was gone or because there was too much clatter out in the hall.

Mr. Barno fell asleep for a while. When he awoke, I asked him, "Why did you do that, at the accident? Why did you say you were driving?"

"It happened. Meeting Celeste helped you to fully accept her and I with compassion, flaws and all. I am glad you finally saw everything."

"Why? Why did you say you were driving?"

"Because I loved her."

"I know you loved her. But she was. She was gone. She was. You didn't know that then, huh? You were trying to protect her, thinking she'd live?"

Mr. Barno lifted himself slightly off the inclined bed and moaned. Finally, he said, "I knew. I saw. A jacket over a body means only one thing."

"Then why do it? She was gone and—" I couldn't say it.

"Couldn't have spent time in prison for killing someone while drinking and driving? I saw the boy before we hit him. On the ladder. Last thing I saw. The car flattening him. The look in his eyes."

I realized Gabi's hand was on my shoulder. I wiped my nose. "Then why?"

"Celeste was, we were trying to start a family. She was pregnant. And, after her mom's sudden death, Celeste started sneaking drinks. She was ashamed. She knew the risks. But she couldn't stop. I didn't want her memory tarnished."

I studied the numbers and letters on the machine that beeped, but I couldn't make sense of them.

Mr. Barno eased back into the bed and said, "She was a good person. She would've been a great mother. She was redeemable. And we had an appointment lined up to help her. And, and then the accident. Back then I feared that people wouldn't forgive her. That they wouldn't allow for redeemable."

I cupped my neck. "So you took the fall? Spent 25 years in prison for a crime you didn't commit?"

Mr. Barno tapped the bed as if nodding with his hand. "I let Celeste take the car keys."

"You must have really loved your wife, Mr. Barno," Gabi said.

"I did and I do." He closed his eyes, his frail head sinking into his pillow. "I don't regret my decision. But I admit I was wrong back then."

"About what?" I asked.

"People can forgive. People can change. It takes a lot. And it's slow. But it's possible. Isn't it Nolan?"

I shook the bed a little so he wouldn't fall asleep. "What kind of tree is that in your yard?"

"An oak tree," he sighed, eyes closed.

"No, I mean—"

"What is it about young people today? They want an answer for everything. Back when I taught, life wasn't about explaining. It was about exploring. Exploring wonders—music, the night sky, nature, art, the human experience."

"At least tell me where it came from," I pleaded.

"The tree Celeste crashed the car into. Before the trial, I was out on bail. I gathered some acorns that must've been shaken loose by the crash. I planted one in my backyard."

Gabi whispered to me, asking me what I was talking about. "I'll tell you later," I whispered back.

"Hi, I'm. My name is. Eh."

When I looked back at Mr. Barno, his eyes were open. He had peeled the mask from his face and was smiling.

"Uh." I turned to Gabi whose palms were up. I cleared my throat. "Uh."

"Welcome. Please excuse the mess, we're renovating." Mr. Barno held a gaunt hand up for me to shake. "My wife should be here any moment. She must've run off somewhere. One second. Celeste, Celeste, where are you?"

After a moment I mustered, "Hi. Hello."

Hello," Mr. Barno echoed. "You are?"

"I'm Nolan," I said, taking his hand. "And this is Gabi."

Twenty Seven

For the rest of the week, Dad let me off work early so I could visit Mr. Barno in the hospital. From the little I understood of what the doctors and nurses were saying, Mr. Barno was receiving close monitoring of his heart and his dementia—the thing that was wrong with his memory.

I Googled dementia and learned what I could. It started with a few hints—forgetfulness, losing track of time, getting lost—and progressed to greater confusion, asking the same questions over and over, and an inability to make good decisions. Some folks became messy and some even stopped taking showers and brushing their teeth.

Eventually, people with dementia would lose time and would even lose familiar people. *Will Barno lose Celeste? Will he lose me?* Some people with dementia may imagine things or hallucinate. The doctors asked me to look for warning signs of depression—they gave me a brochure with info on that—and aggression.

Finally, Mr. Barno would be unable to care for himself. He'd likely be stuck in bed in need of full-time care. And his mind and body would fade away, unable to remember what he ate or how to control the bowels that got rid of the waste.

At dinner on Sunday, I blurted out, "I got to save Mr. Barno's house. It's all he's got."

The inspiration for that outburst? Seeing we were no longer eating meatloaf. And I knew that was because Mom was back at the real estate office working for the evil empire.

Mom cut into her chicken. "It's for the better. He'll be put up in a nursing home where he can get proper care."

"What, so he can die in some cold room with cinder block walls?"

Mom chewed. "I don't know, hun. But he can't stay at that house."

And I almost said, 'Yeah, because you're helping Mr. Lewis sell it out from under him.' But I didn't have the energy for a fight and I didn't want one anyway. I wanted harmony. I wanted help. So I said, "It's special. That tree in his yard is special. I don't know how to explain it to you. But, he uses it to... This is going to sound crazy. Somehow. Alright. You see, somehow he uses the tree to talk to his wife. To see his wife, even."

Mom put her fork down. "I know he may think that. You have to understand, Nolan, Mr. Barno is very sick. His mind is broken in a way. He's sort of lost between reality and somewhere else."

"No, I—" I halted myself and searched for a logical way to explain to my parents that I experienced the magic of the tree, too—that I did the loopy thing. Yet, I could find no rational explanation. Maybe I was losing my mind too—sort of lost between reality and somewhere else like Barno was.

Am I crazy?

No. Mr. Barno said I wasn't. No labels.

But, if he's not all there mentally, maybe he's not the best judge of that stuff. Maybe I really am lost between reality and somewhere else.

Yeah, but you could say that about most people.

That doesn't mean they time travel or meet people who are dead.

Look, there is something to that tree. There may not be an answer—may not be an explanation. Just be okay with that and trust what happened.

A week later, Mr. Barno was still in the hospital. I needed to run. So I ran and ran. South past Neil's house, past Branson's trailer, past the paper mill, then north past Main Street through the historic parts, then up through the neighborhoods past the street sign that read 'Bridge ¼ mile,' and up to the car bridge. I ran across it for the first time since Sarah left. I had always been too afraid to see the other side on foot. Many times, I had been over the bridge in a car—my doctor was up that way, for example—but never on foot. This time, I didn't even stop when I got to the spot where Sarah had gotten into Rafe's car and disappeared.

I ran and ran up to where the orchards were, where the train came from. And when I saw the train tracks cutting past the apple trees, I turned around and ran back across the bridge and into Paxson.

I ran to Mr. Barno's house. I knew it would be empty. I wanted to see it as much as I could before its magic was gone and it was just a house on a street in a neighborhood with an ordinary tree fort in the back-yard. Somewhere in America. Some town where kids went to school and the world just kept spiraling and there was nothing to wonder about, to be in awe of— no difference between the world as it appeared and as it really was. Or, maybe I was wrong. Maybe there were Smart Kids in other towns too. Maybe the Smart Kids in those towns had their own Mr. Barno and they were going to do something to make things a little better.

When I got to Mr. Barno's house, I sat on the drive-way—the driveway that I had resealed way, way back in the summer. A lifetime ago. And as I sat there, I realized something. The Lewis Real Estate Agency sign was gone. "That bastard sold the house already?" I asked the asphalt.

I got the hell out of there. Felt sick. Leaned against a tree a ways down the street and retched. Nothing came out. I was empty.

I ran past Juanita's Taqueria to see if Skyler and Branson or maybe even Neil was there. They weren't. So I ran home. Mom was in the driveway bringing groceries in. "Let me grab some bags," I said.

"Oh, don't worry about it, hun."

"Nah, Ma. Happy to help."

Mom carried bags inside while I went to the trunk. As I grabbed two bags that sat on top of a lawn blanket in the trunk, the corner of the blanket got brushed aside and I saw something red under it. I pulled the blanket back to find a Lewis Real Estate Agency sign with a small sign chained to it that said 'Listing Coming Soon.' I covered the sign, smoothed out the blanket, grabbed the grocery bags, and went inside.

For Halloween, Gabi wanted to hang out and watch the *Scream* movies. There were like 10 of them. I told her I'd watch the first *Scream* if she'd watch the first *Friday the 13th*. And she agreed as long as I promised to watch all the other *Scream* movies someday. And I said, okay, as long as she promised to watch the other *Friday the 13th* movies someday. So we had ourselves a deal. Problem was, where to watch? I wasn't about to go to her house because I figured her mom hated me for hanging with Mr. Barno. And, you know, having a girl over to my house—even if we were just friends— was pretty freaking terrifying considering, of all things, the existence of my parents.

Then, something extraordinary happened. My parents informed me that they were going to some party— the first in the history of their marriage, so far as I could tell. So I sheepishly asked if Gabi could come over and watch *Scream*. And my dad did his shoulder dance and took me aside and—super awkward—gave me 'The Talk' (Which he'd already given me when I was in eighth grade. This time, The Talk consisted of five minutes of me pining for a lobotomy as my dad tried to 'tell it like it is, son' by painting quite the picture with language like 'pleasure,' 'jimmy hat,' 'venereal disease,' and 'baby daddy').

Mom claimed there were security cameras in the home and that they would be watching us through a smartphone app the whole time. She warned that I better not try anything slick or smooth or handsy on Gabi. Which, of course, I wasn't going to try because we were just friends. Except now, I was super paranoid even though I knew my parents were too cheap to spend money on security cameras.

Anyway, I got a bunch of candy and some sodas and was waiting for Gabi to arrive when I started thinking about Sarah. Sarah loved Halloween. I mean she was obsessed with it. She was the one who showed me all the *Friday the 13th* and the *Nightmare on Elm Street* movies and a bunch of others I don't remember when I was way too young to be seeing that stuff. And then I thought about how scary it must be for Mr. Barno to be lost in his own head way up in that hospital with its beeps and clanks. Then I thought about Sarah again. And I decided to do it—to sit down and write her a letter and mail it to her dad, Craig, at the Mecklenburg address she had left in her note. I didn't know if my letter would get to her or not. I just knew I had to try.

I mailed Sarah the following letter and I put my email address at the bottom of it and asked her to write back.

Dear Sarah,

I hope you're doing okay and that you're a big-time music star now. I've tried to find you online but I bet you go by a stage name and that's why I can't find you. What's your stage name? I want to look up your band. I hope the world is everything you want it to be. Most importantly, I hope that you're happy.

I think I'm happy now. At least I'm happier than I've been in a long time and I know that I'm getting there. That's what counts.

There was this teacher at Paxson High School. He wasn't there while you were a student. He was in prison. I wish he was there while you were there, though. I think he would have been great for you and maybe you'd still be around if he had been your teacher.

He's out of prison now. And we're friends. He's helped me a lot. And I guess I've helped him, too. I guess that's what we need. To help each other, I mean, so we can all get through alright.

I wished you were here so many times I can't even count. To answer your question, I don't have a girlfriend. I do have a friend that's a girl. She's really great. She's kind of my best friend right now. The best thing about her is that we lift each other up. I think that's better than having a girlfriend.

Maybe I'm a crow like you. Or maybe I'm not.

Maybe that's what I can do: lift people up. Maybe that's all there is to do. Try to be a little light in an overcast world. Try to be that inch of peace between the sounds.

I used to feel so sad. Sad that you were gone. Sad that Mom and Dad never kiss. Sad that no one's parents ever kiss. Sad that when I'm a parent, I'll never kiss my wife. But I think now that I will kiss my wife. And I'll kiss her a lot and I'll mean it. I'll kiss her till the day I die. It feels like doing that kind of thing really can help. It really can spread out to other people. Does that make sense? Like, if I kiss my wife a lot then maybe if I ever have kids, they'll kiss their spouses till the day they die. Then their kids will do the same. And if there's more kissing, then maybe there's more other stuff. Sorry. I just made myself laugh. I don't mean that kind of stuff. I mean nice things like people being kind. Not just holding doors for others, but really taking a risk to choose to do something good in the world. Not the easy thing. I have to be honest with you, Sarah. I think you did the easy thing. You ran away. You didn't talk to

Mom and Dad about your feelings. You didn't hear their side of the story.

I don't know if you'll ever get this letter. If you do, I want you to know that I'm telling you this stuff not because I don't want you to come back. I'm telling it to you because I do. I love you no matter what choices you made and I think that's what a family is. I don't know him, but I don't think Rafe is your family. Families don't hit each other. They talk to each other.

I used to get afraid that there were no families left anymore. My stomach would hurt and I didn't like to think about any of that. Maybe I got rid of the pain by making new pain. Thing is, I don't know if I can get rid of the pain anymore. Maybe all we can do, crows or not, is make more good, more joy, more friends, more memories. More kissing the people we love.

I've been told that we don't even see most of the miracles in our lives. You were a miracle in my life and I never realized it until you were gone. I want that miracle back.

I'm sorry about Rafe's car. I was trying to save you. I just didn't know how.

Love,
Your full brother. Me. Nolan

The first Friday of November, in Introduction to Journalism, Mrs. de León hounded me about the interview I was supposed to be getting with Mr. Barno. I told her about the heart attack and the hospital and she pulled tissues from her drawer and wiped her face. Then she got up and walked out of the room for a few minutes. When she came back, she apologized to the class. Her makeup was smeared and no one said anything about that. They just worked because that's what comforted Mrs. de León: work.

Mrs. de León had me stay after class that day and we agreed to play things by ear and see how Mr. Barno recovered. Given the circumstances, she said she'd pair me up with another student on one of the other stories. However, I told her I'd get her something on the Protect the Youth of Paxson story, interview with Mr. Barno or not. And she agreed to that.

I wanted to ask Mrs. de León to help me help Mr. Barno with the bank situation and the money. It's just, I figured it was too late. I should've thought of that before Mr. Lewis' real estate agency sold Barno's house out from under him.

I asked her why she didn't speak out in support of Mr. Barno. She said she was a journalist and journalists need to stay objective. Everyone has their own reasons, I suppose, but part of me felt like hers was a load of crap.

It was really weird being in class with Skyler. In the classes we had together since Homecoming, we both just sort of pretended that the other person didn't exist. The same thing happened with Branson and Neil. It was as if we never knew each other. That hurt even worse than it would have hurt if all of them were mean or rude to me—because I know what it's like when someone goes away and basically doesn't exist anymore. It's quiet and empty and you're alone with the gray thoughts that knock around in your head. And you can wait and wait to hear from the people who go away and hope they email you if you mail them a letter and hope they come back. But, see, when you check your email five times a day and you haven't heard from them, you know what gone means.

In Mr. Green's class Friday afternoon, the quote on the chalkboard was written in big block letters. It read: "I am tired and sick of war. Its glory is all moonshine. It is only those who have neither fired a shot nor heard the shrieks and groans of the wounded who cry aloud for blood, for vengeance, for desolation. War is hell." – William Tecumseh Sherman.

Twenty Eight

When I was a kid, I thought being a kid really sucked. I thought when I was a teenager life would finally be good. Then I became a teenager. And boy did that really suck. I mean, it was worse than being a kid. And I thought, *When I'm grown up, life will finally be good. I'll have freedom and money and all that wonderful stuff.*

Then I met Mr. Barno.

I saw him stuck in his house after he came home from the hospital. I set up his bed frame and mattress in the TV room facing the floor-to-ceiling windows and the sliding glass door. I propped him up so he could look out into the backyard at the tree fort. He lay there, his eyes in a haze, and I thought, *Everything is so fragile. Why did I wish all that time away?*

He peed himself. I didn't notice at first until the smell of the urine soured the room. The nurses at the hospital had bathed him so he didn't smell of body odor anymore. So the urine, I noticed the smell pretty quick.

I helped him change and although he was mostly bones and skin that flopped around, he was heavy and he didn't help much. I did most of the lifting and pulling and zipping and buttoning. Amid all that, I had to get the sheets off and change them.

During the changing of clothes and bedsheets, he said to me, "I don't want you to witness anymore."

Some at-home nurse was going to start coming every day to help look after him. There was a mix-up or something and the nurse wasn't scheduled to arrive until that evening.

Mr. Barno's smile was shaky now. I don't mean like tremors. I mean like it sort of came and went and sometimes it didn't seem to have anything behind it. I sat in a chair beside him and read from a book he wanted me to read, *Siddhartha* by Hermann Hesse, while Dodger curled at the foot of the bed.

The house was cold. I put a few blankets on Mr. Barno. Then, I put one over my legs.

"What can we do to change everyone's mind?" I asked.

"What about?"

"The whole town thinks you're this bad person. No one knows you didn't kill your wife and those kids. No one gets that the tree is special. No one believes that you've helped so many students."

"People reflect back what they get—anger, sorrow, violence, greed. If you show them kindness and love, eventually they will give back kindness and love. Be patient."

I pulled the blanket further up my lap. "Why's it so cold in here?"

"Dahlia."

"What?" I got up and tried to turn up the heat. Nothing happened.

"I was married once. Eh. I ever tell you that?"

I sat back down. "Yeah. Yes."

"My wife loved dahlia flowers. Purple and yellow."

I picked up the book and read for a while.

"You're a good soul," Mr. Barno said when I put down the book.

"You are," I replied.

"I'm going to miss you, Nolan."

"I'm going to miss you."

Mr. Barno wiped tears. "You have a kind heart. Scarred, but kind. I sensed that about you."

I rubbed the back of my hand against my nose and sniffled. "Is that why you asked Principal Anand to give me one more chance?"

"Soon, I won't be able to tell you that I remember. But it will always be in here." He pointed to his temple.

I took his hand. It reminded me of a crumpled hamburger wrapper. "I know."

"You go the rest of the way now," he said.

"No. I'll come by all the time."

He shook his head. "You take it the rest of the way. It's your job now."

"What job? What do you mean?"

"You are not alone. I'm always with you, Noah."

"Nolan."

"Did you build that?"

"What?"

"That tree house."

That's when I knew there was no more time for happiness lessons. No more of Mr. Barno left for me to take. I just couldn't do that to him. I wanted it. I wanted to know everything he knew—wanted to live a life as open and beautiful as he had chosen to live his despite the cracks, holes, loss, and anguish. Wanted the peace. The acceptance. The ability to touch the world with wonder.

Thing was, I could not drain that man by asking him to remember what was further and further away from him. And I would not dump my problems at his feet. This was his time now, whatever he had left, to use as he pleased. To be with his wife. When he felt a little better, I would take him up to the tree fort. Yes, that's what I'd do.

I knew I was one of the lucky ones—the kids who got to know Mr. Barno and to learn from him while we were young enough that we still had some heart in us. For us, losing our hearts wasn't a certainty the way it was for so many young people. If I had never gotten to know Mr. Barno, well, let me say it this way: if you've got some heart in you, there's always a chance it can be saved.

I was sad. I don't think that's the right word, actually.

I knew it was my path now.

I suppose that is the magical thing about wisdom— like everything beautiful, wisdom is always within our grasp.

I came back the next day. Iris, the at-home nurse, used her full frame to blockade the door. She said Mr. Barno was resting. I told her that it was against the law not to let me see him, but I had no idea really. She told me she knew I wasn't related to Mr. Barno. Apparently, there had been a search for relatives and it turned out that he didn't have any that were living. I told Nurse Iris I was sorry and when I was walking away she said without a trace of empathy in her voice that it would be okay if I visited once a week. I asked her if I could come by on Monday afternoons since that was our usual time together and she said that maybe, just maybe, that would help Mr. Barno remember me better on those days.

So the next week I came back on Monday afternoon. This time my dad drove me. He waited for me in Mr. Barno's driveway to, "Keep an eye on things."

I asked Nurse Iris to let me take Mr. Barno up into the tree fort. She refused and said it was a horrible idea. "Too much stress. In his condition? Not a chance. A fall. No, it'd be too much."

Well, when Nurse Iris went into the kitchen, I snuck Mr. Barno a cell phone. "Hide this," I whispered. "My phone number is programmed into it. You just have to turn it on and press star and one. It will automatically call me. If you ever need help, just call me or push this button and you can type in a message and send it to me."

He gazed at the phone. Didn't say anything. It might as well have been a rock. I shoved it under his pillow and said, "Don't let her find it. It's not a smartphone, anyway. It's a dumb phone. It just does calls and text messaging."

Mr. Barno didn't yell or get aggressive the way the doctors said he might. His body reminded me of a balloon that was losing air. When I stood to leave, he pointed to something on a little table Nurse Iris had set up next to the bed to hold tissues and a cup with a straw in it.

"For me?"

He nodded with his hand, bending the wrist up and down.

It was a notebook. Beat up. Creased. Edges rubbed away. The cover had faded block letters that read: Atlas to a Kinder Universe. I peeled the notebook open. Inside were pages and pages of notes. It was everything he had learned about life and happiness.

"You go the rest of the way now," he said. "You are not alone, Nolan. You never were. I am always with you."

———————

The Tuesday night before Thanksgiving break, I received a text from Skyler. I froze and put the phone down. I tried to think about how I had not applied to any colleges and how if I did not do it real soon, I was probably going to regret it.

A while later I picked up my phone again to look up application deadlines for Wetton College and a few state schools when I saw multiple texts from Skyler.

Skyler (8:28 pm): Nolan. Can we talk?
Skyler (8:40 pm): You around?
Skyler (8:54 pm): I'm worried about Branson.

So I replied:

Me (9:11 pm): Whats up

We got texting:

Skyler (9:12 pm): He's acting all secretive. I heard him and Neil talking about doing something called Operation Nottingham. They're planning to do it tonight.
Me (9:12 pm): What time
Skyler (9:12 pm): Don't know. We were supposed to be studying. I wasn't supposed to hear.
Skyler (9:12 pm): Do you know what he's up to?

Me (9:12 pm): Ask him

Skyler (9:12 pm): I don't know how. He got all sketchy and went outside when he was talking with Neil.

Me (9:13 pm): Whats your question

Skyler (9:13 pm): Nolan. Please. Tell me what's going on.

Me (9:13 pm): Can't tell you over text

Skyler (9:13 pm): Please

Me (9:14 pm): Look I got it under control. Just dont ever say anything about this to anyone. Ever. Got it

Skyler (9:14 pm): Ok

Skyler (9:14 pm): I promise

Skyler (9:15 pm): Thank you

After my parents went to bed and I waited the customary amount of time for the house to fall still, I snuck out and raced toward Mr. Lewis' house. I wasn't too sure I'd get there in time, but I had to try. I couldn't let Branson and Neil blow up their lives and end up in prison for stealing a bunch of stupid money.

I got to the gate of the Lewis property and paused to catch my breath. I watched the moisture clouds collect in front of me. Each one momentary, vanishing, leaving me alone—the only warmth in the frigid, charcoal night. The low clouds scraped against the trees overhead. Maybe that's where the moisture from my breath went: up, rushing toward something it knew.

It took me three tries to get over that damn stone wall. I scrambled through the trees. I stopped. Saw the silhouette of the fox. It had its head in a hole, its bushy tail spiked up. The fox yanked back out of the hole and shook something.

I kept on—on to the lookout spot.

No Neil. No Branson.

The fog settling over the Lewis property obscured the orange pulse of a fire in a fire pit in the driveway. I crept toward the fire and hid behind the large rock in the landscaping at the edge of the driveway. Through the haze, I saw Mr. Lewis. He sat alone on the other side of the fire pit. Music played from inside the garage—the same woman we had heard months before continued to spill her pain. Mr. Lewis wore a winter cap and a big maroon coat. He was clutching a bottle and every now and then he raised it to his mouth and sloshed his head back. There was something leaning against the chair beside him. It looked like a walking stick. The security camera mounted above him was a faint white blotch.

I listened for the sound of Neil or Branson but everything was muffled by the vapor in the air.

I settled in. My adrenaline cooled. Shivering commenced. I spied over the rock at Mr. Lewis. His head was rolled back, his body drooping to the side. *Passed out drunk. Time to go home*, I thought. *Either the guys postponed Operation Nottingham, wised up and decided it wasn't worth it, or they already pulled it off.*

I readied myself to leave and stole one last look at old Mr. Lewis just to be certain that he was still out. And I could see now that it was no walking stick leaning against the chair.

It was a rifle.

My chest rattled. *Holy shit*, I thought. *So it was old Mr. Lewis I heard shooting a gun that time Neil played war while we were tubing on the river.*

I snuck across the lawn to the lookout spot and through the woods toward the stone wall. I heard something. *The fox?* I froze. Crouched. Slowed my breathing and opened my ears. Listened. Branches crunched to my left. *How far?* I couldn't tell. Too big to be a fox. *A bear? Maybe.* I spread my eyelids as wide as they could go and tried to see through the film between the trees. *Be still. Maybe it won't notice you.*

No, it's not a bear.

I inched toward the sound, slithering over roots, rocks, and fallen branches. I stalked it from a distance. Finally, I stooped behind the trunk of a fallen tree. Maybe a dozen yards away, lurking at the edge of the woods, were the frames of two people—one towering and lanky, the other squat and uneven.

The tall one stood and jogged away from me into the grass and toward the driveway. From the way he moved, I knew. It was Branson.

I surged to my feet. Scrambled through the trees after him. Charged past Neil who was huddled in a ditch, arms cocked on its ledge, eyes locked into his binoculars.

I chased after Branson as we bobbed through the fog. Closing in. Closer. Closer.

I jumped—a soldier in some war movie Neil was watching—and tackled Branson. Our bodies smacked the grass. Rolled.

A sparkle. An explosion.

Its crack reverberated through the trees and rocketed on, out over the river toward the orchards and the cornfields on the other side where it dissipated into the distant mountains.

Pinned myself to the grass. Peeled my head up for a look.

The fox staggered onto the driveway and flopped to the asphalt. Its mouth lay open. Blood pooled by its belly.

On our feet, Branson and I caught a glimpse of each other. Nothing more. And we zoomed across the grass and into the trees. We flung ourselves over the mound into the ditch beside Neil.

"Grab your gear, let's go," I barked at Neil.

"I can't," he stammered. "Can't make it fast enough. Go on without me."

Branson scooped Neil under his shoulder and started to lug him through the woods. I tucked under Neil's other shoulder. The three of us jerked our way through the craggy forest, the light of the Lewis property dimming behind us with every tree we passed. We hoisted Neil over the stone wall. Then Branson helped me topple over. On the other side, Neil collapsed. Branson vaulted over. He and I never left Neil's side as we lurched along the roadside culvert to safety.

We huffed and panted in the trees at the bend in the road at a little clearing that was originally designated as our fallback position for Operation Nottingham.

No one talked. We didn't have the air to.

When I could finally steady myself, I faced Branson. He stared at me. Then he smiled. He grabbed my collar and squeezed me to him, his long arms folded around me. "Yo," he said. "My bad."

"My bad," I echoed. And I would have cried. Really, I wanted to. Problem was, I was a teenage guy. And as much as I tried to let it all flow out, my body wasn't ready to do that in front of them.

Branson held me tight for a minute. And it wasn't a dude hug. It was, like, a real hug. Then he leaned back, put a fist out, and said, "Midnight Warlords forever."

I bumped him back. Neil joined us, and we did the trifecta, the rare and cherished triple fist bump. But it just wasn't the same anymore.

Twenty Nine

In a way, I'm like Gabi. I also don't like heavy coats. That's what I was thinking as I climbed the ladder up to the rafters under the train bridge. My fingers were pink and swollen from the frozen metal ladder and the breeze up there wasn't at all intimidated by my hoodie.

I wanted to be home—warm in bed. Full of the Thanksgiving turkey Dad grilled, and Mom's cranberry sauce, and the stuffing Aunt Jennifer made from scratch, and the pecan pies I have baked every year by myself since Sarah left me as the lone family baker. I was full of all that food—just not in bed.

To get to the ladder, Gabi and I had climbed over a barbed-wire fence and slid along a cliff's ledge.

Gabi had texted me an hour or so before while I was playing Mario Kart in my room. She told me to meet her at Overlook Park at 9 pm. Dad was passed out downstairs on the couch, done in by the turkey, beer, and football combo. Mom had driven to Aunt Jennifer's to stay for the night so they could get up all early and do the whole insane door-buster shopping thing.

When I got to Overlook Park, Gabi pawed at the air and said, "Follow me."

We climbed up the ladder onto a maintenance platform on the bridge—a platform under the train tracks that I had no clue existed. I didn't even know about the ladder.

The platform was the size of a small car. It had a railing bar wrapped around it that was waist-high with no vertical slats to pin you in. There was this one horizontal bar thinner than my wrist to keep you from falling 200 feet or so to a wet and rocky death in the river below. *Terrifying. Absolutely terrifying.*

I couldn't see the river in the dark, but I heard it sliding by, breaking with a catatonic gurgle against the nearby bridge pier.

The maintenance platform was tucked near the first concrete pier between two baseline rows of brown steel triangles that ran the length of the bridge. The triangles were configured into giant boxes. Crosswise, support bars connected the two rows. Above us, maybe 20 feet up, two rows ran parallel to the baseline rows. Upon them, the wooden railroad ties of the train tracks stretched the width of the bridge.

Gabi sat cross-legged on the grate flooring. "You need to invest in a coat."

"Top of my Christmas list, for sure, if we're going to keep hanging out in places like this. Just always hate how puffy they make me feel," I said. "You're not cold?" She was wearing a jean jacket.

"I told you, I run hot."

I sat down across from her and rubbed my hands together inside my hoodie's front pocket. "You're fine, seriously?"

"As long as my head and hands are covered, I stay warm."

"I can see how the beanie and gloves help." I smiled. I was shivering so much I doubt she could tell.

Gabi's gloved fingers spidered along the grate, pressing into the holes every now and then, exploring them.

"So what's up?"

"Shh!"

I pulled my knees to my chest for warmth. "Don't know how quiet I can be with my teeth chattering."

She smiled, her head tilted. "Do your best."

We sat in silence for a long time—together, way up above the river, two kids who had soared out of our little town into a space between the lands. *We're in No Land,* I thought. *No land.* It had a completely different meaning with Gabi.

Looking at it from this angle, the town did seem historic. Candlelit. I had never thought about its history much. Troops had fought and died here. Slaves had escaped north across the shallow waters here. Prisoners had been dragged south across after battles. This was contested land. Full of contested ideas. Ambitions. Dreams. Visions of the future. Interpretations of the past.

"Ever since that day at the hospital, I've been thinking a lot about Mr. Barno," Gabi said. "You texted me that he was helping you. What did ya mean?"

I told her—told her about the tree project and the happiness lessons. I explained about Celeste and filled in the holes from what Gabi overheard at Mr. Barno's hospital bedside. I explained how Mr. Barno saved me. How he gave me hope.

"I want that," she said. "Hope."

"Boomerang?"

She grinned at the edges of her lips and it brought life to her soft cheeks and bronze eyes. "Absolutes. Boomerang."

"You have hope. I see it in you," I said. "Choose to see it, too."

"Thought I knew who I was. Spent years living their life. Turns out, I wasn't that person. So weird, right? You meet someone and poof."

In a lot of ways, I'm like Gabi, I thought.

She held out a hand. I scooched closer and took it. "Do ya know why we're here?" she asked.

I didn't.

"This is where Joshua, my uncle, fell to his death. Twenty-six years ago on Thanksgiving night. My mom swears that Mr. Barno pushed him. I have my doubts. After all the things you said about Mr. Barno, would he really do that? I had to see this place for myself—this place that gashed my mom and left her scarred. Angry. Afraid. When my mom remarried, she went back to her maiden name, Meyers, and had mine changed to Meyers from my dad's last name, Lee. It was to honor her brother and to keep the Meyers name alive in Paxson. I remember seeing Meyers when I wrote my name on my assignments and thinking that was really cool at the time. Now what I see is this thing that happened so long ago that preoccupies my mom—that she's so obsessed with that she can't see any other pain. She can't see anything anymore, just herself."

I felt my phone in my pocket and thought I should text Mr. Barno. He would know what to say. He could come to the bridge and calm Gabi. He could tell us what really happened. Somehow, I stopped those thoughts. I pulled my hand out of my pocket. "I'm so sorry," I said.

"People think they need an enemy, someone to blame for their unhappiness. I felt that way for a long time—was searching for the enemy and finding it at every turn. I think we do that because if the enemy isn't responsible, then the only thing left is to realize that our misery is within our control. And that's a hard responsibility to face. Trust me."

"That's the smartest thing anyone at Paxson High has ever said to me." She laid down and rested her head in my lap. "I know Mr. Barno was there on the night Joshua died. My mom's got this trunk of Joshua's old stuff—recruitment letters from Penn State, Notre Dame, West Virginia University and Florida State—and inside there's a scrapbook. The scrapbook is filled with old newspaper articles about him playing football and winning Homecoming court with his high school sweetheart, a beautiful young woman with a cool name—Holiday Lewis. In the back, there's this one article and there's a quote in it from Mr. Barno who was an eyewitness to Joshua's death. Joshua was part of some after school club that Mr. Barno advised."

"Wow," I said. *That's the connection.*

"Ya know what? I think he jumped. I think Joshua was under so much pressure about which college to play football for. He was trying to please everyone. I bet he was a people pleaser, like I am, and just went along with everything everyone said and never spoke up for himself and never let people know what he really wanted. I bet that's what killed him."

I lay down next to Gabi and held her hand. I closed my eyes and listened to the river as it moved sticks and leaves downstream. That's what rivers did. And I realized, I probably would never know the specifics of what really happened up here on this platform years before. I knew in my heart that Mr. Barno didn't kill Joshua.

What mattered was the pain. And each of us has to learn that we can't prevent all pain—that we can't avoid all pain. And most importantly, we have to learn that we can live with the pain. And we can live a good life. And it's not a bad thing, a shameful thing, to find happiness again. We don't have to punish ourselves.

I wanted Gabi's mom to know that.

While we lay belly up staring at the train tracks above, I thought a few times that Gabi might've been sobbing. I don't know. Maybe it was just the sound of the river below.

"Gabi," I said.

"Yeah?"

"You taught me the difference between being attracted to someone and caring for them." I knew then that I would love Gabi forever for teaching me that, even if we drifted apart after high school—never stayed in touch, never spoke after graduation. Gabi Meyers was part of my story the way Mr. Barno was. We collect people. That's what we do. And who those people are carves the path of our lives. The good people and the terrible people carve the deepest. I lay there and hoped I had carved a deep enough path in Gabi's life. "Thank you. I care about you. I really do."

The day after Thanksgiving, Mom was out shopping. Dad was hungover, I think. I spent it working on the story about Mr. Barno for Mrs. de León.

It took me two weeks, using all of my class time in Introduction to Journalism and staying after school each weekday, to finish it.

One day after school I was going through all the audio I had recorded since I had met Mr. Barno—both the recordings of my time with him and the stuff I had collected around town, like the time down at the boat launch when I was texting with Skyler. I stumbled across a recording I had made but never listened to. I played it and heard the sound of the buzzing of a lawnmower.

The lawnmower stopped and I heard something else—a low hum. A sound I had heard before but couldn't decide where.

I stopped the playback and looked at the date of the recording on the screen of the Zoom recorder: August 26—the last weekend of summer.

I finger-drummed on the editing station desk. *Was that?* I played it again. *Isn't that the same sound I heard in the tree fort when I met Celeste?* I played it again. Again. *What was I doing when I recorded that?* I got up and walked through the school. The halls were empty except for a custodian mopping the floor. I wandered and wandered, down into the Administrative Wing. I remembered that day when I was trudging toward Principal Anand's office and on the other end of the hall I saw Mr. Barno in his long black coat disappearing around the corner. It turned out that Mr. Barno wasn't who I'd thought he was that day. That was for sure. But really, was anyone?

I got back to the editing station and plunked into the chair. *What was I doing? Why was I recording?* I wondered. *What space was I exploring between the sounds?* And suddenly I knew. It was the first recording I made at Mr. Barno's house—the time I had held my microphone over the privacy fence near the oak tree where Mr. Barno tended to the invisible flowers.

When I told my parents I had this big project to complete for Mrs. de León, Dad said I no longer had to help him after school. He said we were doing okay now that my mom was working again.

The only other thing I did besides work on my story for two whole weeks was visit Mr. Barno's house. I helped him pack for his move to the nursing home while my dad waited outside in the driveway. Dad canceled a few work projects and I really appreciated that he did that for me and for Mr. Barno.

On rides home, Dad didn't listen to 90s music. He listened to a lot of Van Morrison—mostly, the song "Moondance." He even played it on an old CD player in the house and it didn't even bother Mom. I thought I saw her actually sway her hips once while it was playing. I started to suspect that they were kissing each other when I wasn't around.

Nurse Iris told me that Mr. Barno would be moved two days after the New Year. Apparently, she wasn't so bad. She helped convince the bank that letting Barno stay through the holidays was in the best interest of his health. And, since they were so 'very generous' and all, they agreed. I guess no one moves over the holidays.

Every day I checked my email as soon as I got up and right before bed. No word from Sarah.

On Friday morning, with two weeks left of classes before winter break, I handed Mrs. de León a flash drive.

She thumbed her glasses up her nose. "What have we here? The interview with Mr. Barno?"

"My opus," I smiled.

Mrs. de León stood and walked over to the computer at the editing station. She plugged the flash drive in, put the earphones over her hive of hair, and listened to my two-and-a-half-minute story. She lifted the earphones off and said, "Not your opus."

I sunk.

"I want you to expand on this. Turn it into your senior project. I want more on each lesson. Also, in the beginning, expand on the backstory of Mr. Barno. The listener needs more context. Let's see, the ending is a touch soft. I think you can strengthen it. Hmm. There's more to this story. I can feel it. Dig deeper. Those critiques aside, you have something special here. And once you have really found your story, then that will be your opus."

"Okay." I sighed. "Alright. Okay. Yes. Yes. I can do that."

"I'm not going to play this as a story on the morning announcements."

"Oh."

"What you have here, it's a bigger story. It needs more space. I'll cut you a deal. Work on the edits I've suggested and expand this out into a few brief episodes. It'll be your own mini podcast. If what you produce is as good as I know it can be, you have a strong shot at being selected for the Fab Five."

"The Fab Five?"

"The top 5 senior projects from this class, the Fab Five, get presented to the school in the assembly hall the last week of classes."

I remembered those. They were a big deal. "For real? That would be awesome."

"Nolan. Have you thought about a future in audio journalism?"

"No."

"The quality of the audio production is impressive for someone so new to this. And the way you approached this from a storytelling perspective, it's emotive, powerful."

"I was just trying to explain some things," I said.

"You did, and quite well. You will explain them even better in the final product. I'm sure of it. Listen, everyone gets feedback, makes edits, and improves their work. This is your first go at it, and it shows a lot of potential. For example, I appreciate how you transitioned with the atmospheric sound effects, how you employed snippets of Mr. Barno speaking, and how you leveraged explanatory narration. Hold on a second." She got up, went to her desk, and took something out of a drawer. I followed her. She gave me a handout with a list of journalism scholarships. "The deadline for the journalism scholarships have passed. There's a scholarship to Wetton College." She pointed about halfway down the handout. "When you do the math, it covers about 75% of tuition. The school is nearby and you could live at home. That may help you save money."

"Wetton?"

"I have a friend who runs a little podcast for the *Post* down in D.C. He takes on a summer intern every year. I want you to apply. It is paid. Normally, it's for college students. Nevertheless, I'm going to write you a strong recommendation letter, send him this piece, and text him until he says yes. Who knows, maybe that internship works out and you get a little job. Then, if you like the work, next fall you could apply for the scholarship at Wetton College and maybe go to school the year after."

"Wetton?" I asked again.

"Wetton. The liberal arts college. They have a great program over there. That's where I went to college."

Thirty

Mr. Barno lay on the bed in the TV room, his feet pointed toward the tree fort that stood unused on the other side of the windows. The sky was clear—a cracked tapestry of a thousand pale blue shards that I could see through the bare tree branches.

Mom, Dad, and I were leaving the next day to drive to Uncle Mitch's house, my dad's brother in Ohio, for Christmas. The good thing about it was that my cousins always had the latest videogame systems and my uncle, who liked any excuse to set off fireworks, set off a crap ton on Christmas Eve.

I sat in the bedside chair reading *Travels with Charley: In Search of America* by John Steinbeck to a sleeping Mr. Barno. I caught the book in the window in the bookstore on Main Street and bought it for him for Christmas because I liked the cover and I liked the idea of searching for a place that was right here but also not really here at all.

In a way, the book was sort of the opposite of everything Mr. Barno had taught me. He taught me to stop searching and to start being. 'It's all right here under your nose,' is what he would say. And I guess that's why I felt like America and happiness had a lot in common. Everyone was looking for it but it was right here and they just didn't want to, or maybe they couldn't accept what it was and be okay with that.

America wasn't perfect and it wasn't a dream. And if you thought about the bad parts, then yeah, it seemed bad. Or, if you thought about the good parts, it seemed good. What I mean is, America was whatever you wanted it to be and also what you didn't. You kind of had to decide for yourself or let everyone else decide for you. The same was true for happiness.

I tried to explain my thoughts about all that to Mr. Barno as he lay in the bed, but his mind was somewhere else. And because I felt awkward rambling on, I just started reading. And then he fell asleep. So I just kept reading. I liked the book, anyway.

A couple of minutes after he fell asleep, there was a knock on the front door. Dodger jumped up and raced to the door, squawking at it. The at-home nurse, Iris, answered it. A man came in, and Nurse Iris showed him into the basement—I hadn't even realized Mr. Barno had a basement. The man was down there for a while, then he came upstairs, fiddled with the thermostat on the wall, and left. After that, the house wasn't so cold.

Maybe fifteen minutes after that guy left, there was another knock on the door. Same thing. Dodger squawked at it and Nurse Iris opened it. And I damn near dropped the Steinbeck book.

Mr. Lewis. He towered in the doorway. He took off his fedora and held it against his black wool jacket as he stepped inside. He handed both to Nurse Iris.

They say the Grim Reaper comes when you least expect it. Well, they were right. Here I am going along, living my life, reading this book about a guy and his dog in a camper, and then, bam. Caught. Busted. Toast, I thought. *No point in fighting it, it'll only drag out the pain and suffering.*

I stood and almost put my hands out in front of me as if Mr. Lewis was going to cuff me. But Mr. Lewis wasn't going to cuff me.

He was mobbed up, if ever anyone in this town was, and mob guys don't cuff you. They hit you over the head with something metal, roll you up in a rug, throw you in a trunk, and bury you in the woods by the glow of car headlights while the instrumental part of "Layla" by Derek and The Dominos plays through the open window on the stereo.

"He asleep?" Mr. Lewis asked me, tipping his head in Mr. Barno's direction.

I nodded.

Nurse Iris brought a chair in from the kitchen.

"Mind if I?"

I nodded again.

I scooted over and Mr. Lewis sat and put his head in his hands by Mr. Barno's pillow.

He sat like that for a while before he said to a sleeping Mr. Barno, "It's done, old friend. Merry Christmas. Apologies it took longer than anticipated. But the house is yours now. Dropped the cash off to the bank this morning. Wish I'd known you were dealing with this, friend——could've taken care of it sooner." He reached out and put a hand atop the blanket that covered Mr. Barno's arm. "What a year."

Holy crap, Lewis didn't sell the house, he paid off the loan, I thought. Then (And I know it's selfish but, come on, minutes earlier I was facing death by mobster), I thought, *Maybe I come out of this alive. Maybe he doesn't know we were going to steal money from him. Maybe Mr. Lewis didn't see us in the fog that night when he shot the fox. Maybe he was just shooting a fox.*

I inspected each part of Mr. Lewis as he sagged, head hung beside the bed. Crisp suit. Shiny dress shoes with gold buckles. Gold cufflinks. Gold watch. Gold rings above chewed fingernails on smooth black skin. Salt and pepper hair. Pulsing vein under his left eye. "Nurse Iris informed me that my HVAC guy came and fixed the furnace. My plumber comes tomorrow to fix the water heater. We'll have you intact before Christmas."

Mr. Lewis turned to me, his almond eyes measuring me from behind his glasses. "Not a word to anyone about any of this."

"I don't—you did something good. Why wouldn't you? I mean, don't you want people to know you're not just this—" I halted myself. *What the heck am I doing? Shut up.*

"Kid, good deeds need no attention. They speak for themselves." *Holy shit. Lewis wasn't squirreling away that money in his garage for his divorce. He was squirreling it away to pay off Mr. Barno's loan in cash. That way, the bank would think the money came from Mr. Barno and not him.*

He made a gun with one hand, pointed it at the wall, made a shooting motion, and said, "Poof." *Wait, so he does know about me and Branson and how I saved Branson before he could shoot him?*

I cowered in my chair. Mr. Lewis eased back and rested his arms on the armrests. I pretended to read *Travels with Charley*. I remembered that my dad was in his truck in the driveway. I figured, if Mr. Lewis was there to kill me, he probably whacked my dad first. After all, that would be the professional thing to do.

I got up and drifted to the window. Nonchalantly, I peeled back a corner of the newspaper. My dad was upright and alive in the truck playing games on his phone.

Back at my chair, I settled beside Mr. Lewis and, I guess because I was trying to be a brave journalist and all like Mrs. de León was teaching me to be, I asked him, "Why are you helping Mr. Barno?"

"I'm not, kid. He's helping me."

Man, that felt familiar. "What do you mean?"

Mr. Lewis pushed his lower lip out with his tongue, signaling toward Mr. Barno. "This saint has kept me going over the years." He surfaced a kerchief and polished a ring. "Young folks don't read the newspaper nowadays, correct?"

"No. Never."

"Let's just say I'm facing some personal challenges right now. I knew if someone could help me find my way through these times, it was my friend Alexis."

"Oh." *I'm not the only one who has been visiting Mr. Barno?*

"See, he and my family go way back to when he taught my daughter, Holiday. She admired him. He helped her through the hardest time of her life, losing her true love. Try and imagine that, kid. For some people, like Holiday, love is ripped away. While most of us, we're just too damn foolish to hold onto it."

"I understand," I said.

"Good old Alexis never left my daughter's side, even when he faced his own tragedy, even when they dragged him through hell and back. Wrote to her every week from behind bars, Alexis did. Now she's all grown up. Never married, no kids, but she's still with us—doing well."

"That sounds like something Mr. Barno would do," I said.

"Doesn't it?" Mr. Lewis leaned forward and covered his nose and mouth. He closed his eyes as if praying. "If you're blessed enough to have a daughter someday, kid, you'll understand how much what Alexis did for Holiday means to me."

Oh wait, I thought. *Holiday. Isn't that? Yes, Holiday Lewis. In the newspaper article that Gabi mentioned when we were on the train platform that night. Joshua Meyers and Holiday Lewis were Homecoming king and queen.*

Mr. Barno's eyes remained closed—asleep, I guess—during the long minutes that Mr. Lewis and I sat there. Nurse Iris was who knows where. Mr. Lewis reached into his suit jacket and revealed a flask. "We helped Alexis the best we could. Holiday spoke up, defended him against the bullshit rumors claiming that he had something to do with her boyfriend's death. And then, Alexis changed after the auto accident. I thought we could still help—paid for the lawyers and a forensic investigator." Mr. Lewis wrapped his fist around the armrest on my chair. "No one knows that and you'll never repeat it."

"Of course. I already forgot it."

The unopened flask hung heavily in his other hand. "The forensic investigator assured me—said, there's no way Alexis was driving based on blood, tissue and clothing fragments collected from the vehicle, not to mention where he and Celeste were found at the crash site. Alexis had a solid shot at proving his innocence." The vein under Mr. Lewis' left eye pulsed faintly. "Wouldn't let them defend him the way they could have. I tried to persuade him. Stubborn bastard wouldn't listen to reason. Never had that before, someone I couldn't persuade."

"If it means anything, I know he wasn't driving and I know he didn't kill your daughter's boyfriend."

Mr. Lewis put a hand on my shoulder and gave it a stiff pat. "Wish there was more I could've done. And now, here we are. The few of us left in his corner are losing him."

"Mr. Lewis, honestly, you've done a lot. You saved him from getting kicked out of his house. You're getting things fixed around here. Plus, it sounds like you did a ton for him back then."

"What did it accomplish, kid? Prison. Reputation ruined. A town turned on him. Nearly lost his home. Why didn't he tell me? Had to find out about it from someone at the bank."

Mt. Lewis unscrewed the cap and eyed the open flask. I watched it fill the space as Mr. Barno slept.

"Mr. Lewis, if you don't mind my asking, I think there's something you could do."

"You got my ear, kid."

"Your daughter Holiday was dating Joshua Meyers. She was there with Mr. Barno when Joshua died, right?"

"Correct."

"I'm, I'm studying journalism in school and I'm doing an audio report about Mr. Barno for my senior project. I'm thinking that if I could get Holiday to go on record stating what she saw on the night of Joshua's death and I had that on a recording, then people my age could hear it for themselves from a credible witness and form their own opinions. I think a lot of us are just listening to what we are hearing our parents say. Much of the truth has been lost over time. Emotions and fears have taken over."

Mr. Lewis screwed the flask closed, having not sipped from it. He turned to me. "I admire your loyalty, young man." He called to Nurse Iris and asked her to bring his coat.

Well, at least I tried.

Mr. Lewis stood and Iris handed him his wool coat. He got into it, reached into a pocket, and took out his smartphone. His fingers pounded on the screen and then he turned the screen toward me and said, "Here's Holiday's number. Send her a text or call. I'm confident she'll do anything she can to help."

———————

I snuck out that night and put Gabi's Christmas gift on her back porch—a case of black cherry soda that I wrapped up and put this great big bow on. Then I texted her and told her where to find it. The next morning, she texted me, "So you're not so cold next time. Hehe." I looked on our back porch and found a present from Gabi—a retro winter jacket from a thrift store. Man, I wore that thing the whole ride to Ohio.

At Christmas I played lots of videogames and the fireworks show that Uncle Mitch put on was his greatest yet. Gabi and her mom spent the holidays with her mom's cousin, Larissa, who went to high school with some famous fugitive or something named Emory. I forget his last name. Gabi texted and told me all about it and how there were a couple books about the guy that she wanted to read.

After the New Year, school started back up. The days slid away and the weeks went right behind them. Still no word from Sarah.

I visited Mr. Barno every Monday like I promised. In addition to Nurse Iris, cleaning people came on Monday afternoons. I bet Mr. Lewis was paying for that.

Mr. Barno languished. He spent most of the time in bed or on the couch. He didn't say much, just asked me to read books I had already read to him. I probably read *Siddhartha* four times. I'd never seen him watch television before, but now the old TV in the TV room was on constantly—I suppose for the noise more than anything because Mr. Barno didn't seem to engage with it.

One day in March, when the weather was unseasonably warm, Nurse Iris and I guided Mr. Barno carefully into the backyard. I sat beside him on the bench that faced the tree fort. Nurse Iris hovered over us, a stern look on her face. Eventually, she went inside.

"Do you want to go sit in the tree? I could help you climb up there. If we're quick, maybe we can get up there before the nurse catches us."

"What tree?"

I pointed. "That one. The tree fort."

Mr. Barno waved dismissively. "Why would I climb into a children's tree house when I've got a perfectly good bench here on the ground?"

Later, I told Mr. Barno my birthday was coming up and I asked him when his birthday was.

"Tomorrow."

On my way out, I asked Nurse Iris if I could stop by the next day with a cake to celebrate Mr. Barno's birthday. She put her hand on my forearm and admonished, "You should know better by now."

I worked and worked on my Senior Project. It was hard but I was proud of it. April came. I still hadn't reached out to Holiday Lewis for that interview. I was avoiding it, wasn't I? Why? Was anyone actually going to listen to my project other than Mrs. de León, anyway? Could I really make something good enough to get selected for the Fab Five?

The email came on a Wednesday afternoon in early May. It wasn't from Sarah. But it was good news. I was offered a phone interview for the internship in Washington, D.C. that Mrs. de León had pushed me to apply for. I told my parents. They were strangely okay with the possibility of me not going to college in the fall and doing the internship instead. Then I texted Gabi and let her know.

Gabi (4:02 pm): Congrats [Party popper emoji]
Gabi (4:02 pm): [GIF of a dancing cat with a party hat on]
Me (4:02 pm): [Cat with tears of joy emoji]
Gabi (4:02 pm): Got some news too. Wanna hear?

Me (4:02 pm): Absolutes

Gabi (4:02 pm): Hey that's my word.

Me (4:03 pm): [Smiley face emoji]

Gabi (4:03 pm): K goof. Meet me at Overlook Park. Wanna tell u in person.

Me (4:03 pm): [Person running emoji]

Gabi (4:03 pm): Wait. First. New game.

Me (4:03 pm): What is it and does it have a good name?

Gabi (4:04 pm): Yes goof. It's called Gabis Delights.

Gabi (4:04 pm): It's when I tell u the little and big things that make me shriek with delight.

Me (4:04 pm): [Smiley face emoji]

I ran to Overlook Park. When Gabi saw me, she shrieked. Really, she did.

"What is it?"

Gabi fluttered on her toes as words leaped from her mouth. "Get this, I'm going to Wetton College next year and I'm studying public relations. I got into both Syracuse and Wetton—found out today when I got home from school. Guess what? I was honest. I told my mom how I wanted to study public relations, not marketing. I told her how I felt about Syracuse and why I wanted to go to a liberal arts college, to a smaller school where I could work one-on-one with the professors. She agreed. I can't believe it. The town fascist agreed."

"She did?"

Gabi threw her arms around me and shrieked again.

"Awesome." I smelled her hair. I didn't mean to. It was up in my face and I couldn't help but absorb her vanilla scent. I closed my eyes and sniffed again and allowed myself for one moment to think, *In another universe*. Then I opened them and shoved the thought away.

Gabi sauntered toward the bench that we had sat on the night last winter when she cried with her head on my lap. "When you nail that interview and land that internship in D.C., you can come visit sometimes, right? We can hang out. You can tell me about city life and I can tell you all about school and classes."

"And hot guys. And frat parties."

"Maybe," Gabi said over her shoulder.

"Of course I'll visit you," I said. "D.C. isn't that far. Plus, we've got like nine more *Scream* films to watch. I'll hold up my end of the deal if you hold up yours."

"What kind of a lady do you think I am? Of course I'll hold up my end. How many more *Friday the 13th* films do we have to slog through?"

"At least nine." I walked toward her. "Can we sit in the grass?"

"Sure," she said.

We sat.

"We're not doing prom, right?" I asked.

"Exactly. Forget prom. We're doing un-prom."

"Un-prom. What's that?"

"Not sure yet. Just made it up. But I'm thinking, our own playlist to your, um, fiercely abstract dance moves, lots of ice cream, and no fake people, and no stress."

"Rad." I did a little shoulder shuffle. "Don't hate on my dancing just because you can't move like this." *Wait, did I just do the same embarrassing move my dad does?*

"Come on now, really? And, rad? That's my word."

"You got full rights to all the dorky words, huh?"

"Maybe, just maybe, I can learn to share."

"Speaking of sharing, give me the deets. How's your senior project going?"

"Pretty good, pretty good. I'm doing a comparative analysis of innovations in public relations. I've got this sci-fi angle about people versus technology. So, the person I'm looking at is Betsy Ann Plank, known as the first woman of public relations. I'm then examining the Cluetrain Manifesto, which was way ahead of its time in declaring how the Internet would make conventional marketing and PR totally obsolete. Basically, I'm using Betsy and Cluetrain as proxies to explore which has had a greater impact on the field: people or technology."

"Sounds pretty rad."

"Again with my words." She picked a daisy and twirled it. "How's yours going?"

"Going alright. I'm working on a story about Mr. Barno."

"Tell, tell."

"It's about the stuff he taught me and a little bit about how your mom and all of them want to kick him out. Hope you don't mind."

"That reminds me, I was going to tell you more big news on the mom front. We had this epic talk two nights ago. We came clean to one another. Well, not everything. I didn't tell her about my stepdad yet. But I'm going to. I feel like she'll listen. Just wasn't ready, ya know?"

"I understand."

"So, and don't be sour at me or anything, but I sort of stole your lines from last Thanksgiving on the train bridge—the ones about how people create enemies because they need someone to blame for their pain. I was thinking about that, about how there are bad people. I've been tortured enough by them to know they're real. But—"

"Yeah, I know. My bad," I apologized. "I didn't mean for you to think. Like, I didn't mean to dismiss your pain. There are bad people who do legitimately bad stuff."

"No, I wasn't trying to say that. I know you understand. You're very understanding. I cherish that about you. I know that's not what you meant. I'm not explaining this well, am I?"

"Sorry. Keep going," I said.

"I told my mom that maybe she was unfairly zeroing in on Mr. Barno and blaming him—that I think the truth is that the whole town was responsible for Joshua's death. Because, if there was all that pressure on him and all those people pulling him this way and that, then, ya know?"

"Wow you said that? And what'd she say?"

"Nothing. She just cried."

"What'd you do?"

"Hugged her."

"And what'd she do?"

"Hugged me back."

"Oh wow. Nice. That's good then."

"Very."

I picked at the grass and threw ripped strands in the air. "Gabi, you're my best friend," I said. "And, well—"

"That title I'm not sharing with anyone else, ya understand buckaroo?" She playfully held up a fist. "Besties. You and me. Who'd have guessed?"

"Wait, I'm yours, too?" That made me feel warm and maybe I blushed.

"For real?"

"I mean, yeah, I totally knew that."

"Don't get too cocky." She tossed her daisy at me. "So what's up?"

"Um. Would you do something for me—something I've always wanted to do with a girl? Wait, that didn't sound right. Trust me, it's not kissing or anything like that. It's harmless. Honest."

Gabi shrugged. "If it's harmless, then, for my best friend? Sure. What is it?"

"Lay down."

"I thought you said this wasn't about kissing."

"It's not, I promise." She laid down and I laid down crosswise and rested my head on her chest. I wrapped her arm over me and said, "I want to hear about your dreams and I want to tell you more about some of mine."

"You're a peculiar guy, Nolan Sussman," she said. I could hear the smile in her voice. "You go first."

Thirty One

The microphone sucked Skyler's soft voice in and blasted it out of the speakers, filling the auditorium. "In conclusion, that is why the future of the restaurant business is intertwined with the future of our planet. Sustainable is not a buzzword, it is an imperative. Economics and ethics do not need to be at odds with one another. I'm Skyler Bell and thank you sincerely for listening to my senior project today."

Amid the applause, I could hear Branson yell out, "Go Sky-Sky!" I chuckled because I could picture him standing and cupping his hands over his mouth.

"Last one. Your time to shine," Mrs. de León said, pointing at me. I was sitting in one in a row of five chairs backstage in the Paxson High auditorium. Gabi, who was sitting next to me in a navy blue pencil skirt suit like an authentic PR executive, gave me a wink. "Fab Five time. You've got this."

I winked back. "You did great."

"You're about to," Gabi grinned. "The Talented Two. Get it?"

"You're such a dork."

She scrunched her nose.

I got up and pushed through the curtains into the bright stage lights. The auditorium was packed with students, teachers, and administrators. A few parents were sprinkled in. At the podium, I scanned for my parents and saw Dad and Mom near the front on my left. Mom was ear-to-ear smiles and Dad was doing what he called his 'Arsenio Hall cheer'—an archaic and embarrassing gesture where he made a fist and swung his hand in a circle near his ear. This display was occasionally accompanied by a "woot, woot" sound. Unfortunately, occasionally included today.

I took a sip from the bottle of water in my hand and set it down on the podium. Man, I was sweating. Those lights. Hot.

I stood there and just looked at everybody. Here I was in front of the whole damn school. And, for the next 20 minutes, they were there to listen to me. A huge room of people. I'd probably spoken to no more than 30 of them over the last 4 years, my parents included.

I finally had something to say to all of them—something worth saying.

I realized that they were staring at me waiting for me to talk. Probably 20 seconds had gone by since my dad had stopped 'Arsenio Halling' and the room had gone quiet.

I cleared my throat.

"Um. Hi everyone. My name is Nolan Sussman. I'm a senior in Mrs. de León's Senior Seminar II - Senior Project class. Well, obviously. Okay. Um. Onto my project. So my project is about—it's a report I did. An audio report. Like a mini podcast series. I recorded all of the sounds you will hear and the people talking—the interviews—and I did all the editing and I produced it. From a career standpoint, I did this project because I'm interested in maybe being an audio journalist on the radio or on a podcast. On the other hand, I might do audio editing or something like that. I'm not sure yet. From a personal standpoint, I did this project because I can't think of anything more important for you to know about before you leave high school and the entropy of your life begins. The story you're about to hear is the story of someone whose name you all know but, the actual person, you probably don't know. And that's a shame."

I sipped my water.

"My project is titled Atlas to a Kinder Universe. What I'll play for you is seven brief episodes. The first episode is an introduction. Then there are five episodes, each about a different topic related to the lessons I've learned during my senior year. The last episode includes an investigative piece that contains an exclusive interview with a former Paxson student. In that episode, I also offer my conclusions. Anyway, I hope you find it interesting and it gets you thinking." I turned over my shoulder and called to Mrs. de León, "Okay, please play it now."

The audio began to play over the auditorium speakers. After the intro music, episode one went like this:

My name is Nolan Sussman and I'm reporting on the Protect the Youth of Paxson movement and the case of Mr. Alexis Barno, a long-time Paxson resident, former Paxson High teacher, and a man who spent 25 years in prison for killing three people in a DUI accident.

Here are the known facts about Mr. Barno.

Over 25 years ago, Mr. Alexis Barno was convicted for killing his wife and two Paxson youths, Marcus Finch and Kyle Warner, while drinking and driving. There is no denying the harm that night caused this community—lives were cut short and families were left to pick up the pieces.

Before that, Mr. Barno was a popular teacher here at Paxson High School. He taught many of the people who are now our parents, teachers, and neighbors.

Mr. Barno was very popular with the students. He was so popular that he ran an after-school club called the Smart Kids where he mentored many students who struggled with many of the things you and I struggle with today—trying to fit in, the search for love, pressure from our parents, trying to figure out what we want to do with the rest of our lives.

I got to know Mr. Barno because of the mistakes I made. As you may know, I vandalized his house, along with lots of other houses in town. What you don't know is that I was facing expulsion from Paxson High School and Mr. Barno gave me a chance to learn from my mistakes. That chance grew into an opportunity to get to know an unusual man that most people in this town fear, despise and want to see gone.

It says in the Declaration of Independence that all people have the unalienable right to pursue happiness. Problem is, no one teaches us how to do that. We don't learn at home or at school. Instead, we are taught to constantly pursue the future. We are taught that's where happiness is and that it can be ours if we don't mess up, get the best grades, marry the right person, and get the best job—essentially, if we are perfect.

Mr. Barno rejected those ideas. He taught me that happiness isn't a prize you win. It's a way of being. Anyone can be happy at any point in their life—things don't have to be perfect and we don't have to wait to be happy. He helped me learn to be happier and to bring more goodness into the world.

In the following episodes, I share with you five lessons Mr. Barno taught me this school year. The lessons are part of what Mr. Barno called The Atlas to a Kinder Universe.

The five episodes played to a still audience, their eyes either on me or on the large speakers that hung on either side of the stage. Each brief episode covered a lesson Mr. Barno had taught me: 1. Happiness, Not Fear. 2. Compassion, Not Judgment. 3. Harmony, Not Rigidity. 4. Gratitude, Not Perfection. 5. Inconvenience, Not Catastrophe.

In each episode, the audience first heard snippets of the recordings I had made of my conversations with Mr. Barno where he explained the lessons to me during our days building the tree project. Then, the audience heard my voice providing summaries of the main points of the lesson that I later recorded when creating the episodes.

Lastly, the final episode played. Here it is:

As a result of my experiences with Mr. Barno, I've wrestled with the following question: How do I come to terms with the possibility that people can make horrible mistakes and still be redeemable?

Sometimes, when I think about this question, I think about the Barnos. Other times, I think about myself. Still other times, I think about other people in this community, even in this school.

Paxson has experienced more than its fair share of tragedy. Some tragedies are senseless mistakes. Other tragedies are premeditated. And other tragedies happen by omission—because people lose sight of what's important.

Here is where the facts about Mr. Barno get fuzzy.

This school year, a movement called Protect the Youth of Paxson was formed. According to their flier, which you may have seen in school or in town, the goal of this group is to, "Lobby our local government to force the relocation of Alexis Barno, a convicted killer who served 25 years in prison."

Why would someone who accidentally killed people in a car accident, an isolated event that surely he deeply regrets, be seen as a continued threat to the young people of our town today? After all, Mr. Barno is a loner who doesn't drive because he had his license revoked.

The reason is the unusual circumstances some 26 years ago surrounding the death of Joshua Meyers, the star quarterback of Paxson High's back-to-back state championship football teams.

Mr. Barno was present when Joshua Meyers fell from the train bridge and died. Did Mr. Barno murder Joshua Meyers, as many have accused? If so, then the fears are warranted because Mr. Barno might strike and kill again.

However, the truth is that Mr. Barno did not kill Joshua. He was trying to help Joshua.

In a moment you will hear an interview I conducted with Holiday Lewis. She was dating Joshua at the time and witnessed the awful death of her boyfriend. She told me that Joshua was a member of the Smart Kids after-school club and that Mr. Barno was a mentor to Joshua. Mr. Barno was the person Holiday called for help from a nearby payphone the night when her boy-friend was planning to jump to his death. Let's hear what she saw:

"Okay, see, it's late—dark out. I'm standing at the cliff watching Mr. B and Josh. It's been raining awful hard and I'm clinging to the fence because the ground's all muddy. The rain turns to sleet. It's getting icy and cold and I'm praying they'll climb down soon. You've got to understand that Josh is in a bad place. He's striving to be Mr. Paxson and make everyone proud—striving to get that third state championship, stressing over which university to play ball at. It just changes him, all that attention. His senior year mid-season—after that close game with Middleview—he starts acting strange. Loses his temper. Freaks out at nothing. One day, the life just seems gone from him. I'm no doctor but... at any rate, up on the platform, Josh and Mr. B talk for a long time and finally I see Mr. B start to climb down the ladder. His foot slips on the icy ladder rung and for a second he has to catch himself. Josh is still up there. I'm looking at Mr. B because of what just happened. Then I look up at Josh, and his arms go up and he falls on his back on the platform— must've slipped. He gets on hands and knees, starts grabbing at the air. I believe he panics because he pushes up to stand, hits his head on the railing, and sort of, sort of goes limp and, and, and tumbles forward through the railing. I watch him—watch him drop. Drop and disappear. I scream. Splash. I'll never forget that sound. And by the time. By the time. That's all. Can we please, can we stop now?"

That was difficult to listen to. As you just heard, Mr. Barno talked Joshua down from the ledge. Joshua chose life. In a tragically ironic twist, he slipped and fell to his death.

Knowing what happened doesn't bring Joshua back. The pain can't be undone.

But, knowing what happened may help us to learn to live with the pain. This town drove one of its teenagers to the edge—a teenager this town professed to love.

Like many of us, Joshua was living with immense pain. We all know some form of pain—unfulfilled dreams, deaths, families torn apart, broken hearts, money troubles, addiction, and so on. We all deal with pain differently. Some people go off to be alone, some rebel, some create a false smile that they show to the world, some run away, and some people hurt others. Some feel driven to the edge and lose hope.

So how do we square the bad with the good? How do we learn to accept? To forgive? To get up and keep going and believe that both today and our future can be bright despite the bad stuff that happens?

Mr. Barno once asked me whether the universe is kind. I thought he was asking whether human nature or maybe our society is full of kindness. It seemed like a stupid question when I thought about all the meanness, bigotry, abuse, jealousy, and judgmental thinking that goes on right here in our own town.

Recently I realized that isn't what he was asking me.

He was asking me to decide how I was going to choose to experience the world. There are so many beautiful and wonderful things in the world and in this town if we choose to see and appreciate them. Swimming and tubing in the river, the feeling of the air washing over your whole body as you run, the views— we live in a place with so much natural beauty —, the song of the trains passing through town, a walk down Main Street. And on and on. And what about the people? We have people who care so much about this town and its people, like Mr. Barno, Mrs. Roland, Mrs. de León, Mr. Green, and yes, even Principal Anand. We have friends, family, and maybe that special someone.

I didn't see any of that before. I saw a small town— a trap. I saw a bunch of other students and adults I didn't understand or care to understand. I saw a place and people to run from, the way my sister Sarah did.

Mr. Barno was also asking what contribution I was going to make to make the universe a kinder place. I'm not 100% sure how I'll make my contribution, but I know that however I do it, I will improve lives and help people—help people see that the world isn't so bad. There is still good out there.

If we just focus on the bad and give up, or if we run away and hide and only ever allow ourselves to experience what's comfortable and what aligns with our preexisting views, then what kind of universe are we accepting?

I believe Mr. Barno's name deserves to be cleared of the accusations surrounding Joshua's death. Mr. Barno is not a threat to the young people in this town. Many people at this school and in this community have passed judgment on Mr. Barno. They've never met him, never spoken to him, never experienced the goodness in his heart. They don't know the other side and haven't heard the stories of the countless Paxson students he helped deal with the difficulties of growing up—the people he was able to save.

This town threw him in prison—threw him away because that felt good. And when he got out, the town tried to do the same thing in a different way. All that did was divert attention from other things we need to address like the happiness and well-being of our community.

We do the same thing to each other every day. We abuse each other for our own satisfaction. It is a sickness and I don't know where it comes from. But I know we have to do something about it.

As I explained in the first episode, Mr. Barno put together the Atlas to a Kinder Universe. Yes, there is a kinder universe out there, but each of us has to choose it. Let's be honest. A kinder universe is not an easy place to get to. That's why getting there requires an atlas. I've been on the journey since the start of the school year, and even with the atlas and a patient and expert guide in Mr. Barno, I struggle every day on my journey. Still, I know it's worth it. I know it's not a destination. It's a permanent voyage—a path you choose to follow every day.

We have a chance to do things differently. I hope we will choose to.

The auditorium speakers fell silent. Everyone was still. I wiped sweat from my forehead and muttered into the microphone, "Thank you for listening." I shuffled toward the side-stage curtain. Then Branson shouted, "Give that man a Pulitzer! That's the best fucking journalism I've ever heard!"

I stopped and turned toward the audience. Branson was standing, his hands cupped over his mouth. He glanced around and, seeing that he was the only one on his feet, the only one making noise, he sank into his chair. I froze in front of the whole school, exposed out there on the stage halfway between the podium and the curtain with nothing to hide behind.

"Nolan," a voice called from over my shoulder. "Nolan. Excellent job. Come on." Next thing I knew, there was a hand on my shoulder—Mrs. de León's. I snapped out of it and turned to head back toward the curtain when out of the corner of my eye I saw him in the back of the auditorium by the exit door. Mr. Barno sat in a wheelchair with Nurse Iris gripping the handles behind him. And he was smiling. He raised a wobbly hand and gave me a thumbs-up.

I waved to him.

"Thank you for the atlas," called a voice from the void. I scanned the expressionless audience. Tyler Pratt-Baldwin stood. "A kinder universe. I want to be a part of that." Neil was sitting next to him. I smiled.

Several rows behind Tyler, I caught Gabi's mom, Penelope Meyers, rise, jostle down the row of seats, pour into the aisle, and scurry out the back.

When I got through the stage curtains, Gabi gave me a big hug and told me that I was brave and that I did excellent. I thought she'd be pissed at me because I had refuted her mom in a super public way. However, Gabi wasn't mad.

"Thanks," I said.

"What for?"

"Believing in me."

Gabi said she'd been drinking so much water because she was nervous before her presentation. Then, she was drinking a bunch during her presentation because her mouth was dry. And now, she laughed, she really needed to pee. I laughed and told her I'd catch her out in the hall in a little bit. She bowed lightheartedly and left.

Skyler congratulated me and said my report was, "Moving and ultra insightful." I told her great job on her project and I said how impressed I was.

I congratulated the other two students who had been selected for the Fab Five: Jamal Young and Becky Stone. Becky didn't congratulate me back. Jamal asked me for a selfie which turned into an extemporaneous video of him with his arm over my shoulder talking into the camera on his phone to his fans about how I was, "If cosmically possible, the lovechild of Katie Couric and John Lennon." I told him thanks, but that the project wasn't about me.

A custodian came in, swept, and shut off the stage lights and main backstage lights. Everyone shuffled out of the backstage door into the wide hallway between the auditorium and the gymnasium. I stayed back and sat in one of the chairs under the dim emergency lights that always stayed on. A couple of minutes later, Mrs. de León came in to grab her bag.

"Excellent work," she said. "I heard from Victor that you were accepted for the internship in Washington and will be working with him on the podcast at the *Post*."

"Yeah, I will be."

"Congratulations, Nolan. You have promise. I'm glad to see that you are using it for good."

"I appreciate you helping me land the internship," I said. "I'm excited."

Mrs. de León walked to the door, her bag in hand. She leaned against the door and said to me, "That was brave, what you did with your project. Very brave. You did the right thing."

"Thanks," I replied. *Why hadn't she? Why hadn't she ever stood up for Mr. Barno? Why hadn't Principal Anand? Why hadn't Mr. Lewis come out from hiding and publicly stood up for Mr. Barno? Why were Holiday and I the only people who publicly stood up and spoke out for Mr. Barno?*

The door opened. Bright light and the chatter from the hallway poured in. Mrs. de León slipped out. The door closed. I went to the curtains and peeped through into the empty auditorium.

In the movies, after something like what I'd done fifteen minutes before, everyone leaps to their feet and applauds while you stand all triumphantly on the stage. And suddenly the jocks are besties with the band geeks, the cheerleaders are making out with the nerds, and two teachers you didn't know were secretly in love with each other are holding hands in the corner. And like that, everyone has changed. No one is mean anymore and grownups are having barbecues as the sun sets, laughing away their past grudges with former enemies while a Coldplay song plays and the camera zooms out. Roll credits. Movie is over. Happy ending.

In real life, you've got to be patient. You've got to go on to the next thing and the next day and keep building toward that kinder universe. And you've got to know that you made a dent, and that, in real life, people need time to change, just like you need time to change. After all, you can't force a miracle.

Thirty Two

Then one day you graduate from high school—just like that. High school is everything. Everyday. Surrounding you. Then it's not. And the road in life widens. That's what my dad said, anyway. He said, "Nolan, today, the road in your life is going to widen. The guardrails are off. You've got to decide how you're going to navigate it." Then he drove me to the high school and as I was hopping out of his truck to find my friends and line up for graduation, he handed me a cigar and a lighter and told me it was "family tradition" and it was "good luck" to light it up on the 50-yard line.

So in the end, I did get to sit in a foldout chair on the Paxson High School football field and listen to the valedictorian, Becky Stone—who pulled off the Triple Crown: Homecoming royalty, Fab Five selectee, and valedictorian—give a speech. And I threw my mortar board up and lit the cigar on the 50-yard line. There were hugs, cheers, decorated mortarboards, and girls running around on grass in high heels.

Some of my family came to town. Uncle Mitch and his kids, Aunt Jennifer and Uncle Benjamin, and even my mom's sister who lived in Georgia—who we called Aunt Cici but whose real name was Carson—flew up. Mom made a roast, I think because that's the only big meal she knows how to make.

I kept watching the door while we ate, hoping to see Sarah pop through it, drop her bag on the floor, and spread her arms wide enough to hug us all. But it never happened. And I never got an email from her.

On Monday morning, our visitors packed up and left—on to the next thing. I had one month before I was to move to Washington, D.C., begin my internship, and try to land a part-time job to help cover expenses. That was the plan: a gap year before college. If I liked the internship, I could apply for that journalism scholarship at Wetton and maybe hang out with Gabi, if she still wanted to be my friend in college.

That afternoon, my dad said it was fine for me to go to Mr. Barno's house alone. Mom and Dad never quite apologized for how they treated Mr. Barno. But after coming to Fab Five and hearing my senior project, they started talking differently about Mr. Barno. And that was progress enough for now.

I ran all the way to Mr. Barno's house—just like I used to. I knew every step, every shortcut I could take that cut through the edge of someone's yard, and every pothole I needed to jump.

Nurse Iris let me in.

"How is he?" I asked.

"One of his better days. He's out back in his wheel-chair."

In the backyard, I found Mr. Barno slouched in the wheelchair facing the flowerbeds that ran along the wall.

Last year, the flowerbeds were freshly mulched and blooming in color. Now, the beds were overgrown with weeds.

"Hey you," he said when he saw me.

"Mr. Barno. How are you?" He looked frail. I knew from Nurse Iris that it was because he wasn't eating much.

"Fantastic," he smiled. "You?"

"I did it. I graduated."

"Well, let's get you a gift."

"No, that's very kind of you but it's not necessary."

Mr. Barno waved to Nurse Iris through the sliding glass door. She came out and handed me an envelope. I opened it. Mr. Barno had signed the card, his handwriting a series of waves like a tiny polygraph. In the card, he had also drawn something, a sort of box or something that was too squiggly to make out. I thanked him and then he said, "Do you like your gift?"

"Yes. Thank you."

"Iris, some alone time with the boy, please."

The nurse's face tensed, but she went back inside.

"Aren't you going to take it for a spin, son?"

"Uh."

Mr. Barno reached slowly into his breast pocket and dangled the keys to the Subaru Impreza that I drove that one time to the hardware store—the Subaru parked in the garage.

"No way," I shouted.

"The dealer said it has all the latest features." He tossed the keys at me unsuccessfully. I reached down and picked them out of the grass.

"Huh?"

He held out his hand. "Don't want it? I can take it back."

I clutched the keys to my chest.

Mr. Barno smirked. "Up for a joy ride?"

Inside, Nurse Iris shook her head. Eventually, she caved in and helped Mr. Barno into the garage and into the Subaru's passenger seat. She gave me a stern talk that I must not drive any further than to the end of the street. She ended with, "Be back immediately."

I hopped in and the Sade tape I had left in the tape deck started playing when I started the car.

"Wait." Mr. Barno held up a hand. He rummaged around until he unearthed the cassette tape for Don Henley's *The End of the Innocence*. He popped it in and hit rewind. "Track one. The End of the Innocence." The song began. "Drive, son."

I eased out of the garage and slipped into the street. As I drove, Mr. Barno sang along. When I glanced over at him, I saw that his eyes were closed and that he wasn't singing to me. He was singing to Celeste—like he must have done many years before when they were young and falling in love.

I drove up and down Mr. Barno's street until the song ended. Here I was, driving an old Subaru that was abruptly mine. My very own old Subaru—just like Sarah. It turned out that was the Sussman fate: to drive an old Subaru, a twinkle car. I never thought I'd say this, but I was sure glad about it. Man, life is funny. Your dreams distract you sometimes from the really good stuff.

Back in the garage, I thanked Mr. Barno over and over for giving me the Subaru as a graduation gift.

He gave me a devious look. "It comes with strings, son. Promise to do some things for me when I'm gone, okay?"

"Please don't talk about that."

"That's the deal or no car."

"Okay, okay. What things?"

"First, smile."

"But —"

He pressed the eject button and the tape popped out. He tucked it in his front pocket.

"I'll come back and visit you all the time," I assured him.

"You've got a life, kids, and a wife of your own. No need to visit so often. Your work is out there now."

I leaned my neck against the headrest, let my head roll back, and closed my eyes.

"Raising you has been the greatest joy of my life, son. A college graduate. I couldn't be more proud of you."

For so many years I had been able to squish everything down and only weep when I was alone. That day I learned that there are some tears you can't keep in no matter how hard you squeeze your eyelids together. The tears broke the barricade and streamed out, painting my face. I licked but I couldn't reach them.

Mr. Barno went for the door handle. "Those are the strings. Smile. And kiss Mom for me every time you see her. Will you do that for your old man?"

Nurse Iris opened the door from the outside and helped Mr. Barno out. She leaned down, gave a curt wave through the open car door, and took Mr. Barno into the house through the door in the garage.

Thirty Three

"What're we doing?" Gabi asked.

"Remember how you shushed me at the train bridge way, way back?"

"Yup. So what if I did?" she mocked.

I shushed her. "Well, this time, it's my turn to show you something."

"Grr," she hissed playfully.

I took her hand. We snuck around the side of Mr. Barno's house and through the privacy fence gate. I didn't recognize the car in the driveway at his house. I figured it was the night nurse and I didn't want her to catch us snooping around in Mr. Barno's backyard. The string lights hanging from the oak tree were lit up and I knew Mr. Barno was on the other side of the glass, sleeping in his bed, not far from the tree project—not far from Celeste.

"Follow me," I instructed. We climbed the ladder through the hole and into the tree fort.

"You two built this?"

"Yeah."

"It's special, Nolan. It's really special. You're a sweet guy."

I smiled. "Thanks. You cut your hair."

Gabi lifted the tips that hung at her neck with her palms. "Always wanted to. Finally did."

"Cool." I said. "Can't believe it's summer and I'm leaving soon."

"I know."

"Will being apart change our friendship?"

"I don't know. I hope not."

"Me too."

"You're going to love D.C.," Gabi said.

"You're going to love college," I replied.

"You're not a cheat are you? We aren't allowed to watch any *Scream* or *Friday the 13th* movies without the other person being present."

"I won't cheat if you don't," I said.

"Never."

"I need to show you something." I took Gabi's hand and sat us down across from each other. "Close your eyes," I said. "I want you to breathe in through your nose and out through your mouth as slowly as possible. Get all the air out of your lungs on the out-breath and completely fill them on the in-breath."

She smiled gently and closed her eyes.

We breathed together.

I opened my eyes. And nothing. Nothing happened.

"Okay, keep them closed," I instructed. "Let's start over. It usually takes a couple tries."

Again we breathed together. And again, when I opened my eyes, nothing happened.

"What're we doing?" Gabi asked.

"Um. Let's try again. Just make sure you breathe real slowly. As slow as possible."

"I was doing that."

"Okay. No, I know. Let's just try it again."

We tried.

Nothing.

We tried a fourth time.

Still, nothing.

Nothing.

Nothing.

Nothing.

Not even on the eighth time. No loopy stuff. No time traveling.

"What's up? Why're we doing this?"

I sighed and climbed to my feet. "I don't know. It's just. It's just not working."

"What's not working?"

Looking out into the yard, I whispered over my shoulder, "I'm not really sure what it is. But it's not working."

"You're peculiar. Anyone ever tell ya that?" She stood, took my hand, and pulled me back down to the floor. She sat across from me and I tried to look away but I couldn't keep my eyes off her.

"You told me that." I smiled. "Why are you looking at me that way?"

"I want you to kiss me."

"What? Why?"

"When you said way back when we were on the train bridge platform that I taught you the difference between being attracted to someone and caring for them, at first I thought what you were saying was that you didn't find me attractive. Then I realized I was doing what I always do and making a judgment—a judgment that I'm never good enough. Then I realized that's the opposite of what you were saying. You were saying that I am good enough—that I'm worth being cared for, weren't ya?"

I nodded. "I was saying that and a lot more."

"So kiss me."

"Are you sure?"

"Yes. I want to be kissed by a guy who loves me, who loves me deeply."

I explored Gabi there across from me under the lights that hung through the tree. And I guess it *was* a magical tree if Gabi wanted me to kiss her in it. I knew that someday some lucky guy would be the person who would help Gabi Meyers learn to love. Problem was, I didn't want to be the guy in the meantime—the guy that Gabi crashed and broke against when she wasn't ready.

My hands were getting damp and I wanted to pull them back. "I don't think it's a good idea."

"Why not?"

"Because," I said looking down. "I don't want to love you more than a friend. I'm afraid of doing that."

"One day, you and I can be more. Just not yet."

I looked up. "What?"

"Nolan Sussman, you're a sweet and brave kid. You listen and understand. You're gentle. You care. You're considerate. You're kind. You're smart. You dance like a madman on Ritalin," She chuckled. "You're cute as all hell. What the heck else do you want me to say, ya goof?"

Maybe for the first time in my life, I really looked into a girl's eyes. And real confidently I said, "I want to know that you like me and that you want me to kiss you—not because you want to be kissed, or because you're in a tree fort with lights hanging overhead and it's all romantic and so kissing is the thing to do, but because you want to be kissed by me."

She held my eyes with hers when she said, "Some things come too soon. Some things come too late. And some never come at all. Yet, true love, it's always there. The way it is for Mr. Barno. So, if we're meant to be, if it is true love, then, when the time comes, after ya know, in a while, when I'm ready, we'll be together. Because you really deserve someone great. And I don't want to be anything less than that for you. What do ya think, we got a deal?"

I thought about what Mr. Barno had gone through, and what he'd lost for this thing called love: everything.

Then I realized something. Maybe I wasn't seeing the circumstances right. It was another one of many moments when it took me a long time to understand what Mr. Barno was saying: life isn't always about changing circumstances, it's about how we relate to circumstances.

Mr. Barno hadn't lost everything for love. He'd gained it.

"We got a deal," I said. Then I leaned over and Gabi and I kissed. We kissed and we kissed. She pulled me down and we kissed and rolled atop each other under the lights for a long time.

Thirty Four

I stepped out of the coffee shop and into the noisy streets of Washington, D.C. to call Mrs. de León.

"I'm so sorry, Nolan," she said when she answered.

"It's okay," I replied. "In a way, I'm happy for him."

"Me too."

"Do you know? Do you know what happened?"

"Heart attack. They found him this morning. It is the oddest thing. He was up in a treehouse in his backyard."

"At least he wasn't alone."

"What?"

"Nothing. Any word on the funeral? I got an interview to conduct here in a few minutes. I could leave tonight and be back in town."

"From what I understand, there are no plans for a ceremony."

"That's unacceptable," I said. "I'll be back tonight."

During the whole drive back to Paxson, I was beating myself up, then forgiving myself, and then beating myself up again. I had written Mr. Barno letters and Nurse Iris would occasionally hand-write a response on his behalf. I called a few times. Not enough. It had been a few months since Mr. Barno had heard from me.

I had done what I promised I wouldn't. Had gotten busy with the internship, my job waiting tables at a little Italian restaurant, life in the city, and occasional trips to Wetton to visit Gabi. I was also finishing up a side audio project, an ode to Mr. Barno—the full story of my time with Mr. Barno: the story of the Atlas to a Kinder Universe.

Back in Paxson, things were a mess at Mr. Barno's house. He didn't have a will or any last wishes—at least none that we could find. I insisted on cremation. I insisted that I got to help scatter his ashes.

Paxson was nice. It really was a special place. Had the circumstances been different, I'd have been glad to be home.

On a Sunday in late February, I called together Mrs. de León, Mrs. Roland, Mr. Lewis, and Principal Anand. Holiday Lewis drove up from Richmond.

We stood in a crispy glaze of snow, blades of grass poking through at the base of the oak tree on the country road where Celeste Barno, Marcus Finch, and Kyle Warner died.

Holiday collapsed. Her dad scooped her out of the snow and propped her against his sturdy frame as she bellowed, his chin a wing over her wool cap.

We all took turns sharing how Mr. Barno had touched our lives—how he'd saved us. I cried too hard to remember much of what was shared. Even so, what Holiday said has stuck with me. She pulled off her glove, pushed up her coat sleeve, touched an elephant tattoo on her wrist, and called Mr. Barno, "The Gardener of the Elephant-Hearted." She said elephants are the noblest creatures because they have strength, wisdom and compassion.

Afterward, I lay purple and yellow dahlia flowers at the base of the tree trunk. We poured most of Mr. Barno's ashes on the gash in the tree. I had never thought before about how that tree had kept standing after the crash, but it did. And much of the wound was grown over.

That night I parked the Subaru in the driveway at Mr. Barno's shuttered house. I pressed through the back gate into the derelict backyard, the place he had once brought to life. I turned on the tree lights, climbed up into the fort, and said goodbye to Mr. and Mrs. Barno—said that I was glad they could be together all the time now. Then I scattered the rest of the ashes all over the tree fort.

I never found out how or why I experienced what I did with that tree in Mr. Barno's backyard—the loopy stuff, the time travel stuff. That night, after I spread the ashes, I tried to do the breathing thing that Mr. Barno had taught me. But nothing happened. And I realized with Mr. Barno gone, it never would again.

And still, I smile.

Thirty Five

Dear Sarah,

The skies are gray sometimes. I will be alright. It's only a passing storm.

I am happy and nothing needs to change. But if it does, I will embrace it. And if it doesn't, I will embrace it. I have happiness inside of me and I will take it with me wherever I go and I will share my happiness in everything I do.

I used to think that chasing success was the most valuable thing to do. Now I know what's rarer and more valuable.

I'm in love with a girl named Gabi Meyers. I don't know if we'll ever be more than friends. It's okay either way. Life isn't about getting the object of your affection. It's about being there for them. Love without conditions.

Isn't that weird, how we get it backward? How we put all our effort into chasing things? How those are the stories we want to tell and hear? People running after stuff and missing everything else and thinking that's their way to happiness someday? I realize now that the problem with someday is that, at its best, it's always at least a day away. You can never get to it. Before I knew that, I wanted my story to be one of those stories.

This is another kind of story. They say each of our lives has at least one magical story in it—the kind where we witness something otherworldly or meet a person who does things that seem impossible and the world is better for it. That was my story.

Some call this stuff divinity. Others say there's a logical explanation that science just hasn't discovered yet. I don't need a reason and I don't need an explanation. I just know Mr. Barno was a miracle. I believe in miracles now. I believe in Mr. Barno.

All of us kids he helped in one way or another are out there in the world—the world within ourselves and in the world of our communities—working to make it a kinder universe. A happier place. We're spreading the Atlas to a Kinder Universe.

The Smart Kids who came before us grew up and did it their way. Our generation will do it our way.

I don't think you'd recognize me if you saw me. And you may not know it if someday you meet one of us. After all, I didn't know it when I met Cammie Roland or Mrs. de León.

So thanks for listening. This was everything I had to say. I'm proud of how it sounds. I recorded it and did all the audio production myself.

Remember what Mr. Barno said: most miracles get overlooked. I think that's because most people aren't paying attention when their magical thing happens. I hope you look up, away from your device and your fears and your ambitions long enough to catch it. Like I said, we're out there. I hope to see you soon, Sarah.

Love,

Your full brother. Me. Nolan

I climbed out of the Subaru Impreza and erected myself in the gravel driveway of a white home with wooden pillars that sat back in the woods on Trough

Road, just outside of Mecklenburg, West Virginia. I held a folded letter in one sweaty hand and a flash drive in the other. It was morning, the sun orange and new.

On the welcome mat on the front porch, a hand-painted sign above a mail bin that hung on the siding read: "Diffendaffer." I shifted the flash drive so it and the letter were in one hand. I wiped my empty palm on my jeans and knocked on the door.

If you enjoyed this book, please help other readers find and enjoy it by reviewing it on Amazon, Goodreads, or social media. A few words helps a lot. Thanks!

Mr. Barno's Atlas to a Kinder Universe

1. Happiness, Not Fear.
2. Compassion, Not Judgment.
3. Harmony, Not Rigidity.
4. Gratitude, Not Perfection.
5. Inconvenience, Not Catastrophe.

To learn more about what inspired Mr. Barno's Atlas to a Kinder Universe and to access learning activities and discussion questions, go to:

MattKushin.com/happiness

Thanks

Thank you to Kelin and Crosbie for the inspiration to write this book and for all you continue to teach.

Thank you to Mom, Dad, Doug and Jarred for your love and support and for a life filled with wonderful, often hilarious memories.

Thank you to Doc for all the wisdom and life lessons.

This project wouldn't exist without the support, encouragement, and editorial guidance of Greg Fields, novelist and friend. I can give no greater compliment.

Thank you to Shepherd University, the professional development committee, and Provost Steven Spencer, Dean Robert Tudor, Dr. Jason McKahan, and President Mary Hendrix.

Huge thanks to Greg Fields, Kelin Kushin, Anna Keys and Owen Rye for their expertise and feedback on scenes from this book. Thanks to Robin Powers for his expertise on trees and thanks to Professor Monica Larson for designing the amazing book cover.

Thank you to the Jared Androzzi Experience for always listening and talking about life.

To the All-Stars: thanks for all the fun, adventure, craziness, friendship and music a kid could ever ask for. You'll never know how much you helped me.

Thanks to the many memorable and dedicated teachers I had in high school. I would not be here without you. Teachers change lives.

Thank you to Jeff Zentner for the inspiration and encouragement. Thanks to J.W.B for paving the way.

And thanks to the bands listed in this book and many more that, throughout the good and the bad, lifteth me up and settith me down gently.

Thanks to the countless students who inspired me over the years. It has been so much fun.

Thank you to every kid who chose kindness growing up. It matters. It really does.

And thanks to you, my friend, the reader. Always remember: you are not alone. You never were.

Matthew J. Kushin, Ph.D. is the author of *Beware the Smart Kids*. He's an award-winning professor, scholar and speaker at Shepherd University. His favorite class to teach is a special topics class on happiness and media use. *Beware the Smart Kids* is a letter to the teenager in all of us.

Matthew follows the atlas wherever it takes him. His home base is in West Virginia.
Follow him online at:
MattKushin.com
Instagram.com/mjkushin
Goodreads.com/mjkushin.